Her face grew flushed, but it was simply the heat of her bathwater, it was not his closeness and the intimate, stroking position of his hands. She certainly did not mean to lean back against him, allowing him to place small kisses against the side of her neck. Nor did she intend to lift suddenly weak hands to stroke his arms and feel the texture of his sun-darkened skin against her palms.

"Cease, MacLeod," she said faintly.

"Do you truly wish me to?" he murmured, his lips sliding over her shoulder.

She did not answer him, which was response enough.

Her head dropped weakly to the back of the tub and he smiled.

"Is this the way the Scots bathe?" she asked, her smile lighting the midnight blue of her eyes. "You have odd customs, MacLeod."

SPINE TINGLING ROMANCE
FROM STELLA CAMERON!

PURE DELIGHTS   (0-8217-4798-3, $5.99)

SHEER PLEASURES   (0-8217-5093-3, $5.99)

TRUE BLISS   (0-8217-5369-X, $5.99)

A PROMISE
OF LOVE

Karen Ranney

Zebra Books
Kensington Publishing Corp.

http://www.zebrabooks.com

ZEBRA BOOKS are published by

Kensington Publishing Corp.
850 Third Avenue
New York, NY 10022

First Printing: September, 1997
10 9 8 7 6 5 4 3 2 1

Printed in the United States of America

To Trudy

For laughter that lasted a lifetime
For understanding, always
For giving me a foundation of love
And teaching me how to share and to give
For instilling in me the joy of learning
The pleasure of reading, the need for self-expression
For sitting in sidewalk cafes with me
And wondering about nationalities from shoes
For agreeing not to sing in public
For asking my opinion
For being my very best friend
And Heaven's greatest guardian angel

I miss you, Mom

Prologue

"By God, not again!" William Cuthbertson glared at his oldest daughter. "You show up more often than a pebble in my shoe, girl! What is it this time?"

Judith Cuthbertson Willoughby Henderson looked down at the stone steps. The lone blue feather from her bonnet was soaked; dye drizzled from its tip to mix with the puddle of muddy water at her feet. The rain had finally stopped, but too late to matter. Her slippers were ruined, her stockings sodden, the hem of her best blue dress was caked with mud.

The coach ride had lasted three days; she'd no coin to purchase accommodations. Sleeping had been accomplished by sitting in the corner of the jostling carriage, wedging herself against the wall. Despite her letter home, there had been no wagon waiting at the crossroads. She'd waited for an hour, then placed the box under her arm, grabbed the weight of her skirt with both hands, and proceeded up the lane she'd walked so many times as a young girl.

Halfway there, the rain had come, a precursor to her welcome.

Standing on the steps of the manor house she'd called home for most of her life, Judith wondered if she had ever before felt as unwelcome as she did at this particular moment.

It came as no surprise that her father insisted upon explanations now, nor was his anger entirely unexpected. Of course he would be enraged that she was, once again, dependent upon his charity. She had managed to anger him by simply breathing.

Judith ignored the familiar flash of pain.

"Have you nothing to say, girl? You, the oldest of my girls and the only one to return home like a bad penny!" he roared.

He lifted his balled fist toward Judith, but she remained rigid, shuttering her eyes against the blur of his descending hand. The air of its passage brushed against her cheek as his fist missed her face by a scant inch.

A long moment later, she looked up and met his angry gaze with a calm and placid facade. It was a lesson she had finally learned.

"The Matthews' family emigrated to the Colonies, sir. There was no coin for my passage." The words were said calmly, softly. Her blue eyes were clear, without guile. No emotion shone at all, except for fatigue, but then, she could not totally mask her exhaustion. There was nothing about the telling of the tale to indicate that it had been conjured up during the long walk home.

"And why did you not become indentured, then?" Her father's face was suffused with red as he continued to glare at her. Judith looked down at her feet, at the small box tied with string which contained all her worldly possessions. What a pitiful sight it was.

Instead of elaborating on her lie, she answered him simply. "I will not be an encumbrance, sir. Perhaps I could find another position, somewhere." Or, was it her burden to fail at servitude as persistently as she had at marriage?

The squire was not appeased. To have her return again was outside of enough! Was she a plague upon his life?

"Is there no welcome for me here, then?" Judith finally asked, screwing up her courage. Where would she go if he would not allow her to stay? Her married sisters were too afraid of her father to give her shelter. Nor would she willingly knock upon the poorhouse door. What, then, would she do? Accept Hiram Matthews' invitation to whoredom?

Not again.

William Cuthbertson stared into his daughter's face knowing that, in this at least, he had no choice. Her presence shamed him, yet his refusal to grant her entrance would only provide fodder for the gossiping harpies in the neighborhood.

He nodded finally and grudgingly stepped aside, allowing her to mount the steps for the comfort of the solar, her mother and her chattering sisters.

Judith summoned the last of her strength as she climbed the stone stairs. At the door, she turned, looking back at her father. It had ever been this way. She had realized long ago that there would never be affection from him. As a child, though, she had prayed to have been left as a fairy changeling's gift, pretending that she was not related to the squire at all. Somehow, it was easier to believe she was not his child than to accept that he truly cared nothing for her.

He watched her close the heavy oak door. So, she was back again, was she?

She was an unnatural female, his daughter. She bore no resemblance to her sisters, or his wife, nothing about her mirrored his own healthy looks. If his wife had been another sort of woman, the squire would have believed himself supporting a bastard all these years. Judith was tall, an oddity in a woman. Her hair was brown, not blond like the Cuthbertsons, her eyes a shade of blue so dark it disquieted him.

Yet, it was not simply her physical appearance which marked her as different. There was a restrained air about her which spoke not of tranquility, but rather of duplicity.

Sometimes, he saw a spark of rage in those odd eyes of hers, but in the next second it was gone, to be replaced by a docility he did not trust.

The girl had not taken to marriage the way a gentle-woman should, resisting from the first. He had wed her to a neighbor, only to have her return within months. He had then wed her to a soldier, whose stern countenance and air of authority should have meant the end of her stubborn ways. A few years later, she was his burden again, a wan shadow of herself, but still determined to plague his old age. Widowed twice over, she should have brought money or land with her, instead, she cost him in room and board.

She'd returned for the last time. She was twenty-four years old, doomed to remain in his household for the rest of her life. Unless he did something to ensure that she never come back.

He almost smiled at the thought.

Madelaine Cuthbertson hugged her oldest daughter tightly, almost in apology for having faced the Squire alone. Once, she had been an attractive woman. Twelve births since she had married at seventeen had aged her until she looked as frail as a fragile summer flower. Only five of those children had survived childhood and, as the Squire was quick to point out, they were all worthless girls.

Madelaine's hair had whitened, like her husband's, nature softly bleaching the soft strands of blond around her face until it appeared as if she wore a halo. In fact, everyone who knew her thought she had a spirit and a personality to match the most devoted of God's angels. She was a peacemaker in a house whose walls trembled with the Squire's temper, a soothing presence in a room filled with the sometimes whiny voices of her daughters, a gentle soul in a life that had not been gentle, although it had not lacked in comfort.

Judith gripped her mother's arms tightly, kissed her

cheeks, and reluctantly pulled away to answer the questions from her sisters.

They were all present in the room, even Sally and Jane, who had both married the year before. Their husbands' farms were not far away, a fact which enabled them to visit their mother often, bringing with them their infant sons, who were feted and spoiled as only boys can be in a totally female household.

Two months had not made a substantial difference in her third sister's appearance, Judith thought, but there seemed to be a serenity about Dorothea which had been missing before. Dorothea did not seem to dread her marriage, but, instead, eagerly anticipated it.

Elizabeth, the youngest of the five, had not changed at all. At fifteen, she was the antithesis of the Cuthbertson females, who matured early. There would always be something childlike about Elizabeth. By unspoken agreement, Judith had been her champion, protecting her from the harsh and sometimes critical judgments of others, including her father. He knew well that Elizabeth was different from his other daughters, but refused to believe that she could not be changed by a little discipline and hard work. The fact that he had not succeeded in his approach was due more to the nature of Elizabeth's malady than to Judith's occasional pleading intervention.

"Tell me what happened, Judith," her mother coaxed, leading her to a cushion by the fire. Even in spring the old house was dank and chill. Judith sank gratefully beside the hearth, allowing Elizabeth to take the box from her hand, and Sally, her still dripping bonnet. She slipped the top two buttons of her dress free, then ignored the clinging of the sodden cloth. She could endure the discomfort a little longer.

She had borne far worse.

Judith knew her mother wasn't speaking about her father's welcome.

"Mr. Matthews and his family were emigrating to the Colonies, Mother," she said, repeating the same lie she'd told her father. Judith fervently hoped her mother wouldn't pry beyond that sketchy explanation.

Hiram Matthews was a fawning, drooling lech, who seemed intent upon waylaying her at every opportunity, even as she escorted his children on their morning walks. He wanted her to accompany him on a journey, true, but it would have lasted no farther than the most convenient inn. Her employer seemed fixed upon the idea that her duties should be nurse to his children, companion to his wife, and his occasional whore, whenever chance and inclination made that possible.

Madelaine Cuthbertson knew there was more to the story than her daughter was telling, but she was also aware that unless Judith chose to divulge it, there was little she would learn. While the other girls seemed to share their every thought, her eldest would often remain quiet and watchful, engrossed not in being the center of attention as much as she was in observing life around her. As an adult, Judith remained as unapproachable as she had been as a child, contained in herself. Madelaine suspected that Judith's silences hid far more than a simple wish to avoid discussing herself.

Yet, despite Madelaine's appearance, she was not a saint, nor did she have the courage of one. There had been times in the past when she might have broached the wall surrounding her oldest child, but she had never done so. And this moment passed also, the opportunity for candor untaken, the bridge untraveled. Judith sat, staring at her hands, trapped in her isolation, and her mother did not disturb the sanctity of it.

Elizabeth sat as quietly beside her, occupied with the box and the string's intricate knots.

"You would be better served by retiring to a nunnery, Judith," Sally said with an edge to her voice. "You would not have half the difficulty you have now, in either keeping a position or a husband."

"I, for one, do not blame Judith for her troubles. First Poor Peter, and then Anthony." Dorothea shivered. She was glad her own prospective groom was strong and handsome.

"Peter Willoughby was simply Peter Willoughby until Judith married him," Sally said, scathingly. "Now he is forever referred to as Poor Peter."

"Do you blame Judith for his death, sister?" Dorothea asked calmly, as if Judith were not sitting five feet from her.

"No, I suppose not," Sally admitted reluctantly, "but it's said that marriage hastened his demise."

"In all fairness, 'tis his mother who spreads that tale." This unexpected defense came from Jane, who glanced at Judith over the skein of wool she was winding. "She blames Judith for Peter succumbing to pneumonia even now."

"Denton's mother is near as bad, Judith," Jane explained, her eyes narrowed at the thought of her own mother-in-law, "but she has not yet taken to carrying a scrap of her son's counterpane through the village like Mrs. Willoughby, using it to mop up her tears. Everyone knows not to ask how she fares; she will tell them straight out that her life is not worth living since Poor Peter's death."

"He had always been a delicate child," Madelaine contributed. "And her only one. It's natural she should be feeling grief."

"Yet, Anthony was not delicate, Mama. He was a soldier."

"It was a chicken bone which ended his life, Sally. He had as good a chance as losing his life in King George's War as choking to death."

"Still, misadventure seems to follow Judith like a lodestone. Tell me, sister, have you brought bad luck to us, now, or are you angling for a husband again?" Sally's look was narrow-eyed. "Surely you do not think there is another man in England who would want you? You have chosen the right road, Judith, in caring for another's children. I might employ you myself, as I am breeding again." Sally preened as she made that announcement, enjoying the cacophony of congratulations and hugs from her mother, Dorothea, and Jane.

She was glad there was no child, Judith thought, either from Peter's apologetic coupling or Anthony's brutality. A child would have bound her to her dead husbands' families with inexorable ties. Now, she had no reason to ever speak to Peter's mother, who had screamed words of accusation at her over Peter's casket, or glimpse the stern, set face of Anthony's brother. For that fact alone, she was grateful.

Judith looked into the fire, wishing the home to which she'd returned was a haven in fact. Yet, she'd always felt the bite of alienation here. While her sisters should have been the closest of friends to her, they remained as far apart as distant strangers. No, strangers will treat each other with civility. Siblings had a way of tearing at wounds until the flesh was free of the bone. She and her sisters were, however connected by blood, worlds apart in temperament and inclination. Like prisoners housed in a common cell, they shared their accommodations, but little else.

She had the feeling, though, that her father would not allow her much time in this genteel prison.

Judith halted before the door to her father's study, wiping her hands nervously down the skirt of her dress before she pushed open the door. This room was where her father conducted his business. Every available surface was filled with open ledgers, yellowed bills of sale, correspondence from the corners of England. It was utilitarian, functional, and dreary, a dismal place to be on a sunny morning.

The rain which had greeted her arrival yesterday had dissipated, to be followed by a wonderfully bright spring morning. Her father's summons, however, chilled any cheer Judith might have felt about the weather.

The squire nodded to Judith, surveyed her in one sweeping look that did little to hide his contempt for her less than fashionable attire, and turned his attention to the man standing beside the window.

Judith glanced at the visitor anxiously, seeking an explanation for her summons in his presence.

His face was as dark and scarred as the old oak in the meadow, his nose askew of the center of his face, his hair silvery brown. He was a broad man with a stocky chest and thin short legs that made him appear like the mismatched halves of two other wholes. He would be more at home, Judith suspected, on the back of a horse or on the deck of a rolling ship then he was here.

Malcolm MacLeod would have been more at home anywhere than here. He watched the Squire with ill-concealed impatience. He did not like the Squire; he was a mealy-mouthed sort of Sassenach who cheated you when your back was turned. But then, Malcolm didn't like being in England. The last time he had been this far south, it had been following the Bonnie Prince on his march to Carlisle, and the Scots weren't exactly trading for sheep then.

However, the MacLeod and the clan still came before his own personal preferences. It was his duty to carry sheep home with him, if possible. The fact that the Squire had refused to talk terms for barter had at first irritated Malcolm, not worried him. But the increasing delay led to the distinct, and disagreeable, feeling that he was being played like a salmon on the end of a line.

The squire leaned back in his chair, unable to mask his feeling of triumph. Soon, one of his greatest sources of trouble would disappear. It would cost him dearly, of course, but by his actions, he would rid himself of Judith once and for all.

"Malcolm, my friend," he began jovially, not noticing the sudden tensing of the man to his left. "I have a proposition for you."

Malcolm MacLeod watched his host with shuttered eyes. No Englishman called him friend. Nor did he doubt that the proposition soon to be offered to him also carried with it a threat. No Englishman had ever played fair with a Scot, and hadn't they a millennium of history to prove that?

"I issue no credit. I have never done so, and will not do so now. Hold, man!" the squire said, half-rising in the chair as the other man made to leave.

"An' why would ye not tell me that in the beginning? Ye think the MacLeods have barrels of gold for yer English sheep?"

"I will *give* you one hundred Leicester sheep," William Cuthbertson continued, forced to look up at the angry Scot. "In exchange for something."

"Name your bargain," Malcolm said curtly. He would play this stupid game to its conclusion, and if it was an Englishman's trick, Malcolm would just as soon gut the fat pig with the dirk hidden in his boot.

William turned to his daughter, who had remained motionless and mute since her entrance into the room. He noted her sudden pallor with indifference.

"The sheep are free if you take my daughter with you," the Squire said, glancing back at the Scot with a small smile playing around his thin lips.

Malcolm looked at the young woman whose presence he had noted and then dismissed. She was tall, and too thin, with hair the color of old, rich leather. He had seen the squire's family, but this one was as unlikely a relation to the others as a Highland deer was from a sheep. She was not petite with plump rounded curves like her sisters; she was lithe and willowy. Nor did she flutter in the silence as if afraid of it; she'd simply stood and waited silently.

She glanced over at him, as if sensing his look and his curiosity. Her eyes reminded him of the waters of a deep loch at gloaming. And like the deepest lake, they were cold. No, they were blank, as expressionless as the eyes of a corpse.

"I am not much of a prize," she said, calmly, addressing her remarks to Malcolm. "You would do well to look elsewhere for a wife."

Her father stirred in his chair, his eyes trained on her as if to pierce her with his look.

"Damn, girl," he growled, "I don't care if he marries you, swives you, or makes you his scullery maid!"

Judith looked down at the oak floor of the room, as if suddenly fascinated with the shape of the boards. She looked up only when Malcolm spoke into the silence.

"I've no wish for a wife, girl. One wife for one life, that's all I need." His words were kind, but it was the softening in his eyes that made her look away again.

"You are married?" she asked quietly.

"I was. Twenty years. I've no wish to repeat the act."

"It's either you or Elizabeth, girl," the Squire said peremptorily. "Make your choice. My house is full to overflowing as it is."

"Elizabeth?" Judith could not mask her look of horror quick enough. The squire only smiled, a thin-lipped smirk of satisfaction.

"It's high time the chit was married, girl. God knows I've tried it with you. If you cannot find a suitable union, then Elizabeth surely can."

Judith thought of her sister, whose sole occupation during the day consisted of wandering from room to room clutching her rag doll. Elizabeth, who could not dress herself, who loved flowers and singing, who flinched when voices were raised either in anger or excitement. Elizabeth, whose mind still remained infantile despite their prayers and their efforts. What would marriage bring to Elizabeth? Judith could not bear to think of it.

"Can you not allow me time to find another position, father?" She clasped her hands tightly in front of her, so that he could not tell they trembled.

"Now, Judith," he said curtly, ignoring her question. "Which of you shall it be?"

"If I go," she said, looking full into his face for the first time, "will you leave Elizabeth in peace? Will you promise not to marry her off?"

"I'll make no promises to you." The squire stood, placed

both palms upon the table, and leaned forward, his small eyes riveted upon his daughter. There was no love in those beady black eyes, Malcolm thought. No concern, no compassion, no emotion at all. He almost felt sorry for the girl. "Either you go, or Elizabeth will find a bridegroom within the month."

Judith had known, then, that her father would do anything to rid himself of her. Known, too, there was no welcome in England.

Chapter 1

"Tynan."

It was a benediction of sound uttered from an otherwise silent Scot. He extended one finger and pointed, as if Judith could not see their destination.

It was twilight and the sea and sky darkened together, a perfect backdrop for the giant black behemoth which huddled at the end of the narrow promontory, its back to the sea. The closer they came, the more Judith could discern the outline of the castle from the ebony shadows of the surrounding moor. The Devil's own lair could not have been more intimidating. It stood like a silent sentinel, guarding the cove and the entrance to the sea, one of its twin towers reduced to rubble, the other scraping the sky with crenelated teeth. An arched doorway, like the maw of some ancient beast, stood open. If not welcoming, it at least beckoned.

Judith shivered.

Her companion said nothing more, but the quick jerk of his head was command enough. Judith sat erect, controlling her fears and her mount with the same dogged determination, eased the mare into a trot and followed Malcolm

MacLeod single file down the narrow track, around the curve of the inlet, and past the gentle waves lapping at the rocky beach.

The sheep grazed in the field behind them, under the watchful guardianship of the twins, David and Daniel. Glancing back, Judith thought the flock looked more like a fog with legs, white-clouded shapes in the encroaching darkness, their incessant bleating more annoying than their odor. Truth to tell, Judith did not like sheep much. They were stupid creatures, with a stubborn will, not at all like the sweet-faced and fluffy pets people would make them out to be. This long journey had neither changed her opinion nor accustomed her to their eternal stench.

Malcolm watched her out of the corner of his eye. She held herself proud, shoulders straight, hands clutching the reins with a little more force than necessary. She seemed alert to any sound or movement, as if she were a forest creature and scented danger at every tree or corner. She did not speak much, but he was used to, and grateful for, her silence. Instead of whining and whimpering, her stoicism had garnered his reluctant admiration during the long trip north.

It had not been an easy journey following the sheep, sleeping on the chilled ground, rising before the sun tipped the trees, riding until it was too dark to prod the sheep further. It had been difficult traversing the distance between England and the Highlands, the drizzling rain drenching them most days, the oozing mud hampering their steps. Even the sheep had become stolidly accepting of the mire after days of trudging through it.

Not once had Judith complained. She did not fit his idea of an Englishwoman. Even now, when most women would have been swooning or filling their handkerchiefs with tears, she simply looked at him with an impassive stare. It was, Malcolm thought, a Scot's trait that sat oddly on an English squire's daughter.

As they neared the open courtyard of Tynan Castle, Malcolm marveled at the more than equitable trade he had made. Not only had he managed to acquire a hundred Leicester sheep for his laird, but he had done something much, much more important.

He had gotten them for free.

Judith's presence did not disturb him much. He had plans for her, too.

He turned back to watch the track behind him. Even though they were only steps away from Tynan, it would not do to forget the threat of mounted English patrols. They crisscrossed the Highlands constantly, seeking violators of the Disarming Act. Malcolm touched the dirk hidden in his boot, well aware he was breaking the law. Yet only an idiot would have made the journey he'd just finished without being armed. Nor would it be the first time he had broken that lunatic decree. Inside his shirt, pinned next to his heart, was a shred of plaid he had torn from his kilt before he had buried it in the secret place.

They entered the narrow opening of the keep-gatehouse and into a large courtyard shadowed by approaching night. The stone of the castle had mellowed to a deep rose, and not the black Judith had originally assumed. The lofty curtain walls, with their flanking towers of massive masonry, rose high above her head. Only one tower was intact, the other pitted and scarred, rubble mounded around its base. At the entrance, stone steps rose four deep to a bronze portal marred by smoke stains that licked around it in memory of hungry flames.

There was an air of decay here, and ruin.

A figure shuffled from the shadows, her passage marked by the imperious *click, click* of her cane. She was tiny, her stooped frame clad in black, her shining white hair wound into a regal crown on top of her head.

She reached Judith's companion first, tapping his knee with the tip of her cane. He remained mounted, looking down at her; his craggy face might have been wreathed in a smile. Except that Judith was certain her companion of the past weeks never smiled.

"Malcolm MacLeod," the old woman said, her voice

sounding rusty and unused, like a gate not often opened, "have you no sense than to come riding in at gloaming? How would we know that you're not the Devil's henchman, or the English come to pay another call?"

"Sophie," he said gruffly, but not unkindly, "all you have to do is look out yon gate and see those damn bleatin' sons of Satan."

Despite her fatigue and her anxiety, Judith almost smiled.

At that moment, the old woman noticed the stranger. She peered through the gloom and then turned to Malcolm with a questioning look. He chuckled and dismounted, bent down and kissed her swiftly on the cheek.

"Peace, Sophie," he said, pulling her tiny, bent frame into a hug. "Ye're still me only love."

"Malcolm, be still," she said brusquely, but Judith could see that she was pleased by the gesture. "Well," she said, addressing her question to Judith, "who are you?"

"In a moment, Sophie, ye'll find out soon enough." When Judith made a motion to dismount, he waved her back into position. She stifled a groan. If she were to travel any further tonight, she didn't think that she could manage it. As it was, she felt permanently welded to the saddle. Riding astride might have been safer during their journey, but weeks of it would no doubt have lasting consequences upon some portions of her anatomy better left unmentioned.

The bronze door opened with a bang, and a white-shirted figure bounded down the steps. He hugged Malcolm with pleasure, gripped his arms, and pulled away as if inspecting for damage.

"You did well, Malcolm. I saw them from the battlements. Well done!" He noticed the direction of the other man's gaze and followed it.

The twilight shadows had deepened in the courtyard; the only way Judith knew he turned in her direction was that the shirt moved as if it belonged to a disembodied ghost.

Judith tensed as the white shape moved closer.

Malcolm quickly strode between them. With one hand, he gripped his laird's well-filled sleeve. With another, he grasped the hem of Judith's riding habit. He grinned, which should have given Judith some indication that all was not well. Unfortunately, either she was too bemused by the sight of those teeth gleaming in the darkness or too exhausted from the long trip to feel much anxiety.

However, Malcolm managed to shock her from fatigue with his next words.

"Judith, meet the Lord o' Tynan, Alisdair MacLeod, yer husband. An'," he quickly amended, before either of them could say a word, "Alisdair, meet Judith, yer wife."

"Wife?" Alisdair roared.

"Husband?" Judith's grip upon Molly's reins was so tight her hands felt burned by the leather.

"Did ye hear that, Sophie?" Malcolm asked calmly of the old woman.

"Yes, Malcolm, I did at that." Her thin lips were pursed in a smile.

"Well, I did, too. Congratulations, ye are now wedded according to the laws o' Scotland."

Chapter 2

"Are you all right, child?" Sophie asked kindly. Judith nodded, bemused. How could she explain that she was teetering between incredulity and a certainty she was dreaming?

"That was simply a farce, was it not? Some odd Scottish greeting? I cannot truly be married." Her face was too white; Sophie wondered if the girl was about to swoon. Her hands were clasped tightly in front of her, the knuckles so bony it was as if no flesh covered them at all.

Sophie passed Judith a candle from its perch inside the double bronze doors. The pitifully small wick did little to illuminate the deep, shaded corners of the Great Hall, merely dancing wildly in the draft, casting unfriendly shadows against already blackened walls. Whoever had burned the castle had done a fine job of it.

The older woman led the way to the rear of the main floor, waved Judith to a chair close to a fire burning brightly in the hearthstone fireplace. She leaned heavily on her cane and studied the young woman. There was a deliberate lack of expression in those dark eyes and she held herself too tightly, elbows pressed against her sides, hands clenched together.

Terrified, that was plain to see.

Sophie bent laboriously, thrusting a long twig into the fire, using its burning tip to light more candles on the mantel, playing for time while her thoughts raced.

"There are four ways to wed in Scotland, my dear," she said finally. "To be wed in the Kirk, by promise of marriage followed by coupling, by living together as man and wife." Sophie looked over at the young girl made luminous by candlelight. Her midnight blue eyes betrayed no emotion, yet she trembled like a foal new born. In that instant, Sophie made her decision. "And by announcing legal ties in front of two witnesses."

A pale face gave way to one suffused by red.

Surely the Scots were not so barbaric as to indulge in this heathen custom. Her wedding to Peter had been held in the small village church; her vows to Anthony had been spoken in her family home. Both ceremonies had been presided over by clergy, duly sanctified unions, blessed by man and supposedly by God.

It was a nightmare, wasn't it?

Judith looked down at her hands. There were scratches on the backs of them and dirt beneath her nails. She was aware of her unkempt appearance, the fact that she'd not bathed in so long she smelled like sheep. Hardly a bride. And yet, if she believed this sweet-looking woman, that's exactly what she was.

"I've been here a scant two minutes and, in that time, I've acquired a husband?" Surely this was one of her nightmares. Except, of course, that Judith could feel the chill air upon her skin. Her lashed lids were too heavy, her eyes felt filled with sand, her fingers trembled even as she clutched them tightly together. And the incongruous smell of turnips. You didn't smell turnips in your dreams, did you?

"I must admit," Sophie said kindly," it's a strange welcome we give you. Perhaps as odd as your presence here."

It was a softly coaxed invitation, one subtly offered. Later, Judith wondered why she said anything, let alone spoke the truth. Perhaps it was due to the fatigue of her journey, or the feeling of being abandoned in a strange country, subjected to odd customs. Or perhaps it was even the sudden wish to cry. This woman with her strange, lyrical accent, her face lined with a hundred small wrinkles, despite her face being heavily rouged and powdered, and her lively, sparkling blue eyes, seemed only kind, not censorious. The story of her father's barter poured from Judith like water from a pitcher.

"Yet, what did you think would happen to you here?" Sophie asked Judith when she'd finished her tale.

It was not something she'd allowed herself to contemplate. Each day, she'd occupied herself with what needed to the done, focusing on ignoring the discomforts, enduring the endless rain, living each day as something whole and complete, as if the journey itself were more important than the destination. She'd not allowed herself to think of the future; it was an interminable pit of blackness into which she could not inject one small spark of hope.

"I had thought to be employed, if nothing else," Judith said finally. "As it is," she said, looking at the pots piled high in the corner, at the crumbs of food scattered over the kitchen table, adorning the floor and every other available surface, "it seems as though I have found work aplenty. I do not have to be married to accomplish it.

"Is there no way to undo this?"

Her eyes appeared like deep pools, Sophie thought, through which one might glimpse the soul. Again, she listened to the voice of her heart before she spoke.

"I'm afraid my dear, that the only way to rid yourself of a healthy spouse is to either be an adulterer, or desert your husband for four years."

Sophie extended her hand, with its wriggling blue veins and horrid brown spots, and placed it on the Judith's young, unlined hand. She looked down at the contrast in their skin, the differences fifty years can make. She was ancient; Judith was only at the beginning of her life. Yet, how like this young girl she had once been, so sure of what she wanted that she did not allow room for fate.

Fate had a way of making things happen.

Especially if it was prodded a bit.

"You old fool, how dare you meddle in my life!"

Alisdair MacLeod wanted to hit something, quickly, and although Malcolm was twenty years his senior, he would do. The fact that Alisdair had to struggle in order to best his old tutor in hand-to-hand combat added another fillip to the situation. He was in the mood for a good fight, a brawl, a skin-tearing, flesh-bruising, bone-crushing bloody melee.

Malcolm eyed the MacLeod warily. Although they were both only long shadows in the courtyard, there was enough light to see the look on the MacLeod's face. It was intent, single-minded, and madder than hell.

Malcolm had thought long and hard before doing what he did. The past two years at Tynan had not been pleasant ones. At first, they'd been too busy trying to survive to spare the time to grieve. But then, memories had a way of seeping in through the cracks of everyday life, hadn't they? He could not help but remember Anne. The laird's young wife was a sweet girl, but had none of the fire a young, healthy man needed. Hadn't he seen the lad, tight-lipped, with a warning glint in his eyes each and every time Alisdair had gone for a long, cold soak in the cove? And hadn't there been too many of those nights?

Of course, the MacLeod would be angry—Malcolm knew there would be repercussions. And although Alisdair wasn't a hothead like his brother, Ian, he was still a Mac-Leod. Every member of that illustrious branch of the clan had a stubborn streak as wide as the glen.

Malcolm had time over the last weeks to take the mettle of the Englishwoman. Time to realize that maybe she wasn't as English as she thought, with her way of scenting the air like a young doe, of her resilience each morning when they'd awakened on the cold wet ground, her and the twins and himself all crabby with the cold, and his bones stiffening up on English soil. Maybe they could make a match of it, these two. The MacLeod with his stubbornness in the face of the English threat, and the Englishwoman who didn't act English at all.

"I could wring that scrawny neck of yours, Malcolm," Alisdair said, watching as the old man remained at least five feet away from him, despite his advance. Inside his castle, or what had once been a castle before the Duke of Cumberland's troops had paid a visit, was a woman to whom, thanks to the Machiavellian maneuvering of his old friend, he was now legally bound.

The very last thing he needed right now was a wife. He preferred a contingent of armed English soldiers, a bout of the plague, or an attack of French pox to marriage.

"Why don't you sleep on it, lad?" Malcolm suggested, the long years of friendship warming his voice.

"Why, Malcolm? Do you lack excitement in your life? Do you miss battle so much that you would bring war to Tynan? Why, man?"

"She's a wee thing, Alisdair."

"She's as tall as me, Malcolm!" Which was only a slight exaggeration. After Malcolm's announcement, he'd pulled his new bride from her saddle. The top of her head came to his nose, a fact he'd discerned only after she'd turned abruptly at the steps and nearly broken it.

"She needs protection."

"Let her hire an armed guard." Alisdair speared his hands through his hair. Malcolm was taking this entire farce too lightly.

"She's been sore used, Alisdair. She's a poor widow."

"Good God, man, now there's something to recommend her! If you must wed me without my consent, at least find me a virgin!"

"Virgins are overrated, MacLeod. Besides, what could I do, post a handbill for a willing English virgin?"

Alisdair halted abruptly, looked at the older man in disbelief. Dark shadows kept him from discerning Malcolm's expression, but not the white flash of smile. He told himself to remain calm.

"She's English, too, Malcolm?"

"Aye, she came with the sheep."

"What, as nursemaid? Drover? Does she perform lambings, or does she shear? Does she card wool, perhaps? What the hell do you mean, she comes with the sheep?" He nearly spit out the words.

"One hundred Leicester sheep, give or take the few we lost on the trip. For free, MacLeod."

"Who sold you this doubtful bit of goods?"

"Her father, the Squire. A true Sassenach." Malcolm's grimace seemed to convey his exact impression of Squire Cuthbertson.

"Her father?"

"Aye."

"Are you saying her father traded her?" Despite his intentions, his voice lost the restrained tone he had managed in the last few minutes, and rose to a roar.

"He's no' a likable mon, MacLeod."

"Is she deformed?" He had not seen her, only felt the strong resistance of her thin frame bouncing against his. That, and the violent thrust of her head against his nose. He fingered the bridge of it gently.

"No, MacLeod, she's no' deformed. Just a mite skinny."

"So you bring her here, to feast on turnips and cabbages and potato pancakes," he said sardonically.

"Aye, and mutton, too."

Alisdair stared at his old friend, now only a black shape in the darkness, and tried to prevent his lips from twitching, but it was a losing battle. He finally could not stop his laughter.

Alisdair wondered later what the hell he found so amusing.

Chapter 3

His head hurt, but Alisdair would pay that price gladly. He and Malcolm had sampled a few bottles of Squire Cuthbertson's brandy. How the old Scot had acquired it, Alisdair had not asked. There were some things he preferred not to know. The squire, however unwittingly, had provided the two of them a glorious night of celibate debauchery. Well, it had been a glorious drunk, anyway. Heather ale was all well and good, but brandy, now there was a drink. Not as smooth as Scots whiskey, of course, but still, a fine golden taste on the tongue. In his youth, in Edinburgh and in Belgium, he had consumed many a glass of strong spirits, with never a thought to the cost. But drink, like all other things youth thought so necessary, now demanded a price both in pain of the body and in good honest coin that was too dear.

Alisdair felt every day of his thirty-two years.

He shifted, and wondered why his bed was so hard. He slitted open one eye and gazed at the feeble rays of sunrise through the gate. Good God, he had slept in the courtyard all night. He looked to his left, but Malcolm was gone.

He blinked, flinching with the pain of that simple gesture. God, he hurt. Something was rolling around in his head, a thought that he must remember.

Woman . . . Wife . . .

He'd forgotten.

He levered himself up on his knees and tried to pretend that the pain in his head was only a temporary thing. Pressing both hands against his temples seemed to be a necessary action in order to prevent his brain from oozing out his ears. His stomach urged him to retch, and wouldn't that be a waste of a good drunk?

He finally managed to straighten by the simple trick of leaning against the wall until the dizziness eased somewhat and he could bear it. He was getting too old for this. He wondered how Malcolm did it. He hoped, fervently, that the old man was suffering in a similar way.

God saw fit to deny his prayer.

He heard his cheerful whistle before he saw him, and with a last, stoic effort, Alisdair raised himself straight and stepped away from the wall, hoping that his face did not look as green as it felt.

"Good morning, MacLeod," Malcolm said, cheerfully, "an' a fine, fine mornin' it is."

Alisdair nodded weakly.

He asked about the woman's whereabouts, and Malcolm's response was a taciturn growl and an equally short-tempered snarl.

"And why would ye be wantin' to know?" Malcolm slitted his eyes at him, and Alisdair scowled at the condemnation in their depths. Malcolm should feel the inside of his head—he doubted his dour friend would feel such charity, then.

"To beat her, of course," he said caustically, leveling an intent look at his companion. It was a look that several members of his clan would correctly identify as a warning— one that cautioned against pursuing a certain course of action. In Malcolm's case, it did not deter him one bit.

"I'm thinkin' ye'll be leavin' the lass alone. She should be sleeping like the dead."

"Where?" An economy of words kept the pain in his head to a tolerable level.

"And where do ye ken? Four rooms fit for a mousie to live in."

Malcolm had found her asleep in the chair beside the fire. He'd led her, then, to the room that had been Ian's chamber. The other rooms stood open and gaping, their wooden doors burned to ash, their interiors nothing but blackened shells. Yet, some sentimental notion had prompted the women of the clan to ready Ian's room as though Alisdair's brother had not been lost at Culloden.

Alisdair threw him another fierce scowl, but Malcolm only turned away, hiding his wide grin.

If he hadn't drunk enough brandy last night to summon forth a regiment of drummers in his brain, Alisdair wouldn't have minded that the roof frame was to be raised onto the new weavers' hut this morning. Now, he groaned at the thought of climbing twenty feet in the air while his stomach rolled and his head pounded and every limb felt dangerously weak. It was, he thought with a self-deprecating smile, enough of a lesson to keep him away from the brandy for months.

He'd taken the time to inspect the sheep. They looked healthy enough, but their fleece should be spun of gold thread for the aggravation they'd brought with them.

Yet, his only thought the minute he mounted the fragile wooden frame of the half-completed weavers' hut was his clan's welfare.

The crofters needed income. Income that was fixed and permanent and not subject to excess taxes or the fortunes of war. The Leicester sheep Malcolm had brought home would be cross bred to their native black-faced breed, and the result would be longer fleece, and a thriving industry from the wool they would produce and weave. England paid dearly for Irish linen; Alisdair had long since vowed they would pay as well for Scots wool.

As he stretched and pulled the lattice work of the roof

frame in place, he was not aware of anything but the task at hand.

Malcolm, however, made sure Alisdair didn't forget his new wife.

From his viewpoint twenty feet off the ground, Alisdair could see Malcolm striding toward him, accompanied by the Englishwoman. His clansman made a point of stopping at several of the crofters' cottages and introducing Judith. Alisdair could imagine what was said by the sharp looks directed his way. It would take only minutes before the knowledge of his new bride swept the village.

Damn Malcolm!

He looked down at the woman standing in a pool of light. The darkness had not flattered her. Here, at least, the sunlight picked up the tints of red and gold in her hair, turning the mousy brown into a rich hue. She was taller than most of the women in his clan, and although slender, the bodice of her dress strained over breasts most men would pay money to touch.

There was promise in that face, he thought, as he watched her with a physician's detachment, colored as it was with his own personal thoughts. Her skin was so fair that it was almost translucent. Her face was too thin, accentuating the high angle of her cheekbones and that autocratic-looking nose. No Roman god would be complete without a nose that patrician. Her lips, full and tinged a pale coral, pursed at the sight of him.

Her eyes were black, he realized with a start, as she raised her face and stared at him. No, blue. Midnight blue, like the color of the sea during a storm.

He pulled the ladder from its perch near the frame, hooked a boot on the top rung, and lowered himself to the ground, jumping the last three rungs. His head thumped with discomfort.

She tensed, the closer he came.

He had only been a vision of sweeping shadows before. That, and a long, lean column of strength as he had propelled her off her saddle. Now she could see him clearly. It was not a reassuring sight.

Alisdair MacLeod was a large man. He was tall, and the black trousers he wore did nothing to hide the muscles outlined in his widespread legs. Nor did the white shirt, rolled to the elbows, conceal the strength of his forearms or the breadth of his shoulders.

He could snap her in two.

She took a tiny step backwards, and he smiled. The gesture only focused her attention on his face. She wished he were ugly. Her gaze traveled up from that strong column of neck, fully exposed by the open collar of his shirt, past the strong cleft chin that she suspected jutted out at the world in stubborn defiance. Her eyes swept past the molded lips, aristocratic and now quirked in ironic humor, up the nose which changed direction once, to meet his eyes. They were fixed on her with a directness that left her gasping. They were brown, hinting at gold. Here, in the sunlight, they seemed to gleam with hidden depths, like the finest brandy sparkling in the light of a hundred candles. His hair was black, long and curling, and swept from his face by an impatient gesture and a short leather tie.

She shuddered.

"That bad?" he asked, having borne her inspection without a word, although it had, unaccountably, made him acutely uncomfortable. But shuddering was a bit much, wasn't it? Granted, they had all fallen upon hard times, but he was still as clean as possible under the circumstances. He shaved each morning, he changed his clothes each day, he brushed his teeth with a tiny brush dipped in precious salt, he bathed often, even if that bath was no more than a quick dip in the cove.

He glared at her. She stared back. The clanspeople muttered.

Malcolm, damn him, smiled.

"I want out of this marriage," she said, in a clear, ringing voice. It could have carried to Edinburgh, he thought. She also sounded too damn English. He could feel the tension in the people around him, as the shock of her voice filled the air.

"Good, so do I."

"Fine, would you give me some money, please, and I'll desert you for four years. That will do it, won't it, Malcolm?" She looked to the other man for assent.

"Aye, lass, it will."

"Malcolm," Alisdair said, turning to the other man, who stood grinning at both of them, "since you are the fount of so many wonderful ideas, perhaps you'll tell me what I'm to use for coin." His tone was conversational, as though he did not have the sudden urge to begin shouting.

"Money could be a problem, lass," Malcolm said, nodding wisely.

Judith gripped her hands tightly.

"Have *you* any money, Malcolm?" she asked shortly.

He thought for a moment, as if considering the matter. "No, lass, I don't."

There were too many people about, all silent, their gaze fixed on her. Even the clan's leader stood with his feet braced apart, his arms crossed in front of his chest, studying her. The silence was oppressive, the regard too intent.

Judith knew too well what she looked like. She was too tall, too thin, with long legs and lean hips. Anthony had once told her it looked as if she'd been stretched between two trees. Her shoulders were too broad, her breasts too large, as if nature, having granted her little grace and few womanly attributes, felt justified in giving her a doxy's chest.

Her nose jutted out like the prow of a ship, her lips were too full, her eyes too strange a color, her hair dung-colored and straight. If anything, Judith felt more plain than before, standing before this magnificent-looking man with his casual elegance despite the sweat stains on his shirt, and the dust of his trousers.

The ghost of a smile on his tanned face made her feel even more ridiculous.

She turned to leave, but he moved quickly to intercept

her. He was suddenly beside her, one large, tanned hand on the sleeve of her dress.

For a second, she believed the look of compassion on his face. Only a second, until she remembered the lessons of the past—that emotions were easily manipulated, and that it would be safer simply not to trust anyone.

"Unhand me. Now." She pulled away, but he gripped her tightly.

"Guard your words with care, woman," he said, hearing the barely audible collective gasp. None dared issue orders to the MacLeod.

The sudden fire in her eyes surprised him, almost as much as what she did next. She looked into his face, studying him, as if searching for something visible there. What she saw caused her to glance down at her feet, as if her dusty boots were worthy of immediate and fascinating scrutiny.

"Forgive me," she said, the words well practiced, easily said. They meant nothing. She'd said those words all her life, easy words to excuse her very existence. Forgive me. Judith gave them to him freely and gained herself some safety.

Alisdair cautioned himself to think nothing of the fine tremor that skated along her skin, to ignore the flinch she thought to hide. He released his grip on her arm, intrigued despite himself by the way the texture of her skin changed, the bumps mottling her flesh as if she'd been chilled by a gust of icy wind.

He extended one finger, tilted up her chin. She didn't want to acquiesce to such an inspection, but he was resolute, the pressure under her chin more forceful than it appeared, less tender. But this was not a tender moment between them, reluctant bride and unwilling groom.

Finally, she looked at him, surrendering to his stubbornness. If it was submission he wanted, she gave it to him then, her long lashes drooping over an impassive glance. The only thing lacking was a sweeping curtsey, a kowtow of homage. Her lips closed; they breathed no words, neither censure nor conciliation. Her face paled, but a tinge of color, a faint shadow of pink appeared above the collar of her ugly dress.

What emotion drove her to grant herself so easily to him? Or did she do so at all? Did this woman hide with the alacrity of a winter-traveling rabbit, in plain sight? Who was she, that she could disappear so quickly even as he held her within his grasp?

Alisdair considered himself a rational man, an educated man, yet he was still a Scot. And his ancestors, long gone and buried in the earth that surrounded his burnt-out home, bequeathed him a thousand years of belief in omens, signs, and that feeling which now trickled from the back of his neck in an icy stream down his spine.

This woman stood silent and still, a sentinel announcing danger at the same time she declared herself a mystery imploring to be solved. Alisdair knew he would be better off forgetting he'd ever touched her, knowing in that uncanny way given to a Scot that she posed more problems than he had time to solve.

He could almost hear the warning in the wind.

Chapter 4

Bennett wiped the blood off himself, carefully, deliberately. He was disappointed, but then, he had been thwarted often in the last two years.

Pity the sport had ended so quickly, but he'd grown tired of her witless pleading, had ended up stuffing her mouth with her own petticoat. Such tactics only spoiled the rest of the sport.

He finished tying his ascot, blessing the fact that his valet had left his employ three years ago over the paltry inconvenience of being unpaid. Bennett had learned to fend for himself since then. Doing so in such circumstances as he found himself in now only simplified things.

He kicked at the stiffening body at his feet, wondering if he should bury this one, then shrugged. What was one more carrion in this land of walking skeletons? He'd thought the slut was going to give him a good game. True, her backside was a little too bony, her tits too small. Still, she'd had a hot little cavern and a scream that had made him as hard as the rocks surrounding this godforsaken trysting place.

He donned his waistcoat, straightened it by pulling on

the front and, jerking it into place, riffled a long-fingered hand through his bright blond hair. Her golden boy, she'd called him. He chuckled. It was both a pity and a necessity that his victims be so idiotic and devoid of sense. They must be romantics, these Highland whores, the better to believe him.

How many did that make now? Six? Seven? No, eight, counting this one.

The first one had been Moira, barely seventeen, with the palest milky skin and the faintest of freckles. Her hair was the color of a dawn sky—or at least that's what he had told her—softly auburn, nearly red. Her fingers were long-boned and fine, and had performed the most exquisite of functions, trailing over his skin with eagerness, willing to learn all that he'd taught her. She had been so pathetically grateful for his attention that she would have done anything he asked.

Looking back, Bennett believed she might have been the best of all of them.

He'd met her on the moors, where she'd been filling her apron with odd-shaped purple flowers—for heather ale, she told him later.

"If it's gathering of the flowers you're doing, lass, you've missed a few."

She whirled and stood, facing him. Wordlessly, she stared at him, shook her head, and then smiled brightly at the picture he'd presented.

He was not such an idiot to seek out his victims dressed in his regimentals. It pleased him, however, to pretend to be a fool, to solicit humor and even pathos. In this disguise, he was a wool factor from Inverness. He wore brightly colored green trousers, a dun-colored shirt, the outfit topped by a long ankle-length outer coat of a mud color. His boots were coated with muck, his hat was a floppy thing a cavalier would have worn in another century.

"It's the weather," Bennett said, almost apologetically, to the girl who stood looking at him with wonder in her eyes and a small smile around her mouth. "Never can get warm enough, even in summer, especially traipsing over these hills." He studied the ground carefully as he slowly approached her. "Tripped a while ago, I did," he explained, with a grin, glancing up at her. "Rabbits, or some such."

"You're English," she said, her amusement replaced by Scots caution.

"Half. Only half. Father English, Mother a good Scots lass from Inverness."

"You don't sound Scots."

"The English say I don't sound English. What is a man to do?" His mobile lips turned up into a comical quirk.

He extended one gloved hand to her, grasped her fingers, and kissed the air above her hand. With a flourish, he lifted off his hat and swept it into a low arc, causing the poor feather to sweep the ground. She smiled and her smile was answered by his.

Ah, Moira, how much fun they'd had. She even believed he was going to marry her, enough to gather her small parcel of possessions and meet him on the outskirts of her village. She did not know that he would never allow a child of his to be the get of a whore. She'd cried the day he'd taken her virginity, but then, she'd been easily placated by empty words and a hint of a bright, loving future.

Perhaps he'd gone a bit far too soon with dear Moira. Yet, she'd lived two whole days, for all her delicacy. Of all the women who followed her, he remembered her with the most fondness.

For the last two years, he'd been assigned to this hellish spot, a boil on the arse of humanity. Routine patrols only took so much time, his companions' diversions bored him more often than not. He amused himself by selecting his women with patience, wooing them with words and a genteel cavalier approach. Such a painstakingly planned strategy was designed to occupy his free hours. All in all, it was not a difficult deception. To play the fool, a little food, a smile or two, a few tender kisses, and each woman willingly met him in a deserted spot like this one, their final resting place spotted with gorse and blooming flowers.

The lonely women of Scotland were like fish caught in a leaking pond, dying of their circumstances. He was their friend, their lover, and ultimately, their savior. He saved them from the drab existence of their own lives. It was not a role which displeased him.

This one—what was her name again, oh yes, Mary—had come eagerly to this deserted place, fed for weeks on scant kisses and tender touches. She'd fallen to the ground skirt up, bodice open, mouth hungry to feed off him. She loved him, she loved him, she loved him, she said, murmuring the words over and over like a benediction of the damned.

Her eager compliance was not what he'd wanted, but it was not until she'd seen the knife that she'd suspected anything was amiss. Even then, she'd not believed, not entirely. Not until a crimson line had appeared upon her chest—a bridge linking her two small breasts—had she comprehended that he was not gentle suitor as much as victor, that he wanted not her pleading nor her submission.

He wanted her terror.

His victims' intense and unrelenting fear was the greatest aphrodisiac, filling Bennett with blood lust, an almost mindless passion that made him dizzy when they died, mouths open and screaming to the four winds as if beseeching someone for help.

Of course, no one ever came.

Mary had finally fought him towards the end, not liking the pain. It had taken too much effort on his part to maintain her fear, the silly cow. She'd retained that befuddled look almost to the end. Her soft brown eyes had worn a look of surprise, shock, and finally horror in their depths, as if she could not quite believe what he was doing.

Bennett smiled again and did up his trousers, patting the cloth over his now dwindled member in approbation. He stared down without interest at the body rapidly cooling on the harsh grasses of the moor. It no longer bled as copiously, but a hundred slivers colored first scarlet and then nearly black with congealed blood told the tale of these past hours. His talented knife was cleaned by the simple expedient of wiping it on the tall grass. He would sharpen it later; it was amazing how dull it became after one of these afternoons.

He wondered what his sister-in-law would have said about his newest penchant. His dear brother's wife, loaned on more than one occasion. God, he'd lusted after her, hadn't he? So silent, so still, until he came for her. All he had to do was smile at her and she would whimper. He had her tied at first, but later, even that was unnecessary. He'd barely had to touch her before her screams began. But she'd had the stamina to take whatever he gave her, didn't she? He'd never used the knife on her, though. What would she have done? The thought of it engorged him again, and he cursed the dead and useless woman at his feet.

Too bad she was not nearby. Too bad.

He really missed Judith.

Chapter 5

"Aye, lass, it's a bonny sight ye are."

Judith wanted to tell Malcolm to save his compliments for someone who would believe him. Instead, she opted for silence.

She'd been left alone all afternoon, and while idle hands might be the devil's tools, her equally unoccupied brain focused on the absurdity of her situation. She had not, however, found a way to end her enforced visit to Scotland. She had no friends, no funds, and she dared not return to her family. What was she to do now?

Finally, having no outlet nor answer for her worrisome thoughts, she occupied herself with the basics of life. By the end of the day, Judith was certain that being clean was considered a luxury in Scotland. She had trudged up the steep, downward sloping stairs with three buckets of warm water, willing to endure any hardship in order to wash the scent of sheep from her skin. Only when her standing bath was complete did she use the last of the warm water to wash her hair. The meager contents of her valise yielded a boar bristle brush, which she used to brush her hair free of tangles while it dried.

Her ablutions were completed with thoughts of comfort, rather than beauty. There was no vanity in the fact that her hair fell at the midpoint of her back, or that it was thick, rife with red and gold highlights and curled on its own. There was no mirror to see if her dress fit well, or if the color flattered her complexion. She did not care if her lips appeared bloodless or her cheeks were too pale. She'd long since avoided mirrors, it being too painful to see the person reflected there. As long as her laces were tied tightly and her hair pinned back from her face, that was as much as Judith cared about, that was all the vanity she required.

If she wished, sometimes, to be different, then those were silly dreams. There was no point in pretending that things would ever be different. She was simply who she was, both outer plainness and inner soil. Dreaming and wishing wouldn't make it better, wouldn't change it.

The summons to dinner had come just as she was deciding whether or not she should venture from the room again. The fact that the MacLeod stood imperiously at the bottom of the stairs, glowering up at her, almost changed her mind about following Malcolm down the steps. Only the hunger gnawing at her stomach convinced her to continue.

Judith thought later that she should have stayed in her room and demanded bread and water. It might have been edible.

She sat between Malcolm and Sophie and poked suspiciously at her dinner of translucent vegetables and a gruel that tasted of laundry water. They served themselves, and she watched in wonder as Malcolm returned to the pot simmering above the fire time and time again. He must have a cast-iron stomach, she mused, as she forced down a potato. Even the MacLeod, sitting on the other side of the broad oak table, picked at his dinner fastidiously, as if he, too, were concerned about its ingredients.

One of their clanswomen had prepared the meal, she was told at her tentative inquiry. Judith could begin to understand Malcolm's desperation in obtaining a wife for the MacLeod. Yet, she could have chopped, diced, pared, boiled, and stewed just as well in an unmarried state as she could being linked to the lord of this pile of bricks.

The lord in question ignored her presence as studiously as she would have liked to ignore his. Her eyes scanned the tall form seated across the table, noting his broad shoulders, the tanned arms, the large hands with their fingers blunted by calluses, marred by a hundred tiny scrapes and cuts. His head was bent upon his task of consuming his meal, but although he ate with diligence, his manners were better than Anthony's or even Peter's.

Nor was that the only way he differed from her two previous husbands.

He had a scent about him not redolent of the sickroom, like Peter reeking of camphor, or of blood and sweat, like Anthony. His was a clean, crisp scent, like pine and the outdoors. His black hair was thick, as shiny as a raven's wing, not blond or thinning. He was taller and broader than both her husbands; his shoulders strained the seams of his worn white shirt, his thighs pressed against the fabric of his trousers too well, leaving nothing to the imagination.

His face was marked by strong, decisive features. Twin lines bracketed his jaw as if leading the way to a full, squared-off bottom lip. Sun or wind, or life itself, had carved faint lines around his eyes, but instead of detracting from his appearance, they only added depth and substance to that face. He used his eyes like weapons; a direct amber stare from the MacLeod was like an invasion of the soul. And when he smiled and those white, even teeth flashed in that strong, tanned face, a flutter of fear spiraled in her belly.

Sophie felt the barely hidden currents between Judith and her grandson and smiled.

"Malcolm," she said to her clansman who was obviously, and loudly, enjoying his meal, "would you mind leaving us alone, please?"

Malcolm looked to the MacLeod, who barely nodded,

then at Judith, who only concentrated on her bowl. Finally, he glanced again at Sophie, who smiled softly at him. He filled his bowl once more before leaving the kitchen, to Judith's repugnance and the MacLeod's amusement.

Sophie had thought all day about what she would say. Age and wisdom had given her the will, her courage had been fortified by the knowledge that time, itself, was slipping from her grasp. These days, Sophie could remember her childhood on her father's estate in France with more clarity than she could the previous hour. Such ability amused her, proving her finally old in the way her ancient, wrinkled grandmother had been old. Strange, but there were times she didn't feel elderly at all. Inside, she felt like a young girl, except for possessing the memories of a well-lived, well-loved life.

Oh, Gerald, it would not be long, would it? It did not strike her as strange that she prayed to him more often than the God of her youth. She had loved him so, this proud, vital man who had become her husband, her heart. But, ah, not without a struggle.

There were things to do before she could be with him again, things she must accomplish, duties she must discharge, not the least her grandson's happiness. What a stubborn man he was. Almost as stubborn as his grandfather. Sophie sighed, but the sound was accompanied by the wisp of a smile. Aye, as loving, too, she thought, remembering.

Judith reminded Sophie too much of herself. She, too, had come reluctantly to Scotland, many years ago. And she, too, had fought against the union planned for her without her consent. The Agincourt family in France had long ties with the MacLeods, and Sophie's marriage helped ensure the continuation of that relationship. Yet, despite her initial unwillingness, this land of fierce Scots had become a land of beauty for her, the initial loneliness she'd felt had shifted to become a deep and abiding love.

If she could, she would grant such an opportunity to these young people.

Sophie folded her hands upon the top of her cane. That they waited for her words was evident, that each waited with their own dread was also clear. Judith's head was bowed over her bowl, but Sophie did not need to see her face to know that her eyes would be dark and filled with emotion. Nor did she need to decipher the fixed and tensile strength of her grandson's jaw. Such stubborn people, each in their own way.

"I will give you three months, children," she said, a soft smile softening the edge of her words, "to see if you do not truly suit. At the end of that time, if you do not feel that you can make a life together, then I will evaluate my words in the courtyard. It is quite possible that I made a mistake, and did not say anything binding when Malcolm asked it of me." She looked at Alisdair as she spoke.

At question was the intent of their declaration in the courtyard. A couple must wish to be married to each other for such a bond to be recognized. Yet, by his actions today, by introducing Judith as the laird's wife throughout the clan, Malcolm had made Alisdair's willingness perfectly clear, a declaration as binding as wedding lines. They were considered wed by the clan and by their own customs.

There was silence while each evaluated her words. When Judith spoke, her words echoed Alisdair's thoughts, a coincidence which did not dull the edge of his irritation.

"I could save you the time," Judith said softly. "I know we will not suit."

Alisdair nodded in complete accord.

"If you do not at least try, then my memory is without fault, child."

"Granmere, as much as I would wish an end to this farce, I do not ask you to lie."

"Alisdair, it is my fondest wish to see you settled before I die. Life is too short to spend it in regret or pain. I would do anything to bring about your peace, even if it means forgetting a few details." She smiled fondly at her grandson. He reminded her so much of her own beloved Gerald.

"Never doubt one thing, my dear," she said addressing

Judith, "if you doubt all other things in life. This land breeds a fierce people. Stubborn, loyal to a fault, believing in causes the rest of the world would sooner disavow. My grandson is the epitome of all that is good about this land. You could do worse for a husband."

Perhaps it might be said that he could do better for a wife, Judith thought, looking down at the table before her, intent upon her inner thoughts and not the unpalatable bowl of watery soup. She glanced up only once at the frail woman who wore such determination on her features, and caught a glimpse of the strange flush upon the MacLeod's face. If she did not know better, she would have thought the MacLeod embarrassed by his grandmother's fulsome praise. Embarrassed, indeed.

"If, at the end of this time," Sophie continued, as if she had not seen the look Judith directed towards Alisdair, "you do not feel content here, then you are free to go. Although there is little in the way of actual coin, there is my jewelry. It would enable you to live for some time."

"I could not do that," Judith protested.

"Nor will I allow you to," Alisdair said curtly. In the last two years, despite the hardships, near starvation, and deprivation they had all suffered, he had not touched his grandmother's jewelry.

It was not pride. Pride had died when he harnessed himself in front of a plow. Pride had died when he'd broken up furniture for firewood, deep in the winter when the snows were too thick and the winds too fierce and howling to venture from Tynan's walls. Pride had died when he had returned home to Tynan, sick with grief and despair, only to stare in horror at the assembled scarecrows who were his clan. And the remnants of that pride—frail wisps that they were—had died an ignominious death when he scrabbled in the earth, finding long-forgotten potato mounds, unearthing food, any food, for his starving people. No, it was not pride, but a curious sort of sentiment, out of place for this time perhaps, but still powerful.

There was little they had left that belonged to the past. They had been stripped of their heritage and forbidden their culture. All that was accessible to them were memories and a few trinkets. Sophie's jewelry may have purchased temporary comfort, but their loss would have been greater than what they bought. The brooches, the necklaces she hid away, a few bracelets of gold, and the sparkling gems which had never been mounted, were gifts from his grandfather. Although she would not have begrudged selling them, Alisdair had seen the way she occasionally took them from their safekeeping and traced the line of each one, silent tears falling down her cheeks. He would not touch his grandmother's memories. Nor would he let this Englishwoman leave with them.

"We all do what we must, children, at the time," Sophie said, her stubbornness, if he'd realized it, the match of her grandson's. "My jewels are mine to do with as I will. Besides, have you forgotten something? Your parting is not a fait accompli. I will be the arbiter here. If I feel you have not honestly tried, then you remain wed.

"Child," she said, glancing at Judith, "we do not live in ordinary times, and it is not as if you were a maiden. If you were, this agreement between us would not be possible. You have been wed before. Therefore, a few months with Alisdair will neither enhance your reputation nor destroy it. Do you understand?"

"I think you are hinting at warmer relations, Granmere," Alisdair interrupted, "but such a thing will not happen." He had no desire to compound the complexities of his life by welcoming this Englishwoman to his bed.

Judith forced herself not to look up from the scarred oak boards of the table.

"But you will try, won't you, to get along? You will try," Sophie admonished them, "because if you don't, be prepared to spend the rest of your lives together."

It was a sobering enough thought to make Judith look at the MacLeod full-faced. It was such a frightening thought that he stared back at the Englishwoman without scowling.

A spark has often kindled a big fire, Sophie thought, and smiled.

Chapter 6

Something was hurting.

Her eyes would not open. No, that was not right. Judith tried to blink again, fighting against the heaviness of her lids. She reached to press her hand against her eyes, to free herself from the cloth, only then realizing that her hands were tied. Bound together over her head so tightly that her arms ached with the discomfort. She pulled on them, but all she accomplished by that futile gesture was to tighten the rope that bit into her wrists. Terror washed through her like a fountain of fear, bathing every pore in sour-smelling sweat.

She let out a startled scream when a voice spoke near her ear. "Ah," it said, in a low, almost considerate tone, as a hand reached out and covered her mouth, "you are awake. Good. I would hate to think that you would be missing this next part."

"Please," she pleaded, her words muffled by the pressure of that hand.

"And rob us of our fun?" Another low chuckle. "I think not." The hand was replaced by lips that were too hot and too wet, and she almost gagged at the insertion of a tongue into her mouth. He tasted of brandy and tobacco. The revulsion she felt was enough to clamp her teeth firmly against that intrusion.

He recoiled immediately, his gasp of pain her only reward for momentary courage. That, and the vicious blow strong enough to knock her head to the side. She screamed then, as loudly and as strongly as she could. It was the only thing she had left, the only defense. But they only laughed at her screams, as if the sound of her terror excited them, wolves amused by the plaintive sound of fear.

The blanket was stripped from her body; the cool rush of air chilled her sweating skin. She kicked out with legs that were free of bindings, but her thrashing movements only encouraged masculine laughter, they did not stop the stroking hand which obscenely and leisurely explored her body. Nor did her struggles impede the invading fingers, which cruelly poked and probed. Her hips bucked up from the mattress at the pain from those thrusting fingers, but that movement only seemed to foster ribald comments from those in the room.

The mattress sagged with one man's weight. His legs brushed her own, the rough hair upon them scraping against her skin. Judith lunged upwards again, as if to dislodge him. A muffled groan followed by an oath indicated that she had managed to inflict some pain on her assailant.

"Stretch her legs out, Anthony, and fasten her ankles to the bedposts."

She did not make it easy for them. Yet, even her strength, born of terror and underlaid with rage, was not enough in the end. The manacles fastened around her ankles were red with blood before she collapsed against the mattress. Still, she did not meekly acquiesce to their plans for her.

As she squirmed in abhorrence at the touch of the hands and lips which explored her body at will, arching her torso from side to side in the only movement allowed her, laughter was interspersed by coarse encouragement.

"By god, she loves it!" one voice shouted.

"Your bitch needs taming, Anthony!"

As if in punishment for her defiance, her breasts were tightly squeezed by brutal fingers. She moaned in pain, but that slight sound seemed to encourage her assailant, who bit her nipples *cruelly in a parody of pleasure. Yet, even that pain was easily forgotten in the agony that followed.*

Thrusting fingers were replaced by his male member, as it ruthlessly invaded her, tearing the walls of her dry passage, lubricating his rape with her own blood. Her assailant's grunt of pleasure accompanied her own muffled screams.

Nor did it stop there.

His release found, the first one left, only to be replaced by another. Still another took his place, marking her body with a series of vicious bites and sucking marks, driving into her until agony was just a mild word compared to the writhing torment that was her body.

Her mind was not occupied in this battle for survival, it sat outside of her body, watching with dumbstruck eyes as she was made victim. Wet warmth seeped from between her legs and she knew that she was bleeding freely. With each thrust, part of her soul was injured along with her body.

Judith's first waking thought was that she was alone, that the nightmare which had left her trembling and spent was only the stuff of memories. It was not real. Not anymore. Anthony was dead and his brother far away. She was safe in this burnt-out castle. And that was the most fitting irony of all, wasn't it? That her father had unwittingly sent her to a sanctuary.

And Sophie MacLeod had offered an incredible bargain.

That the Scots found it necessary to honor such a bizarre ritual as her courtyard marriage was odd in itself; honor not having been a commodity highly revered in her past experience. Her father thought it only a word used by weaklings, but then, he routinely cheated and lied if it meant reaping more profit. Nor had either of her previous husbands seemed overly endowed with what might be called character.

Judith sat on the edge of the sagging mattress, her hands still trembling. The nightmare hadn't come in months, but she was not unduly surprised it had visited her last night. This place summoned ghosts and memories, this desolate castle with its burnt walls and its constant smell of soot.

She stood, looking out the window and the view of dawn which beckoned. The scene itself was an oddity, so different from her first view of Tynan, so changed from somber night. It was as if nature had arranged a sampler for her taste, a teasing bit of topography to stir the eye. A gray angle of mountain sat far in the distance, its color dark mist topped by white, like foaming milk upon a slab of chocolate. Tall pines thrust from a promontory to her left to soar to the sky, their branches so thick, the covering so solid, it was as if the earth were bearded in green. The cliff fell to a sea which boiled up and crashed against huge boulders, then subsided into the gentle rock-lined cove surrounding Tynan on three sides. The slash of color was brilliant on this fine morning in the Highlands. Deep cerulean blues from both the sky and the sea, emerald from the forests, white from the flecked waves and far-off snows, gray from the shadowed mountains and deep waves.

Judith closed her eyes and sniffed. The tang of the air was so different from London; it did not come from emptied chamber pots, her neighbors' cooking, or the stench from the Thames. It was pleasant and crisp, a hint of ocean salt and recently turned earth. Nature's scent, not man's.

Three months was a relatively short time when her marriage to Anthony had lasted an interminable four years. Three months was nothing, really, especially if it promised safety and freedom at the end of it. Three months would carry her to autumn, when the roads should still be passable. But she wouldn't go back to England. She would start a new life, begin again some place new and as fresh as this dawn morning.

Judith would have washed with cold water and enjoyed it, had she remembered to fill the ewer the night before. She'd been too eager to escape the kitchen table to concern herself with that chore. Now, she simply sighed, dressed in the same dress she had carefully removed last night, scraping her hair back into a serviceable bun. She squared her shoulders, drew a deep breath, and opened the door leading to the hall.

And nearly collided with the object of her thoughts.

The MacLeod stopped, looked her over without comment, a sweeping inspection that carried with it neither derision nor approval. It was a totally expressionless examination, as if she'd not been there at all, and he studied the wall behind her.

Neither said a word, and yet a volume had been spoken.

She knew only too well what he thought of her. Men like the MacLeod—graced with aristocratic good looks, strength of body, and firmness of resolve—normally wanted only one thing from a woman. And usually experienced no difficulty obtaining it. Judith thanked the heavens that he didn't seem to wish it from her. Yet, what if he changed his mind, and that look came into his eyes, and his stare focused on her chest? There seemed to be something magical about the size of her breasts which sucked the brains from even an intelligent man. Would he, too, make comments about her physical shape? Brush by her accidentally, liken her to a mare eager to be mounted?

Without a word, he was gone, down the curving staircase.

Moments later, she followed the route the MacLeod had taken, peering into the kitchen before she entered it. The room was empty, so Judith grabbed a grimy turnip for a solitary breakfast and sat upon one of the scarred wooden benches.

Would it be like this for three months? Her heart in her throat, her blood only pooling ice. How could she do it? How could she possibly do it? Three months stretched out in one-minute increments. And yet, she had played that game before, hadn't she?

What other choice did she have?

She listed the alternatives in her mind the way a shopkeeper would tally his profits, except the list was pitifully small and there was no joy at the sum. In the end, she had no other choice.

Seated upon the bench in the kitchen, with only the scrabbling sounds of vermin accompanying her thoughts, Judith Cuthbertson Willoughby Henderson MacLeod reluctantly conceded that there was, after all, only one option open. As much as it frightened her, she would have to remain married to the MacLeod.

But only for a little while.

Chapter 7

"Come on, man, we've almost got it!" Alisdair MacLeod shouted at his ancient clansman.

The faltering Geddes was no match for the plow that stubbornly skidded along the weed-choked ground. A few moments later, Alisdair dropped the leather straps wound around his shoulders and torso and wearily walked back to where Geddes stood, bent over with age and the shame of being unable to contribute to even this simple task. Alisdair, well aware of the state of the old man's pride, clapped him encouragingly on the shoulder as he thrust his worn boot at the metal flange, stomping and kicking at it until it found purchase in the stubborn soil. Grasping the wooden handles of the plow between two large, callused hands, he showed Geddes how to hold them firmly as his laird acted as their draft horse.

Alisdair disliked having his ancient clansman help in the rough work, but Geddes needed to feel useful. That, coupled with the fact that there was no one else to do this chore adequately, subdued Alisdair's conscience.

The Englishwoman was still on his mind, damn her, despite the plowing to be done.

Alisdair could not recall one instance when he had frightened a woman. When he was young, studying at the University, he'd no complaints. The girls, well, the girls of Edinburgh and Brussels had thought he was a fine enough companion for winter nights and summer dreamings. And Anne, she was the most gentle creature of all; he'd never disquieted poor dear Anne.

Even lately, when care and worry was ever present on his mind, he was gentle with the women of his clan. He'd never frightened them, not even Fiona, who might have benefited from a good scold.

Yet, he'd managed to scare the Englishwoman, hadn't he? She'd jumped when he'd seen her this morning, dropping the skirts clutched in her right hand, paling so much that he wondered if she were going to faint. A pulse at her neck had throbbed so violently he could count the beats, and his physician's mind had discerned it too rapid not to indicate distress.

For a moment this morning, when Ian's door creaked open, his own heart had stilled. Instead of his golden-haired brother, the Englishwoman had stepped out, and then simply stopped, fear so much a part of her that he could almost smell it flooding the pores of her skin.

He looped the leather straps over his back, inserting his arms in holes designed for the haunches of a four-legged animal. He was the MacLeod beast of burden, had been since Malcolm had taken their one horse south to England. That poor beast had earned a well-deserved rest, being fattened up with that other skeleton of an animal the Englishwoman had ridden north. He was surprised the emaciated creature had made it this far. Woman or beast? Aye, the woman could use some fattening up, too.

And gentling.

Alisdair bent against the resistance of heather-choked soil, pulled until clods of earth flew from Geddes' feet, unearthing one row, then another and another. The muscles of his back and shoulders flexed with the strain and ached in protest, but he didn't stop.

He couldn't stop.

Habit and strength of will made him ignore the pain in his shoulders and back. The discomfort of his body was a small price to pay next to that of his conscience if he did not work as hard as he could.

Fate had made him laird; he would not compound the tragedy which had elevated him to that status by being a poor leader. Nor would he abdicate his responsibilities, either by selling his own clansmen into slavery as had been rumored of other chiefs, or by demanding rents from tacksmen who were living from day to day on the meager produce garnered from their hidden root crops.

"I've a stable you can muck out when you're finished, brother." The memory of his brother's teasing words hung in the air.

It was ironic that after all the hell he had taken from Ian, it was, after all, his fancy education that had saved their lives. Not the education garnered at Edinburgh and on the continent, as he struggled to learn his profession of physician, but the training received, quite literally, at the feet of one of his professors. Dominic Starn was not only a famous biologist, but he had a peculiar leaning for root crops and an affinity for Scottish soil. Alisdair often dug in the earth of his don's small yard in Edinburgh while being lectured on muscles, veins, ligaments, and bone. He'd done the same here, at Tynan, to the mocking accompaniment of his brother's amusement. Yet, it was those same turnips and cabbages and potatoes which had ultimately fed the clan, kept the old from dying too young and the young from dying before learning to live.

He and Anne had returned to Tynan after the calling of the clans to the doomed cause of the Bonnie Prince. They had left their home in Edinburgh and returned to the Highlands because he was a MacLeod, not because he wished to fight. After Culloden, he had taken his wife and escaped to the continent, in hopes that his child would be born safe from the bloodbath that had been Scotland. But, such was not to be, and once again, he had returned to the place he called home.

Wholesale genocide was the Duke of Cumberland's aim, but he was not going to succeed if Alisdair MacLeod had anything to say about it. As long as a breath of air filtered through his lungs, and his arms could raise the long leather straps of a harness, and his back could bend beneath the savage demands of a plow, he would fight for his people. If once he thought that the drudgery of endless nights of study for exams and tedious days of listening to interminable lectures were hellish, it was little compared to his life of the past two years.

Sometimes, at night, he would nearly sob with fatigue, or genuine pleasure, at the feel of his body lying straight upon his bed. Tears would sometimes squeeze from beneath clenched lids in those stolen moments in the darkness and silence of the night, but Alisdair wouldn't feel ashamed. He was too exhausted to feel shame. Or grief. Or a thousand other emotions that would only hamper his driving ambition to be a leader for the ragtag, haunted-looking group that was his clan.

He did feel regret, however, that he had not taken the time in the past to realize how precious life truly was. As a physician, he had been prepared for death, but Alisdair realized he had never lived so fully as during the last two years. He had never appreciated the heather blooming on the moors as he did now, stooped to the plow. Nor had he smelled the sea with quite the sense of wonder, when each wave washed up the briny scent and carried with it the hope of a fresh catch in the morning. He had never before appreciated a clean, soft linen shirt with the same, singular joy as now.

Simple things measured the clicking of each day on some celestial clock, like rising in the morning and striding barefoot on a cool, wet patch of dew, the plucking of a rosy turnip from the ground, a filling meal of potato pancakes, the tangy sweetness of heather ale.

He appreciated, too, no matter how paradoxical it

seemed, his struggles. The hardships proved he still drew breath, that he still lived. Therefore, he was unperturbed by small events which would have left him irritated in the past. He repaired fallen roofs without cursing God for bringing the rain, played the part of plow horse without complaint. When his belly growled with hunger, he anticipated their meager rations and was grateful. He no longer questioned the unjustness of life, simply experienced it, with all its glories and disappointments, accepting the bad along with the good.

Hope was an emotion of choice, one of the few liberties still left him. Hope had made him agree to the terms of his conditional pardon. Hope had made him discount the feeling that he'd betrayed his country, his heritage, his ancestry, as he signed his name to the document which lashed him to English terms of justice. If he were lucky enough, did not die of starvation, or incur the wrath of the English, perhaps he would one day become a bitter old man feasting on the alum taste of memories grown vivid with age. But for now, he clung to the feeble ray of hope, shielding it like a candle in a gale, cupping it protectively in his hands and his heart, choosing not to remember as much as to dream.

Only now had his memories achieved a distance in which he could view them without anguish. His poor, dear Anne whom he had been unable, with all of his skill, to save. His father, the debonair laird, laughing at the thought of death and championing lost causes with riotous disregard for reality. And Ian, his older brother, who stood just an arm's length away as nine thousand well-trained, well-equipped, and well-fed troops of Cumberland's army swarmed across the glen. The fierceness of the Highlanders had counted as nothing that day.

Perhaps that was why he worked so hard to feed his people, to make a way for the crofters to subsist, to prepare them for an uncertain future, to hope in a land where hope had been burned and starved out of its people.

He had not believed.

He had never believed.

He had always despised lost causes.

His voice had been joined with the pitifully small minority who urged caution, who pleaded with Lochiel and the other influential clan chiefs to wait, to negotiate, to investigate the promises of the Bonnie Prince.

Even Ian had not cared that the man who would be king was a self-centered twenty-three-year-old weakling.

"He sees nothing wrong with the sacrifice of five thousand ill-equipped troops who left home and hearth behind to follow a doomed dream, Ian, yet your prince has not once provided the aid he promised." Even today, he could recall that conversation. Ian had only smiled at him, patient in the way a man is who does not listen to dissension.

"It will come, Alisdair. You must have faith in the cause." How like Ian to have believed so readily, to have embraced so avidly something so dangerous, so potentially disastrous.

"He wants silk and satin in his tent instead of coarse linen. He complains of the rough food of the Scots. This is the man you would have as king."

"His name alone will unite the clans, Alisdair."

"He whines when no one will plan strategy with him, as if it were a game with toy soldiers. Then he refuses to listen to his own generals."

"Then why are you here, brother, if you find him so lacking?" Ian had looked him up and down, as if he had been the smaller of the two. In truth, Alisdair towered over his older brother, had done so since they were boys. How could he tell Ian of the dread he felt, not only for battle, for killing, but for the future?

"Because you're my brother. Because I'm a MacLeod." They had looked at each other then, knowing that a chasm of thought and reason lay between them, but their love for each other would remain a bridge, a greater bond.

So, in the end, Alisdair stood beside Ian, and together the sons of the MacLeod marched with their father. Alisdair had stood and faced the charging men and felt terror break out on his skin, heard the pipes which echoed his own trembling wish to scream and run. He had glimpsed the grinning, bone-white face of death, but instead of fleeing the scene of carnage, Alisdair had killed in the name of freedom.

The life he lived now was a singular paradise of simple pleasures in comparison to that moment.

Alisdair had begun to find peace.

Until the woman arrived.

What on earth had come over his grandmother? Why did she think that he and that Englishwoman would ever make a match of it? Why had he not shouted her down? Because he respected her. Because, other than his absent mother, she was his only surviving relative. Because, her way was the only chink of light showing in this idiotic situation. Because, honor still mattered.

The reason Alisdair was not living a life of courtly luxury in Paris, instead of coaxing a living from scrubby soil and persuading his clan to turn their backs on the past, was the same reason he could not pretend this farce of a marriage had not occurred. Honor. A conscience. A heritage that demanded more of him, more from him. The old rules were easy to break, but what would that make of him, if he did? His clan would be as loath as he to take an Englishwoman into their midst, but a man who broke his word, who would lie once, would lie twice. Even if he did choose to ignore his country's traditions, he could not ignore his honor. Hope and honor were all he had to call his.

Still, he remembered her start of fright, the paleness of her face, the expression frozen in those deep blue eyes.

He had never frightened a woman in his life.

Chapter 8

Sophie Elizabeth Agincourt MacLeod leaned heavily upon the ivory-handled cane, her deeply sunk but still brilliant blue eyes watching as Judith climbed the small hillock leading to the crofters' cottages.

The first part of her plan had been put into action. At least they had agreed to her terms.

The second part had not been accomplished without some difficulty. Judith was surprisingly stubborn. The girl acted as if someone had once told her she was ugly and had set about proving them correct. Those glorious auburn curls, as richly colored as a sunset crowning Ben Nevis, were always worn scraped back and fashioned in a frowzy knot at the base of her neck. Sophie had coaxed them free, brushing them loose and finally convincing Judith that a hair ribbon would be as practical as all those gouging pins. If Judith had her way, she would still be clad in the same threadbare blue dress, so deeply dyed it appeared black, hanging so slack around her frame as if purposely designed to conceal any womanly asset.

Alisdair's mother would scream in sheer horror at the thought of her clothing being worn by another, yet Louise's armoire was the first place Sophie had gone in search of serviceable garments that could be altered. The signs of violation were as visible in Louise's dressing room as any other section of Tynan. Sophie recalled the thousands of schillings that had been used to purchase the embroidered curtains with their heavy gilt thread, the chaise upholstered in scarlet and gold. Now the furniture was ash and the draperies hung tattered, soot-filled, upon the windows. Yet even the looters who had defiled Tynan could not manage the great feat of stealing all of Louise's many gowns.

"Sophie, I do not require a new dress," Judith insisted this morning, clutching the skirt of her blue wool with two determined hands. Ever since she was a child growing up in tightfisted Squire Cuthbertson's house, Judith's clothes had been crafted of the coarsest and most sturdy materials, always of a serviceable brown or dark blue so as not to show either wear or soil. Marriage had not varied her wardrobe. Peter's mother grudged any extra coin for her son's bride, and what funds could be spared for luxuries from Anthony's pay were more often than not used for his drink or gambling, not his wife's apparel.

Judith had long since given up the notion of pretty dresses or perky bonnets, or other accessories that would enhance her appearance. Those frivolities were for women with petite, rounded curves and heart-shaped, winsome faces. Nothing would change the shape of her face, or make her less tall and gangly, or transform the color of her hair. Clothing served only a utilitarian purpose—to hide her nakedness, not enhance fictional charms.

A point Sophie calmly, and stubbornly, refuted.

"It is one thing for me to wear dark colors, dear child," Sophie said calmly, marking a line on the cloth. "I am old, my life is behind me. But you should wear vibrant colors to enhance your looks. Did you know," she asked, with a twinkle in her eye, "that you have the coloring of a lovely Scottish lass?"

Judith's look was a mixture of incredulity over Sophie's statement and tenderness towards the frail woman who was kind enough to utter such a falsehood. She'd learned how generous Sophie's nature was these past weeks. The older woman had turned over the keys of the castle to her, had taught her the workings of the massive fireplace, praised her efforts at cooking. At no time did she scold or criticize, and Judith treasured their many conversations, but for the constant references to the MacLeod's innumerable virtues.

"Another man might be measured by his words, Judith. Alisdair should be judged by his deeds. He does not speak of duty, yet the weight of responsibility hangs heavy on his shoulders. He does not speak of fairness, but he strives, above all, to be just. You could do worse for a husband," she finished, reasoning that she had rambled on long enough. She squinted down at the garment in her hands. The hem would need to be let down, but that minor chore was less difficult than obtaining a length of cloth for a new dress.

"While I salute your efforts at Tynan, my dear, there are not that many days of sunshine in the Highlands that you can afford to shun them. There's a storm brewing, Judith, see the sun while you may." Such had been her banishment from Tynan—gentle words spoken with a soft smile and an implacable nature.

Now, Judith stood at the crest of the hill, her hair brushed until it shone, lifted by the wind riffling from the west. Her dress had been altered with tiny stitches, her cheeks had been touched with red flannel dipped in hot water.

Judith watched the horizon and the clouds boiling black and dangerous a few miles away. Did it rain forever in the Highlands? The air was heavy with the hint of storm, the wind combed through the moor grasses and soughed through the pines.

Beside the sheltered cove was a narrow footpath curling up to the top of the moor, its serpentine trail finally culminating in a flat grassy site about five feet wide. From here, Judith could see the blue finger of the cove stretching out

to the ocean, or turn her head slightly and view the glen
sweeping down to the village. Straight ahead, the path
branched off in three directions, the center track leading
to broad, cultivated fields.

Judith glanced at the line of cottages arrayed along a
twisting path and the unsmiling women standing in front
of each one, their dresses identical in style and shade of
black, crows perched upon a tree limb. Their midday meal
had evidently been supplanted by curiosity about the
woman who strode through their village.

Malcolm watched her for a long time before approaching, slipping away from the others when he saw her stop
and study the horizon. She smiled as he fell into step beside
her as together they walked through the clachan. He'd
brought her this way on her first day at Tynan, had stopped
in the doorway of a few of these cottages, introduced her
as the laird's new wife. The mood was more amiable now
than on that day, when Judith had wished to bind her
hand over Malcolm's volubleness and prevent his words
from being spoken.

Three weeks in the Highlands and she'd come to no
harm. Still, Judith knew how deceptive peace was, even in
this place of rolling storms and silver mist.

"I've been inspected by the women of your clan," Judith
said softly, glancing at the women who nodded curtly as
they passed. "Sophie has had visitors who come less to see
her, I suspect, than to view the oddity in their midst."
Being raised in a family with four sisters had made Judith
familiar with being around groups of women—not necessarily comfortable. She disliked being the subject of their
speculation. Only two women had seemed genuinely
friendly, the sisters, Meggie and Janet. Janet was in the
advanced stages of pregnancy and relied on Meggie to
assist her in both standing and sitting. She took it with
good grace and not a little pride, as she smoothed her
hands over the firm mound of her belly.

"He'll be big like his da," Janet said proudly, and it
was only later that Judith learned her husband had been

drowned two months earlier. Meggie had tentatively offered a smile and an invitation to come and visit, such a welcome and rare overture that Judith almost hugged her for it.

"And why not?" Malcolm asked her impatiently "Ye're married to their laird, an' English for all that. Do ye not think that there might be some fear in the glen? Ye must change their minds, Judith."

"I cannot help that I was born English, Malcolm," she said, "and the subject of my marriage is one not quite decided, if you recall."

"Still, they canna help fearing ye. 'Twere the English who burned the castle an' stripped the land. 'Twere the English who killed their men an' let their bairns starve. Do ye ken the Butcher's rule, Judith?"

She glanced over at Malcolm, but he wouldn't meet her eyes.

"None of his men could give aid to the enemy. The Scot." His mouth twisted. "If they gave food ta anyone, Judith—even a babe in swaddlin'—they could be flogged or hanged. So they sat, an' they ate, an' they filled their fat bellies, while mothers begged for their children ta be able ta drink the blood of the animals the English had slaughtered." His eyes met Judith's finally, and it was her turn to look away. "So, if they look on ye with suspicion, an' aye, a little fear, it's kinder than yer own countrymen did for them. The clan used ta number over seven hundred strong, Judith. Barely a hundred are left."

"Why, Malcolm, knowing that, did you see fit to wed me to the MacLeod?"

"Because, lass, ye didn't strike me as English. Don't go an' disappoint me now. Ye've ignored the MacLeod like a skitterin' crab. Leavin' a room when he was enterin' it, hidin' in yer room as if feared he would touch ye. Ye've gone an' gotten all ninnylike, lass, an' it's no' a good change. Ye've no reason ta fear the MacLeod."

Easy words. Softly spoken. But many was the night Judith had heard the MacLeod pacing in the room above hers, his footfalls a metronome which seemed to measure each breath she took. When they halted, her breath stopped, only to resume when the footsteps began again.

Yet, he had not once attempted liberties.

Still, there was something about him to inspire caution. A fluttering in her belly when he smiled, a trembling of her limbs when he grew too near. No, Malcolm was wrong. There was ample reason to fear the MacLeod.

She had only a short time left until she could experience true freedom. In two months and a week, her heart would no longer lurch at the thud of boots echoing on a wooden floor; she needn't cringe at the slam of a door. A man's booming voice would not induce anxiety or his anger a paralyzing fear. Her life would be of her making, not lived because of the sudden and changeable whims of a husband. But to tell Malcolm these things would be to expose too many other, darker, secrets. It was better, in the end, to simply remain silent.

They passed at least forty of the small crofters' huts. Their roofs of thatch and heather merged with the rolling hills so well, they blended into the landscape. Only their rock walls declared their man-made construction. Judith was surprised at the number and the tidiness of the community, but noticed that several of the cottages were empty.

"Emigrated," Malcolm said shortly when she asked about their inhabitants, "or didn't survive the last few years. 'Twas the bairns, mostly, who didn't make it. Only two bairns born since the '45, but one is my own wee Douglas."

"Your son?"

"Bless you, lass," he said, smiling, "my grandson. I'm surprised ye haven't seen him yet; Fiona fair dotes on the lad, she does. Would ye like ta see him now?"

Judith nodded, following Malcolm down the track to where it veered left towards the cultivated fields. Immediately she wanted to stop him, to say she changed her mind, but by then it was too late. The MacLeod had already seen them.

"Does he work all the time?" she asked, not realizing how much her question betrayed her growing curiosity about him.

"Aye," Malcolm said, "but then he's always been a demon for work, the MacLeod. There's work aplenty for all here in the Highlands, lass."

The MacLeod was standing at the end of one field, removing his shirt. His bronzed back was wide and glistening with sweat. A feminine hand smoothed down the droplets on his spine, curved around, and grasped him firmly by the waist. They made a handsome pair. The woman's head barely reached his chin, making him appear larger and more formidable. As he bent and whispered something to her, her smile broadened. Her eyes had not left Judith since she spotted her following Malcolm.

Fiona reached up and pulled his head down for an unsolicited kiss. It was damned bad timing, Alisdair thought, pushing his clanswoman gently away. The flush on Judith's face disappeared, to be replaced by a stark whiteness.

At Malcolm's request, Fiona fetched her son, returning with a wide-hipped walk that appeared deliberately saucy, Judith thought.

And the MacLeod did not have the grace to look ashamed.

Fiona's son had the dark amber eyes of the MacLeod, lit by golden flecks. It was plain that Fiona was not the only one who doted on the child. Malcolm oohed and aahed over the baby, who was proudly displayed by his mother. Proudly and with a challenging smile.

It was the MacLeod Douglas reached for, however, and he took him easily from Fiona's arms, cradling him against his bare chest. Judith was not the least bit interested in his paternal leanings. Nor was she concerned that his face softened or the light in his eyes was a glow of love. He was so gentle with the child, as if an errant movement would hurt him, holding the baby easily in the crook of one arm, a stance that denoted much practice.

It was, after all, none of her concern.

Fiona took the baby back to his basket, not resisting a backward glance at the still, stiff figure of the English-woman as she did so. Judith did not miss her mocking smile and schooled her own features into a perfect mask, giving nothing of her thoughts away. She did not realize that her eyes turned flat, betraying little, appearing like the calm waters of the deepest loch.

It was grating on his nerves.

Alisdair told himself that he had been as polite as possible, but she continued to be perverse. She fled from a room if he entered it, refused to speak to him when he was being civil, stared at him when she thought he was unaware. If he had to spend the rest of the term of his grandmother's idiotic scheme coupled with such an antagonist, he would cheerfully strangle her. Let the English hang him for that.

If Malcolm had to bind him to an Englishwoman, he should have at least noted whether she grew pale around a man, if her breathing accelerated and was faint at the same time, if she looked as though she would rather die than be caressed. It was the least the old matchmaker could do. But, no, Malcolm had forgotten those little details, and Alisdair was tied to a cold spinster, no matter how many times she'd been wed.

Thank God this unholy bond would last only a little while. It was a thought he should have remembered. Instead, that flat expression on Judith's face goaded him to thoughts best left unvoiced. Or, was it the fact that her hair seemed to shine even in the gloom of an approaching storm. Her lips seemed too full for fretfulness, and her soft, pillowy breasts gave the lie to her coldness, coaxed his palms to curl.

"Do you not think the lad bonny, Judith?"

His voice was too smooth, too honeyed, as soft as velvet, as dark as a moonlit moor. The wind tossed his hair from his face, the darkening sky was a perfect backdrop for the tanned expanse of his bare torso. He was an avenging god of storm and dark anger.

Judith took one step back, so slight that he should not have noticed. Yet, he did, and the sway of her skirts as she did so. He noted, too, that the pulse beat at her neck accelerated, as if he had touched her with more than his mind.

She was silent still, yet the air swirled with heaviness, as if her thoughts added weight to it.

"I thought all women grew soft and maternal at the sight of a babe. Are the English so different then? Is it that Douglas is only a Scot? Do you English consider him only half-human?"

When she did not speak, he grabbed her arm and pulled her closer. Perhaps she should have pulled away then. If she had distanced herself from him, she would not have felt the warmth of the hand which lay upon her arm. Skin against skin. Too intimate.

He forced her chin up so that he could see her eyes, staring into her face with studied intent before he abruptly released her. There was no expression at all in those azure eyes, and the total absence of emotion disturbed him. It was as if part of his English wife had disappeared somehow, as if she'd retreated from his words, from his very presence, from his punishing grip upon her forearm.

Something made him want to banish that calm, nothing-look on her face. Any emotion was preferable to that flat look in her eyes.

"Or is it that you have no maternal leanings yourself, Judith? Twice married and no bairn. Yet you," he continued, his thin-edged smile infinitely cruel, "have the hips of a born breeder. You could spit babes into the world without a gasp."

She didn't bother to respond. His words did not surprise her; she was immune to ridicule. Her father had not ceased commenting upon her appearance since she was a child. Peter's mother had read her a litany of her faults from daybreak to dusk, and Anthony had not abstained in his scathing remarks about her looks, her abilities, her many liabilities. The MacLeod's words paled in comparison to those she'd received in the past.

The thunder rolled, a drum beat of punctuation to her silence.

"Yet, it's true ice is not a fertile ground," he said brutally. "Were you never warm and willing, then? Only cold like now? If so, I can see why no man's seed found purchase in your pristine English womb."

Her pallor was replaced by blotches of red, the flat look in her eyes gone, supplanted by a look so fierce he almost recoiled from it. Yet she did not speak, and as he stared, she changed again, cloaking her rage in something he could not describe. There was no hushed comfort in her silence, nothing restful. It bubbled like an underground stream.

Then she did the one thing designed to infuriate him.

Judith turned and walked away.

He had had enough.

She felt the jolt at her knees and would have fallen if he hadn't scooped her up and thrown her over his shoulder. She screamed, which only fueled the laughter of those who'd followed her through the village despite the oncoming storm. Judith beat on his bare back, but all he did was hook his free arm around her legs and drop her by the ankles, until the long mass of her hair uncoiled and touched the ground.

The eternal Highland rain began to fall, full, fat drops accompanying the symphony of thunder. It was, Alisdair thought, a curious diorama they enacted, complete with nature's cooperation.

Her nose was at the level of his knees. Judith was beyond humiliation. Her skirt was sliding down and, in a moment, her legs would be bared to the shuffling mass of people who relentlessly followed them despite the MacLeod's quick and determined strides. She ceased pounding on his back, replacing that futile gesture with one far more practical.

She bit him.

He dropped her with a shout.

She landed on her back, momentarily winded. She stared up at the furious face of the MacLeod and realized that modesty was going to demand a price. She crept up on her hands and knees, brushed her hair back from her face with one wet hand, never shifting her gaze from him. She watched him warily as he rubbed that portion of his anatomy which had been the softest and most accessible to her teeth. When he came after her, she was prepared. She leapt to her feet, looked to the left, but darted to the right.

They raced towards the castle and Judith knew that she was going to pay for her impulsive gesture but not, she vowed, in view of a hundred people. She gathered the skirts of her new dress in her fists and, without a thought to the modesty she had protected only moments earlier, lifted the folds of material above her pistoning knees and sprinted for her life.

The storm was full upon them now, but Judith didn't notice the pelting rain, her only thought was to escape the retribution she would receive at the MacLeod's hands. The path she'd taken only moments earlier became as slippery as a stream bed, but still she ran.

If he caught her, he was going to kill her, Alisdair decided. One less Englishwoman was not going to be a loss to the world. Especially, this one. But, damn, the woman could run. The rain was icy upon his bare chest, but he was immune to such petty discomfort.

Alisdair caught her just inside the bronze doors. He swept her up in his arms despite her struggles. The crowd cheered as he disappeared from sight with his sodden English wife momentarily tamed. Well, if nothing else, Alisdair thought, she had been an entertaining diversion.

He swayed against the stone steps that led to the living quarters. She had not stopped fighting him, but he lacked the energy to throw her over his shoulder again. He'd been working in the fields since dawn while she, no doubt, had been saving her strength for their encounter. He scowled at her, a gesture that would have given a sane person a reason to cease their shouts and blows. No, his English wife was as stubborn as she was athletic.

"Shut up, woman!" he finally shouted, and the sound bounced off the stone walls and seemed to echo down the long corridors.

"Let me go!" she yelled in response. She had nothing to lose; she knew what punishment awaited her in the room atop the stairs. If she could only delay it, she would forestall the pain, also.

Alisdair wondered exactly who Judith was, that she could hate as deeply as a Scot, and tremble with fear at the same moment. For all she wished to hide herself, he'd read those emotions well enough.

Rain had plastered her hair down, sheened her face. Her lashes were long, spiky, her lips were full and wet. Alisdair wanted to tell her that a mouth could be used to better pursuits, a voice to softer demands. Instead, he only stopped and stared at her, wondering why the rhythm of her heart would be so audible to him, why his own breath, raspy and winded, would echo hers so exactly.

The staircase had no railing, no banister. Those were frivolous notions for manor houses and estates. This staircase had been built with defense in mind, steep downward sloping steps that were difficult to mount if one were tired, or sick, or like Sophie, aged and frail.

At this moment, Alisdair felt all four.

Despite the trembling in his arms, he held his temporary English wife out over the sheer drop.

"Now?" he hissed.

She felt the tremors in his arms and held onto his bare chest. He grimaced at the discomfort of her nails digging into his skin.

"Now?" he repeated.

"No," she said softly, defeated.

"Are you sure? It would be no trouble at all." He could

feel his own heart pounding so loudly that surely she could hear it. He was tempted to throw her over, anyway.

She shook her head, frantically, and he stepped back and wearily leaned against the wall. He lowered her legs and allowed her to stand, but kept a firm hold on her upper arm. He pulled her inside Ian's room, and swung her around as if she weighed no more than a feather. Her skirts slapped around her, wet, muddy. The beautiful blue sprigged dress—the prettiest dress she'd ever worn—was ruined.

Alisdair stood, hands on hips, and watched his newest burden as she scrambled up on the sagging mattress. She remained on her knees, her eyes flashing fire. Such temper was still a welcome change from the vacuity they displayed so often.

He smiled, a particularly infuriating grin that prodded her to words more prudently left unsaid. Yet, if she was going to be punished, then let it be for something, not simply the innocence of self.

"Is it that you wish me to fawn over your bastard, MacLeod? Your prowess as a male applauded and saluted? Very well, I applaud and salute you. You have fathered a child. Congratulations."

"I am not Douglas's father."

"And I am the King of England, MacLeod."

"Do you call me a liar then?" His scowl was too fierce. Her heart beat strongly, urging her to caution.

"No," she said, scooting away from him.

"I am sick unto death of you slithering away from me," he ground out between thinned lips, his voice low and intense. "I am not a monster, nor am I a lovesick fool. You have nothing to fear from me." Because he was irritated and not a little confused by the emotion he'd felt in the stairwell, he frowned fiercely at her, determined not to allow compassion to soften his words, or lead him into dangerous thoughts.

"If your husbands craved you with carnal lust, then it's because they had not seen another woman in months!"

His conscience cringed at his cruelty, his manhood relished the open battle at last. "You are not Helen of Troy, nor are you an ethereal vision of loveliness. You are in a word, my English wife, a scrawny, sour-tongued hag!"

He left the room in a whirl of motion and rage, leaving Judith staring after him.

Her eyes felt as though they had been dusted with pepper, tiny pinpricks of hurt.

It was only the rain in her eyes.

Chapter 9

"Was it very bad, Alisdair?" Sophie asked. Her soft voice conveyed compassion, her worried eyes concern for his obvious fatigue.

Judith watched the MacLeod warily. They had not spoken since his outburst a few days earlier. She had managed to avoid him since then, wanting nothing to do with the MacLeod, or his precious Tynan. She cared less than nothing for either of them.

Nor did she care about the errand which had kept him abroad all night. No doubt looting and pillaging. His eyes were shadowed and sunken, their edges looked red. His beard was full-blown; he looked a marauder in truth.

Judith dished him up a bowl of porridge, which he ate standing up. He did not look at her, but concentrated on his meal as if he had not eaten for days. For some reason, the Scots did not refer to their meal of boiled oats as an "it," as in a leg of lamb or a haunch of beef. Instead, porridge was a "they" and best consumed standing up. It was one of those oddities of the Scots that Judith simply accepted. Explanations were better left for someone who was interested.

He gave the empty bowl to Judith, and without a word, went into the pantry where he poured himself a stiff measure of her father's brandy. He swallowed it without seeming to breathe.

Only then did he speak, his voice gravelly without sleep. He rubbed his eyes fiercely as if to further open them.

"It was bad," he said simply. "The babe never drew breath."

Sophie looked at him sadly. She wished she could have spared him his memories, but that was beyond her province. His recollections of Anne would cease in time, but not if he were forced to relive them, again and again, as he had last night.

Judith looked at them curiously. Their cryptic conversation spurred an interest she pretended not to feel.

"And Janet?" Sophie asked.

There was only silence for a moment, as he leaned against the door frame and shut his eyes tightly. The light was too bright. The long, sleepless night had been filled with activity and not a little praying as he had attempted to save at least one life. All for naught.

"She really had no chance from the beginning," he said, somberly. "Too little nourishment, too much work, too much grief."

Sophie stood, her demeanor that of someone who has witnessed enough sadness in the world. No one said a word as she shuffled to her room and gently closed the door behind her.

She did not like this land, Judith thought, as she bent to scrub the table. It sucked dry the energy of its people; it demanded too high a toll. Granted, it was no different in England, young women still died in childbirth. Yet Scotland seemed harsher somehow, as if life had been stripped of all of its beauty and only the bare essentials remained. There was no softness here, no frailty. The soft did not survive, the frail fell beneath the burden of day-to-day living. It was wild, untamed, mocking its recent conquest by the English, stark and as desolate as Tynan itself.

Judith knew every foot of the castle so well she could have drawn its plan by memory. Most of the rooms were now shut off; in certain spots not even the wooden doors had been replaced, leaving gaping black holes which exposed the degree of ruin the fire had caused. The dining hall was intact, but so gloomy and dim she could understand why the inhabitants of Tynan used the kitchen for their meals. In addition to her room and Sophie's niche beside the kitchen, one room in the retainers' hall had been cleaned, and the lord's room, in which the wheel staircase, the only access to the battlements, was located. The castle was a labyrinth of rooms hidden beyond rooms. It took long moments to finally find her way around the second floor, and she had climbed the sloping steps to the third floor only once. She did not venture inside the MacLeod's room. It was enough to simply stand at the doorway and scan the immense dimensions of the room with wide eyes. Here, too, the windows overlooked the sea, but there were no panes of precious glass in their large rectangular openings. A massive bed, only one poster remaining, dominated one entire wall. Without much effort, she could envision the MacLeod there, his long legs stretched full-length, his body occupying more than half its broad width. There was, however, still room for a wife. She had left the room quickly. It was not as easy to banish the chamber's occupant from her mind.

Alisdair opened his eyes to study his English wife.

He told himself that it was not his conscience that bothered him as much as his sense of fairness, a different thing entirely. Every crofter in his clan was welcome to come to him with a complaint, and would be listened to because his word had merit. Every child was protected by every adult, because life was valued and cherished here. Every woman in his village could expect to be treated with honor, both by their husbands and by all other men who lived in the glen inhabited by the MacLeods. The old were cosseted and excused. The imperfect were protected. Those who did wrong were chastised and corrected, not shamed.

He was too aware that he had not acted with fairness, but with a brutal cruelty. He had tried to wound her with words, and from the look on her face now, he had succeeded beyond his expectations.

Although leadership came more easily to him than apologies, Alisdair forced himself to face her and utter words he'd never thought to voice to an English subject.

"Forgive me," he said, his voice flat, exhausted, "for saying what I did." Two fingers pressed against his eyelids as if to minimize their sting, so he did not see the sudden surprised look she directed at him. "You did not deserve my crudeness."

It was bewilderment that kept her mute, but he only noted her silence with irritation, an emotion not easily banished in her presence.

"Granmere means a great deal to me," he said, another statement that caught her off guard. She stopped wiping the table and straightened, watching him warily. He remained slumped against the door, head bent back as if he studied the ceiling with infinite patience. His soft tone was strangely somber, intensified by the silence in the room. Judith could hear the rustling of something suspiciously mouselike, the MacLeod's breathing, the pounding beat of her heart. "I would not have her hurt," he said, "for all that she means well."

His face was set into stern lines, an uncompromising look, which gave little or nothing away. As if he buried his emotions so deep that none could find them. It prompted an unwilling feeling of empathy.

"I would not hurt her, MacLeod." It was easier, somehow, to concentrate her attention on the rag held tightly in one hand than to meet his gaze. It did not mean, however, that she was unaware of him. If anything, the room seemed to shrink, or he grow larger. Or was it because there were only inches between them?

He reached out and casually stroked a lock of her hair where it had come loose from the bun she habitually wore. The tips of his fingers brushed against the side of her neck, and a shiver of sensation followed their passage to her shoulder. Slowly, too slowly, dangerously slow, she moved away, and his hand dropped.

She faced him then, arms wrapped around her middle as if to protect herself. It was a telling gesture, and one he noted with less detachment than he would have wished. He did not want to notice anything about this particular woman.

"Shall we call a truce?" he asked her, a small smile playing around his lips. "Rest assured, Judith, you have nothing to fear from me. I prefer a celibate bed to one occupied by a frosty English statue."

"What exactly does your truce include then?"

He laughed, the mocking sound of it echoing through the room, prickling her skin. "What did your poor husbands do, to earn your enmity? Did they not give you enough of an allowance? Pay you no heed? Question your expenditures? If so, then you have not improved your lot. We are farmers here, without access to funds that are not reserved for grain or seed."

Judith looked at him as if he had sprouted two heads. Would that had been all Anthony had demanded.

She clenched her teeth. "Let us say that I am not a marital prize. To put it into words a farmer could understand, label me as stupid as a sheep, as stubborn as a goat, as hysterical as a chicken."

"You do not, perhaps, have the loyalty of a favored horse, the placid disposition of a cow, or the intelligence of a pig?" He was grinning, his fatigue forgotten, his grief muted by this sudden, fascinating side of his silent wife. Judith wished she had the courage to wipe that idiotic smirk from his face.

"No."

"Then it does not bode well for the next few weeks, does it?"

They stood for long moments staring at each other, and his sense of irony surfaced from the burden of day-to-day

living, from the grief he felt for Janet and her babe, for
Anne. Indeed, for the ruin of his life.

"Shall we call it peace, then," he asked, "if for no other
reason than for Granmere's sake?"

"And your conditions, MacLeod?"

"A smile, from time to time, perhaps? A word spoken
without rancor, the cessation of your eternal silence. If I
should enter a room, you will not disappear from it. Your
chastity, my companionship?"

After a long moment, she nodded.

"I would have your word, woman."

"My word?" she questioned shortly. "Would you take
the word of your horse? Perhaps you could make your pig
swear." Her eyes widened at her own words, two fingers
pressed against her lips as if to test their ownership. His
grin grew broader in scope. So, his English wife had a
temper, too, when nudged from her silence.

"If you do not value your own word, woman," he said
softly, "then it truly lacks worth."

"Is a Scotswoman's promise more valuable?" Her tone
left little doubt of her thoughts.

"You are woefully ignorant of our world, woman. You
have evidently not been in a Scotswoman's presence, or
else you would not speak so stupidly. She is the helpmate
of her husband, works beside him, shares his life. Has been
known to take up weapons beside him, and yes, to die with
him, if need be."

"I would not mind dying with you, MacLeod," she said
bluntly, her scowl a study in irritation. "It's living with you
I balk at."

His bark of surprised laughter followed her from the
room.

Chapter 10

Bennett Henderson stepped carefully around the puddle of vomit. Young Hartley was not up to drinking all night. The youngest of his group, the boy naturally gravitated to Bennett, had even taken to emulating his own taste in liquor and its quantity. The fact that Hartley was not quite up to the challenge was amusing, as was the puppylike adoration.

What Bennett really wanted was a companion of the soul, someone who would understand his deepest desires and most forbidden aspirations. Someone who would encourage his most terrible of wants.

Anthony had done that.

Sweet Anthony, two years his junior; Anthony would have done anything for him. The times they'd had, the debaucheries they'd practiced, it was almost too much, the memories. They summoned up a longing he could not dismiss.

The last two years hadn't been the same without him. Not only had he lost his brother, but his best friend, his gambling companion, and more. How many times had they shared a woman between them? How many times had they shared a look of such utter understanding across the body of a spent and sweat-dampened female body?

Anthony was his other half.

Hartley staggered from the corner, where he'd pissed again, too drunk or uncaring to find a chamber pot. The stench in the common room was growing, but none of the inhabitants seemed to mind it. It was just another of those subtleties of his life which differentiated him from the rank and file of his fellow soldiers.

In this year of Our Gracious King, George II, the most favored and least onerous duty was that of soldiering. For a small fortune, a captaincy could be purchased, with the result that most of the officers in King George's army were noble second or third sons, or like himself and Anthony, the sons of a minor peer. The ranks of English officers, therefore, were less concerned with changing the world for the better than simply staying alive. They led their men the way a hundred generations of gentlemen had before them, with haughty superiority and an inbred belief in the rightness of themselves and England, if not their cause.

If the Scots suffered for their invasion, it was because the upstarts had the audacity to challenge the world's greatest power. If fields were burned and houses razed, and babies slaughtered and women raped, it was no less deserving of their insurrection and rebellion.

Bennett no longer bothered to listen to his companion's conversation, his attention on the ashes of the fire, allowed to grow cold not because the air was less chilly than before, but because none of their group would stoop to refuel it.

Bunch of trailing sycophants. But they, too, had their place in the world, he thought with a smile. It was not a warm or a comforting smile, but one that held a hint of rapaciousness to it, a tinge of cruelty to the upper lip, a mocking derision in the ice blue eyes. It was, a casual observer might feel, a look to cause one to wish his doors locked firmly, his windows shut tight against the evil night air.

"Where is dear Lawrence, that he has not refueled our

fire?'' In his voice was more than a question, it was an invitation, a luring finger beckoning all who would be led toward the most immoral carnality.

As obtuse as the group was, they caught his meaning well enough.

The young subaltern was terrified.

The pitiful mewling of his approach made Bennett Henderson smile. Two of them divested the poor fool of his uniform without haste, their tender strokes and intrusive touch softening the edge of his fear. His arousal was a pitiful thing, half-masted, more pulled from him than generated by true lust. He was too frightened to feel anything but the spiking of his fear.

But his buttocks were so beautifully round, their whiteness only newly marked. Dear Lawrence was an apt plaything for when the storms of this godforsaken place precluded their patrols, when the rain promised only floods and Scotland's eternal chill.

Bennett lounged in his chair, watching as his companions kissed and readied their victim. He flicked his fingers, and the instrument of his choice was placed upon his palm. Standing, he surveyed their prize, the trembling young he-goat, nearly hairless, frightened, so afraid that the air was colored red with it.

He breathed it in deeply, the stench of this fear, and smiled.

Without subtlety, Bennett swung his arm and the whip sliced through the air, the keening sound seeming to strip the tint from the young man's face until it was whiter than parchment, paler than a winter's moon.

He relished these moments, craved them the way some of his brother officers lusted after virgins. When he tasted blood, it was of his own making, and the anticipation of it was almost as heady as the deed itself.

Almost.

His smile was sharp, grinning, his feet widespread, his stance poised and in control. Bennett opened the placard of his pantaloons, prepared himself. But for the state of his rampant arousal, he would have been mistaken for a victorious soldier, exhilarated from a battle hard-won. This was a battle of sorts, he supposed, but there was never a question of victor.

He moved closer, near enough to see the tears coursing down the young man's face, close enough to smell the cloying sweet scent of terror that jerked his arousal even tighter, harder. He bent, tenderly placed the young man into position, and flicked the whip gently, almost lovingly across the spread buttocks. His companions merely laughed, ennui giving way to anticipation, buggery an apt sport for a wet night in the Highlands.

At the bellow of pain, he nearly laughed, so great was his euphoria at this moment. But the scream was almost too guttural, too masculine, lacking the real tones of pure terror. He pretended though, closing his eyes as he thrust himself forward. His arm lifted and the high-pitched whine of the whip's strokes were a complement to his own shout of release.

"Judith!" he nearly screamed, and it was rage that brought him to his senses at last.

It should have been her white body beneath him, her moans he heard, her blood he spilled.

One day, he would find her. Until then, he had her memory. Long nights filled with ecstasy.

And the sound of her screams.

Chapter 11

"The best wool," Judith explained," is behind the shoulders and down the front legs. Here and here." With a few practiced strokes, the hapless ewe was shorn of half its coat. "Always cut from the legs towards the back, and it doesn't matter if you do it in one pass or not. Most of the time, the wool will have to be separated anyway. It saves a step if you grade it while you shear it." She flung one section of fleece towards the small pile to her right, another to the growing pile to her left.

So far, only the twins had spotted the MacLeod, not his surprising English wife.

"It's best if you wash the sheep before you shear, but you'll still need to wash the wool, too."

Alisdair had expected many things of Judith. He had anticipated that she would stir his clan to irritation, possibly anger. Perhaps she would bedevil them the way she did him. But, in all his thirty-two years, Alisdair could not have imagined a scene like the one he came upon after returning from Inverness, with the sun beginning its downward journey into night.

She was, his English wife, astride a sheep.

Her skirt was tucked into her waistband, her bare legs pressed against the woolly sides of a protesting ewe. The sleeves of her bodice were tied back to the elbows, her hair fixed in a haphazard knot, curls tumbling from it as though she were a well-used doxy at the end of a prosperous night. Her hands were buried in the long fleece, her face brightened by a sheen of sweat, and a dark swipe of something whose origins he preferred not to guess marred her forehead.

A rim of men stood leaning idly against the fence shouting instructions, a gaggle of women stood in a tight circle muttering. With one hand, Alisdair dismissed the men; a look was all it took to send the women scurrying for cover. The twins stood on either side of his wife, each grasping two legs of the hapless ewe while she lectured them upon the serious business of shearing.

When Judith noticed that neither of her helpers was moving to control the heavy ewe, she prodded Daniel—or was it David?—in the side with her elbow, her only free appendage, then glanced up to see the source of his fascination.

The MacLeod's smile was not so much mocking as it was rooted in surprise.

Judith forgot how to make a sound, and even now, when the most prudent person would have looked away from the amber gleam of those eyes, she found herself staring like a lackwit at him.

His trousers were not new, but they encased legs too broad and brawny to need any English padding. His white shirt was old, but constructed of the finest linen and still carelessly elegant. His coat was blue superfine, his boots polished black. It was not sartorial elegance Alisdair Mac-Leod portrayed as he casually leaned back against a fence post, legs crossed at the ankles, hands resting on hips. He was too tall, too muscled, too tan to be truly a dandy. Judith had the oddest thought that while he may have only been the chief of a tired clan, his home a burnt-out castle, Alisdair MacLeod greeted the world with as much pride as a duke, as much arrogance as a prince.

"Dare I wonder exactly what you're doing, wife?" he asked, his tone one not of a half-civilized Highlander, but of a bored effeminate indolently lounging in a London drawing room. For a moment, she could imagine him the medical student in Brussels, or Edinburgh, half his time analyzing the human body, the rest engaged in intense and intimate scrutiny of only female limbs.

"I am shearing your sheep," she said, finally, straightening from her task and placing one hand against her lower back. David and Daniel were still on either side of her, both hands in identical position on the back of the sheep's neck, both legs clamped on either side of the bleating prisoner.

At least twenty naked sheep, their forms curiously fragile shorn of their coat, were bleating their displeasure loudly and furiously nearby.

A nod was all it required to banish the twins. The trapped ewe was released and scrambled up the slope. Judith pulled at the hem of her skirt until it fell from her waistband, fluffing out the material in a vain attempt to ignore the MacLeod. It was no use, she could better ignore an oncoming storm than she could his tall and broad figure.

Whatever she felt about the man, there was no mistaking the fact that it was intensified in his presence. He was a puzzle, this new, and unwanted, husband of hers. He treated her with civility, was polite without being overly cordial, deferential without one word of mockery. He greeted her when they met with a smile which seemed genuine, if a bit tinted by the sardonic twinkle in his eyes. He inquired as to her health, asked about her daily pursuits as if genuinely interested, wished her a restful sleep. Once, they'd even discussed Brussels, his travels upon the continent, his studies. Not once had he broken their truce, not one time had she cause to fear him. A month had passed and she had been left at peace.

She wanted to repay him for it.

When she looked up, it was to see a strange assessing look on his face, as if he judged her with some secret knowledge.

Judith could feel the flush rise from her toes to her cheeks.

"Why?"

"It is already summer, MacLeod, and the sheep are fat with wool."

"I'd thought to hire some sheep men," he said, his voice soft, almost soothing.

Neither one of them mentioned that if there was coin to be had for hiring men, she would not still be at Tynan.

"I doubt you'd find many to come this far north," she said, partly to ease his pride, and partly to ease the silence between them. It was the first time she'd felt disturbed by the utter absence of sound. Even the incessant noise of the sheep seemed muffled, as if a great glass jar separated them from the rest of the world.

"I know a great deal about sheep, MacLeod, more than I ever wished to know. My father saw to that." Squire Cuthbertson had insisted all of his daughters earn their keep, despite the fact that raising sheep required hard physical labor. At nine, Judith had learned to shepherd the stupid things, walking from hilltop to hilltop on her father's vast acreage. She'd learned to wash the long virgin fibers and card the wool before she was twelve.

"And so, you'd teach what you've learned."

"That, and the weaving, if you wish." All of them, even Elizabeth, had worked the looms, and if Judith had a favorite activity of all of them, it was that. She could sit on the hard bench behind the six-foot-wide loom, pressing the long narrow board with her feet, while her hands automatically placed the threads in position. She'd become so adept at it that she could spend hours weaving, mesmerized by the *click, clack* of the boards shunting across the tight threads, lost in her own world of thoughts and dreams.

Alisdair found himself curiously entranced.

Her face was dirty, her hair a tousled mess of long dusty

locks, a thousand small white curling strands of fleece clung to her clothing; she smelled of sheep and good, honest labor.

Her eyes flickered like a candle flame, he thought, wondering what caused her more consternation, the fact that he emulated her way of mute defense, or that he could not help but be captivated by this new, unanticipated side of her.

She raised her eyes to examine his face and found herself oddly trapped by the look in his eyes. It was not censorious, or even angry, but filled with the strangest sort of curiosity, and if she didn't imagine it, a hint of vulnerability. As if he dearly wished to know who she was and what she was about, and such inquisitiveness rendered him open and susceptible.

"Why do you care, Judith?" he asked softly. Calling herself back to the present, she spoke in as soft a tone, as if the world had suddenly become still with listening and their conversation too intimate to be overheard.

"If you cannot import shearers or weavers," she said, answering his question in a roundabout way, "then you need to train your people, MacLeod. Women have more patience for the weaving, and men more strength for the shearing."

She turned away, but her movement was not quick enough to escape the arm that easily grasped her around the waist.

"Why, Judith?" he asked, when he tilted her chin up so that her eyes could meet his. They were too close, too near to each other, which was why she could barely breathe, and why her heart was beating so quickly. The wisp of his breath brushed across her cheek, the hand upon her waist spread until it nearly reached her underarm and the curve of one breast.

Her lashes fluttered like the wings of a trapped bird, he thought. And her pulsed raced as rapidly. If he had not thought she would have fled his touch, Alisdair would have placed his finger there, to prove to his eyes how quickly

her heart beat. Or breathe upon it, his lips only an inch
from the softness of her skin, his warm breath a comfort.
Instead, he plucked one curling wool fiber from her bodice, wondering if the pressure of his fingers singed her
skin as ably as the touch of her softness made his fingers
itch.

"You've been fair in your truce, MacLeod. I'd thought
to repay you, that is all." She looked away, down at the
ground, up at the darkening sky, anywhere but at him.

"Has your life been so devoid of simple kindness, Judith,
that you would feel a debt for it?"

His words coaxed her attention. She glanced at him,
away, then slowly back.

On his face was a look he'd worn for Douglas—how often
had she seen him look so?—sweet patience and gentleness.

Judith wanted, in that moment, to tell him everything.
This man enticed her strangely to honesty, coaxed her to
feel safe in a world still strange and foreign. In a moment
of time, outlined against a world hastening to dusk, a
second passed, and then another, in which she pretended
that he might be unlike any man she'd ever known or that
she might not be the person she knew herself to be. A
fleeting clutch of seconds, a silver drop of purity, only a
moment passed, but it was gilded with a thought as errant
as a rainbow in her palm, precious, but impossible. What
would it be like to speak the truth? The moment passed;
Judith did nothing more dangerous than continue to look
at him, wondering if the last chance for expiation vanished
also.

"It will make the time go faster, MacLeod."

One finger touched the bridge of her nose and then
slipped softly to her temple. It was such an odd gesture
for someone to make, especially someone as large and
strong and Scots as the MacLeod, that for a moment she
forgot that she was trapped so close to him that a mere
inch would cause her lips to meet his tanned skin. For a
second, she almost forgot that danger came with closeness,

and kindness often masked cruelty. Gentleness. Tenderness. The two worst lies.

She stiffened in his arms, and it was a response Alisdair had waited for from the first moment he touched her. The delay pleased him. Perhaps his English hedgehog could be gentled after all.

"Your help would be welcome," he said then, as he released her. She was unprepared for the full effect of his smile. It was too charming, too intense. She swallowed heavily, gripped her hands before her and nodded, not looking at the MacLeod after all, but forced by something—some fleeting emotion which tickled her stomach and made her heart lurch in her chest—to stare, wordless, at the stony ground in front of her.

She nodded then, mutely. With the sun having tinted her nose pink, her long lashes brushing against the curve of her cheek, and her lips tilted to a self-conscious half smile, Alisdair MacLeod had the strange and sudden thought that beauty was more than just good looks, that it came from the soul. That it was more than a ripe figure pressing against the bodice of a too snug gown, more than shapely ankles and long, long legs. It was more than a face as delicately carved as a bust from ancient Greece. More than a simple smile. That beauty was kindness and concern. Maternal nurturing, friendship, love. That in the soul of her, Judith MacLeod had all the raw material for true, exquisite beauty, and he probably had willfully and willingly ignored it until now.

Dangerous thoughts for a man counting the days until his freedom.

Chapter 12

Twenty women appeared, as if by sorcery, the first day the MacLeod called them together. Judith remembered some of the women from their visits to Tynan's kitchen. Some had glanced at her from the doorway of their cottages, some had followed down the hill when the MacLeod chased her back to Tynan, but still others she'd never met before.

Meggie came, too, and the two women shared a smile of tentative friendship.

Judith had taken her a kettle of stew the day after learning of Janet's death. If her kindness was thrown back in her face, Judith had reasoned, then at least she had made the effort. Instead, Meggie had welcomed her.

Her cottage was dark, barely lit by the chimney flue located in the middle of the thatch roof. Judith stood on the threshold, uncertain whether she truly wanted to go inside. But she had, because of the smile on Meggie's face, and the sorrow on her face.

"Thank ye," she said quietly, as she took the covered kettle from Judith, who stood peering into the gloom with surprise and not a little shock. How could anyone live in such conditions? She had gone from her own spacious home to Peter's, from there to a small, rented house in London. Yet, none of those dwellings had been as cramped and as gloomy as this rickety structure.

The cottage was only one small room. The floor was packed earth swept clean by the bristles of an improvised broom. A narrow board nailed to the side of the frame served as the only table. Other than one small chair and a cot, there was no furniture. It was neat and orderly, however, with shelves containing all of Meggie's possessions in tidy rows.

Judith had no choice but to sit on the wobbly chair Meggie hastily provided. She did not know what to say. What words could possibly help?. Even so, she had tried.

Her husband had been a MacLeod, Meggie told Judith that day, as if explaining her presence in the glen. She herself had been a McDougal, her brown eyes alight with memory as she told Judith of the day a MacLeod had come to her clan, seeking a woman with hair as blond as the sun and eyes as blue as the sky. What he'd got, Meggie said, smiling, was a woman with dark brown hair and eyes the color of soil, but he had never admitted to feeling the lack.

Such reminiscent joy was beyond Judith's understanding, but she wished there was some way she could banish the look of sorrow in Meggie's eyes. Yet, that look was not far from any of these Scots. Sorrow, however, never stopped these people. They rose at dawn and challenged nature, worked as hard as the most humble serf in the fields, labored days upon weeks and weeks into months. They took pride in their heritage, in their uniqueness, in their very stubbornness. They relished their songs, their language, and themselves. They held fast to beliefs passed down for generations, in the strength of clan and clansman, legend and pipes.

It was daunting to be in their midst, to witness firsthand how they accepted their troubles, yet never bowed beneath the weight of them.

Judith didn't know if she could ever understand these

Scots. She suspected that she would never be as strong, nor as resilient, nor as stubborn. Even as she stood here, waiting to help them, they looked at her with suspicion.

"I know that you're here either to spread your knowledge of weaving, or to learn the craft, and I'm glad to share with you what I know. Are there any among you who have used this loom before?" And a paltry excuse it was for a loom, too, Judith thought, staring at it accusingly, as if the frame of warped wood was responsible for its own condition.

A knurled hand was extended into the air, and Judith craned forward to see its owner.

"I've knowledge o' the loom," Grizzelle said, and Judith almost groaned when the woman stood. She looked to be ninety, nearly bent over with age, but her wizened appearance did not seem to affect the resolve in her step. Slowly, she walked down the aisle between the rows of benches to stop before the old loom.

Large, broad-knuckled fingers stroked the wood, pulled impatiently upon old threads left to rot in the delicately carved prongs. Despite Grizelle's advanced years, her hands were not knotted with age.

"It ne'r worked right twenty years ago, an' I doubt if time's added ta its worth," she said, her voice crackling with irritation. "It should ha' been burned ta the ground, but I ken that the good tends to go first, an' the bad linger on."

The women chuckled, and Judith smiled.

The time sped by, day after day, from sunup to gloaming, what the Scots called the time when the light abruptly vanished into mist. Day in, day out, Grizzelle taught the intricacies of the old loom, while Judith guided unskilled fingers with her own, praising the rudimentary efforts of each woman as they learned.

The air in the weaving hut was warm, occasionally stuffy, the air filled with wool fibers, but enlivened by the quick, easy conversation of women who'd known each other all their lives, who'd shared heartache and joy. They created a pocket of companionship and camaraderie, labor made palatable by the presence of others.

Judith began to anticipate her days. By midafternoon Friday of the second week, their first weaving was finished. There were gaps in the threads and knots where there shouldn't be, but the overall result was something to be proud of, their first completed length of cloth.

"Aye, an' it's time for a celebration, I'm thinking, "Sara said. "Take a wee nip o' the ale," she insisted, passing an ornately ugly pewter bottle with a cork stopper to Judith. "It's from my own barm, an' a finer brew ye'll not find in the glen."

Because the woman had gone to the effort of fetching the ale from her own cottage and partly because she was being watched intently by the rest of the women, Judith ignored the fact that Meggie was shaking her head and rolling her eyes heavenward. She drank deeply of the heather ale.

It was surprisingly sweet. Brandy carried with it too many memories; Judith could not abide the taste. Nor did she care for wine because of its bitterness. Heather ale was different from both.

It was only when her giggles appeared like bubbles from a batch of soap that Judith realized how strong it was. She clasped her hand over her mouth in surprise, turning wide eyes to the women, who were swaying where they sat, and had the oddest ability to duplicate themselves until there was a whole roomful of twos.

It was the MacLeod who lifted her in his arms a scant hour later. He muttered something about the English being unable to hold their liquor, but somehow, it didn't seem important. Nothing was important, and wasn't that simply wonderful?

Judith liked the ride back to Tynan curled against his chest. She especially liked it when they mounted the stairs. It was comfortable bouncing against him like this, mainly because he smelled of the fields and of sunlight, and in a strange way, of heather.

Or, was that her?

Her head dropped back upon his arm and she breathed deeply. Why did some men always smell bad, and others never smell bad when they should? She nuzzled her head into his armpit and heard the strangest sound, like the rumbling of thunder.

Judith raised her head, looked around, and then decided she was safer with her head level. That way, the stairs didn't spin quite so much, nor did her stomach lurch as though she had just sniffed a vat of wet wool. She truly liked the MacLeod's strength. He did not puff, nor did he huff. She giggled. He said something, and she squinted up at him, but still could not decipher his words.

He was so handsome, with his mane of black hair and his golden brown eyes and his deeply tanned face. And that mouth, looking as though it had kissed a thousand willing women.

Judith tried to touch his face, but missed on the first try. The second time, she succeeded, touching his lips quickly with one finger. They were soft, too soft for a man's lips. They felt like velvet or the down from the belly of a goose.

She sighed happily.

He balanced her precariously as he opened the door to her room. She held on by the simple means of gripping his shirt, once more oblivious to the fact that she had also grabbed a handful of chest hair. He grimaced, but didn't bother to try to extricate her hand.

Alisdair was glad that his English wife was a friendly little thing when inebriated. She could have been maudlin, or worse, mean. She did not seem to know what she was doing, however, and that colored his actions as he gently lay her on her bed.

She would have said something, but the words and the deed whirled out of her head just as the room spun and blackened without warning.

He stepped back and removed her shoes. She had a time of it, his English wife. For two weeks, he had seen

her rise at dawn and lift herself wearily up the stairs at
night, all without a word of complaint.

Tonight, he'd watched her as she sat and giggled with
the women. Now, she was dead to the world with her mouth
hanging open and her face flushed with drink. She would
hate herself in the morning and wouldn't that be a pity.
He had laughed at her antics, she had been so un-Judith-
like.

He had not told her how much he admired her efforts.

Yet, it was the sound of her laughter which had arrested
him in mid-stride. It was lilting and lyrical and, he suspected, rare. If it took a jug full of heather ale to transform
this English wife into a pretty Scots lass, he himself would
gladly brew a barrel a day.

He did not undress her, only tucked her in gently, covering her with the soft linen sheet and blanket, a protective,
tender gesture unseen by any other eyes.

He had been right to think she would bring him problems. Why did she hate as strongly as she feared? Why was
her smile such a rarity? Why did she deem herself unworthy
of kindness? When had the answers to all his questions
become so necessary?

He only had a few weeks of civil behavior to be gotten
through. Surely, he could manage that. This fascination
with his English wife had, at its root, the simple fact that
he'd been without a woman too long.

After Anne's death, he had led an almost monastic life,
finally easing his urges in the silken body of a friendly
woman in Inverness. Yet, he'd declined to take advantage
of her presence during that last visit. Why?

He was not such a weakling that another person, let
alone an Englishwoman with Loch dark eyes and a too
full lower lip, could make him lose control over his own
emotions. She did not have that power over him.

Yet, why did he ache to shut her mouth when she spoke
in that godawful accent—and not just with his hands? Why,
on God's earth, did he want to discover why her eyes
darkened sometimes until they were almost black, and

her gaze journeyed to some far-off distant place where he suspected no one else could travel? Why, in the name of Scotland and all that was holy to him, did he have this strange feeling that he should ride to Inverness and remain there until their three-month marriage was finished?

Alisdair determined, in that moment, that he would simply increase his pace. He would work harder than ever, and then this inconvenient curiosity and even more intransigent need of his would simply be buried beneath fatigue.

He stood at the doorway for a long time, his hand on the frame, his eyes on the bed. Judith slept heavily, her slight snores causing an amused grin to dance upon his mouth.

It would have been better if he had not seen her smile.

It would have been easier if he had never heard her laughter.

Chapter 13

"You could use time away from all your chores. I'd not thought to see anyone match my zeal, but your industry tops even mine," Alisdair said the next morning. He smiled at the untouched bowl of porridge beside Judith. He could imagine the state of her stomach. Heather ale not only produced an unexpected kick, but it left a distinct longing for death the next day.

"I'll not ask for mercy, MacLeod. It was my own foolishness that has my stomach in knots." Judith stood and disposed of the contents of the bowl in the slops jar.

"Do you not ever allow yourself to play, Judith?"

She turned confused eyes to him.

"There is too much to be done and not enough time."

"But chores will always be there and time will not."

"Is this Alisdair MacLeod speaking? The man who rises at dawn and only rests at midnight?" Her smile was oddly crooked and totally mesmerizing. Yet, her eyes were filled with caution and there were shadows beneath them.

He wondered if she dreamed again last night, or had her indulgence in heather ale also gifted her with one night of forgetfulness? For weeks now, he'd heard the sounds of her crying, became as accustomed to it as he did the waves crashing to the shore outside his window.

Another question, unanswered.

He extended his hand, and she stared at it. Hard, callused, large, it was offered palm up, a wordless invitation to come to him. For long moments, her gaze shifted from his hand to his face, as if the study of both would offer insight into his actions. Finally, she stepped forward, her breath caught oddly in her chest, and placed her palm over his.

What she expected, she didn't know, but it wasn't that the MacLeod would suddenly smile at her, and loop her arm over his.

"We've a sun to catch, Granmere," he said, his eyes never leaving Judith's flushed face.

Sophie thought it an excellent sign. Alisdair was beginning to look at Judith with interest. He was a lonely man, for all his work and worry. He needed someone to talk to, someone who could share his burdens, bring a little laughter into his life, a little comfort.

There was still time.

Alisdair held her hand as they moved up the track to the top of the moor. It was a strange sensation, Judith thought, but one not altogether unpleasant. They were silent, each trapped within a bubble of thought and unspoken wishes, a comforting silence for all that it teemed with unvoiced yearnings. He led her onto the path to the left, to a place beyond the fields, one littered with large stones bathed bright by the morning sun. On the horizon, dark clouds rolled incessantly onward, a constant presence of rain, of warning, of promise.

Judith pulled her hand free, went to the largest stone, moving her fingers over strange markings carved into the surface.

"I could tell you were English if you spoke not a word," he said behind her. "You touch a place none dare venture near," he said, smiling.

She stepped back, her hand still outstretched. Other

than a few scrawled markings, unintelligible to her, there was nothing to indicate the purpose of the stone. She hoped, fervently, that she had not just touched an ancient tomb. Her face must have registered her horror, because he only laughed, and led her to another rock, carved smooth by the forces of nature, not man, and sat beside her, looking out onto the moor that swept down to the rolling white sea of sheep, and further to the track to Tynan.

"No," he said, alleviating her all too obvious fears. " 'Tis not a sacred place, simply a mysterious one. We are a strange people, full of superstition. It is an unlucky spot. The villagers think that *Domhnull Dubh* emerges from the ground here, and those markings are his hoof prints."

"Who?" she asked, unable to repeat the strange syllables.

"Domhnull Dubh, Black Donald. The English call him the Devil, which is a case of the pot calling the kettle black, I think. Did you ever hang a horseshoe at home?" he asked, the question coming before she'd had time to tense at the mention of nationality.

"Yes, of course, for good luck." She glanced over at him, too bemused by the softness of his voice and his sudden, winsome smile to spoil the mood by questioning it.

"We do the same. Except, of course, that the English hang it open side up. We don't care about its placement, but there's a reason for that, too. Would you like to hear the story?" His smile was boyish, filled with a charm she'd seen hints of before, but nothing like this windswept stranger whose gaze roamed the land before him with an odd blend of possessiveness and sadness.

She nodded.

"Once upon a time," he began, as if he were a father telling a bedtime story to his enraptured daughter, "Black Donald pulled a smith from his bed. He needed him to shoe his hoof, you see. The smith was frightened by Black Donald, but still angry that he had been awakened at midnight. So, when he drove the first nail in, he sank it deep, past the horn of Black Donald's hoof and into the fleshy part of his foot. Black Donald hopped about in great pain, furious at the smith, demanding that he finish the job properly, else he would visit great misfortune on him and his family.''

Judith's head was bent, her hands were stilled. There was such an air of intensity about her that Alisdair knew she listened like a child, eager to grasp holes in the telling of his tale. He smiled and continued. ''Well, with that threat, the smith realized he had better make a bargain with the devil. He refused to finish the work until Black Donald granted him a wish. That wish was, whenever the devil saw a horseshoe, whether it was sitting on the ground, or hanging, he would do no mischief. Black Donald, who was hopping around on one foot, reluctantly agreed. Before the smith finished the job, however, he first surrounded his entire house with horseshoes. And because of Black Donald's bargain, the smith's family was left alone. That's why we don't care how a horseshoe is hung, just that it's there to prevent Black Donald from making mischief.''

Judith smiled. He wished she would smile again. It brought sunlight into her eyes and a hidden dimple to her cheek.

''I think it Pictish markings, myself,'' he said, motioning to the stone, ''but none will ever know, I suspect.''

''Pictish?''

''The Picts were an ancient people. They may well have been the first Scots. They did, at least, predate the Romans.''

''I did not know the Romans occupied the Highlands.''

''Oh, they did not occupy them,'' he said with a smile. ''They, too, tried in vain to conquer us. It seems as though half the invaders in the world's history have attempted it and failed. At least, until the English came.''

It was too good to be true, this easy companionship.

''No, Judith,'' he said softly, ''do not get all stiff and rigid. I do not fault you for your birth. It is, after all, a fact that you could not help. I do, however, fault the English government and that pack of wolves let loose by Cumberland. I fault each and every one of those beasts.''

Judith sat with the wind blowing her hair around her shoulders, her hands clenched tightly on her lap.

He liked her hair this way, strewn around her shoulders like a wild woman's, or a good Scots lass. He absently imprisoned one errant curl and rubbed the softness of it between his fingers, noting that the color was a rich brown with glinting red and gold highlights. ''Your hair has a hundred colors in it,'' he said, ignoring the fact that she was edging away from him more each moment. Shortly, he mused, she would fall off the rock and he supposed she would find some way to retreat from him then, too.

She pulled loose from his grasp, and patted her hair into some semblance of order. ''It is not practical,'' she said shortly, frowning.

''Ah, that word.'' He smiled softly. ''There is much duty attached to being practical. For example,'' he said, rising, and again extending a hand to her, ''practicality demands that I not forget that I have work to do. While it is pleasant sunning on the rocks, I have duties and obligations.''

''I, too,'' she admitted reluctantly, surprised at the sudden feeling of regret which poured over her. One small part wished she could find a way to keep him here for a little while longer. Another, saner part of her mind welcomed the release from his presence. It was a paradox, those emotions, and they caused her to step away from him.

''Do you know,'' he said absently, ''there is a story about the Picts and heather ale. Remind me to tell you some time, after you've recovered from it.''

''Your heather ale is deceptive, MacLeod.'' Her smile was wide, disclosing white, even teeth. It was a smile untinged by mockery, alight with mischief.

He wondered if she knew how pretty she was when she smiled.

They walked down past the milling sheep again, but

before they parted, he stopped and grasped one of her hands. He held it, studying it, seeing the strength of it and the fine suppleness of her fingers. She pulled it from his grip before he could remark on its size and the fact that blisters were forming on her palm.

"I have not thanked you, Judith," he said softly, "for your efforts and your work. For caring." He smiled a little at her confused look.

"It made the time go by faster."

"Ah, yes, time. We haven't much left, have we?" There was an intentness about his look, as if he gauged her words, her expression.

"A month." It ticked through her mind like a symphony of raindrops, one perfect sphere at a time. There was only a month left at this ramshackle old castle. How odd that each day seemed to remind her of something she would regret leaving behind. Oh, Sophie, of a certainty. Judith would never forget those sparkling blue eyes and that mouth always pursed in a laugh or a smile. She would miss this sweet lady who seemed to grow more fragile each passing hour.

A month, then, to savor the sunset over the cove, the sweet scent of pine wafting into her bedroom window at night. A month in which to learn to live without the burr of Malcolm's accent, or the soft breeze which billowed like a lover around Tynan.

"Twenty-eight days," Alisdair corrected softly. "I can count, also."

His voice seemed to lower when he spoke to her, as if that tone was reserved only for her. If anything was dangerous, it was the sound of that voice, skittering over her skin like the lightest touch of a feather.

In twenty-eight days, then, her mind would become hers once more, and she would not be lulled into thinking forbidden thoughts. No more silly games and sillier notions and childish dreams that should have died when she was a child. No more thoughts of him, unbidden and dangerous.

Did he know how different he appeared even from his

own kind? His clean-shaven face was as out of place among these bearded Highlanders as a cow among the sheep. And yet, it suited him, the same way his smile suited him. Judith had witnessed at least ten versions of them—the tender smile when he nuzzled Douglas's hair with his chin, the smile he gave to Granmere when she said something outrageous that quirked his humor, the grin he gave to Malcolm when the old Scot refused to back down and gave him measure for measure, the smile of accomplishment as he looked out over his crops, his land, his sheep. And the odd, almost tender smile Judith noted on more than one occasion, when she turned and found him studying her again.

Twenty-eight days, four weeks. No more wondering, at the end of those days, what life would have been like if she were different. No more pretending that the past had not happened, that she was untouched by it. No more wishing, in odd little moments, that it could have been different if they had met somewhere else, some earlier time. Perhaps they could have greeted each other in the way civil strangers do. Perhaps even become friends. That bond would have allowed her to ask him all the questions she so longed to ask, questions forbidden because of their intrinsically personal nature.

She would be gone soon, Alisdair thought, and this strange link welded between them by Malcolm's words and his grandmother's good intentions would be sundered.

He should feel triumphant, should he not?

Instead, he was suddenly irritated beyond belief, and his aggravation had at its center his English wife. Now was not the time to notice that her face softened more often into a smile, to linger upon her full lips, or remember that her eyes darkened at night until they were almost black and reminded him of a storm at sea during the day. He did not want to recall the long line of her magnificent legs outlined in the threadbare cloth of her dress.

Nor did Alisdair wish to remember the night before, when her laughter had stirred his interest and something more, and her smile had lit up her face until she was almost beautiful. He had no wish to encourage the curious protective impulse, that feeling that he alone could banish the look of sadness she unwittingly divulged or the flicker of quickly masked fear in her eyes. It was a foolish thought. As idiotic and nonsensical as the curiosity which made him wonder why she still eyed him with caution, as if she were a Highland deer, and he a skilled hunter. It would do no good to open doors not easily closed again.

Yet, he was not a bad prize as husbands go. He was a learned man, a man of principles. And although he might not be Adonis, at least he did not frighten children. Of a certainty, he did not possess the legendary experience of his fallen brother, but at least he knew what pleased a woman. He was getting older, true, but he still had strength in his limbs, was able to work as hard as he had in the past. Other than a tumbler full of brandy now and then, he had no terrible habits. While it was true that the legacy of Tynan was more a millstone around his neck than a blessed inheritance, still, he possessed a castle and not many men could boast of that, could they?

He was not *that* bad a prize.

His nod was curt, dismissive. His look was filled with irritation.

Judith watched him as he walked down the glen, wondering what she had done to spark his displeasure. It was difficult not to notice how his trousers were pulled tight against his legs by his long, firm strides, or that the sun made his hair appear almost blue black, or his broad back strained the seams of his white shirt.

What manner of man was he, this laird MacLeod, who could tell a tale with such charm one moment, then become almost frosty with rudeness.

Who was he, really?

She should not wish to know.

Chapter 14

There were fourteen days left when the English came.

Malcolm rushed in from the seaside door, shouting at both women that the English troops under Colonel Harrison were assembling on the moors. The MacLeod followed close behind, scooping up a clean shirt from the wooden hook mounted near the kitchen door.

"They'll be gathering the clan, next," Malcolm warned, "ta check for contraband."

"It's the pipes they're looking for, Judith," Sophie said gently, correctly interpreting Judith's confusion.

"The pipes are outlawed," the MacLeod said shortly.

"Aye, and our weapons," Malcolm added. He held out his arm and helped Sophie rise from her chair.

"And the kilt," Sophie contributed with a smile.

"Why?" It seemed an innocent enough question, but it began a spate of conversation unlike their usual topics of crops and sheep.

"They are symbols of our heritage, Judith," the Mac-Leod said, as he stood at the bronze doors. Along the horizon, the mounted troops appeared, backlit by the sun. From here, their crimson tunics were almost unrecognizable. "Without our heritage, we are less a threat. We will be assimilated into English society without the blink of an eye. Soon, all of our poets and scientists and men of promise will call themselves English, and the heritage of Scotland will be no more than a little finger on the hand that is England."

"Aye," Malcolm said, joining him, "the fist that is England. We're no' allowed our pipes, because they stir the blood. We're no' allowed our weapons, lass, because we might revolt against tyranny."

"And the men aren't allowed kilts, child," Sophie interrupted, "because there is not a more thrilling sight than a handsome man without his trousers." Her gentle laughter diffused the gloom which had fallen over the men.

Malcolm hugged her tightly. "Sophie, if I were only a few years younger, I would show you handsome."

"But then think of the scandal we'd cause," Sophie teased, smiling at him.

The MacLeod went first through the bronze door and into the courtyard. Malcolm helped Sophie slowly down the steps. Judith reluctantly followed.

There, on the hillock, where the moors swept down to the track leading to Tynan, stretched a long line of mounted English soldiers, their crimson tunics as bright as blood.

Everyone assembled quickly, not daring to anger the English soldiers by their dawdling. The entire clan was crowded into the courtyard; a hundred people pulled from their daily occupations. Geddes hobbled in on a twisted cane which looked too frail to support him. He was only one of the elders of the clan, the other men followed behind. Hamish, nearly blind from cataracts, was assisted by Alex, who glowered at the assorted English with none of his hatred masked. Of the elders, only Geddes seemed prudent, walking heavily to the curved side of the keep and remaining there, resting wearily against the brick. The women from the weaving shed arrived as a group led by Sara, her old wool dress threadbare and worn, but topped with a white, starched apron. The rest of the women of the clan, most clutching children barely old enough to be counted as more than babes, followed behind. Grizzelle seemed to draw strength from Meggie, as she leaned heavily against the younger woman. Fiona clutched Douglas to her chest in a frantic effort to soothe the child's wails. Her usual sneer was replaced by the look they all wore on their faces.

Fear.

Judith had been a witness to the Duke of Cumberland's triumphant return to London, had thrilled to the sound of "Hail the Conquering Hero Comes," as the Duke had garnered a riotous welcome from London's usually cynical inhabitants. Column after column of soldiers, in full military regalia, had marched before the overflowing crowds as the country had celebrated an important victory.

Now, Judith only watched the redcoated soldiers with wide eyes, the memory of an English victory submerged beneath anxiety for these vanquished Scots.

In the center of the courtyard was the MacLeod. He stood, calmly donning his shirt, as if the colonel of the regiment were not marching closer to him, his stallion's shod hooves imperially striking sparks against the stone cobbles of the courtyard.

The Colonel did not have to push his way towards the MacLeod, the group parted automatically, pressing back from his presence as if fearing to be soiled.

Only the MacLeod remained fixed and still, his eyes scanning the horizon now filled with mounted troops. His eyes dropped and then lifted again, to meet the Colonel's sharp stare.

"MacLeod."

"Colonel."

Neither man smiled in greeting. Judith could feel the tension in the people around her as each man intently eyed the other.

"Have you anything to report?" the Colonel asked, his

eyes sweeping down the tall, muscular frame of the Mac-Leod.

Harrison was damned tired of playing nursemaid to this group of misfits, having to ride the interminable length of the lonely moors from Fort George specifically to act as father confessor to a bunch of defeated Scots. Rumors spread like a grass fire from one glen to another, but he didn't have to like his assignment of ferreting out each tale told by a traitor. Yet, he knew full well that Alisdair MacLeod had been at Culloden, had marched with his own Highland brigade into England itself. The terms of his surrender must have been particularly onerous to a man whose male relatives had perished at England hands.

"We have been but good subjects of the Crown, Colonel." Alisdair was not unduly impressed by Colonel Harrison's show of force. His clan would be, though, and he could feel the frisson of fear which swept through them. The Colonel was not like the Butcher's men, who had looted, burned, and raped their way through the Highlands. But the Colonel was a stickler for orders, and his instructions were to continue to monitor and subdue the clans under his command, especially those headed by men under the confines of a conditional pardon.

Alisdair had long since decided they could have fared worse.

"Yes, MacLeod, but are you obedient subjects of the Crown?"

"We are a small and puny bunch here," Alisdair said calmly, "not apt to make much trouble. I doubt any of our clan have the strength to disobey the Disarming Act, let alone the wherewithall to do so."

"And your pipes have been destroyed, and your tartans burned?" The Colonel scanned the group surrounding him. They were poorly dressed, the strain of constant hunger only recently eradicated from their faces. The children looked at him wide-eyed, and their mothers stared at him in fear. What did they think he would do, he thought irately, seize babies to serve the King?

Judith edged to the rear of the crowd, each tiny movement a study in restraint. Her face was bleached white, her lips clamped together, her stomach boiled with a sickness too deep and vile to call simple nausea. The fist made by her left hand pressed against her mouth so hard that the edges of her teeth tore her inner lip. Her right hand bunched up her skirts, preparatory for flight. Still, she barely moved, trapped by the feral smile from across the courtyard, the gleam in eyes she had not seen for over two years.

Judith would have greeted Hell with more welcome than the sight of Bennett Henderson among Colonel Harrison's cadre of officers.

Only he noticed when she backed up to the ruined tower, following the curve of it until she broke free, circling it in a desperate and futile bid for freedom.

Bennett Henderson nearly laughed aloud. Of all the presents this pit of earth could have delivered to him, this was the most delicious. The smile that lanced his face was anticipatory, sharpening its long, lean lines, a perfect counterpart to pale blue eyes, as cold and as hard as shards of ice.

He edged his horse away from the knot of people surrounding his commanding officer and the intractable leader of this dung-filled courtyard and circled around the keep.

Dear God, Judith thought, why him? Of all the people in the world who might ride into the courtyard of Tynan, why did it have to be him?

It did not enter Judith's mind to seek safety inside Tynan. She could not bear the thought of being trapped inside four sturdy walls, while outside he would be waiting, cunning, savage, patient. Instead, she bolted for the open countryside, racing across the moor, feet flying across the grass, her heart straining in her chest, her breath exhaled in short, choppy gasps. She was silhouetted against the hillock for just a second, but it was all the man on horseback needed. Moments later, he effortlessly overcame her and

would have run her down had she not turned at the last
second.

Bennett was tempted to see how long she would last.
The chase could be lengthened pleasurably, the sight of
her attempting to outrace his stallion almost comical in
the extreme. His mount was bred for speed; his stallion's
achievements had lined Bennett's pockets more than once
in the Officer's Mess. Still, there was his commanding
officer to remember. Yet, he was beyond the rise of earth,
too far away to hear a woman scream.

Bennett cornered her again, leaned down, gripped
Judith's flailing wrist, twisting it cruelly, but she whirled
on him, sinking her teeth into the back of his hand. Her
reward was a muffled oath and temporary freedom. She
changed directions, racing down the track towards Tynan.

"Bitch." A mocking smile curved his lips as Bennett
sucked on the blood she'd drawn. No wonder he'd missed
her. What an enjoyment it would be to tame her again.

Bennett raced toward her again, overtook her easily.
Still, Judith fought him, her battle no less intense for its
silence. The skittish horse reared, disliking Judith's flailing
limbs. The stallion was high-strung, volatile, tamed only
by the centaur grace of its rider. Judith took advantage of
the moment by flinging herself near the rear legs of the
black beast and kicking out with one foot.

It was a suicidal move. Bennett had more concern for
his stallion than his victim; he was off the back of the horse
before she could flee again, throwing her to the ground
with such force that Judith hit the earth hard on her stomach, the breath escaping from her lungs, her mouth tasting
dirt.

A guttural sound escaped her lips as Bennett turned her
over, flattening her to the ground with his body. Even her
rage and fear were no match for his tensile strength. He
laughed, deeply aroused by her struggles and memories
of other occasions when she had shown as much spirit.

"Anthony's bitch," he said softly, his bright smile at
odds with the cruel look of his blazing blue eyes. The only

sign of his exertion was his flushed face; otherwise, he could have been a country gentleman out on a stroll. Except, of course, that the object of his affections was pinned effectively between his outstretched thighs, her thrashing legs attempting to dislodge him from her body.

"And here I thought you would be welcoming me, Judith, as you have so many times before." One hand effortlessly imprisoned her flailing hands, the other contemptuously flattened against one breast, pinching flesh through layers of cloth. "Have you missed me, bitch?"

Judith spat into his face. His response was a casual backhanded slap, hard enough to force her head around. She tasted blood where the edge of his ring cut her lip.

"Imagine, Judith, when I had despaired of this backwater, to find such entertainment in such an unlikely place. But then, you always were a surprise, weren't you? Tell me, have you grieved these last two years?"

"Let me go, Bennett." It was not a demand, but rather a plea, breathed in such a frail voice that she barely recognized it as hers.

"What? And be deprived of family, Judith? I think not. I think you owe me something, don't you? Something for not voicing my suspicions to the magistrates? Something to pay me back for all those days of mourning my dear brother's untimely demise? English justice, Judith. Even here." He pulled a lace handkerchief from his tunic pocket and thrust the edge of it in her mouth, effectively gagging her. It was a pity to silence her, still, there was the presence of the regiment to consider. He would slake himself in her once, and then arrange for a more leisurely reunion.

"Come, Judith, we've played this game before, haven't we?" He discounted her struggles as he casually unbuttoned the first button of his trousers.

Judith clenched her eyes tight and prayed for deliverance. It came in the softly mocking tones of the MacLeod.

"Is this the way your officers greet a new arrival to the Highlands, Colonel? If so, then I must insist upon correcting your manners."

One moment he was astride her; the next, Bennett was rolling across the ground. The MacLeod's fury was evident in the gleam of his eyes and the sardonic grin that wreathed his mouth. As Bennett stood, the MacLeod turned, as if asking the Colonel's permission, then lashed out with one powerful fist. It was a deceptive blow, seemingly casual, but with enough strength to knock the Englishman to the ground again. Alisdair did not bother to hit him again, but hauled him up and shoved him toward the Colonel, whose only response was to direct a look of utter disgust at his officer.

Alisdair held one hand out for Judith, neither bending down to assist her or looking in her direction. She spit out the handkerchief, scrambled up from the ground, and stood behind him, still not quite believing that she had been rescued.

Without being aware of it, she moved closer to Alisdair. She placed her hand on his arm, the first time she'd ever voluntarily touched him. At another time, she might have noticed that he jumped at her touch, or that there were soft hairs upon his golden skin which tickled her palm. Perhaps she would have noted, in some other circumstance, the smooth strength of his barely flexed muscles or the fact that they were clenched tightly, as if in reaction to her touch.

Instead, she only wondered how much he'd hate her when he knew.

"Captain Henderson," Colonel Harrison demanded, "what is the meaning of this?"

All eyes turned in the direction of the officer who stood stonily beside his mount, staring at Judith with such a malevolent expression that she flinched. How well she remembered the promise of that look.

"A misunderstanding, sir," he said, speaking slowly, still not turning his gaze from Judith. "This woman, sir, is my beloved sister-in-law. Imagine my delight in finding her here. Yet, instead of us sharing our mutual grief for my brother, sir, she flew at me. I can only surmise that grief has loosened her wits."

"Your brother, Captain?" The Colonel's look was filled with confusion overlaid with anger. He was here to restore peace in the Highlands, not assault helpless women. He didn't like Bennett Henderson, there was something about the man that made his skin crawl, but he was still an officer of the Crown. "Wasn't your brother in the service of the Duke?"

Judith did not imagine the murmurs that rose from the hastily assembled clan. It seemed that each member had followed the MacLeod and had witnessed Bennett's assault.

Alisdair felt Judith's tension, looked down into her white, set face, and then up again into Colonel Harrison's glower.

The Colonel drew himself up to his full height and glared at her from his perch in the saddle. He had not missed the fact that she had sought protection from the MacLeod.

"Why, Madam, would the window of a decorated Cumberland veteran be in such a godforsaken place as this?"

Judith felt the shock whip through the MacLeod. She also sensed the horror of the group behind her, as if they'd taken a collective gasp. She was not surprised by such a reaction; she would have felt it herself had she been a Scot. Anthony had taunted her with descriptions of the battle of Culloden, regaling her with details of blood and gore too horrible to visualize. Anthony had bragged that he'd killed many a wounded Scot, but his brutality hadn't ended there. He'd slain women and children, too, his contempt for his victims as chillingly obvious as the delight in which he'd relayed his tale. For that, England had awarded him a medal.

Judith didn't move, nor did she speak.

"She is my wife, Colonel," Alisdair said shortly. His tone indicated that he would prefer she be anything else.

"I don't believe it," the Colonel said skeptically. It would be just like the Scot to protect himself by marrying an English widow. One of the Duke's men at that.

"How is it that you come to marry a Scot, woman, when your husband fought at Culloden? Are you in truth wed to this man?"

Judith removed her hand from the MacLeod's arm and took a tiny step away from him. With one word, she could disavow their union, but at what price? The hope of freedom was gone now. The moment she had seen Bennett, she'd realized that.

Yet, she had more than Bennett to worry about now. The fury the MacLeod barely held in check would soon find an outlet. Judith knew she would bear the brunt of it. Yet, she would gladly exchange the MacLeod's rage for Bennett's sadism.

"Well?" the Colonel demanded, irritated by her hesitation, angered by his officer's actions, acutely aware of the mumbling of the assorted people who had joined this comedic farce.

Judith looked up at the MacLeod who stood so stoic and silent beside her. He would not meet her eyes, choosing instead to focus his attention on the far horizon. She took a deep breath and answered him.

"Yes, Colonel, I am married to Alisdair MacLeod," she said firmly.

"Very well," Colonel Harrison said abruptly, motioning to Bennett Henderson to mount. "MacLeod, I will leave you to the care of your English wife. It seems an apt irony. And," he said, leaning down from the saddle and peering into Judith's face, so closely that she could see the flecks of black in his gray eyes, "as an English citizen, you will let me know if aught goes amiss here, won't you, Mistress Henderson?" She did not falter beneath his stare.

"MacLeod," Alisdair corrected harshly. "Her name is MacLeod."

"Indeed, I will, Colonel," Judith said, deliberately distancing herself still further from the immobile, taut figure of her husband.

"I'll hold you to that. MacLeod," he added, before he turned his mount, "let no danger face your new wife. If I hear of any harm to her, it will not go well for you or your clan. She is an English subject and the might of the Crown protects her. Remember that.''

Bennett Henderson mimicked his commanding officer's movement, bending low near Judith. Because she was standing a few feet away from Alisdair, he did not hear the words the English officer whispered to her, but he saw the sudden blanching of her face. Her wide, frightened eyes watched the man canter from the moor and join the rest of his regiment.

No one moved. The clan remained still and frozen as if waiting for a signal to disperse. All eyes were on Judith. Malcolm did not speak, and would not look in her direction, as he assisted a trembling Sophie down a path that suddenly seemed too difficult to traverse unaided.

The MacLeod's grip on her arm ended the suspense.

Now, the punishment would come. Judith turned and looked at him, her only emotion an odd resignation. She seemed to sag, Alisdair thought, as if the bravado was now spent, leaving only exhaustion in its place.

He did not speak as he grabbed her arm. Alisdair thought it not unlike hauling a sack of meal as he pulled her down the path and through the courtyard of Tynan. Only when they had mounted the steep steps and entered the laird's room did he fling her from him. The massive bed halted her momentum.

She didn't struggle, nor did she speak, and it was her strange lack of protest that goaded his rage.

''Why did you not tell me?'' he shouted, and the words could be heard in the kitchen where Malcolm and Sophie were helping themselves to an abundant quantity of purloined brandy.

''I could not help his occupation, MacLeod,'' Judith said wearily. She did not have the strength to fight him. The scene on the moor, her struggle with Bennett, had taken what reserves were left.

''And your brother-in-law, Judith? Did you not think that little scrap of knowledge was important? Such a tender family reunion. You seemed somewhat reluctant to greet your long-lost relative.''

She did not wish to discuss Bennett. Not now. Dear God, not ever. Yet, the MacLeod deserved some scrap of truth. "I did not know he was in Scotland."

Silence. He wanted to shout at her, to warn her that her speechlessness was dangerous, that remaining mute was not the best course. He wanted answers, and her reticence was only a stimulus to the fury he restrained by a thread.

"Good God, woman, do you realize what you've done? Do you have any idea?" He advanced on her as she leaned against the bed, but she did not recoil. She only stood, resolutely staring at him with wide blue eyes that seemed to grow darker and more lustrous with every passing minute.

He wanted her to defy him, so that his own rage would find a worthy escape. Instead, she only bowed her head and curved her shoulders inward as if to protect herself from a blow.

"Granmere's plan is so much smoke in the wind, woman," he said. "I have not begged and groveled to acquire a conditional pardon to be hanged because of a woman. You are now and truly wed, my lovely soldier's widow. To me, the enemy!"

"You are not my enemy, MacLeod," she said, her own voice so low that he had to strain to hear it.

"By the end of this day, you will think it," he snarled.

He could not help raising his voice in anger. He had, after all, great provocation. Not only had she lied to him, but there was that scene on the moor, the sight of his wife lying acquiescent beneath an English soldier. He wanted to punish her for that, and for her eternal, damnable silence.

Alisdair paid no attention to the voice of his conscience which urged him look coolly at the situation, to heed the signs that were there in Judith's eyes and in her stance. He was not calm enough for that. Reason should have stopped him from gripping her arms painfully and jerking her close. He felt her trembling and it angered him more.

He was too enraged to be logical. Despite all of the causes, all of the provocations, he thought later, he should have been able to prevent his next actions.

"You might as well be made wife," he said, his face contorted by rage, by jealousy, by something he would only later identify as betrayal. With one tear, he ripped the dress from her body. Nor did he stop there, but tore each of the garments from her until she stood clutching the bedpost, facing the wall, naked and as afraid as she'd ever been in her life.

Alisdair looked at her with eyes that widened as he stared, his rage changing to confusion, his frown replaced by a look of horror.

And wanted to weep.

Chapter 15

There were evidently more secrets in Judith's life.

Crisscrossing her back and her buttocks were deep red scars. They ranged from inch-wide scarlet welts which faded to a purplish hue, to delicate fronds of pink which extended around her waist to her belly. It looked as though she had been scourged, her back mutilated with a cat-o'-nine-tails. Not once, but many times.

Judith calmly stepped back from the side of the bed, removed the remnants of her torn clothing as if he weren't standing there horror struck by the sight of her exposed back. She took the clothing he had just ripped and painstakingly folded it without a word, until the torn cloth was assembled into a neat little square. This she placed on the bedside table and then walked, impervious to her nakedness, around the bed, to the long line of windows overlooking the sea. She stood there looking at the sun beginning to set, an orange disk disappearing into the dark blue expanse of water.

She was not thinking. She did not think at times like these. She did not feel, either. She shut off her emotions and her thoughts and disappeared somewhere where there was no pain, no anguish, no humiliation. No shame.

She would not beg. She had learned, long ago, that begging only made it worse. It only lengthened her torture. It was simpler just to exist somewhere in a timeless state while she endured it.

Judith heard his soft steps behind her and, despite her resolve, a tiny shudder shook her body.

Alisdair said nothing, only smoothed his hand over her back, feeling the deep indentations on her mutilated flesh. His fingers trailed from the nape of her neck to where her buttocks curved back to her thighs, smooth, long strokes as if to ease the memory of her pain.

She must have been in agony.

"Who did this to you?" he said, unaware that his voice rasped with emotion. "Your father?"

She shook her head.

Then it must have been her husband.

"Why?" It seemed the only question.

What did she tell him? How many times had she thought of this moment, of this revelation? Too many times and each ended with this question. She never had the answer and now a lie was all she had to offer him.

"The width of a man's thumb, MacLeod," she replied in a low monotone. "It is the law in England." There was absolutely no inflection in her voice.

"What does a wife do in England to deserve such punishment?" It was difficult to touch her as she stood so courageously waiting to be hurt again. He was filled with anger at the monster who had inflicted such pain on the body and on the soul. It sickened him to the core.

It explained, however, both her hatred and her fear.

"Be a woman, MacLeod, that is all. So simple, so ridiculously easy."

Her loathing of marriage now made sense. Her resistance to their union, to him, was an act of desperation. What had she ever learned from marriage, but pain and anguish? She had experienced nothing of the joys, of the feelings of belonging, of contentment, or solace a union can bring. Perhaps he had not loved Anne as she deserved, but their marriage had brought him contentment, some measure of happiness.

In that crucible of time, when Alisdair stood mute and still with his hand pressed firmly against her back as if to wipe clean the scars he felt there, he began to be aware of what he, himself, had done to cause Judith pain.

He had called her scrawny. She had only been thin.

He had called her a hag. She had only been tired.

He had called her sharp-tongued. She had only been frightened.

He wondered what he would have done, in a similar situation, if he had been uprooted from his home and forced to travel across a country, be tricked into marriage and expected to merge into an alien culture overnight?

His thoughts stopped suddenly, as he realized with shock that their circumstances were not as different as they appeared on the surface. He, too, had been forced to march across a country. His own. Alisdair had been expected to join in the uprising along with his father and his brother, despite the fact that he had argued vehemently against its lunacy. He had been tricked into this selfsame marriage, and the English expected him to be assimilated into their culture with nary a ripple on the surface of his heritage.

And his response? Anger.

The fact that it emerged from him in the guise of determination did not discount its source. He was still angry at his slain father and brother, at his own country for turning its back on survival. He was angry that Malcolm had tricked him into this marriage, and his honor insisted he continue with it. He was angry because he was expected to become all things English without a heed to the soul inside him that was blatantly Scot.

His anger had forced him to challenge his world. It was his way of coping with the changes in his life, to the presence of grief and loss. This new world the English had foisted upon him would be altered by his determination. He would not crumble beneath its demands.

He looked at his wife with new eyes.

Judith had fought for her survival by protecting herself in the only way she knew how. She surrounded herself with a mantle of silence, restraint. Even now, standing naked in front of him, she did not move to cover herself. She had retreated into detachment where pain or humiliation could not affect her. It was as much camouflage as whistling in the dark.

It was her only way of living through the horror she had experienced.

He turned her so that she faced him. The cut on her lip still oozed blood. He hadn't noticed it until now. He touched it gently with one finger, thinking it should be washed. Still, she did not raise her eyes even after he'd gone to the ewer and dampened a cloth, ministering to the cut with the gentlest touch.

He spread his arms around her and she flinched, even though the embrace was light and tender. She stood straight in his arms, until he pulled her head down, into the curve between his shoulder and his neck.

Such tenderness was unknown to her. Such compassion suspect.

"I will not beat you, Judith," Alisdair said softly, as if he heard her unvoiced thoughts. "I never touched a woman except in pleasure and passion. My wife had nothing to fear from me."

"I did not know you had been married before, MacLeod."

"There seems to be much we do not know of each other. Have you any more secrets to reveal?" he asked, in the first attempt at humor since the scene on the moors.

"I stand before you naked, MacLeod. Surely if there were any more secrets to divulge, you would see them readily." Her eyes glittered in the faint light from the window. She did not speak of other, darker secrets, whose knowledge was emblazoned on her soul. Those she would share with no one but God.

He moved to the bed and pulled the sheet from it. With infinite tenderness, Alisdair placed it around her and held her, covered, in his arms.

It came as a shock to him, after he had tucked her in like a child and left Ian's room, that Judith's presence as his wife could be a benefit. He had worked hard to acquire legitimacy for them all, and his conditional pardon was a noose around his neck. However, his English wife could garner them all another measure of freedom.

He wondered if Granmere had already figured that out. She probably had.

Chapter 16

"I'll go," Judith said, when Granmere insisted they needed milk from the milch cow and eggs. Although she had no wish to savor the clan's displeasure, it was the only way to escape Malcolm.

Every communal meal had become a misery. Malcolm watched her constantly, as though she were the embodiment of all things evil and English. He rarely spoke, simply glaring at her over his plate as if he viewed the revelation of her past as a direct insult to him and to his choice of her as wife to his laird.

Judith could understand his anger, but she could do nothing about it, nor alter its cause. The old Scot evidently felt she was as guilty of the atrocities committed by Cumberland's troops as if she had performed them herself. What Malcolm did not know was that she had despised Anthony from the first, with a hatred and a loathing that only grew with time.

Her marriage to Anthony Henderson had been arranged by Squire Cuthbertson, barely six months after she'd returned home following Peter's death. His regiment had been successful in putting down the food riots in Yorkshire, where her father had no qualms about selling his produce above market prices. Judith had wondered, then, if she were being given as a prize to the soldier who had so helped her father. Otherwise, it was unlikely that a man without property or prospects would have been an adequate candidate for a son-in-law. Perhaps though, like her banishment to Scotland, her father simply hadn't cared about her bridegroom, as long as she was gone from his house.

She met her new husband on the day of their wedding and although her sisters had commented on his good looks and military bearing, she had only seen the contempt in his eyes for the daughter of a tradesman. A contempt that carried over to her wedding night and resulted in nothing less than his feral savagery. She had been married before, but Peter's absentminded, apologetic coupling had not prepared her for Anthony's cruelty. Nothing would have. She had emerged from the small room at the inn the next day with a dawning horror in her eyes. Nor had her lot improved from that day on.

The worst memories were from those long months when Anthony's regiment had been billeted in London. His dislike of his new assignment had been translated into daily abuse. There were great blocks of time unset in her mind about those days, as if they had happened to another, or she had lived them from a distance.

When she was a child, Judith had rolled up a paper into a cylinder and peered through one end. The view seemed distorted, as though it were faraway. Her life with Anthony seemed the same. Remote, as though someone else had lived it, and she were trespassing into their mind and their memories.

Nature had provided for her survival by cushioning those days in a dense fog, accessible only in bleak nightmares.

The revelations of her past had destroyed the camaraderie Judith was beginning to establish with the women of the clan. She was not treated badly, she was simply ignored, in such a finite way that she felt invisible. When one of the village women would call on Sophie, her eyes would simply slide though Judith, as if she were not standing there, a welcoming smile on her face. If a chore took her from the confines of Tynan, it was to meet a silence so profound it seemed she could hear the whisper of the wind upon the moor grasses. All activity in the weaving shed had ceased, as if her presence there soiled the very wool they carded and spun. Stupid women. They were as foolish as they were stubborn, Judith thought. Their actions would not hurt her, but only themselves.

Judith had thought she'd grown accustomed to feeling unwelcome, but the glacial treatment by the MacLeod women taught her that she was still capable of being hurt, after all.

Only Meggie continued with her unconditional friendship. Meggie's gentle smile was as welcome as her knowledge of farm animals, as she took Judith to the communal barnyard.

Judith relied on her friend's help to retrieve the eggs that Granmere requested. She'd been in such a hurry to withdraw her hand from their angry, pecking beaks that she'd pulled out the sitting stones, instead.

"They're placed there to give the hens the idea of what to do," Meggie said, chuckling as she replaced the stones.

"It was so much easier simply to go to the meat seller's stall in London and point," Judith admitted, smiling wryly. "I'm a poor farmer's daughter."

"Not so," Alisdair said from behind them. "I remember a lass with a penchant for shaving my sheep."

"Shearing," she said as she glanced back at him, although she knew he teased.

Alisdair smiled at Meggie, thanked her, and escorted his wife back to Tynan.

"Are you well?" he asked, noting her sudden flush with interest.

"Well enough, I suppose," she answered shortly.

"I have not seen you much in the last few days," he said, smiling at the fact that her eyes looked everywhere but at him. "Have you been avoiding me?" She never left her room until he was in the fields, refusing to sup with him at night, creeping around his castle for days, as if to spare herself his presence. It was rare she ventured from Tynan's walls, and when his patience had finally been rewarded and he'd seen her, he'd left the other men, claiming the need to stretch his legs a bit. He chose to ignore their disbelieving stares.

"Yes," she answered honestly. "I have been an unwelcome addition to your clan, MacLeod. I'd thought to spare you and your people my presence." She did not tell him that she had spent the last few days alternating between faint hope and more confusion than she wished. He had had ample reason to punish her, yet had not. He had, instead, comforted her, holding her against his chest in the most tender of touches, like a parent would soothe a child.

"I regret that my countrymen are as stubborn as they are," he said, smiling. Judith wished his teeth were rotted, his skin mottled, or his hair falling out. Anything to make him appear less attractive and daunting in his good looks. They came to a rise in the hill, MacLeod holding the basket with the eggs as nonchalantly as a lady's parcels on the streets of London. She concentrated on the path, the dust swirling over her scuffed boots.

"It is to be expected," she admitted, finally. "They would no doubt receive the same treatment in England. But I would have thought that Malcolm would understand."

"Is he giving you trouble?"

She finally looked directly at him. He wanted to tell her that the shade of her eyes reminded him of the mists over the mountains just before sunset, deep and rich and mysterious. Instead he only smiled at her, thinking that he could restrain himself a little while longer.

"Malcolm thinks I am no better than Black Donald's mistress, MacLeod."

He laughed. "Aye, that sounds like Malcolm. He's an old bear of a man, a true Scot. Born to the land, tied to it for life, whether that life be long or short. He and a few others like him will find a way to keep the battle raging until he dies.''

"What would you consider yourself, then, MacLeod, if not a true Scot?"

"Oh, I am one, at that. But I have had the blessings of seeing the world, Judith. I know our paltry problems here are of no concern to others. If they were, the Pope would have long since recognized the claims of the Bonnie Prince and his father. What Malcolm and others like him would have us do is don our kilts and march proudly from glen to glen, summoning the clans until blood washed Scotland clean.''

"You speak as one who hates war, MacLeod."

"I see no shame in admitting it. No, our industry is better used by preparing for the future than for mourning the past.''

"Do you truly think your future lies with England? It seems a strange view for a Scot to take."

"A practical approach, however. Did I not state that I was a practical person, also? Trade with England is our only hope.'' He would have preferred another country's coin, but was prevented not only by geography but by English ships which lay in wait off the coast of Scotland for just such enterprising commerce.

Alisdair did not tell her there were times he could not quite forget Culloden and the loss of friends and family. Memories, however, had become an impediment to the future. Just as Judith's recollections kept her awake at night, nearly screaming.

"No wonder you sought to buy sheep from my father. He is a great believer in free enterprise," she said wryly. "Everything is a commodity to him. Even his daughters are only goods to be sold on the matrimonial market.''

"He is not the first father to want to profit from marriage, Judith," he reminded her gently. "How would you have it, if it were not so?"

"I would be free, MacLeod. Free to do what I would,

when I would, as I would." She did not mean for her words to sound bitter, but he thought he understood the reason for such a tone.

"Freedom. Do any of us have it?" He looked around the path they were taking, to the broad moors that slipped down to the sea. "I am not free," he said in explanation. "I have duties and obligations that will not cease even when I lie in my bed at night."

"Because you are a man, you could never understand." The look she gave him was new and fascinating. He wondered if she knew her eyes flashed as if lightning lit their depths.

"I am a man with a brain." His grin was challenging. "Explain it to me. Any idea which makes you crinkle your nose with such disdain can surely be spoken."

She thought for a moment, trying to find the words. "Men are capable of living their lives like islands, MacLeod. They are not dependent upon anyone in order to survive. A man is either a noble, a soldier, or he has a trade. He can decide whether he wishes to live in Yorkshire or Kent, whether he marries or does not. He can make the choice to have a child, ten children, or none. But none of these things are possible for women. Our occupation is wife, harlot, or spinster, all dependent upon a man's convenience. We've no option to refuse our husband's mating, no way to prevent the seventh child or the seventeenth. Men are islands. Women are captive birds. Freedom? Some of us have it more than others, MacLeod."

He had never heard her speak so many words at one time. It was with delicacy that he disagreed, hoping that by doing so, he didn't push her back into the shell she'd worn so comfortably since coming to Tynan. This new and voluble Judith was a singular pleasure.

"Yet, you said it yourself. A man is dependent upon no one. If he succeeds, it is because of his own work. If he fails, then that, too, is laid at his door. A woman has no such burdens. She is taken care of and cared for. It seems a fair trade."

"I wonder how many women would trade their husbands for their freedom, and being taken care of for the ability to care for themselves," she said, and it was suddenly not a simple question she asked, nor so much a rhetorical one.

"Aye, that's true enough, I suppose," he said, thinking of her tortured back and the deep darkness of her troubled eyes. "Yet, you did not trade this husband for freedom, Judith. One word would have made you a guest of Colonel Harrison's, safely under the protection of the regiment. Why did you not speak that word?" His look was amber directness, allowing for no lies nor reservations.

How could she tell him that he offered less danger than Bennett?

"Perhaps I had no ability to care for myself." It was not a complete answer, yet he did not question it. The key to Judith was perseverance, Alisdair thought. She divulged snippets of information about herself a bit at a time, and only then when they were pulled from her.

"And your brother-in-law? Would he not have cared for you?" The question, posed in a reasonable voice, made her wonder if he'd been privy to her unspoken thoughts.

"I dislike him."

The best course was understatement. Those who embellish are quickly branded as liars. She would not tell him about Bennett, or that other part of her life. Those secrets would be better left unsaid, and unthought. To do otherwise would be to condemn herself to purgatory on earth. It was enough that she was destined for Hell itself.

Such prevarication would have worked, had he not been watching her when he'd asked the question. A blankness appeared in her eyes as if she'd simply walked into a room and shut the door behind her. It was the same response she'd had when she'd waited for him to punish her. There was a mystery here, and he would pursue it. Thanks to the English, he had the rest of his life to solve this puzzle.

Alisdair stood aside for her to precede him up the stairs, through the bronze door. They walked quietly into the kitchen, where he placed the basket containing the eggs on the large, scarred oak table. Smiling at his grandmother, Alisdair reached for his wife.

Judith brushed his hands aside, but he would not be denied. He effortlessly lifted her into his arms, one arm beneath her legs, the other encircling her shoulders. It was not unlike, she thought, the way he might carry a lamb, gently, but with stubborn intent.

"It is daylight, MacLeod." It was neither a command nor a request. Instead, it was said with a sense of fatality. Hadn't she been waiting for this moment ever since he'd rescued her from Bennett? It was the price she had to pay for solidifying their marriage.

"So it is," he said, as if just noticing the sun rising high in the stairwell window.

"I have chores to do."

"So you have. Obeying your husband." His lips quirked.

"What instructions would you have me heed?" Her voice was low and serious. He gently pried her fingers from his shirt front, and his chest hairs, well aware of the fear that filled her face and made her eyes wide and as deep as the sea.

"At this moment? To cease struggling."

She turned her cheek away from the warmth of his chest, choosing, instead, to stare at the moving ceiling.

The sunlight streamed in through the windows of the lord's room, and it was the first place she went when he finally released her. She breathed in the salt air that blew in from the sea.

"Do you never get cold in the winter, MacLeod?" she asked, anxious to enliven the heavy silence. She wanted to postpone what would happen between them. She had begun to feel a softness for him, a respect she'd not had for any man. The feeling was so precious that she wanted to hoard it a little longer, keep it safe before it was shattered, forever destroyed.

"I have never spent a winter in this room," he said, calmly.

She turned to look at him, a small frown upon her face.

He would give half his sheep to see her smile, to keep her standing there, with the sunlight touching her hair the way it was right now.

Of course, this was the laird's room, and until his father and Ian had died, Alisdair was only the younger son. She wished she had not asked.

"I winter in Ian's room, Judith. Or at least I did before I acquired a soft, warm wife who could ease the chill."

He walked to her, slowly turned her to face him, and began unlacing her dress. She didn't move, simply closed her eyes. He smiled, softly, an infinitely tender smile she didn't see.

It would have been a blessing to tear this ugly dress from her body, but that would leave her only the black which sagged along the neckline and was too tight in the bodice. Alisdair wished he had extra coin to spend on fripperies for her, a bonnet to accentuate the color of her eyes, to enhance the unusual shade of her hair, a pretty dress that was not so snug across her beautiful breasts. It would be a joy to spoil her, pamper her in a way he suspected she'd never before been treated.

"Come," he said, when the unlacing was completed, and her bodice hung gaping and open. His gaze memorized the soft swell of alabaster skin, the hint of generous pink nipples. If this moment had been other than what it was, he would have slid his palm into the opening there, feeling the warmth of her skin, the back of his hand abrading one sweet nipple.

Alisdair extended a hand to her and led her to a chair seated in front of the window, its back to the room. He smiled tenderly at her look of discomfiture.

While she sat, hands clenched upon her lap, he stripped off his shirt in one clean movement. His chest was as densely blanketed with black hair as she remembered, sworls of it encircling bronze discs of masculine nipples. She watched him warily for a moment, until she caught herself, then directed her gaze outward, towards the sea.

Alisdair smiled at her studied unconcern, keeping his movements slow and unhurried.

Her mouth went dry. She did not want this to happen. Why were men so insistent upon spilling their seed? They were no more selective than a dog marking its territory. In this eternal battle between men and women, why couldn't women simply wave a flag of surrender, rather than being physically dominated, invaded, mounted like a beast of the field?

Alisdair sat on the edge of the bed, removed his shoes, then his stockings and finally stood to unbutton his trousers. He watched her without speaking. Judith had not moved an inch in the last few minutes, unless one counted the frantic darting of her eyes or their quick shuttering. He knew she wanted to disappear inside herself, but curiosity kept her moored here, watching him the way a beaten puppy would note the movements of a cruel master.

Her eyes were so wide they could swallow him whole.

He removed his trousers, wishing he wore a kilt still. It was less cumbersome and certainly less threatening to let yards of plaid drop to the floor. Not like the stance one was expected to maintain while pulling off a trouser leg. He smiled at his less than graceful actions, but Judith didn't notice.

Naked, he moved towards her and she looked frantically for an escape route, but there was no place to hide. She uttered only one small gasp of protest as he extended one hand around her arm and gently pulled her up from the chair.

Judith lifted her eyes to his and kept them studiously on his face. One small glimpse of his nakedness had been enough. He was bronzed all over, except for a small area of white buttocks and upper thighs glimpsed when he had bent down to pick up his trousers. She'd closed her eyes tight before he'd turned around. Never had she seen a naked man like this, in the bright light of day, with the sun burning white through the window, with motes of dust dancing in the beams which licked his skin.

Her hands trembled, her knees felt soggy like overripe turnips. The memory of pain and degradation turned the brightness of the room to midnight, the aching breath in her chest became stifled screams.

Could she bear the pain?

Alisdair slowly pushed the bodice of her dress to her waist, and then over her hips. Other than the pulse frantically beating at the side of her neck, she gave no sign of her fear. Nor did she protest his undressing of her, only closed her eyes and allowed him to remove the remainder of her garments.

For a moment, he allowed himself to look, seeing what he had not seen before in this room, with her naked and stripped bare to the soul. Her skin was the purest white, like virgin milk, her breasts were heavy, pendulous but proud, large pink nipples jutting out from their pink areolas like tiny fingers begging to be kissed, to be sucked. Her waist curved to perfect hips and then to long, luscious legs. The vee at the notch of her legs was shielded with auburn hair, curly and curiously beckoning.

His fingers itched to touch her just once, to see if she was as soft there as she looked. His mind urged him to explore, to discover if those pink nipples would draw up and nearly disappear at the touch of his mouth, or pout proudly. His palms urged him to forget his plans and stroke down one hip to see if she trembled beneath his touch.

Instead, he sat down in the large overstuffed chair and pulled his reluctant wife onto his lap. Her eyes opened and she stared at him in surprise.

Alisdair placed one hand on the back of her neck, gently urging her head down until her cheek rested upon his chest. The look in her eyes was suddenly too much to witness—hurt, pain, and fear, silent emotions all the more powerful for being unspoken.

Judith curled into herself, placing her arms across her breasts, drawing up her knees, as if to hide herself from his interested gaze. It did not mean, however, that her skin lacked sensation, that she could not feel the mat of his hair against her right arm and cheek, or the smooth warmth of his golden flesh.

Her body was soft where his was hard, curving inward where his barely tapered.

Alisdair placed both hands on the arms of the chair and looked out the window, wishing he could view the sea. It would be a paltry diversion to feeling her flesh against his. Yet, Judith was so armored by her own fear it was as if there were a suit of chain mail between their bodies.

The hammer beat of his heart boomed loudly against her ear. Would he not hurry then, or was this some sort of slow torture?

Judith didn't move, not because he restrained her, but because she felt exposed in the sunlight, more so than the time when she had stood before him naked.

"Did you know I studied at Edinburgh?" he asked.

It was not the question she was expecting. She nodded, remembering their conversations.

He reached out suddenly and grabbed her foot before she could jerk it from his grasp. A tiny frown marred her brow as she sat, contorted, her foot in his hand, his fingers gently tickling her toes. Alisdair wondered if she realized her frowns had been growing more frequent of late. The perfect mask she'd worn was cracking, and beneath its surface lay a woman he wished to know. One who felt anger and joy and a hundred other emotions once buried under an exquisite facade of blankness.

"There are more bones in the foot," he said absently, as if not noticing her nudity, "then in any other part of the body. Did you know that?"

"No."

He stroked her foot from her ankle to her toes. "You have long toes," he said with a smile. "It is a very aristocratic-looking foot." She peered over her clenched knees as if never having seen it before.

"I, however, have wolf feet," he said, extending one of his own so that she could see it. Even his toes were hairy, and the black hair extended up his ankle and over the corded muscles of his calf. "One of the women of our clan used to say that it looked as though the kelpies had stretched my feet at birth." It did look that way, she thought. The space between his toes and heel was long and flat, with barely an arch.

He gently released her foot, again pushing her head down upon his chest before returning his hand to the arm of the chair. They sat for a long time in silence, the beating of his heart the only sound she heard. That, and the faint breath which emerged from his chest. Occasionally, his chest hair would tickle her cheek, and she would rub it absently, then return to her original position.

She did not like waiting for the pain. Perhaps he would not hurt her as much as Anthony had, or degrade her as much as the other, but it was still a duty she wished fervently to avoid. The feeling of his skin against hers, especially that warmth that lay just beneath her buttocks, was disconcerting. She was not so scarred there that she could not feel.

"Will you not just do it, MacLeod?" she asked finally in the silence.

"My name is Alisdair," he corrected her absently.

"Very well, Alisdair," she said shortly, "will you not just do it?"

"Do what?" he asked, smiling.

"Mount me. Spill your seed. Seek your pleasure."

"Good God, Judith," he said, that infernal smile still playing around his lips, "you have a variety of descriptions for the act, don't you? It is sad that none of them is correct."

"What would you call it, then?" She squinted up at him, and he chuckled.

"Making love, coupling, sharing passion. They all seem more apt than your rather coarse terms."

"Fine, call it whatever you will. Will you not just get it over with?"

"That is not my purpose, Judith," he said softly, countering her sudden panic. It showed in her eyes and in the stiffness of her body, curled though it was over his.

The sun touched her skin and made her warmer. She squirmed, and Alisdair fervently wished that she would not move. It was damnable practice, this, and he could not focus on other thoughts if she was forever moving about. He was very grateful her husband had not only been a sadist, but that he had also been a lousy lover. That was plain by the contempt with which Judith viewed lovemaking. If Anthony had compounded his sins by teaching Judith pleasure, then she would have learned to equate it with pain. As it was, she knew a great deal about torture and nothing about passion. Even now she sat, fearing to move much lest it stir some great dormant desire of his.

If she knew anything, she would have realized that his desire hadn't been dormant for quite a while.

For almost an hour, they sat in the sunlight. With the warmth of the room, and the warmth of his skin, Judith began to feel drowsy. She sighed, heavily, and allowed herself to relax a little. He smiled again, nudging the top of her head with his chin. The soft movement did not disturb her, nor did the placement of his hand upon her knee.

He traced a path with that broad palm of his, over her knee, down the length of her leg to her ankle. She moved, fitfully, against the tickling sensation. He slowed his touch and removed all but one finger from her skin. He traced an imaginary circle around her knee slowly, so delicately that it felt as though a fly brushed across her skin.

He chuckled when her knee jerked, as if to dislodge his finger. He moved slowly, extending his right hand over her body, and clasping it with his left so that she sat within the circle of his arms. She opened her eyes and looked at him accusingly, but he did not remove his arm, nor did he go any further.

He broke their look, staring out the window at the clouds massing above the promontory. From here he could see the very tops of the pines, but no more.

"Anne was very young when we married," he said, as if she had asked the question. "Barely grown. All of my skill, what there was of it, could not save her. My child died with her, struggling to find life."

She kept his eyes upon his profile, that jutting chin that spoke so eloquently of his stubbornness, that nose which looked to have been broken once, she wondered how. His hair curled around the shells of his ears, and the shadow of his beard was showing through the tanned expanse of his cheeks. It was his eyes that drew her attention the most, though, and the soft, pained look within them. It seemed to alter their color to molten copper.

"You could not prevent a death in childbirth, MacLeod. It happens all the time. It happened to Janet," she reminded him.

"Too often, Judith. Surely a bountiful God would not make it so. In Anne's case, it was a forced escape from a place she'd learned to call home, the terror of fleeing in the dead of night, her youth, perhaps, and a body not built for birthing that caused her death. Not to mention the futile and puny skill of her husband. It was too much to ask of her."

She wanted to ask why he left Scotland, but then realized the timing of his exodus, shortly after Culloden. Then, she wanted to ask why he had returned, to this isolated spot, when he would have been welcomed anywhere with his skill and his education, but realized that what she knew about the man answered that question. Alisdair MacLeod had a deep and abiding sense of obligation and responsibility. He would not turn his back on the people who, for generations, had looked to their laird for sustenance and protection. Nor could Judith picture him enjoying a carefree life while those who had once depended on him tried to survive. No, he would either lead them to victory, or die with them.

"Did you love her very much?" The answer was somehow important.

He sighed. "Perhaps part of the guilt I sheltered and

protected for so long was because I did not love Anne as much as she deserved. Is that truth enough for you?"

She nodded.

"And Anthony? Did you love him?"

Her horrified glance was answer enough.

"I tell you of Anne for one reason, Judith. I berate myself for what happened to her, even though in my mind I know I did all that I knew to do. It is human nature to try and apportion blame, to capture some of it for ourselves. I think you must do the same, without knowing. But what was visited upon you was not of your doing."

He spoke of the scars on her back; he did not know of the scars on her soul. Too many times, Judith had awakened with the sickening awareness of her own actions.

"Your union with Anne was not like my marriage." He waited, but she said nothing else. Perhaps that acrid statement was enough, after all. A small vent hole of rage. Alisdair could imagine what she buried beneath the crust of it.

He held her still, within his arms. It came to her then, with a shock, that she was not as frightened as she had been earlier.

"It is still possible for me to leave," she said slowly. "It would spare you a marriage to me."

Alisdair glanced down at her, liking the way her chin jutted out when she was being defensive. He wanted to applaud every instance in which she expressed emotion. He suspected that she had, for too long, simply shut herself off from feeling in order to survive. Yet, in order to heal, Judith needed to recognize the emotions she had kept suppressed, dampened.

"I'm afraid if you left now, Judith," he said, with a hint of amusement in his voice, "the good Colonel would hold me accountable for your disappearance. Although life at Tynan is not as pleasant as I would wish at present, it is still life. I find the thought of my hanging somewhat daunting."

She looked up at him, her eyes a deeper blue than before.

"You could do so much better than to take me to wife, MacLeod."

"Alisdair," he said automatically. "And what is so wrong about you that I would have cause to put you aside?"

It was the perfect opportunity, if perhaps an odd one, sitting naked upon the MacLeod's lap, to tell him of other secrets. Secrets that would endanger him and the clan. The moment passed, however, and she wondered at the sense of relief she felt when the truth remained unspoken.

"I am barren, Alisdair," she said, instead.

"We live in uncertain times, Judith. It may not be safe enough to bring a child into this world," he said calmly.

"You are the last of your line, MacLeod. It is fitting that you have an heir."

"It is more fitting, perhaps, that I simply survive," he said calmly. "Let others found their dynasties. I do not crave a mirror image of myself."

Why should you want what you already have? Douglas looks just like you.

"I am too tall for a woman. I am not delicate like a woman is supposed to be. My eyes are an odd color, and my hair will not be pressed into curls no matter how hot the iron." She focused her gaze on her clenched hands. It was the only way she could be as honest as she was. She did not want to see the acknowledgment of her own defects in his eyes.

Alisdair wondered why she chose to believe the worst of herself. He, too, had been mocked for his differences, mainly by his brother and those who would follow him. Yet, that condemnation had been laid over a foundation of stone. Since he was a child, he had been praised for his very being. He was, after all, a MacLeod. His first steps were feted, if not by his mother, then by the father he'd grown to worship and the family relationship of his clan. Even when he'd made mistakes, they had been brushed off as the growing spirit of a MacLeod. He was set apart and excused, but most of all, he had been encouraged. His early life had been spent around the crofters' huts, where members of his clan were his surrogate parents, correcting, scolding, but above all, loving. He had always appreciated his heritage, but never more so than now, when he realized with a jolt how much his clan had brought to him.

Total acceptance.

Had she never felt it? Had she never been loved?

"Is there a reason for this litany of concerns, Judith?"

"It was you who wished for the telling of my faults."

After another long silence, he spoke again. "Do you remember the little lamb we saw on the hill the other day?"

"Yes," she answered cautiously.

"It was black, was it not, although the other lambs were white?"

She nodded.

"Was it still a lamb?"

"You know it was."

"Then know this, too, Judith," he said, nuzzling the top of her head again. "Your differences do not set you apart, they simply define you. One day, you will see yourself differently, I promise that. You will accept yourself and all that has happened to you as only a part of who you are, as I am comprised of my past, my present, and my hopes for the future."

"I think I'd rather be a lamb, MacLeod," she said, an unwilling smile upon her lips.

"You have the stubbornness for it, I think," he said, chuckling.

He leaned down and kissed her, quickly, but she did not draw back. It was a light, unthreatening kiss, a benediction of friendship more than lovemaking. When it was over, she held two fingers to her lips. He smiled at the gesture, the bemusement it unwillingly divulged.

He stretched out one hand and cupped her left breast lightly. She shivered in response, but it was not in passion.

"You have beautiful breasts, Judith," he said softly, his fingers softly stroking. "Full and luscious, they have always caught my eye. Your nipples peek from their resting place like tiny hillocks, proud and tall."

She shivered at his touch, that one finger placed tenderly on her nipple. He smiled at her, bent closer to kiss her forehead, a calming, gentle touch.

His right hand descended to the nip of her waist, and he drew her closer so that she could feel his breath on her cheek. "Your curves are a woman's curves. Soft, sweet, desirable. You are not petite, Judith, but I would have no dolls in my bed. You match my height perfectly, you know. I will not need to bend my back like a bow when I enter you."

He lightly brushed her cheeks with his lips, felt the warmth of the flush that changed their paleness to deep rose. He smiled softly, as he continued to move his hands down her body. "Your legs, Judith, are long enough to wrap around mine, to encase my waist," he whispered. "How beautifully slender they are, neither stocky nor plump." He clasped his hands around her, trapping her within his arms once again. "Do you not know how much desire you instill in me?"

Her eyes widened again. "MacLeod . . ."

"Judith," he interrupted softly, "you may dress now."

"What?"

He brushed his lips against the tip of her nose. "You may dress," he repeated, the smile never leaving his mouth.

She looked at him as though he had lost his mind. Did he imagine that flicker of disappointment? He hoped he had not.

"What are you about, MacLeod?" she asked him warily.

"I think that since we have decided it is safer for the sake of my neck to remain married, Judith, then it would be a nice change for you to call me Alisdair. Don't you think so?"

"And you stripped me naked so that I would call you by your rightful name?"

He laughed. "No, Judith, I stripped you naked so that you would not fear me. And, too, so you would listen. There were things you needed to hear."

"My ears are here, Alisdair," she said, pointing to them.

"Very nice ears, they are, too. But would you have listened, truly, being so afraid of me pouncing at any moment?" She remembered her feelings before he had placed her on his lap. She'd not been able to swallow, the blind panic was so great.

"No, probably not," she admitted reluctantly.

He stood, holding her in his arms, then deposited her gently on the bed. He leaned over her, placing both hands on either side of her face.

"Listen to me, Judith, listen well. Whether our union was a good thing that happened, or simply an accident of fate that we must make good, we are now married. Gone is our temporary bargain, thanks to the English. We are now husband and wife. Part of that belonging is sharing this." He stroked the flesh on the top of her breast with the back of one hand and watched her eyes. She did not flinch and draw away, but looked surprised at the feelings his touch evoked.

"Do you think we shall spend the rest of our lives without touching, Judith? Do you think never to seek my warmth, or to always deny me the pleasure of yours? Your words betray you, not your body. You have intelligence and wit and a spark of fury. I can provide a haven for you within the walls of Tynan, but I cannot guarantee a world without men, especially if that means never being husband to you."

He placed his palm against her left breast, feeling the impudent nipple bury into his skin as if seeking a home. He wanted, desperately, to bend down and place a welcoming kiss upon that nipple, a warm and wet suckle. Instead, he smiled, then bent over her. His tongue traced the line of her lips, his teeth nipped playfully at her bottom lip, coaxing it to yield to him. Her eyes were open, a startled fawn's, but still, he did not deepen the kiss. Even when his tongue intruded through the seam of her lips, he did not succumb to the warm invitation of her mouth. He kept the caress light, sweetly imploring, leading her to deeper pleasures.

Only when her lids drooped, did he allow himself one tiny taste of fullness, one sweeping invasion of lip and tongue and wetness. Too soon, too quickly, he forced himself to pull back. Her eyes opened wide as she studied him, her own lips licking where his had just been.

He stifled a groan, raised himself away from her.

Judith watched him dress and leave the room. He was smiling and whistling, which irritated her. Which was the only reason her palms were damp, of course, and her heart racing.

Chapter 17

The room was blessedly dim, lit by a single sputtering taper on the mantel. Only embers remained in the hearth, crimson dots of color amidst black and gray. Judith was cold, but it no longer mattered. The chill of her flesh seeped into the depths of her body until it seemed to touch her mind, her soul, with tendrils of icy fear.

She blinked, knowing that Bennett would be displeased unless she opened her eyes and watched him. His mocking displeasure would be an excuse to inflict more pain. He would either grasp her nipple between two fingers and twist until the sensation was unbearable, or he would thrust exploring fingers into her dry passage, deriding her lack of desire. As if she could ever feel desire for this man. As if she could ever feel anything but horror.

If she were lucky, the pain would be fierce enough at the beginning that she would lose consciousness again, depriving him of her participation in his little games. If she were lucky, he would be alone tonight and the depravity would last only minutes instead of hours. Lucky? It had nothing to do with luck. Nor did prayers seem to matter, because if God had answered her prayers, she would not awaken in the morning, nausea her rooster, despair her morning sun.

Bennett came closer to the side of the bed, and Judith blinked again, willing the fear to be banished from her eyes. He would seek it, revel in it. Something dangled from his hand, one of his toys, and despite herself, she flinched. He laughed, pleased, and tapped the riding crop against one hand rhythmically. What would he do tonight? Thrust the long, broad handle almost to her womb, pleased at the blood he induced to flow between her thighs, or claim she was his recalcitrant mount, and thrust himself between her buttocks, his lust fired not only by her screams of pain from his perverted invasion, but by the scourge marks he inflicted in his frenzy.

Judith moaned, a small sound of more than despair. It would soon be followed by screams, as the small sane corner of her mind retreated beneath pain.

She was crying again.

Was she doing it on purpose, rubbing raw every nerve he possessed?

He should be able to sleep; he needed his rest, he was tired enough. He should not be staring at the ceiling for long hours, listening to the sobbing beneath him and praying for it to stop. The sound permeated the walls of his room as if some ancestral ghost demanded to be heard. Alisdair levered himself up on one elbow thinking oddly that if Scotland had a lament, it would sound like this— a woman's soft, grief-induced keening.

He could not tolerate any more. Each night it had been the same, seemingly hours of this low moaning sob, followed by unearthly screams, the sound of which were cut off suddenly, as if Judith awakened herself with her own terror.

This night would be different.

The moon was only a thin sliver of light reflected by the soft lapping waters of the cove. It was by this faint illumination that he saw her, dappled in moonlight, frozen by terror.

Judith was as rigid as the boards beneath his feet, her

arms pressed together at the wrists and extended up above her head as if tied there by unseen cords. She blinked, eyes open, and at his approach, she screamed again, the muscles of her neck forced into prominence by the effort. She arched against an unseen touch, twisting violently as if to ward off a ghostly presence. The hairs on the back of his neck elected to begin a primeval dance.

"Hush, Judith," he murmured, thinking his dark shrouded appearance must appear ghostlike to her. She saw him only as an apparition of the past, a naked man with strength in his arms, his shoulders broad, his size alone enough to overpower her. She screamed again as his large hands grasped her wrists and attempted to force them down into some semblance of normalcy. Her wide unseeing eyes were open, fixed on him as if he were the devil himself.

Only one word forced its way through her clenched lips. One word, and one word only. The sound of it, along with her obvious terror, speared through his heart. Alisdair sat on the edge of the bed and gathered Judith up in his arms, oblivious to his nudity as she was supremely aware and frightened by it.

"Please," she continued to say, as though it were a magical chant, the word itself uttered in painful resignation. "Please," and the sound of it seeped through the armor of his self-restraint with the sharpness of forged steel. "Please," she begged, her hands forced between them, her body as taut as the tightest bowstring, her eyes focused unseeing upon the mat of hair on his chest. "Please," she breathed as he placed the palm of his left hand firm against the back of her head, feeling the rich softness of her free flowing hair. He gently urged her head forward, until the word was muffled against his chest, as her flushed cheek was flattened against his skin. His other hand curled protectively around her back, feeling the homespun texture of her bedgown and the soft woman flesh beneath.

Judith flinched, then shivered against his touch. A wry smile etched Alisdair's lips, a strange counterpart to his worried frown. She had nothing to fear. He had never been so lacking in desire as now.

Alisdair rocked her as he would a child racked with terror, her soft moaning word the only speech which passed between them. Occasionally, he would mutter a soft "shhhh," which passed as comfort, the only thing he could think of to say or to do, other than the rocking motion which seemed to soothe her.

How long it took for the stiffness to leave her limbs, a rigidity not unlike that of death, he did not know. Gradually, though, she slumped against him, the sound of her pleading finally silenced.

Without a word, he picked her up, carried her up the stairs to his room, moved to the edge of the bed, then settled her on his lap. He placed her arms around his neck; her head bowed until she snuffled into his neck like a child. Her tears wet his neck.

Once he'd seen her back, he no longer wondered about the subject of her nightmares. Still, he asked.

"Will you tell me of it?"

Her head wagged from side to side, a gentle movement which seemed to spread her scent around them, a delicate blooming of sweetly perfumed air, redolent of soap and Judith.

"I dislike the sounds of your screams, wife." His words were gruff, his voice devoid of passion. Tenderness, however, laced his words and caused his hands to gently smooth her back. Even now, she trembled.

"Forgive me," she said, her voice muffled, her lips too close to his bare shoulder. He slept in the nude like any good Scot, a fact she'd no doubt discerned the moment he'd placed her on his lap.

"I do not want your apology, Judith. I want an explanation."

"I cannot give you one, MacLeod." Her voice was heavy, laced with her tears, a caramel whisper in the dark. It struck him then that perhaps his passion was not muted beneath tenderness. He wanted to kiss her, to taste her lips and see if they were full and swollen and sweet.

"Cannot or will not?"

There was no answer to that riddle. Judith sat silent, tense, upon his lap. It was a replay of a few days ago, when it had taken nearly an hour for her to lose her fear of him, for those muscles to unclamp and those nerves to unstring themselves like violin strings too tightly tuned. He sighed. Each step with her was to be measured by a snail's daily pace, then.

"Has the act of loving given you nothing but pain, Judith?" His voice was a warm whisper in the darkness.

It was disconcerting to be holding a conversation with him when her nightdress was twisted up about her middle. Her bare buttocks rested on his thighs, just as they had days before. She could remember every moment on his lap, every nuance of feeling, the rasp of hair against her back, his gentle stroking with one finger down her leg, circling her knee. She would hear his voice, talking to Malcolm, and recalled feeling it rumbling from his chest. She watched him stride from the room and remembered his long, bare feet. Occasionally, she would blush at the thought of his nakedness, at the solid warmth of his large body.

And now, they repeated that act, the only difference being that they were seated on the side of Alisdair's massive bed, in the dead of night, with only the sound of the incoming tide and the calling of the sea birds to mar the silence of the darkness.

Judith wished that he would just do what he wanted and be done with it. She did not want to talk endlessly about it.

"Does it matter?"

"Yes," he said thoughtfully, "I find that it does. Have you never felt enjoyment, even with your first husband?"

"No," she said, when it was evident he was not joking. "Not really." She had barely noticed Peter's tentative love-making. He had slipped into her room only after midnight, his billowing nightgown ample covering for his thin form. He had apologized all through the act, even on their wedding night, when she'd been left bemused and curiously disappointed, but not in pain. Nor did Peter seem to wish the act as often as Anthony, content to regard her as sister more than wife.

Alisdair laughed mirthlessly. He stood with her in his arms, then calmly laid her down on the bed, covering her. Without comment, he dragged her close to him so that she was tucked beside him, her head resting on his shoulder. He kept perfectly still, so still that he could feel the tremors that shook her body.

"Tell me of your family."

"My family?" She looked startled. "I hardly think my family belongs in my marriage bed, MacLeod."

"Is that what this is, then?" he mused. "Your marriage bed?"

"Of course," she replied crossly. "If you wish to mount me, MacLeod, please finish the act. I am tired, and wish to sleep." He grinned in the darkness, thinking that she was more like an English hedgehog than she knew, frightened, yet prickly.

"Then sleep," he said softly, placing one finger upon both eyelids in turn. Both eyelids shot open.

"But I am ready."

"But I am not."

"Oh." That one word was brimming with relief.

She pulled away from him and would have left the bed had he not grabbed one arm and restrained her.

"Where do you think you're going?"

"To my bed. To sleep. Or had you not decided that?"

"From now on, Judith, when you wish to sleep, it shall be here, in this bed." There was a pause during which she measured his intent. He knew it, remaining silent, a figure of shadow and stubbornness.

"With me." It was an answer to a question she'd not asked.

"I am the oldest of five girls," she said stubbornly, as

she reluctantly allowed him to tuck her close again. She did not like the feeling of his hairy skin next to hers. It gave her the strangest sensation, as though her skin were shivering inside. "There is no history to our family's line," she continued, resolutely ignoring the pounding of his heart so close to her ear, and the warmth of his skin next to hers. "Our manor house is drafty and cold even in summer, although it is a pretty place."

"What do you like best about it?" he asked, his chin nuzzling her hair. She wished he would stop that. She also did not like the fact that she was so close to him that she could again feel his voice, in addition to simply hearing it.

"I have a secret spot, which is hidden to all but the drovers. It is tucked up in the hills, a small cave, really. I used to go there, when I was sad or lonely."

"It seems a strange thing to seek solitude when lonely," he said, brushing his lips against her forehead. She wrinkled her brow against the tickling sensation.

"Loneliness is worse, I think, when you are surrounded by people."

He thought of the feeling he had experienced at Culloden. In the midst of thousands of men, he had felt horribly alone. "Were you a lonely child?" he asked softly, touching his finger to her lips in a darting, teasing gesture.

"I was a strange child, my mother used to say." She turned her face away from his touch. "Always wanting something I couldn't have."

"What did you want, Judith, that was denied you?" He pulled her back into his embrace, tucked her close so that her lips brushed against his chest. She nuzzled there for a moment before she realized what she was doing. Once more, she pulled away, and this time he allowed her to keep a little distance between them.

How could she put into words what she had felt? She had wanted to belong, but amidst her chattering sisters, the noise of her home, she had felt strangely out of place. She wanted some place where she fit, where she would not be thought of as strange, or difficult, or different. But most of all, Judith wanted someone to accept her as she was and find that good enough, after all.

That dream was impossible, now. She could not even accept herself.

Alisdair wished, not for the first time, that he could penetrate her silence. He had been right in sensing dimensions to her. Although she had fought against their marriage, she had not complained since about her situation. Each day saw her laboring as diligently as any other inhabitant of Tynan, yet she did not protest the volume of her duties. Not once had she mentioned her lack of clothes, the state of her hands, the deprivation of life at Tynan. She hoarded her feelings aid her observations with a miser's care.

Judith had come to Scotland with a doubtful dowry. Instead of coin, she brought memories and assumptions and pain. Although life at Tynan was comprised of a series of struggles, Alisdair recognized that there would always be problems even in the most perfect of worlds. Yet, with joy and laughter and love, the sun was still worth greeting each day.

In the darkness of the room, with Judith cuddled up next to him, yawning, Alisdair MacLeod admitted to himself, finally, that maybe it was a good thing Colonel Harrison had come to Tynan.

Chapter 18

Judith awoke to a feeling of being caressed by a sea of flesh. Her nose was pressed up against Alisdair's underarm, her arm was thrown across his wide chest, her leg bent and draped over his hard and muscled thigh. She cocked open one eye, enough to see that her knee rested too close to the juncture of his thighs, to the living reminder that her Scots husband was all male.

She drew back slowly, as if afraid to awaken him, but his eyes were open and watching her intently. He said nothing, nor did he move as she slowly slid one long leg from beneath the covers. She would have left the bed then, had she not been naked. She glanced down at herself, wondered when she'd lost the nightgown she'd gone to sleep in, then spied it hanging like a flag of surrender from the one remaining poster of the bed. She frowned at him, but still he made no comment, nor explanation. Nor did he move to free her from the prison of his long and intent stare.

He smiled finally, a particularly lupine expression she'd not seen before. His eyes were still dusted with sleep, his hair unruly; the morning stubble made Judith want to reach out and see if the skin of his face was as abrasive as it looked. He was strangely appealing in this guise, if a little frightening, like taking a puppy to raise only to discover that you'd petted and cooed to a wolf.

She eyed him suspiciously, but he continued to grin at her, a promise of incipient mischief.

Alisdair extended one arm and flung back the sheet. Judith moved to cover herself, but he only chuckled, grabbed one arm, and propelled her out of the bed. Before she could flush, before she had time to become embarrassed and barely before she could glimpse more than a flash of tanned skin and white buttocks, Alisdair had dragged her through the room and down the stairs.

He passed Ian's room, ignoring her whispered protests as he pulled her down the next flight of stairs and into the great hall. He opened the door to the courtyard, now brightly lit by a dawn sky. With her hands, Judith was desperately trying to cover parts of her body, but even that was a futile attempt with him gripping one arm so tightly. It was not a harsh grasp, just one filled with maddening resolve.

"MacLeod, we are naked!" she hissed frantically, looking around for signs of early morning activity. She tried not to notice his bare body, but it was difficult when pressed against his naked back and buttocks. She thought it unfair that he looked as magnificent without clothes as he did with them. Nor did it seem right that his backside had an alluring dimple at the top and curved so entrancingly down to his legs.

He tugged her onward, discounting the increasing volume of her voice and her pleas. Her nakedness was intentional, not accidental. He'd spent the night dreaming of the taste of those luscious breasts, the feel of her skin rubbed against his in affection and not simply comfort. He'd edged her nightgown off as she slept, one inch at a time, creating for himself an agony of restraint and delight.

Alisdair had finally slept, only to awaken to find her curled around him like a very warm and replete kitten, stroking him in her sleep with one insistent knee. Such a friendly gesture had made him hard as an iron staff.

And determined that this Englishwoman be made wife.

"MacLeod! We have no clothes on! Someone will see!"

Alisdair pulled her into his arms, raised her high to protect her feet from the sharp stones of the shore, and waded into the waters of the cove. Twenty feet out, the bottom dropped, and it was here that Alisdair MacLeod threw his new wife.

Judith descended like a stone into the icy water. She emerged in a desperate bobbing motion, shouting for him, for air itself.

"MacLeod," she sputtered, "I cannot swim!"

He suspected as much with the care she avoided the cove. He extended his arms, brought her to rest against his chest, her hands curled over his shoulders as if he were the only way to avoid drowning.

He wanted her dependent upon him, wanted her mind active and alert, filled with possibilities and promises, but he didn't want her to forget that she needed him to stay afloat.

MacLeod was hard all over, an observation Judith had made to herself many times. Her nails gripped his shoulders tight enough to leave marks, but he didn't flinch. The mischief in his eyes had been supplanted by something else, serious and somber.

He was taller than she, and had no trouble touching his feet to the rocky bottom. But he didn't bother telling her that safety was only a few feet away. He wanted her clinging reluctantly to his shoulders and glaring at him with her blue eyes turned dark with storm clouds.

The tide had come in and washed the beach clean. Although the water was crystal clear, it looked Stygian due to the ebony rock beneath his feet. Over Judith's shoulder, the rising sun heralded the dawn in pink and yellow and coral. To the left, the towering pines seemed colored black, as if needing the filtering sun to change to emerald green. Eerie cries of nature surviving itself sounded through the forest; birds chattered and sang the approach of a new dawn. It was a newly created world, harsh, starkly beautiful in a way that tore the soul to shreds.

"Shall we pretend, Judith, that we are creatures out of time? Shall we be newly discovered, each of us? No husbands for you, no Anne for me?" He smiled at the look of confusion that crossed her face.

She didn't answer him, but then, he'd not expected her to. When she was confused or wary, Judith took refuge in silence.

"If I were a new creature, come upon you in my self-discovery, I would marvel at the sameness of you to me." He placed his hands upon hers where they rested on his shoulders. "You have hands like mine. And arms," he continued, as he traced two fingers down each of her arms. "Your shoulders are not unlike mine, but they are so much more rounded and soft, as if to entice a kiss upon their surface." Suiting actions to words, he dipped his head and tasted her, brine and Judith, warm flesh and cold water, bare essence of life itself. His hands dipped beneath the water to encompass her waist, his fingers brushing against her like a mischievous sea urchin, fingers creating rivulets of sensation wherever they met her skin.

"Your waist is so much more narrow than mine, your hips curve where mine do not, although your legs are formed for the same purpose, and your feet designed to walk the earth. But there our differences end, do they not? If I were newly created, filled with curiosity as to this Eden, I would think that our Creator had erred in the pattern."

"What are you about, MacLeod?" She was filled with puzzlement as to this man, who would induce whimsy on a chilly dawn.

"Call me Adam. And you shall be Eve. And together we will be the first inhabitants of this world, with minds aglow with curiosity and memories like empty baskets, ready to be filled and stuffed with happy times. There is no past, Eve. No yesterday. Only this moment, and as many futures as we could wish."

She would have demurred, refused to play his game, but for the look of something in his eyes, a hint of pain as he glanced back at the ruin of his home. A second, that was all it took, and it told her too much of the vulnerabilities of this man who would parade through his home without a stitch of clothing upon his nakedness, but who bared his soul with as little ease as she did herself. Perhaps he, too, wished to deny the pull of memory for just a while.

He was not unkind, this MacLeod who would be Adam. Yet she could never be innocent enough to be his Eve.

Long fingers of dawn light lit the crown of Judith's head, her shoulders, revealing the pale milky whiteness of her skin. Alisdair wished he could banish the look upon her face, one of resignation, stoic acceptance. He wondered if she knew how deeply he'd studied her over the last weeks. Her expressions, the fleeting pleasure which lit her eyes, the anxiety she was so careful not to show to others, seemed to him to be so easily discernible on her mobile face, in her deep, lake eyes.

Nor was she aware that he had, for days, sought to acquaint her with his touch. When she handed him his porridge in the morning, he thanked her with a soft smile which held promise in its gentle curve. As he passed her, he casually hugged her, a gesture which no longer caused her to flinch. Those nights when he worked late and was not at their meal, Granmere told him that Judith's eyes would stray to the door as if seeking his presence.

Aye, there was promise here.

Alisdair turned his head to the briny wetness of her wrist and licked gently. He was amazed at his own restraint. He'd wanted her with a fever since he'd awakened to find her burrowing next to him. Her inadvertent touch had done things to him no dream had ever accomplished, and his dreams of her had fired his nights.

His hands remained on her waist, supporting her, but his eyes were focused on the alluring sight of her breasts bobbing in the water like white, pink-tipped islands.

"I think the Creator has crafted an intriguing delicacy

here, do you not think, Eve?" One hand cupped a buoyant breast, lifted it free of the water. Droplets ran down, caught, sparkled on the nipple. He seemed fascinated by the sight, entranced by the pink pearliness of her flesh puckering as he watched. "I have never seen such a thing before, the symmetry of this plump flesh, the darkening of the skin here," he said, touching the areola growing darker in the cold water. "I am but an innocent in this raw world, but I am of a mind to taste it, and this cold little nubbin here."

He lifted her easily in the water, until her breasts were exposed. The chill dawn air puckered her wet nipples even further. It only required a tiny movement on his part to bend his head and capture one pink nub in his mouth. How had he restrained himself all this time? Her taste was uniquely Judith; he wanted to burrow his nose into her flesh and inhale her.

His lips were warm; his mouth was hot. Judith looked down, her hands fastened on his shoulders, frozen into immobility by the sight of his mouth fastened on one breast. His lips and teeth created a shiver of sensation, nothing more. Not a taming, not even a taunting, but something else. He glanced up at her, tiny golden lights warming his eyes, as he changed breasts, leaving the nipple he'd suckled traitorously craving further attention. She flushed and looked away, as if the sight of him feasting on her flesh was not emblazoned on her eyelids.

With a calm far in excess of what he was feeling, Alisdair placed the flat of his tongue against one nipple. Only that. A soft inducement, a sweet benediction, an unbearable torture. His tongue was hot, her nipple struggled against it like a proud warrior, rising firm and stiff against its gentle abrasion. Only when she moaned did he raise his eyes to hers again. She bit her lower lip, he made a cavern of his mouth and sucked the nipple within its hot depths, all the while watching her. It was as if he were waiting for something, some reaction from her, some movement, some sound.

He lowered her into the water again, until her breasts

were nearly covered, only, she discovered, that he might bend his head and whisper more naughtiness into her ear.

"It felt so right, Eve, to have you in my mouth. Strange and welcome feelings have coursed through my body at the taste of you. Shall I show you where?"

She licked her lips, but remained silent.

Her breasts had always been an embarrassment to her, her too full bosom an object of scorn from her sisters, and one of ribald comments from Anthony. Even here, in the cove, with her breasts being washed by the sea and Alisdair's lips, she would just as soon they were near to invisible. Yet, he seemed to enjoy the touch of them, their plumpness, suckling her like he was a babe. He feasted, plumping up one breast with a free hand as if he wished to devour the whole of her into his mouth. He nibbled and licked and groaned when she moved suddenly under the unbearable pressure of it. Her nipples felt swollen and oddly warm, not uncomfortably so, merely a different sensation.

He raised her higher in the water, slid a hot and wet tongue under one breast. "Oh, Eve, I should sing hosannas to our differences." he said, his smile enticing, filled with devilment. He removed one hand from her waist and captured the breast his mouth had just left. His fingers plucked her flesh, causing shivers of sensation where they touched.

The shivers were from the cold, not from his touch.

He smiled and licked the space between her neck and shoulder. She tasted of the morning sea and Judith, woman and nature, as heady a combination as he could ever wish. He felt himself swelling even further. His hands cupped her buttocks, the tender flesh, the inviting cleft.

"Your bottom is so sweetly curved, Eve, it could be a pillow for my lips, a sweetmeat for my teeth."

Her eyes opened wide at the meaning of that, and she splashed the smile from his lips with one flattened hand against the surface of the water.

"That's enough, MacLeod. Just let me go."

He did, and she sank. He pulled her up by one arm, sputtering, holding her within the safety of his arms.

"You see, Judith," he said, grinning, "I will always do as you request. All you have to do is ask me."

"Take me back to Tynan," she said, glaring at him. One hand wiped her face dry, but moisture still sparkled on her lashes, gleaned on her cheeks, wet her lips. Alisdair thought he'd never seen such a beauty as his English wife at this moment.

The fact that she was physically *safe*, whether or not she was conscious of it, had begun to alter the way Judith responded to the world. She was unaware that she walked with long-legged grace, her hips swinging with unpracticed and unconscious seduction, not the jerky movements of only weeks before as if her legs impelled her in directions she was unwilling to go. Nor did she hunch over herself, rounding her shoulders and bringing her arms close in to her sides, as if protecting herself, but stood tall, her height and slenderness enhancing the curves of her womanly body.

And at this moment, with the sun rising above the horizon, with her deep blue eyes shooting lightning bolts of irritation, anger, and something akin to frustration at him, Alisdair MacLeod realized that his wife was more than simply pretty, she was beautiful the way Scotland was majestic. Not a common beauty, but something unique, made precious by its rarity.

"I will, sweet. But in a moment," he murmured, concentrating on the sensitive tip of one breast again. It puckered still tighter at his delicate touch, as if it remembered and sought further attention. He stroked the skin beneath one breast with a patient finger, feeling the texture of her flesh, memorizing it and the soft gasp which accompanied his touch.

Her knee brushed against something unbelievably long and hard. Her eyes widened and he smiled.

"Kiss me, Eve," he said, lowering his mouth to hers.

She did, a short, darting kiss, which was about as passionate as a snowflake.

He grinned. She was so damned stubborn. He lowered

his mouth to hers and kissed her with endless weeks of hunger. His lips were both hard and soft and tasted of the sea. They molded to hers, opening them wider for the assault of his tongue. She could only hang onto his shoulders and hope she didn't drown. After a moment, Judith felt as though she were drowning anyway. How hot his mouth was, and how deep and dark.

She did not fear him; she had weeks in which to study him, gauge his measure. Nor did she fear this act he played at with such devilment. She was very much afraid she was immune to what the MacLeod called passion, as if each tender spot in her mind and body had been cauterized by fire itself. There was nothing left to feel.

Yet, she shuddered again as his tongue licked the outline of her lips, lapping the droplets of water from her skin. She buried her face in the nape of his neck, and shivered. She was so cold and so hot at the same time.

"Our mouths will be swollen from our kisses, Eve. Is that what a tongue is for? To soothe and anoint?" His voice was husky and low. Alisdair placed one hand beneath her chin and led her mouth once more to his. His tongue dueled with hers, touched the molten warmth of her inner lips and the cavern of her mouth.

He pulled her close to him, the buoyancy of the water bringing her effortlessly near the apex of his thighs and to the evidence of his desire for her.

"You are so beautiful, Eve," he said in a hushed voice. "A perfect creation on this first morning." He bent and kissed her again.

She made a small noise next to his skin, and could not resist the lure of it. Her tongue licked where her mouth rested, and she tasted salt, and the warmth of his golden flesh. She wrapped her arms around his neck, and closed her eyes with the feeling of it.

He nudged her closer, wrapped her fallen hair around her shoulders and played with the ends of it. He wound its wet length around one fist and pulled her head back so that he could reach her lips. Again, he pillaged her mouth, robbing her of her last defenses in the whirling heat of his tongue.

His hand descended from her breast and smoothed its way down past her waist to her hips and lower, until he touched her intimately at the top of her thighs. She flinched, but he pulled her closer into his embrace, soothing her, gentling her as his fingers invaded her warmth and found the spot he sought. She was hot, and wet, slick with a moisture that did not come solely from the sea. He lifted her slightly and eased a finger inside, slowly slipping in and out, as his mouth sought her breasts. His thumb slid through the folds of her flesh, and rotated slightly.

"The most perfect difference of all, sweet Eve."

They were floating on the slight current. He, supported by his feet touching the rocky bottom; she, bolstered only by the touch of his hands and his mouth.

He lifted her slowly, brought her closer, and in one smooth stroke, entered her.

"This is the most magnificent of all the Creator's gifts, sweet Eve, that we come together in effortless match, drugged with pleasure, each needing the other."

Alisdair gripped her shoulders, bending her gently back so that he could see her face.

He filled her completely. Judith felt stretched by his width and by his length, but not painfully so. When her eyes closed, he stilled his movements until they opened again. She was impaled by the swollen heat of him, and by his look, somber, serious, lit by the dawn sun and by passion and intent.

He moved slightly, spreading his feet.

God, she was hot, and she clung to him as though he were life itself. He moved again and a slight sound emerged from her parted lips. He bent and kissed those lips again, his tongue playing on hers, at the same time his fingers delved, again, into that secret, slippery place.

He grit his teeth against the feeling of her gripping him. She sank against him, her mouth, swollen and open, resting against his neck. The little gasps she uttered aroused him further.

He tried to think about the shearing still to be done, the mending of harness, and a million other unnecessary and calming thoughts. Instead, all he could thing about was Judith. Her arms were loosely draped about his shoulders, one hand tangled in the length of his hair at his nape. Her mouth was warm and wet against his collarbone. Occasionally, her tongue would dart out and touch his skin. The water was icy, but Judith was fire. Teasing flames of gold red hair and the hot promise of shadowed eyes. Flushed cheeks and taunting nipples, and the silken feel of her surrounding him.

He had not wanted to spill inside of her yet. She, on the other hand, had other ideas. He was hanging onto the last vestiges of his mental and physical stamina when she moved. It was an innocent action, of instinct rather than skill, but her legs locked around his calves and brought him deeper still.

She stroked his lips with one wet finger and he wanted to kiss her again. He did, and once more she moved, a gentle bobbing that made him explode. He groaned into her mouth as he filled her. She took the sound and changed it into her own slight moan.

When he could breathe again, he shifted his weight slowly, moving back so that her feet finally rested on the rocks below.

She leaned her head against his chest, shivering in the chill. It had not hurt, this mating with the MacLeod. It had been different, a game of sensations and silliness she'd not thought him capable of, ending in an emptiness which made her feel oddly cross. Judith did not think, however, that she could ever look at the cove again without blushing.

He sighed against her, knowing that he had not brought her to fulfillment. Damn, but the woman was a living contradiction. She had the body of a siren and the innocence of a child. Nor had their first experience together abruptly altered that state.

She looked at him as though she was surprised at his sudden fatigue, and then looked beyond his shoulder. He watched the expression on her face change from bemusement to horror.

He turned to see what would cause her such consternation.

There, on the shore, stood what looked to be the entire clan.

Chapter 19

Judith was beyond humiliation.

Alisdair only grinned.

He emerged from the water with her draped in his arms as if he were truly Adam and she Eve. The people on the shore, especially the men, winked their approval. The women only glared.

"Do they have nothing to do but gape?" Judith hissed, burying her face against his chest. She tried to pretend that she did not hear Malcolm's curt greeting, or the MacLeod's jaunty response.

"Good morning, Granmere," he said, responding to his grandmother's shaking head with a broad smile. Judith groaned something that sounded suspiciously like, "Oh, God," and buried her head further into his armpit. She squinched her eyes shut, trying to pretend that she would awake in a few moments, in her own bed.

Sophie smiled, watching her naked grandson carry his equally naked wife up the stairs. Judith's past had resulted, not in disaster, but in the final impetus to bring these two together.

The MacLeod released her and Judith bounced upon

the bed, grabbing the covers and burrowing into them until she had at least two layers of cloth around her.

"You are a barbarian, MacLeod," she said angrily.

"So I might be, Judith," he agreed complacently.

"Must we have relations in broad daylight? And in front of others?"

"I refuse to accept all of the blame. Neither of us were paying much attention to the shore, were we?" He turned, that stupid grin still playing about his mouth, and began to wash, not affected by the chill water in the ewer. "Besides, Judith, we did not have relations," he added, turning to face her, "we made love."

He walked back to the bed, sat on the edge of it, and hauled her close to him. "Daylight or dark, Judith, there is nothing to be ashamed of."

"But in the cove, MacLeod?"

"Yes, Judith, in the cove. You were, perhaps, too occupied with treading water to fear me so much, were you not?"

She looked at him, the truth apparent in her eyes. Although one part of her had not believed he would let her drown, the fact that she could not swim had occupied most of her mind. There had been no room for terror, or anything other than the thought of all that water beneath her feet.

At least at first.

She blushed, and he thought that she had never looked so lovely. Her hair was mussed around her face in damp curls, her skin still held a rosy glow—although how much came from his loving and how much from simple embarrassment, he did not know—her lips looked swollen and well kissed. It was the expression in her eyes, however, that caused his breath to still and his heart to turn over in his chest.

They held no fear.

They were, however, still misted with anger.

He bent down and kissed her, hard, and for the briefest

of moments, she opened her lips under his. She moved away and he chuckled.

"Get used to it, Judith," he said softly, "we will do it often, I think. And now," he said, rising, "get dressed. I have many things to do today, and wish you with me."

"Perform your own chores, MacLeod, without me. I have my own duties," she said, emerging from the other side of the bed, the sheet wrapped around her.

"No," he said, the smile still playing around his lips. "Not today." He did not tell her that he wanted her with him to spare her long thoughts. She would do nothing but hoard up her embarrassment until nightfall.

She only saw the implacable set of his chin, and sighed.

"Very well, MacLeod," she said stonily. "But," she announced, her own stubbornness adding a glint to her eye, "do not expect to tumble me on the moors."

"Judith, your inventiveness intrigues me. Think you the sheep will mind?"

She wished she had something to throw at him.

Judith did not have time to be humiliated.

The MacLeod was a busy man, and it was difficult to keep up with him and remember her embarrassment.

She followed him over the track through the moors, trying to match his broad strides, but even so, he would not wait for her. She found him, finally, and stood and waited while he gave the older men instructions on how to care for the newly sheared sheep. It was important for them to be watched carefully for the first few days after their protective coat of fleece was gone. Parasites could bore within a cut or scrape, and the MacLeod was taking no chances on losing any of them. She and Alisdair skirted the empty weaving shed, but neither spoke of the fact that it was empty, that the women of the clan still refused to return to the weaving.

Judith followed him to the fishing huts, located some distance away from the main village. The stench of curing fish permeated the air, along with the odor from the huge fields of seaweed spread out to dry.

Each activity was an industry unto itself, each populated by members of the clan, some of whom glared at Judith. The others simply smirked.

The MacLeod was having none of it.

Without seeming to do anything out of the ordinary, he would pull Judith into the circle of his arms, introduce her to people she had not met formally before, and by doing so, announced his message as clearly as if he had signaled a trumpeter.

None of them missed his meaning.

Their eyes would meet the MacLeod's over Judith's head, or when she turned away. Without a word spoken, his intent was conveyed to every member of his clan.

She was his wife. What you do to her, you do to me.

Some would remember the scene in the cove and wonder at the sight of her now clothed in the crow's dress that hid every inch of skin from their gaze. They would remember the sight of her wrapped around the sturdy length of the MacLeod, but these memories were only indulged in after their laird strode away, his wife struggling to keep up. Still others would recall the scene in the glen, when she'd admitted being an English soldier's widow. Those clan members could only wonder at the MacLeod's actions. Their criticism was never voiced aloud—there were many people in the glen who owed their survival to Alisdair MacLeod's efforts.

Judith thought it strange that Fiona was not present. Did she have no duties to perform? When she said as much to Alisdair, he only grinned, wondering if it was jealousy that made her eyes sparkle, and turned her blush a deeper rose.

"She is in Inverness, Judith, visiting her aunt. Do you miss her presence?"

"She is allowed much freedom for an unmarried woman. Is that usual in Scotland?"

"I am sorry that you have not become friends," he said,

ignoring her question. He did not want to talk about Fiona's marital state, or in this case, the lack of it. His kinship with Fiona did not dictate that he was responsible for her morals. He did not know who Douglas's father was, but he did not condemn her for the child's illegitimate birth. In the last few years, other priorities had supplanted the rigid teachings of the Kirk. As long as they did not include him—although he knew that Fiona wished otherwise—he was not overly concerned as to her plans for the future. He had no doubt that she would eventually find some eager mate willing to pay for her favors by offering marriage.

"Friends?" Judith looked at him in wonder. How could he be so obtuse?

He grinned again and could not resist fueling the fire. "She thinks you're a cuif," he said calmly, waiting for the question. It was not long in coming.

"What's a cuif?"

"A ninny."

"I'll ninny her," Judith snarled, and for the next few minutes, strode angrily in front of the MacLeod. He thought her anger a glorious thing.

She thought him the strangest man she'd ever known.

He could not have protected her more, if he had wrapped her in a blanket and carried her from place to place. By keeping her with him, he announced their bond. She was not part of this land, nor was she part of the clan. Nor, in honesty, did she know if she ever would be. She belonged to the MacLeod, however, and not only was that message becoming apparent to every member of the clan, it was also becoming very obvious to Judith.

She began to wonder about this man who had accepted her into his life with more grace than she had acknowledged her own place in it.

Who was he?

He was not like her father, whose contempt for her had punctuated her childhood. She suspected that Alisdair would treat a daughter of his with as much tender care as he lavished on Douglas. Nor was this new Scots husband of hers like Peter, whose gentleness was only a mask for weakness. The MacLeod did not claim to be gentle, yet his actions of the past days had proven he was both compassionate and kind. He was not like Anthony, who had wielded his sword with cruelty and his husbandry of her in the same way. Yet, the MacLeod had fought in battle, surviving when many had not. He had yelled and roared at her, but had held her close to comfort her. He had charm, and wit, and patience, and at the same time could be caustic and surly and unkind.

He had told her she was beautiful.

By dusk, Judith was no closer to understanding him then she had been at dawn. By the time they returned to Tynan, it was turning to night, and with night came another problem. What would happen now?

Alisdair had noted her glances when she'd thought he was not looking. He'd seen how her brow wrinkled when she was deep in thought, and noticed the frown that marred the space above her nose when she was perplexed about something. It had come as no surprise that her humiliation had dissipated. It was difficult to feel anything but fatigue after walking for miles across the moors.

Alisdair was not unduly surprised, either, by the sight of her anxiously scanning the skies as if to hold off the night, or her faltering steps as she reluctantly entered the courtyard.

The key to alleviating Judith's fears, he had decided, was the same response he'd had when trying to restore his life after the decimation of his family and his clan. It was impossible to live as he had once lived. Alisdair had realized, upon returning to Tynan, that the only way to abide with, and accept, his past was to alter the present. Memories hung like dripping shadows from each room of Tynan, and he consciously sought not to replicate them. He never ventured near the suite of rooms he had once shared with Anne. He would not sit by the fire in the great hall, as he had so many times with his father and his brother. He never took his meals in the dining hall, where they had all supped before, amidst rollicking discussions and fierce debates. He would not even leave Tynan by the seaside door, as he had as a young boy.

He would never, consciously, duplicate Judith's past, either. Judith's horror bloomed in silence, so he would show her that words could cure. She had feared being punished for her feelings, therefore he would encourage each one of her many and varied emotions. Whatever had made her uneasy, he would make normal. Whatever she had known as normal, he would make rare.

It was both a vow and a promise.

Chapter 20

The slut was in Scotland.

The smile he wore was not one of humor, a fact more than a few members of his regiment had discerned over the last year. When Bennett Henderson had that expression on his face, it did not mean he was in charity with the world.

How utterly perfect that she was here. And how like her to have found a protector. She was a survivor, he had to give her that. It was that very quality which had made mounting her such delicious enjoyment. All those nights, when she'd fought him, it had made the pleasure that much greater. To know that he'd mastered her, conquered her, beaten her, wiped the rage from her eyes and replaced it with fear, ah, it almost made him laugh.

She was growing brave again.

He would leave her alone, then, until she thought herself safe. Until she began to believe that a Scot could protect her from him. Until she began to think he planned no retribution, no vengeance for her act. Only then, when she'd become hopeful, when her tenseness melted to relaxation and her fears to laughter, would he visit her again.

Perhaps then, he would introduce his group into a different pleasure, show them what treasure these barren hills and misty glens could hide.

Until then, he ached for another woman, one who could keep him satisfied until he saw Judith again. A temporary replacement, that was all, to assuage his body while his mind fed on the anticipation of it all.

Judith.

He could hardly wait.

Chapter 21

He had barely spoken ten words to her all day and now he wanted to talk!

Judith rolled over and tried to ignore him, but it was the sound of his voice as much as his words which drew her attention. It was too deep and alluring, she thought, undoubtedly the result of much practice. She punched the nearly flat pillow into shape and edged closer to the side of the bed. It was no use. The MacLeod was too big and the bed too small. Each time she moved, he followed her.

She squinched shut her eyes, trying to sleep despite the fact that he had insisted upon lighting a branch of candles on the bedside table. Finally, in desperation, she turned and glared at him.

"MacLeod, do you never cease? Are you more than human? Do you never sleep?"

Alisdair drew her up next to him and she sighed again, loudly. Judith would much rather be in another bed, but he had refused to allow her to return to her old room.

"Judith," he coaxed, "were you not paying attention? Here I thought you hung onto my very words."

"I do not want to talk about it, MacLeod."

"Alisdair," he corrected softly.

"Very well. Alisdair, I do not want to talk about it." She turned her head away when he would have kissed her. He nuzzled her cheek, instead.

"But, Judith, it is a subject I could warm to, without much encouragement."

"You seem to be warming to it without any at all, Mac-Leod." She frowned at him.

He chuckled. "I think they're very nice breasts and your waist curves so sweetly to your hips."

"Will you cease?"

It did not escape his attention that her face was flushed. The candles also illuminated her full lips, the sheen of her hair, the budding perfection of her breasts.

She wished he would stop looking at her that way—it made the sheer nightgown seem even more transparent. She should have refused the gift in the first place, but Granmere had labored so long over it that she did not have the heart to do so. Now, she felt exposed, inviting.

He reached out one finger and touched the tip of her breast through the cloth, but she jerked away and pulled up the sheet. It was a futile protection, she thought, against his words.

"Your nipples felt so good in my mouth, Judith," he said, a small smile curving his lips, "but not as good as you felt when I entered you, all hot and soft and liquid."

She rolled over onto her side, away from him. Would he not simply hush? Her body felt ablaze with embarrassment.

"You seem intent upon reliving the entire experience, MacLeod, word for word!"

"I seem to remember it being a very nice experience, Judith, although you did not enjoy it as much as I," he said softly, leaning towards her and pulling the sheet from her grasp. He turned her over until she was flat on her back.

A hand trailed up one leg, slid beneath the gauzy cotton of her gown.

"MacLeod!" she said, placing her own hand upon his, stopping his gentle exploration, "what are you doing?"

"Alisdair," he corrected calmly, with a smile.

She could feel each separate finger on her flesh, five places of heat and sensation. It was like playing with fire itself, the pain of being burned following the sensation of it by long moments. His hand undulated under hers, a teasing touch, one that let her know he was acquiescent only because he wished it, not because she was strong enough to prevent him.

Yet, he had said he would do whatever she wished. Did she truly wish him to stop?

Mating with the MacLeod carried overtones with it, buried laughter, a hint of teasing, qualities she wasn't sure she understood or could even accept in such context. There was more, too, a hint of something stronger, feelings which swelled the heart and expanded the soul.

Did she truly wish him to stop?

He smiled at her, his lips dusted with light and mischief. He bent slowly, giving her ample time to escape, testing her with resolve and a bit of dare. If she wanted to escape, it was now she should move, now she should protest, now she should refuse.

The touch of his lips was warm, full, soft. A gentle invitation to proceed down a road she was unfamiliar traveling. She lay quiescent, waiting, but he did nothing more than lay his lips tenderly there, as if implanting the feel of him upon her. When he did not move, did not deepen the embrace, she breathed slowly, a small gasp of air escaped her lips, brushed against his. He opened his mouth as if to receive a treat, inhaling deeply.

Intimacy in a breath.

She shivered.

He drew back, studying her, his eyes the color of molten gold, the expression in them too deep to read. Or was it simply too uncomfortable? There was restraint there, and something else wild and needy and frightening. But even more fear-provoking was the tenderness.

She could not fight his empathy.

Her eyes were as wide as the ocean and as deep, made mysterious by a thin film of tears.

A tear slid from her eye. He traced its path with his tongue, buried his hands and his mouth into the mass of hair at her temple, breathing slowly, fighting back the insensate rage he felt. Not for her. Never for her. But only for the man who had done this to her.

She turned her head, found his cheek, pressed a soft kiss upon it. He raised his head and studied her face. Such a gentle gesture of acceptance, such a tender bestowal of permission. He did not discount the meaning of that kiss.

"Ah, Judith." It was the only thing he could say, the rage fading beneath the swelling of more tender emotion.

A long finger reached up and traced the outline of her lips. Would it frighten her to know the extent of his need?

"You have such beautiful lips." He stopped what she would have said by the simple expedient of placing two fingers atop her mouth. "For kissing, Judith, not for speech."

He kissed her then, like he had in the cove, a mouth-hungry kiss that demanded reciprocity, not surrender. He led the pace, but he did not force it. When he lifted himself away from her, her lips were pink, full. A tender touch of tongue anointed them, his and hers alike.

Her eyes were open wide, her cheeks flushed, her fists no longer gripping the sheet, but instead his shoulders, as if she once again feared drowning.

His hand continued its gentle exploration under her nightgown, as if there'd been no interruption, no long mind-drugging kisses.

They watched each other, only inches apart, his eyes lit with mischief, hers with something that looked like fear but tasted only of inexperience. He was prepared to stop the moment she asked him to, she was ready to ask him the moment he stopped.

"I didn't pleasure you in the cove, Judith," he said softly, his voice like the flutter of a butterfly's wings on her skin.

Was it possible for her skin to become more flushed? She looked as ripe as a fall apple ready to be plucked from the tree. He grinned at her embarrassment, bent down, and nuzzled her neck with his lips.

With a sweep of hand, he divested her of the sheet. In a flash of seconds, he had her nightgown at her waist, her limbs exposed to night air and candlelight. When she would have brushed his hands aside and covered herself, he kissed her again, his lips as mind-numbing as laudanum, as addictive.

One moment he was smiling gently at her, tracing the line of her chin with a teasing finger, the next, he was kissing her belly, anointing those scars which trailed from her back, lacerating the tender flesh of her stomach.

His touch was gentle, almost tender, but stubbornly insistent.

"MacLeod."

Her entreaty had no effect. Yet, she remained still and unmoving, bound not by cords, but by the sensations which swept up from each of his touches on her body.

Bold fingers trailed through the curls at the apex of her thighs, combing them, patting, petting.

"Forgive me for being an impatient lover, before," he said. The words were nearly obscured by her gasp of shock.

His tongue traced an imaginary line from her thighs to their juncture, and she squirmed in his grasp until his hands gently pushed apart her legs.

"MacLeod!" Her opposition had no effect on him.

"Hush, Judith."

She lay back against the pillow, her focus on the ceiling above her. Strange darts of fire strummed in her belly when she had seen him tasting her. The tenderest of touches and yet, they had the ability to make her shiver. What power did he have, that he could make her feel such things?

He opened her legs wider, as if demanding access to the very core of her. It was not fear which made her part her thighs, or even the heat which poured over her skin until she felt molten with it, but a strange, compelling, curiosity.

Resistance faded beneath his touch, her will melted beneath the sensations he was stirring in her. It seemed as though he had all the time in the world, hours and hours in which to tease and taunt, all the while whispering to her of the sweetness of her taste, the need he felt for the tasting. His tongue touched her everywhere, short darting strokes that were fast, and then slow, and then fast again, circling, stroking, a parody of soothing. His touch did not placate, it incited, it stirred. It raised a fire from ember to conflagration. He seemed pleased by her reaction, delighting in the soft moan which slipped from her wet lips, defying restraint.

"Alisdair," she mumbled softly, his name an incantation. He ignored her summons, denied anything but the sensation he was experiencing. She opened for him, a flower blooming wetly in the candlelight, her petals swollen and deeply red. Her hips were pinned gently beneath his arms, but he could feel the thrumming rhythm in her trembling, knew that she would arch toward his touch if he gave her enough freedom. He wanted her captive, instead, a prisoner of delicate, repetitive, insistent demand. He wanted her to come apart in his arms, fold into herself, weep her woman's rain onto his hands and flood his mouth.

He raised himself up and studied her, at the dark blue eyes that were wide and open, their pupils dilated, their color deeper than ever before. His own needs threatened to swamp his restraint then. It was almost pain, this urge to be inside her, to see her eyes open as she welcomed him, to feel her shudder and gasp with the sensation of it.

Instead, he returned to his delightful occupation, not ceasing until he heard her unmistakable moans of surrender. She shuddered, imploding into herself, her climax so powerful that he clutched the mattress with both hands to prevent the sweeping urge to be inside of her, sharing, melting into her warmth. There would be times for them both, but tonight was hers, only hers.

Only when he'd gained control over himself did he move back to her side.

"Goodnight, wife," he said, leaning over her to extinguish the candles. He hesitated for a moment, debated the wisdom of kissing those too full lips, knew then that he could not trust himself. He wanted her too badly.

A soft sigh was her only response. It sounded, to his eager mind, wistful and nearly as needy as he felt. She roused herself, as if gathering all the pieces of her body back together, turned until her back was to him, extended the sheet over her shoulders.

Alisdair pulled the sheet down, baring her back. Even now, he could feel the tremors which still racked her, sensations he could feel duplicated in his own flesh, a drumbeat of insistence which demanded relief.

He kissed her above the deeply scooped neck of the gown, tracing the scars there with his tongue, so faintly and so tenderly that she might have imagined it.

She lay taut until he finished saluting each separate scar with his lips, kissing her, branding her with his painless touch. He covered her again and whispered in the darkness.

"They are a mark of your courage, Judith," he said, his hand smoothing the sheet and venturing up to her hair, which lay heavy and unbraided upon the pillow. "Not a sign of your shame."

Judith lay awake for a long time.

Chapter 22

"It's a foolish thing we do here, Malcolm," Geddes mumbled, his shuffling gait in the ancient rushes the only sound in the room. To his ears, perhaps. But not to Malcolm, whose glower intensified with every harsh breath exhaled by the other three occupants. Stealth was what was needed here, not complaints, not the wheezing protests of an ill assorted band of conspirators. Not that he had much choice, now, did he? These were the elders of the clan, as pitiful a sight as they were, but he still punctuated his displeasure by glaring at his kinsmen.

They were a sorry bunch. Old Geddes, arthritis crippling him so badly that he walked in a permanently stooped position. Hamish, his one remaining eye so filmed over that he needed help to see even on the brightest of days. Alex, however, was the worst of the lot, and if they were caught, it would be because of his infirmity—one leg replaced by a crooked, whittled stick of a limb which fit so painfully that every piercing scratch upon the floor was accompanied by a muffled groan of pain.

"Quiet!" Malcolm hissed, his brow furrowed, his irritation growing with each precious second they lingered.

They were the wise men of the clan, yet all they had done since they had met in Geddes's cottage an hour earlier was moan and groan or bicker like old women.

It was Alex's accusations which pierced him to the core, though, for all their muttering. He whirled and faced his detractor. "Would ye have the English take it a' away, mon?"

"What they've no' taken, Malcolm, is our lives," Alex said stubbornly. "As puny an' as ill fed a lot we are."

"I'd no' thought to hear a coward's voice from yer throat."

"A coward is it? A coward? When I lost my own son? When his bairn died because there was nothin' for her to eat except for the grubs an' the worms of burned out fields? I answered the call as willingly as the next." His words were whispered, but no less vehement for their lack of volume. Nor was the look he shot Malcolm softened by the gloom of the keep.

"Then ye' should ken, mon, more than the rest."

"What is there to understand, Malcolm?" he said tiredly. "Would ye have the four of us take on England's army, now?" Mockery tinged his words, and an odd sort of sadness.

"Aye, Malcolm, do ye preach rebellion?" The question came from Hamish, standing alone and apart from the others. He, too, had buried kin and mourned even now for their loss. What Malcolm wanted was a return to days of glory, as few as they were. He could appreciate the sentiment at the same time he realized its stupidity. What Malcolm wanted was as futile as their own march to Carlisle, but oh, those had been days to recall for the rest of their lives, weren't they? They had marched into England behind the Bonnie Prince filled with dreams and exhilaration, knowing that, for once, the men of Scotland had occupied English soil and not the other way around. For a few blessed days, the sons of Scotland had determined the course of events, not England. For a few glorious days, there had been change in the air and Scotland had been considered more than a nuisance, more than a wayward child. Aye, he could well understand why Malcolm preached insurrection now. But the days of Carlisle had been pre-Culloden. Before the end to the rebellion, before most of the able-bodied men of the Highlands had died in a battle so unevenly matched. Surrender was what the English had wanted and surrender they had gotten, and sent the Duke of Cumberland, the Butcher, to make it so.

"Rebellion, is it now?" Malcolm answered angrily. "Is it rebellion to want a Scotland filled wi' Scots, then, Hamish, an' no' the Sassenach?" he said, his spine stiffened by the accusations of his longtime friends.

"It's rebellion against the laird I'm speaking of. Have ye forgotten what the lad wants? Have ye forgotten the pardon?" His soft words were accompanied by a muttering of assent from the others. Alisdair's dreams of economic independence had found strong supporters in the glen. It was a sad fact of life, but one undeniably true, that they could not beat the English. The dreams of a Jacobite rebellion were only that; the prince had returned to the continent, and the men who'd so gladly followed him were either dead or stripped of their possessions, titles, and estates, or like Alisdair, living a tenuous existence with a conditional pardon.

The dream of out trading the English was their only way of retaliation, not to mention what would happen to Alisdair and the rest of the clan if insurrection could be proven. Alisdair's conditional pardon was exactly that— based upon a series of conditions, none of which included meeting in a deserted keep for the purpose of anarchy.

"Besides, Malcolm, what about the English wife you brought to the glen? It was your idea to wed her to the MacLeod." They were Hamish's words, but he uttered the thoughts of all of them.

"An' I'll go to my grave regrettin' it. Is tha' what you want to hear?"

Hamish did not reply.

"It's time to arm oursel's, for each member of the clan

to have a weapon to protect against the English. Are ye for me, or no?'' Malcolm asked, turning and fixing them with a steady look. Hamish sighed and reached out one arm, which was taken by Alex, who lurched forward with him. Old Geddes shambled towards them, his step as shuffling as before, echoing his reluctance.

Malcolm crossed the room swifter then the others, pushing back the rushes to expose the metal ring hidden in the floor.

"We're for ye', Malcolm," Hamish said, when his companions remained mute. "Please God, this decision will no' bring tragedy down on our heads."

Chapter 23

Alisdair and Malcolm had taken the first shipment of their raw wool to Inverness. Without a goodbye, without a word spoken, he had simply left. Judith couldn't say she was ungrateful to be spared Malcolm's presence for a few days, but the least Alisdair could have done was to inform her of his plans.

Judith had the whole day to think of the fact he had let Sophie do the chore for him.

"The chicken is already dead, Judith," Sophie said mildly. Judith only slammed it harder on the board. She wielded a mean knife, too, and it was Sophie's sudden thought that Judith was wishing it was another body laying upon that board, other than a scrawny hen with its neck about to be chopped off.

Judith looked down at the exposed neck of the chicken, took a deep breath, and closed her eyes. She hated this chore. But, they still had to eat, and if she were to consume another meal consisting of colcannon, it would be one too many. Anything, even chopping the head off a chicken, was preferable to eating another turnip.

She was cutting the onions into fine dices when Fiona

opened the seaside door, entering the kitchen as if she
needed no invitation. Truth to tell, none of the women
ever knocked, simply entered Tynan as if the laird's home
was as open to them as family. It was, after all, the clan
system. Related or no, the clan was kindred and all its
members as close as siblings.

Still, Judith frowned at the woman who dared to invade
her kitchen.

"Yer daein brawlie wi' the cloker," Fiona said, the sweetness in her voice at odds with the contemptuous sneer
on her full lips. Her accent seemed oddly thicker, Judith
thought, as if it were a thinly veiled insult at her nationality.
Not that Fiona ever needed an excuse to mock her. The
woman had been a splinter under her skin since the first
moment she'd seen her, always sauntering up to Alisdair,
rubbing herself around him like a purring cat.

Even now, when Alisdair was in Inverness, she'd doxied
herself up for him. Her blouse was scarlet, loose-fitting
with full, gathered sleeves and a neckline scooped low in
the front, revealing the swell of plump, uncorseted breasts.
A woolen skirt, not long enough to cover her ankles, also
exposed bare feet. Her curly black hair was artfully tousled,
as if she'd just risen from bed, leaving the impression that
both the sheets and their recent occupant were still warm,
sultry, and scented with sex.

Douglas was perched on one hip, eagerly patting his
mother's cheek. Fiona did not distract him, only smiled
fondly into his infant face. A face which bore the unmistakable stamp of Alisdair's parentage.

"Douglas cam ta bide a wee wi' the laird," Fiona
announced, not bothering to mask the sneer on her face.

"Alisdair's no' here," Judith said, in a parody of Fiona's
accent. One hand held the onion steady, the other held
the knife, a pose that would have given any other woman
a reason to retreat.

Fiona, however, sauntered closer.

There was a faint smile on Fiona's lips as she lowered

Douglas to the floor, and fetched him a piece of bread from the table.

"He'll be the laird one day, will my Douglas."

Judith did not bother to respond, only began disemboweling the chicken with a fierceness far in excess of the need.

"De ye no' think he looks like Alisdair?"

Judith's temper was pushed one notch higher.

Fiona smiled down into her son's face. For a long moment, Judith did not raise her eyes from the much abused chicken.

"Alisdair says he is not Douglas's father."

Fiona only shrugged and then looked meaningfully at Judith's apron-covered stomach. "He'll ne're have another, though, will he? Ye wi' yer empty womb. Two husbands afore Alisdair, an' nothin' to show for it."

It was too much.

Judith picked up the chicken by its still attached neck and threw it at the other woman.

Fiona shrieked as the chicken hit her, dripping blood and entrails over her best blouse. The noise was enough to rouse Sophie from her doze in the chair by the fire. His mother's scream was enough to send Douglas into a rousing wail.

Judith lost what composure she had left. As Fiona continued screaming, Judith continued throwing. Whatever was at hand was hurled at the woman who had the nerve to flaunt her relationship and her child in front of Judith. Chopped onions followed the greens. The boiled oats and stale bread were next.

At each successive hit, Judith grinned broadly. Fiona's face was flushed with ugly blotches of chicken blood, her hair was streaked with guts and boiled oats, the swelling bodice of her blouse was filled with chopped onions.

Fiona went for her throat.

Judith was ready for her.

Douglas cried louder.

Sophie started laughing, an odd crackling sound that sputtered and then stopped, as she gasped for breath.

Alisdair froze in mid-step.

He retrieved Douglas from the floor, set him on Sophie's lap. Then he returned to the women, neither of whom, he was disconcerted to note, had ceased in their efforts to throttle the other. Fiona was smaller, but heavier, while Judith's rage had given impetus to her strength.

"Enough!" he shouted, but even that was not enough to part them. They had to be bodily separated. Malcolm, with a frown, managed to restrain his daughter, while Alisdair hauled Judith up against him until she felt his full length against her body.

"Ye should have let the English take her, lad," Fiona shouted. "She doesn't belong here a' Tynan. She's no' for the likes of you."

She smiled, a curve of full, carmined lips, and dropped her lashes, a coy imitation of a maiden's distress despite being restrained by her father's arms. It would have been more effective if she'd not had a gizzard stuck in her hair.

Alisdair, however, would never have been enticed, despite how well she dressed for seduction.

"Since when do you know what's right for me, Fiona?"

"Since ye were a lad, Alisdair," she said softly, her sultry voice evoking thoughts of warm flesh and cool nights, "I've known what you wanted." She had the right of it, he supposed. Once, when he was just a boy, he'd flushed whenever she came around, her plush beauty and plump curves fueling his adolescent fantasies. He'd longed for a sight of her, near panted when she'd artfully stretched, or accidentally showed a length of leg. He could not be around her without wondering if her breasts would fill his hands to overflowing, and how they'd taste.

But that had been years ago, when he was a youth and starved for the touch of a woman, any woman.

He had become more discriminating with age. Now he longed for wit as well as upthrust breasts, for intelligence that sparkled behind sultry blue black eyes, for long legs and a challenging smile. He craved the sound of throaty laughter and an unflagging courage as laudable as any man's. He wanted affection with his sex, and a touch of spicy wit, and something else. He wanted loyalty, unquenchable passion, and love. He suspected that only one woman was capable of giving him those things.

The look he gave Fiona was not as sharp as it should have been, nor as condemnatory as his wife would have preferred. She was not only his clanswoman, she was a companion of his youth. The look, however, carried with it such indifference that even Fiona noted it.

"I'd never thought ta see the day, my laird," she said, her pride stung, "when you'd prefer an English bitch ta warm your bed. Tell me, do the English do it differently?"

"Do not presume upon our kinship, Fiona," he said, his voice as somber as a gray day, no emotion in its depths. The very lack of it stilled her in the act of pulling away.

"So, it's like that, is it?" she said, her look searching the depths of his amber eyes. Whatever she saw in them dissatisfied her.

"It's like that," he agreed. From this day forward, things would not be the same between them, and both of them knew it. He would no longer be able to accept her flirtation for the innocence it was not. She would not be able to be around him and remember he'd rejected her. Their bond of kinship had been traded for stronger emotions. Love, pride, desire, and anger.

He wished it were not so.

She pulled away from her father's grip and straightened her blouse. " 'Tis a pity, that," she said, not looking at him as both hands smoothed the material down over rounded breasts. " 'Tis a shame she's not more comely."

Her own beauty was never in doubt. She had been raised with the notion that she was the clan's reigning beauty, the way a person born with brown eyes is conscious of that color. Her beauty simply was, like an appendage, or a name, or a talent. Even Ian had been no match for her wiles, nor had Douglas's father.

Alisdair met Malcolm's eyes over the heads of the women. Malcolm nodded to an unspoken command and removed Fiona forcibly from the kitchen. He returned a moment later for Douglas, who had still not ceased his wailing.

Only then did the kitchen begin to resemble the oasis of peace and quiet it had always been. All except for the bloody chicken and a medley of vegetables strewn across the floor.

Alisdair turned his wife in his arms.

The flush was still on Judith's face. Damp tendrils of hair fell below the bodice of her dress.

His eyes were flecked with gold, and a small, wry smile appeared on his face, as he continued to study her. Judith could see the day's stubble of his beard and, despite her intention, one hand strayed to that bristly chin.

"Fiona is a kinswoman," he said softly, the touch of her palm on his face fueling desires never quite dormant around her. He had only to smell her scent and he felt needy, hot-blooded, stallion-ready.

She pulled away from him and turned her back, blinking away the sudden sting in her eyes. It was the onion, of course. Everyone knew they made you cry. It was not the sudden show of loyalty from Alisdair which prompted her tears.

"Kinswoman or not," Judith said, "that woman has to go. It is my kitchen, MacLeod," she said, stooping to pick up the chicken, chunks of onions and greens from the floor. "I've a right to who comes in it." Chicken blood was splattered over the stone and she washed out a rag to begin cleaning it.

Alisdair had waited for the day when Judith felt secure enough with him to express her anger. He had expected it, anticipated it. Yet, he could not reconcile the stiff, silent woman he'd first met to the virago he'd seen when he walked into the kitchen.

He grinned, the effort of restraining his laughter almost too much. He reached for her, but she evaded his touch.

She didn't like the twinkling light of merriment in his eyes. It was not funny. Fiona was a constant thorn in her flesh.

"Come here, wife," Alisdair said, his smile still in place, a different note in his voice. Not so much teasing as it was promising.

Instead, Judith backed away slowly, toes of one foot placed carefully behind the heel of the other. It was a gentle gesture of escape that did not go unnoticed.

"Come here, Judith," he said, still in that calm, reasonable tone. She distrusted it. Each time Alisdair adopted that unhurried, narrating tone of voice, it meant he was about to do something bizarre or wicked.

She did not mean to, but when he raised his hands to put them on her shoulders, she flinched. It was as if time itself stopped at her unbidden gesture. The very stillness of his stance made her look up, to see his eyes fixed steadily on hers.

An eternity of speech passed between them in those long seconds, words unvoiced, yet spoken all the same. *Trust me,* his look said, *I will not hurt you. I know,* she answered, *but there are times I forget.* An admission that was as hard to reveal to him as it was to herself. She wanted to shut her eyes against his tense regard. Instead, she allowed him to see what she felt, exposing herself in a way she'd never done before.

Alisdair wondered if she knew that her eyes always gave her away. He could measure her feelings by their expression. In their depths was uncertainty, wrapped in a cloak fashioned from bravado. He smiled, lifted her chin with the tip of one finger, and bent to kiss her swiftly, hard, a kiss to brand.

"Go upstairs, Judith. Wait for me."

She'd been given that command too many times in her married life. It had never struck sparks of anticipation before, only fear. A finger pressed to her lips halted her words, the message in his eyes as old as time and as solemn as church vows.

"I will be obeyed, my stubborn wife." His eyes glittered as he gently kissed her.

She tried to stifle a smile, but it burst forth anyway, a small slip of one, as if she were a child and at some solemn gathering and forbidden to grin.

"This time, MacLeod."

Her grandson had a unique laugh, Sophie thought, as she lay her head back in her chair, thinking that this evening was too eventful for an old woman like her. Still, the sound of Alisdair's laughter was a pleasant thing. Almost as lovely as Gerald's.

Chapter 24

Alisdair hauled the old tub from the pantry, emptied it of the potatoes usually stored there, and began to scrub it mercilessly. The tub had been one of his mother's extravagances. Why she had required a hip bath whose surface was etched in bronze, he had never known. Louise's peculiar and frivolous purchases had only one thing in common. They were exclusively for her enjoyment and comfort. The tapers especially scented with sandalwood, made to her order in Edinburgh, were to illuminate her suite of rooms. The wine sent in crates from France was for her troubled digestion, and not shared with other members of the family. The soap milled in Germany from the finest ingredients was for her delicate skin, roughened and chapped by the Scottish seasons.

She had not, although she had certainly tried, exceeded Tynan's coffers. That had been accomplished by the '45. Louise had simply removed what coin had remained, prior to her self-imposed exile to France. It was a good thing, Alisdair thought, that his mother had not chosen to remain. She could never have borne their hardships.

Alisdair hefted the tub up the stairs, not an easy chore.

Nor was lifting the buckets of heated water. The result, however, was worth any discomfort.

Despite Judith's protests, he lifted the soiled dress over her head, followed by her undergarments. She fussed the entire time. He ignored her.

"Is it your aim to cook me, Alisdair?" she sputtered, as Alisdair helped her into the bath.

She lifted one foot, then another, and stepped from the water, all the while scowling at him.

"Come, Judith, it's not that hot," he said mildly.

"Is this penance of some sort, MacLeod?" He seemed preoccupied with every exposed inch of skin, so she reluctantly sat in the tub again, raising her knees to shield herself from his eyes. The heat of the water did feel good, but it did not mean that she chose to bathe in front of him. Just because he gloried in his nakedness was no reason for him to think she would likewise be as shameless.

She began to wash her face with the scrap of linen he handed her, and thus did not see him kneel behind her and take another cloth in his hand.

His first touch upon her back was startling. His strokes were sure and firm, unlike the gentle touch of his lips the other night. No, these were strong kneading motions using the palms of his hands. She relaxed, reluctantly, under his ministrations.

"Does your back hurt in damp weather?" he asked, noting that many of her muscles seemed knotted and twisted. She turned and looked directly into amber eyes only inches from her own.

"Sometimes."

"Did you have no treatment for it?"

She stared at him as though he had lost his reason. The man who would have summoned aid would not have perpetrated this persecution in the first place.

"No," she said, her voice clipped. She acted very English sometimes, he thought, as if she were drawing on a protective cloak of reserve. "I was expected to act as though nothing had occurred. Anything that would have indicated my discomfort would only have brought more down upon me."

His eyes flickered with an expression she could not read. "Is it the norm in England, this treatment of wives?"

"I do not know, MacLeod. I did not boast of it, you can be assured of that."

"Your family? Were they not prepared to assist you?"

"Again, I do not know. I never spoke of it."

"So you have grown stoic," he said, soaping the linen square and then her back. He swept the length of her hair aside and continued his bathing of her neck and shoulders.

She thought it a strange duty he had taken on, bathing his wife.

Yet, there was nothing ordinary about the MacLeod.

It was not the first time in her life a man had ever spoken softly to her and offered her consolation. Alisdair had comforted her when he had first seen her scars. It was not the first time a man had ever stroked her skin gently, tenderly, with no thought of exchange. Alisdair had done so, causing riotous feelings in her body. It was not the first time a man had ever wished to know of her life. Alisdair had evinced an endless curiosity from the first moment she'd seen him.

It had always, and only, been Alisdair.

Judith did not realize she had spoken about her scars without tears in her eyes, in a voice that, although it indicated past anguish, held none of the terror or active pain of a few weeks ago. He did, however. Nor did she realize that by turning the conversation to her past, he had adroitly banished her of embarrassment or shame about her nakedness.

"Hardly stoic, MacLeod," she answered him finally, thinking of those days filled with passionate hatred for Anthony and his brother.

"What would you call it, then, Judith," he asked, "to not seek assistance or protection?"

"Where would I go? To my father? He would have sent me back. My mother? She was as much a pawn as myself. To my sisters? They would not wish me in their households."

"So you said nothing, and became a martyr."

"I haven't the temperament for martyrdom" she said, and he smiled, thinking her right.

"Did you find it easy to kill, Alisdair?" she asked suddenly, her abrupt question stilling his hands upon the rounded curves of her shoulders. "You with the training to heal?" She turned her head to look at him. Her lovely blue eyes were troubled, but he had the strangest feeling that the emotion in their depths was something he did not wish to plumb.

"No, Judith, I found it very difficult. It is harder, I think, to live with the memory of it."

A strange comment from a man who lived every day as though he squeezed each hour dry, who looked at the sky and noted the clouds, the expanse of horizon, and nodded as if satisfied with God's handiwork. She'd seen him stopping to study the bloom of an isolated flower, bravely growing beside a pebble-strewn path. She'd seen him do all these things and more, and it was not the behavior of someone who wished to forget the actions of his life.

What had life been like for him during the past two years? She found, and not for the first time, that she very much wanted to know.

The MacLeod had other ideas.

He dropped the square of cloth, letting it float gently to the bottom of the tub as he took the soap between his large hands. He smoothed his slippery fingers over her shoulders, and down toward her breasts, only smiling at her futile gestures, at the hands that pulled against his wrists but were powerless to prevent his actions.

"I think that being stoic is a fine emotion for some situations," he said, paying close attention to her nipples, tracing circles around their pink length with his soapy fingers, then cupping her breasts in his hands, feeling their fullness, their plump heaviness. "But I think it loses its appeal in some circumstances."

"What circumstances would those be?" she asked, in a tremulous voice, thinking that it was a strange man, indeed, who would insist on touching her in such an intimate way, but continued to converse as if they were taking tea in the drawing room.

"Have you not noticed?" He bent close to her and she turned, noting the tender smile on his lips and the gleam in his eyes accentuated by some mischief there. His fingers were splayed across her skin, tracing the symmetry of waist to hip, from hip to thigh.

Once more, she tried to dislodge his hands, but they were firmly planted and would not budge.

"I am clean, MacLeod," she said between clenched teeth, trying to dismiss the sudden feeling of warmth where his fingers explored, then lingered.

"Oh? So you wish me to move on to another spot?"

He almost laughed at her quick nod. She glared at him when he did.

Did the man have a thing for water, she wondered, trying to concentrate on something other than the placement of his hands. It was not easy, this detachment. Her face grew flushed, but it was simply the heat of her bathwater, it was not his closeness and the intimate, stroking position of his hands. His mouth licked the outline of her ear, and then swooped to caress the heated scent of her neck.

She closed her eyes.

She certainly did not mean to lean back against him, allowing him to place small, sucking kisses against the side of her neck. Nor did she intend to lift suddenly weak hands to stroke his arms and feel the texture of his sun-darkened skin against her palms.

"You no longer need to be stoic, Judith," he said, a light rasp to his voice. "I'll never let you be hurt again."

"Then cease, MacLeod," she said faintly, her voice not as strong as she would have wished, her tone not as forceful.

"Do you truly wish me to?" he murmured, his lips sliding over her shoulder.

She did not answer him, which was response enough.

His fingers combed through the silken curls nestled between her thighs, his thumbs parted the folds of her submerged skin and delved even further. She was startled by his touch, would have raised up in the water, but he held her imprisoned by his mouth, by the gentle nip of his teeth at her neck.

"It's all right, sweet," he whispered. His arms rested on either side of her breasts, lifting them up so that her nipples peeked through the soapy water. She sank back against him, not protesting when he touched her ear with the tip of his tongue and breathed words that would have embarrassed her at another time.

This was not another time, this was now, and she was without thought or reason or logic as his fingers spread her wide and entered her. She could do no more than feel as he stroked her with hands that were suddenly too knowing, too experienced.

Her head twisted away from him, her eyes were tightly shut, but she was more aware of him than she'd ever been before. The feel of his lips on her neck, his tongue dancing lightly against the line of her jaw, the sinewy muscles of his arms as they rested against her breasts, the long fingers that were sending darts of feeling spiraling through her body as an indefinable ache began somewhere deep and dark. He removed one hand from her slippery wetness and cupped her breast, gently pulling on an engorged nipple. He began to whisper to her, provocative words that echoed the feelings inside of her that were straining for something, something.

"Please," she said finally, when she could bear it no longer.

"Not yet." He nuzzled her neck and stroked her breasts with gentle, teasing motions.

He returned his fingers to that one spot that was so swollen and distended. He moved his body slightly, turning her chin so that he could reach her open lips. He kissed her then, tasting her passion as the feeling overwhelmed her, slowly licking her lips, their corners when she arched and shuddered. He slid his hands to her breasts, widening his fingers so that her nipples slid between them. He drew them out, slowly, his lips still fastened on hers, her hands clenching his wrists as if he were a lifeline.

Her head dropped weakly to the back of the tub and he smiled. She opened her eyes, and he saw the widened pupils, the lambent look, and his smile broadened.

"Is this the way the Scots bathe?" she asked, her smile lighting the midnight blue of her eyes.

He grinned as he lifted her from the tub, then gently dried her, then tucked her into one side of the bed and lowered himself to the other. She did not even mind the faint chuckle that she heard, as he hauled her close to him.

"You Scots have odd customs, MacLeod."

"You don't care for the practice?" One eyebrow winged heavenward and a knowing glint in his eyes made her turn her face into the pillow.

He laughed, that great barking laugh that filled the room. Extending one arm, he pulled her close.

"Would you like to hear the story of the Picts and heather ale?" he said, absently stroking her hair back from her face.

"Tell your story, MacLeod," she said, feeling as if every muscle in her body had gone limp. It could have been the hot bath, but she suspected it was due more to the MacLeod's ministrations.

She allowed him to cuddle her closer.

"Well," he began, "I've already told you that the Romans came to the Highlands, but they couldn't subdue the Picts. However, another tribe of people, probably another branch of the first Scots, decided to have a try. They had heard the story of the mystic heather ale, which had a rare and wonderful bouquet, a sweet and tangy taste, far superior to the brew we know today. The secret was passed from the king of the Picts down to his firstborn son, which is how the secret was kept for so many years. The king of the Scots captured the king of the Picts and demanded to know the secret. The king said that he would tell him, but only if he killed his son first. For he meant that the secret would never be known, you see. There is a verse about it, too.

> *My son ye maun kill,*
> *Before you I will tell*
> *How we brew the yill*
> *Frae the heather bell!*"

Judith stirred, thinking that this was a strange bedtime story. Alisdair only nuzzled her closer, and continued.

"The king of the Scots complied, murdering the young man. When he returned to the king of the Picts, having killed his son, he demanded again to know the secret. The king of the Picts just looked at him calmly, replying that he could kill him now, because the secret would never be known:

> *And though ye may kill,*
> *I winna you tell*
> *How we brew the yill*
> *Frae the heather bell!*

And that's how the secret died, and why the ale we brew today is only a puny replica of the original. Did you like the story?"

"I think it mirrors Scotland well, MacLeod," Judith said wryly. "Bloodthirsty, stubborn, and stupid."

"Ah, but Judith," he said softly, "we can also be loyal and brave. Cunning and quick." He raised himself up, peering down into her face. "We value courage and reward honor." He bent to kiss her lips, a soft and gentle kiss.

He held her in his arms until she slept. She did not

dream of long shadows and torture, nor had she since the first time she'd slept beside him. He wondered if she realized that, or that she cuddled next to him in her sleep, all warm and soft and inviting.

Chapter 25

"You'll do just fine, Meggie," Judith explained patiently for the fifth time. "Your greatest danger will be in falling asleep, not in being a bad shepherdess," she said, in an effort to reassure her. There were no natural predators around Tynan. Wild dogs did not seem to be a problem, and the Highlands were too isolated for poachers.

Meggie reluctantly followed Judith up the path worn into the hillside by a hundred sheep over the past weeks. Her look was grim, as if she were walking to the gallows, rather than assuming her new chore.

The few young men who could have been spared to shepherd were needed at other occupations which required strength, like harvesting the huge nets strung at the entrance to the cove, or helping to build new dwellings. The elders of the clan, those old men who sat outside their cottages and commented on the comings and goings of everything and everyone, had balked at being sequestered on a hilltop with nothing but sheep as company. Therefore, the women took turns on the hills, ensuring that the sheep didn't stray too far from MacLeod holdings.

"None of the new lambs will be born until next spring,"

Judith said, "and by that time, you'll be an old master with sheep. I wouldn't be at all surprised if you were not Tynan's resident animal midwife by then."

To the left, Judith could see Tynan, perched like the sentinel it was, guarding the MacLeods. Perhaps it was not black and brooding now, but it was just as ugly, just as ruined as the day she first saw it. But nearly everything else had changed, hadn't it?

Meggie still wore that look of unrepentant unwillingness, but at least she was no longer chuckling about Judith's encounter with Fiona, an episode that brought a blush to Judith's cheek even now.

One moment, the two women were walking up the track, the next, Judith had grabbed Meggie by the arm and was roughly jerking her down into the waist-high moor grass. Meggie's mouth was open to loudly protest Judith's actions, when she glanced past her friend's suddenly stricken face.

At the top of the hill, set in bold relief, their tunics a crimson slash against a gray Highland sky, were six mounted British soldiers. All but one of them controlled his mount with ease. The sixth held a squirming lamb, who in its fright was causing him no end of grief, not to mention the caterwauling sounds it gave off to signal its mother.

Meggie glanced at Judith, who motioned for quiet, one finger to her lips, her eyes never straying from the mounted patrol. With her left hand, she pointed to her left, to a gouge carved into the earth as if a giant had scooped it free with a huge spoon. The embankment above it, only two feet wide and weed-choked, was the only place to hide on the whole hillock. Any second now, the English soldiers would cease their torturing of the hapless lamb and might chance to glance down the hill.

She and Meggie edged slowly to their left, cautious that movement alone would signal their presence. The sound of panicked bleating became more audible, but there was nothing they could do. The lamb would be slaughtered, if not the entire flock. Even in the best of times, however, two lone women were no match for six men. This was a scant three years after Culloden, and those were English soldiers.

Bennett Henderson led them. His blond hair was a beacon, drawing Judith's attention to the thin, aquiline face, the cold blue eyes, the thin lips curled into a smile as he watched one of his men sever the lamb's tail with a flick of his wrist and a wickedly sharp dagger.

All the English had to do was move five feet in either direction, and they could easily spot the two women cowering below them. Tynan was a long way away, and no men worked these deserted hills where the sheep roamed freely. Their only chance was to remain silent and hope the English patrol passed them by, that the only cruelty they showed this day was for a poor animal.

They reached the relative safety of the embankment, the sight of the soldiers blocked from view by the same gorse-choked earth that might save them. Judith shivered, crossed her arms around her stomach, pressing her back against the concave earth, almost as if she wished to press herself into it.

This was a nightmare, revisited and sunlit. In her dreams, she could never outlast him, never escape him. Judith could only pray reality did not mirror her dreams.

The sound of the lamb's distress was growing louder. So, too, the masculine laughter that punctuated it. Judith put her hands over her ears and turned, pressing the side of her face into the earthen bank, absorbing the smell of it, the cleanness of it, the rightness of it. If she trembled, she held herself too tightly to feel it, pacing the moments by the feverish beat of her heart, by her shallow, open-mouthed breaths. She willed herself to be anywhere but here, with Bennett no more than fifty feet away.

Meggie, beside her, was just as still, her own panic fueled by the stark terror on Judith's face.

There was silence now. The birds did not call, the waves ceased their rolling to shore, the gentle bleating of the sheep had ceased. It was as if everything were waiting. An eternity of time measured in long, breathless moments. For discovery or freedom?

It was to be discovery.

Judith saw the sleeve of his tunic first, just as she pushed Meggie from the gorse-choked earth and downwards toward Tynan.

"Run, Meggie, run!" Her voice sounded raw, as if a scream were trapped against her throat.

Meggie, damn her, did not move, frozen into immobility by the sight of the five soldiers who surrounded her, their grins enlivened by anticipation. She slowly backed away from them, careful steps accompanied by wide-eyed fear.

Judith wanted to scream at her, shout, beat her hands against the other woman's back. Anything to get her to move, to make her feet pound against the track, to force her to run for shelter, protection! But a hand gloved in leather was clamped cruelly against Judith's mouth, an arm rigid in its strength was pulling her inexorably back against a male body she knew too well. Her struggles were futile, her kicking found nothing but air.

"Sweet Judith," Bennett Henderson said, his breath upon her cheek oddly fresh and smelling of mint. It should have been fetid and foul. "I have missed you. Dare I tell you how much?"

Judith closed her eyes against his words, against the sight of the men approaching Meggie. They laughed and taunted her with promises of what would happen next.

Please God. What a useless prayer. How many nights had she prayed that worthless prayer?

"Shall we watch, dearest Judith? Although it was Anthony's bent, more than mine. Tell me, dearest," Bennett said, his hand inching down her bodice, cupping the softness he found there with the most gentle of touches, "have you missed our little soirees?"

The arm tightened against her throat as she pulled away, the red wool abraded her skin, her words of loathing muffled behind a leather-gauntleted hand.

Meggie's screams lanced the air, sharp, shrill. Judith

struggled again, but it was as if she were moving against air, there was nothing she could do to hurt her attacker. That was the most horrible part of it all. If she could have inflicted any pain, however small, it would have made her feel less powerless, less a victim. Her blows, however, were ineffectual; her struggles were as impotent as praying to God for relief.

Bennett turned her in the direction where Meggie now lay, her skirts around her waist, her legs held apart by two of the men. A third pumped rhythmically into her while scratching her breasts, freed from her ripped bodice. Another soldier held her arms while she struggled, one other waited impatiently for his companion to finish. A section of her own petticoat had been ripped and thrust into her mouth, but it was not enough to totally silence Meggie's frantic cries.

"You are next, sweet," Bennett said, pushing his arousal against her back. "I'm not a selfish man, I share what I have."

Hate was too small a word to hold all the feelings Bennett's touch invoked. If emotions had colors, the rage she felt would be bloody black, the color of witch's sabbaths, unholy practice, and congealed blood. Could it be possible to live with so much rage? And how impotent this feeling. How empty her hate. It could not save Meggie. It would not protect her.

It was, strangely, the sheep which saved Judith. The lamb's cries had alerted its mother, which had parted from the flock in search of her lost offspring. The flock, more than willing to follow anything at its head, had swung off from their determined trek across the moors. It was as if a giant sea of white undulated over the short grass.

"Get your mind back where it should be, laddie," Malcolm said with a none too gentle push. He had stood on the top of the ladder handing thatch up to the MacLeod for what seemed like hours, and now the man had his sights not turned on the nearly completed roof, but on the rise of land near Tynan. There was a frown of concentration on the MacLeod's face.

"Malcolm," he said, the tone of his voice sharp and oddly urgent, "did we ever finish the fence near the southeast pasture?"

"I've only got two hands, lad," Malcolm said, grunting under the weight of the thatch, "it's on my list of chores to do." He dropped the thatch onto the ground below.

"Well," Alisdair said, moving across the front of the roof in preparation for descent, "unless we get there first, it looks like the sheep will harvest those fields before we get a chance."

The mere mention of danger to the food supply was a great motivator with Malcolm, who in turn rallied the rest of the building crew.

The English soldiers, brave and dauntless when accosting two women, chose not to confront thirty angry Highlanders armed with timbers and hammers.

They were too late, however, to save Meggie.

Chapter 26

"How is she, today, Alisdair?" Judith asked in a low tone, careful not to disturb the sleeping occupant of the bed. She looked down at the huddled form of her friend under the bedcovers and wanted to weep. Again.

Judith had spent the last two weeks here, in Ian's room converted for Meggie's use. The stairs were too steep for Sophie to climb and Malcolm did not intrude. Here, she was not subjected to the contempt of the clan, and Alisdair had become only physician, not husband.

Meggie was turned into herself, into a place so deep and so dark that Judith wondered if she would ever return from the journey.

"No better and no worse, I'm afraid," Alisdair answered quietly. He didn't know if Meggie would heal. Body, yes, but mind? How did he tell that to Judith? When Meggie slept, it was too deep, an abyss that ended in horrible nightmares, from which she surfaced with high-pitched screams and flailing arms. She reminded him too much of Judith, of that void into which he could never reach, never help her heal. Awake, Meggie lay wide-eyed in Ian's bed, staring up at the ceiling as if the Holy Writ were engraved there. She didn't speak, nor did it appear that she heard his words or Judith's coaxing entreaties.

Alisdair's intent gaze fixed upon his wife both with a physician's eye and a husband's concern. The incident in the glen had affected more than just Meggie.

His fists clenched as he recalled the scene upon the hillside. His breath had nearly stopped when he had come over the rise and seen Meggie being raped and Judith entrapped in another soldier's arms. The English had mounted their horses with a speed he'd damned them for. Alisdair had nearly reached their leader when Bennett Henderson had spurred that stallion from hell and escaped his reach. He wanted to go after the mounted soldiers, despite the fact they were English and only English justice prevailed in the Highlands now. He wanted to kill the men who had dared touch his wife and raped one of his clanswomen. Yet, he was prevented by law from arming his people, prevented by the lack of horseflesh from chasing after the English patrol, prevented by his nationality from demanding justice.

English justice did not extend to inhabitants of Scotland.

Alisdair remembered too well how he'd found his wife. Judith remained frozen against the embankment, her eyes fixed upon Meggie, who lay sprawled on the grass like a broken and discarded doll.

Judith had flinched when he gently laid a hand upon her arm.

"They've gone, Judith," he said, his face a study in worry. Long moments later, she stirred, stepping away from the indentation in the earth she had created in her terror. She would have willingly crawled into an open grave to avoid Bennett Henderson.

Alisdair extended an arm around her shoulders, hugged her tightly against him until her trembling eased a little. He carried her to a small clutch of stones not far from the hillock, while Meggie was covered and slowly borne to Tynan. There was a muttering of angry voices and Alisdair pulled his wife tighter into his arms, so that she was concealed from prying eyes and vicious words.

Her nationality was not to blame. English or Scot, this was an act of cruelty, of the strong victimizing the weak. It was not one of borders, of politics, or one nation against another. It was man against woman.

He held Judith until her tremors began to subside. Only then did he raise her in his arms and carry her gently home.

Judith had not spoken of that day since, but in her eyes was a despair as evident as their azure color. Her face was drawn and taut, she'd lost weight. Because he was so attuned to her, because he had once won the battle of overcoming her fear, Alisdair recognized the depths of her retreat. Although she did not shrink from his touch, she had gone to that other place in her mind, a place where nightmares were the only constant.

For that, he damned the English.

"Did she eat today, then?"

"A little broth, a few scraps of bread. Not very much." He arranged the coverings over Meggie and stepped back from the bed.

Judith stood so still, so tightly held within her own composure, that she appeared as brittle, and as breakable, as glass. Could anyone touch her? As a man, could he ever reach her? He felt unwanted and superfluous, both as a physician and as a husband. Even as laird, he could do nothing. The knowledge clawed at him with a hundred talons.

Alisdair could do no more than what he did now, extend his arms around his wife, imparting wordless comfort and an offer of refuge while she stood rigid and unmoving within his embrace.

He placed a soft and passionless kiss upon her forehead, then moved to the door. "Time is all she needs," he said, wanting to say something to dispel the look in Judith's eyes.

Judith accepted his words the same way she would have

accepted a bouquet of poison ivy from a child, with kindness and tenderness, appreciating the sentiment, if not the gift. Alisdair didn't understand, not truly, but the words sounded well meaning and caring.

Time. Such a pleasant notion. As if time alone could salve some wounds. As if time would matter a tinker's damn. The clicking of a clock altered nothing. Oh, outward wounds healed, bruises faded, bones knitted. But what about the other wounds, less readily apparent, just as deep, just as painful? They ate away at the soul.

Judith stared out at the sea.

Time.

It was a panacea held out to the despairing. Get through today and tomorrow will be better. But when tomorrow was no better, hope was held out in the other hand. The day after will be much better than today. And on and on and on until time became only a way to measure misery. And the blinding expectation that it would one day cease became only a small pulsating light in the star-filled heavens. A small star to wish upon. Please, God, make it better.

Time would not heal this wound.

Judith knew it better than anyone.

Time would do nothing but dull the sense of invasion, it would not erase it. It would not negate the knowledge that her body had betrayed her by its very receptiveness. As if she could have sealed it up to prevent the intrusion. Time would not mitigate the sick horror of being violated in spirit as well as in flesh. Of being unable to prevent it. Of living through it.

She sat on the edge of the bed and looked at Meggie's pale face.

"Have you ever seen evil, Meggie?" she asked in a calm, dispassionate voice, as though her listener were awake. On some level, however, she knew Meggie heard; the only reason she knew was that she had been as Meggie was right now. She slept, but it was not sleep she craved as much as the opiate of oblivion. After a while, the body had rested enough, but the mind remained in a white cloud of almost wakefulness, prevented from rousing by a wounded soul.

The torpor was never quite deep enough.

So Judith gave her friend the only gift that might help. The truth.

"I know the face of it well," Judith said softly, looking down at her hands. They were entwined with each other, normal hands, if a bit wear-worn and red. There was a scratch on her thumb where a splinter had pierced the skin. Alisdair had washed it with something that had burned, while he'd lectured her on the dangers of open wounds. As if she'd not known.

The words Judith spoke were halting, their slow cadence came not from reluctance as much as a sense of being dredged from the bottom of a pit. Once she had a nightmare of falling down, down into blackness, tumbling into a deep, bottomless void—nothing to reach for, nothing to hold onto, nothing to stop that endless fall. The poisonous shame she felt about herself lived in that endless well, a night creature slithering away from light, exposure. It was not an easy thing to speak the words, to tell the tale. She spoke of herself in the third person, as if Judith were the name of a woman she knew, a close friend. As if the story had not happened to her, but to someone else, some poor creature who should now only be pitied.

After a while, her voice lost its plodding quality and Judith forget to say "she" instead of "I." Instead of a monotone, grief began to tinge her voice, her speech was higher, more finely honed. A deep need to swallow stopped her for a few moments and it was tears she drank down, unknown and unaware. They splashed against her face, too, inner nature's rain. It was the first time she'd ever told the entire story to anyone. Her marriage to Anthony, her terror at learning what kind of union she'd been tied to, Bennett, and the fear he brought to the once simple and ordinary occurrence of nightfall.

When Meggie's eyes opened, fixed upon the face of her

friend, Judith was unaware, as trapped in the telling of the story as she'd been living it.

"Anthony first introduced me to his brother the night we arrived in London. It seemed that Anthony and Bennett were very close, had always shared things. Little things like shirts, cravats, boots. Then, bigger things like horses, careers, whores. And then a wife."

Anthony especially like to watch Bennett strike her, whipping her until the blood flowed freely. Bennett enjoyed her screams more than a stunned and docile acceptance. She had been the plaything for his restless nights, when the barmaids or tavern wenches were either unavailable, too highly priced, or boring in their mute response to his cruelty. She had been the victim of his experiments in pain.

"The first time, they had to tie me down. The second time, they simply force fed me enough brandy. Maybe it was the fifth time, I don't know, but all they had to do was tie me loosely. I wouldn't have escaped by then. I was too disgusted about what they had done to my body, to my mind, that I could barely show my face in the light of day. I could not bear to share the sunlight with others. Whenever I chanced to meet someone's eyes, I was the one who looked away. I was too dirty."

Judith had thought, at first, that she would die from it. She had even prayed for death as her husband helped tie her to the bed willingly, eagerly, watching with enthusiasm as she was brutally raped. Her nights were filled with terror, days encircled in numbness, aching shame. But she did not die. The body did not expire that quickly; the spirit succumbed much easier.

Her fingers loosened their death grip upon themselves, her eyes raised to the open window. "Part of me just closed; my humanness, I think. I wasn't a person anymore, I was no more important than a thing, like a candle, or a chair. I wouldn't let myself feel anything when it was happening."

One terrible morning, Judith came too close to losing herself, becoming like the poor demented creatures at St.

Mary of Bethlehem Hospital. She was alone in the house, the silence of it surrounding her like a cloud. Instead of rising at dawn, she'd remained in her chamber, sitting in the middle of the bed, her arms crossed over the top of her head, rocking back and forth endlessly, the sounds from her lips that of the keening of some poor trapped animal in desperate pain. It was almost as if she were not in her body anymore, but floating nearby, powerless to silence herself, or heal her mind. For most of the morning, she remained like this, until sanity returned, a drop at a time.

She had been too much like Meggie, trapped in a world of no thoughts, no memories, simply experiencing an endless white fog that cushioned pain and despair. Yet, she discovered that that world demanded too much in order to become a lifelong inhabitant. Into this whiteness, this blankness, had come a spark, a chance to survive, an opportunity to overcome. Hope, itself.

From that day on, Judith planned.

"Forgive me, Meggie. Forgive me, for bringing you pain. For bringing him here."

Because of her, Meggie had been raped. Because of her, Alisdair was in danger. Because of her, the clan was in peril. She had, unknowingly and certainly unwillingly, brought danger to the Highlands, in its most odious form—true evil. An evil which had not altered despite place or time. It remained the same, an asp in a basket, ready to strike when the lid was raised.

"How did ye' escape?" Malcolm's voice came from far away. Judith turned to find him standing in the doorway, his scowl replaced by features carefully wiped clean of any emotion. Any other time, she'd have felt an aching shame that he'd heard her story. Now, that emotion was simply buried beneath the guilt and grief she felt.

Judith smiled, a sad-tipped smile that Malcolm found particularly hard to bear, especially since she looked straight at him, her Loch eyes betraying not a ripple.

What would Malcolm say if she told him the truth, that

the final indignity had been hers, the final barbarism had not been Anthony's, nor Bennett's, but her own?

She had endured the brutality until she no longer fought, and it was that very submission that had finally pummeled through to her brain and compelled her to survive. It had taken a year to grow the little plant with its silvery leaves—a year in which to hoard enough of the precious buds and grind them into powder. That night, she'd basted the roasted chicken with her poisonous nature.

Murderess.

She had never forgotten Bennett's whisper to her in the courtyard.

But Malcolm would not understand. Would anyone?

"He died," she said, simply.

When she'd stepped away from the stiff and cold figure of her husband and watched as the lid was nailed upon his wooden casket, not all of her relief was due to Anthony's death. King George II had done her a favor, too, by posting Bennett's regiment far away.

Into Scotland, and she'd not known.

Chapter 27

Sophie roused slowly, her dreams having more substance than the present day. She blinked several times until they slowly faded. They had been too real, these recollections, too filled with the faces and the voices of those who no longer lived. She sighed, feeling the pain again, as if losing them once more.

She waved away the plate Judith offered.

"No, child, I am not hungry."

Sophie looked pale, with splotches of red upon her face. Judith bent and kissed her brow, feeling the papery dryness of the woman's skin.

Judith returned the plate to the kitchen. She'd taken a tray to Meggie's room, but her friend had only turned away when she'd offered it. Still, she'd left the food.

The hours Meggie slept had become fewer, her waking hours spent staring out the window. Still, she did not speak. Silence could both heal and imprison, Judith knew. It was Meggie's decision which it would be. They'd not spoken of Judith's confession a week ago. Occasionally, Meggie's eyes would meet hers and there would be questions in their depths, but they were left unasked.

Judith returned to Sophie's room with a basin of warm water and would have assisted the woman from her gown, a French confection of black, inset with rusty lace, but Sophie waved her away.

"I've plenty of time to sleep, child," she said with a smile. "It is time with you I lack. I should spend my remaining hours with those I love, not dozing like a cat in the sun."

Judith had no answer to such words. There was much about the Highlands that she could live without, but not Sophie's kindness and gentleness. What would she do without her?

"Is anyone still in the kitchen?" Sophie asked, straightening her legs painfully.

"Alisdair is helping with a difficult lambing." Malcolm had not shared their meal since the day he learned of her past.

Strangely enough, he had not repeated what he'd heard at Meggie's bedside. Judith had expected him to gloat of his knowledge of the depths of her degradation, waited for him to spread the story throughout the glen, but he'd evidently said nothing.

She, herself, had not waited for the clan to ease their condemnation of her. Every day for the last week, she'd gone to the weaver's hut, one of the twins her escort on Alisdair's orders. Every day, she was shunned by the women, who knew she went to weave, to sit behind the clacking old loom and hum softly to herself while pretending her meager labor would make a difference. It wouldn't, and everyone knew it. But it was a testament to her stubbornness, and theirs, that they continued to play this little game each day.

Judith wished she could say that her hours alone in the weaving shed gave her something to think about other than Meggie. It would be a lie. The endless solitude, the rhythmic noise of the loom became second nature, and only guilt occupied her thoughts. What emotions remained were apportioned for the MacLeod.

"Come, child, for these old bones are telling me that I may not have much time."

Judith placed her hand underneath Sophie's elbow and helped her to rise. Sophie smiled her thanks. She retrieved the candle from its holder beside the bed and held it out for Judith.

"I have something to show you, child. You are the only one who can make a promise to me. The one I trust most to protect Alisdair when I'm no longer here."

"Nonsense," Judith said, with a faint attempt at heartiness. "You will probably outlive us all, Granmere."

"This is not the time to humor an old woman, child," Sophie said firmly, leaning a little on Judith. "I see death at my door each night, and bid him wait until the morrow before he summons me. He sits upon my bedstead during the long hours and counts my breaths. I cannot see the future, Judith, but I can feel it. What I feel tells me that there is little time left."

Again, Judith had no answer for her words, she could only assist the woman from the room and follow where that imperious cane pointed.

It took them much longer than it would have a month ago, because of Sophie's waning strength. The only assistance Judith could offer was not to argue as she was led through the darkened courtyard and into the deserted keep.

Their two horses were contentedly munching on feed stored in what looked to have been a baptismal font. The room bore little resemblance to its former function as family chapel. The darkening sky peeped through the top of the tower, smoke stains marred the gutted interior. Something which looked like mildew, but smelled worse, grew latticelike upon the inner walls. Only the altar remained intact, a stone edifice too large to have been torn down, its altar pieces melted to molten and twisted lumps of metal. It now served only as a storage shelf. The room stunk of animals and dampness and the lingering odor of burnt cloth. Not even the flooring had been spared. The colored tiles were chipped badly in places, and severely gouged in others. It was a scene of degradation and ruin that marked the rest of Tynan Castle.

Sophie stopped and motioned for Judith to unlatch the heavy oak door leading to the other tower. She did, pushing the bar aside.

They stood in the deserted circular room, bare except for the hay piled upon the floor, alone in the company of spiders and industrious mice. Judith fervently hoped that nothing else lurked there in the cover of darkness, that the candle would last as long as it was needed, that the sputter she heard was not a herald of total darkness.

"Close the door, child," Sophie said, leaning weakly against one wall. She looked at the window, then the broad expanse of the hay-strewn floor. Judith wondered if she were getting her bearings. Why were they here?

"I feel the burden of my secret," Sophie whispered, acutely conscious that the sound circled the room and seemed to bounce back against them. "I would divulge it to you this night, before death robs me of my voice." She turned to Judith, but all that she could see of her was the shadowy outline of her pale face. The lone candle did little to illuminate either the room or its occupants.

"Do you swear," Sophie said in a voice that echoed solemnly in the empty room, like a ghostly voice in a sepulcher, "to never speak of what you see this night to anyone outside of the clan MacLeod?"

Judith nodded, bemused by the ceremonious and grave nature of Sophie's request.

"Then come, Judith," Sophie said, satisfied.

She shuffled to the wall upon which the high window was mounted, and walked slowly back to the door. Judith was not sure, but it looked as though the older woman was counting her steps. When Sophie summoned her, she knelt to where her cane pointed and began to shift the rushes from the floor. There, hidden by the matted hay, barely visible in the gloom, was an iron ring. Sophie stepped back, pleased. So, she had truly remembered.

" 'Tis the opening, Judith. Pull upon the ring, and we shall see what awaits us.''

Judith did what she was told, which was more difficult than expected. The door was cut from the same stone which made up the keep. Long moments later, she had finally lifted it a few inches from the ground. She placed both hands beneath it, and with a strength she had not known she possessed, flung the door away from its opening. It fell open with a thud, the sound only partially muted by the hay. She and Sophie looked at each other, and then stood waiting. There were no sounds of rushing feet, no one came to investigate.

Sophie handed her the candle and urged her down the steps. By the glow of the flickering light, Judith could see the lines of worry etched upon the older woman's face, and it was this concern, coupled with Granmere's flagging energy, which propelled her down the steps. They were carved into the earth, no more than a few downward sloping niches wet with dampness.

At first, the well exposed by the door was only a darkened pit. It was not until she reached the bottom step, when she lifted the candle, that Judith realized what she was seeing. Glints of metal and shining things transformed themselves into claymores, dirks, ancient broadswords arrayed in long lines, only their hilts showing, their blades protected from the damp by the plaid of the MacLeod. On a rough shelf built into the side of the hidden cave, stood the rusted shields of a hundred long-dead ancestors. Near the bottom stood silver porringers, pitchers now almost black with tarnish, cutlery that gleamed brightly in the light of the candle. Off to the right sat the etched glass which belonged in the windows of the Lord's room. Almost at her feet sat a strange collection of long, round wooden reeds, with holes along their lengths and attached to a sunken bag.

She knew exactly what she was looking at.

The treasure of the MacLeods. It was not the silver or the etched glass, or even the buried plaid or the presence of the pipes that would cause disaster to the clan MacLeod. It was the existence of the hoard of weapons arrayed with more care than the other valuables. The sight lingered in her mind long after she had emerged from the dirt room, handed the candle back to Sophie, and as quietly as possible, lowered the stone door back into place.

"Why?" was the only question she could think of. Her only thought was the memory of the English soldiers, their presence in the courtyard, only a few feet from this room.

"There are those in the clan, child, who would wish a return to the old days. To days of glory," Sophie said sadly. "Perhaps my grief allowed me to believe that their dreams had substance. Perhaps, though, I was simply a foolish old woman. When they came to me, I showed them this place, and now its contents threaten my peace. I would ask one more thing from you, child," she told Judith somberly.

In the darkness of the keep, amid the flickering shadows created by the lone candle, Sophie carefully instructed the young woman she had come to know and love in her last request. Judith listened, and nodded, and although her heart beat quickly in her chest and her breath halted as she heard, finally she agreed.

Sophie placed her hand upon Judith's cheek and then bent with a fragile gesture and placed dry lips against the warm skin of the younger woman.

"It is not an easy thing I've asked of you, child. I know this."

"I will help if I can. But they may not listen to me."

"They will listen, Judith. They will know I would never have trusted you without cause."

"Why have you?"

"You would ask why, Judith? Because of the look in your eyes when you see my grandson. Because of the smile on your lips when you think no one is looking. Because your cheeks flush when he announces that it is late and time for bed, and yet, your eyes light up with expectation and eagerness. That is why, child. Because of the great goodness of your heart and your capacity to love."

"How do I know if I can love, Granmere? How does anyone?" There was a world of pain in her voice, Sophie thought, a world of disillusionment.

Sophie cupped her hand around Judith's cheek. Her voice was soft, her smile as misty as Judith's. "When you wake in the morning and anticipate the day, Judith, or ache to talk with the one special person in your life, when circumstances no longer look hopeless, when things can happen this side of miracles, you'll recognize that love has changed it all. There is a promise to love, Judith, something bright and sparkling and as brilliant as the most radiant of stars. Look for the promise, my child, and you'll recognize love.

"I bless the day you rode into our courtyard, my child," Sophie said softly. "Are you happy to have come to our land?"

"I hadn't much choice," Judith said ruefully.

"And what would you say if given that choice, now?"

There was silence, a lengthy uncomfortable one, in which Judith pondered the danger she'd brought to Alisdair and the clan MacLeod. She could not think of love. How could she ever render herself worthy enough for it?

"Do not fight against love when it comes to you, child," Sophie said gently when the younger woman didn't answer. "Alisdair needs your love. He will especially need it when I am gone."

Judith hugged the older woman. Although Sophie felt so frail and tiny, she seemed to glow with vibrant life.

"Do not plan to leave me so soon, Granmere," Judith said softly, feeling her eyes mist over again. "I may need more advice."

"Whatever God wills, child," Sophie said, smiling gently. "Remember, always, that I loved you as if you were my own child. My love will be with you and Alisdair long after my bones have become mixed with the earth of Tynan."

How could anyone love her, knowing the truth?

Chapter 28

The candles flickered in the darkness, casting long shadows in the room.

Judith hugged herself against the chill and stared into the black opening of the massive fireplace in the laird's room. Its cavernous depths could hold a six-foot length of tree trunk, but now it lay bare and cold; the last fire blazing in this room had been the one sparked by the Duke of Cumberland's troops.

But Judith wasn't thinking about her ties to the Duke's army, of Bennett or Anthony. She was thinking of Granmere's words in the keep, of the duty she'd asked of Judith, of words spoken about love.

Alisdair thought her smile sad and strange. He had been right, those months ago, to think that this Englishwoman would bedevil him. She charmed him, too, promising secrets not quite revealed and hints of passion never quite released. He'd suspected much about this accidental bride of his, but he hadn't realized that he would wish to protect her, that one of her uncommon smiles would cause a rush of joy through his veins.

Since Meggie's rape, he'd been careful of his wife, recognizing in her a great and borderless grief she would not share with him. Did she think him so unaware that he would not know? All anyone need do was look into her eyes, see the old pain there, and know that what had happened to Meggie had once happened to Judith. It made it all so clear, the nightmares, the stifled screams, the terror. It was more than a bad marriage Judith feared, but a man's domination itself.

"I'd not thought you the type to seek out self-punishment, myself," he said now, brushing aside his rage for gentle humor. "It is a cold place, our room."

She looked at him over her shoulder, met his smile with a small one of her own.

"Are you practicing for winter, then?" he asked, noting her shivers and the fact that both her arms were wrapped around herself. The breeze from the open window was not chilly to a Scot, but raw to one accustomed to English climes.

"I'm not sure I can take one of your winters, MacLeod," Judith confessed. "I'm nearly freezing now."

"Then, let me warm you," he coaxed, coming up behind her and putting his arms around her, holding her fiercely in a tight embrace. It was the first time in a long time she'd accepted his touch, and he was not going to let her go so easily.

So a bear must feel, she thought whimsically, as she leaned back against his chest. His head nuzzled the top of her chin, and for a perfect moment, they stood, untouched by the cares of the day, unaware of the half-burned room, each immersed in thoughts of the other.

"Did the lambing go well?"

"We have yet another wool producer, my sweet. All matted and wet and bleating like hell for its mam."

He thought she smelled of open air and rare English roses, that her hair was as soft as the downy thatch on Douglas's head, that her skin was like satin against his callused palms.

Judith melted into his tenderness, an emotion she would

not have ascribed to another living male. But the MacLeod was a different sort of man, wasn't he? This was the same man whose hand effortlessly assisted Geddes up a steep set of stairs, or who lifted Douglas until he shouted with glee.

She cared for this man, in a way that surpassed anything she'd ever felt before. When he coughed in the night, it woke her, and she would lay there for long seconds before falling back to sleep herself, calmed that he was not suffering from the ague or from some other swift and deadly illness. When he sweated, as his large body was wont to do under even a thin sheet, she checked him for fever, as though he were no older than a two-year-old child. She cosseted him, protected him, nurtured him, and if those gestures went no further than her mind, at least there, she could fuss and flutter and be concerned and none would know.

She wanted to hold Alisdair within her arms, kiss his broad back, and trace words of possession upon his warm, bare skin. The depth of her emotions scared her, as Anthony had never been able to frighten her. As Bennett, despite his attempts, had never accomplished.

But was that what Granmere called love? Judith didn't know. How could you recognize it, if you've never experienced it before?

Judith suspected that to love Alisdair MacLeod was to surrender herself. To trust, wholly and completely. To believe in goodness and right, nobility and honor. So easy, and so difficult for someone tinged by guilt and touched by evil.

She sighed heavily and he caught the sound, spun her in his embrace as if she were no heavier than a feather. His brandy eyes sparkled, a finger tipped her chin up so that he could inspect her face, his lips tilted in a restrained smile.

So might a wolf have looked before stalking the sheep.

"Did everyone adore Anne?"

The question so surprised Alisdair that his mind froze in mid-thought. He glanced down at his wife.

"Anne?"

"Yes, your wife."

"I'm aware of her identity, Judith," he said, irritation swamping his senses. She never did what he expected, did she? She was always full of surprises. He smiled, then, at the thought that the next twenty years would not be boring.

Judith felt something inside her twist at the tender reminiscent look. She looked down at her clenched hands and wondered why she dared to ask. Except for that one day, when he'd held her so gently upon his lap, Anne's name had not been broached between them. A picture of her had grown in Judith's mind. A gentle sweet face, filled with patience and kindness, a Madonna glow of purity around her. She would have been the beloved wife of the laird, a fitting mate.

"Anne suffered as well during the winters," he said. "Is that what you wished to know?" His forehead wrinkled in confusion.

"I never said I wanted to know anything, MacLeod."

"I'll not argue the point, Judith. I'm not yet as addled as Geddes. I heard the question. I just can't comprehend why the answer is so important to you."

"It was but a passing comment, MacLeod, as insubstantial as inquiring about the weather."

"I think not," he said, not allowing her to escape from his embrace despite her wriggling. "As far as affection, I never heard any ill words spoken of her."

"Not even from Fiona?" Judith mumbled, her forehead pressed against the great expanse of Alisdair's chest. Not for the world would she have looked up into those too knowing eyes.

"Not even Fiona," he said. The words held no mocking humor, only a depth of understanding she recognized and which made her jealousy feel childish.

"I think you would have liked Anne," Alisdair said, his wish to ease Judith's discomfort giving voice to words better left unsaid. "She was sweet and kind, with never a thought for herself. She was too gentle for life at Tynan, though, I see that now. Sometimes, I think she was too good for life at all."

It had been difficult living with a saintly wife, Alisdair remembered. Anne never spoke above a whisper, her smiles were tremulous and timid, she never reached out to touch him, or to initiate their love play. She lay docile, sacrifice not so much her aim as to retain a ladylike and demure pose while engaged in the least polite of human occupations. Yes, everyone at Tynan had loved her, but it was the gentle-natured affection of those who care for one in their midst not as strong.

Judith, for all her travails, had the soul of a survivor, not an angel.

It was a real woman who stared back at him, eyes darkened to nearly black, an unrecognizable expression molding Judith's features into a mask of perfect, polite, unrevealing restraint.

Too good for life. Not like a slightly used English wife with a soul-destroying secret. Not sweet, nor kind. Certainly not selfless. Anne would not have been racked by guilt, by a culpability that sickened her.

Who wouldn't have loved such a paragon of virtue? Who wouldn't have adored such an angelic personage? It was a wonder the MacLeod didn't have a statue erected in her honor or a shrine built with her name inscribed on it.

Saint Anne.

"Excuse me," Judith said, feeling all too human at this particular moment. Her words were clipped and very English, her tone cold as she slipped from his arms and would have escaped. Except of course, that one left the MacLeod's presence only when the MacLeod allowed it. She tugged, he pulled. She jerked, he only drew her closer. She tensed, he tumbled her onto the bed.

She lay where he placed her, not moving when he lay beside her. When his arm reached out to pull her close, she did not demur but lay stiffly against him, her head cradled reluctantly on one of his arms. His fingers idly traced a path against her temple. She sighed, a grumbling sound of surrender. He reached out one hand and twisted a tendril of her hair around his wrist.

"What is it, my little English wife?"

"Do not call me that," she said fiercely, "do not ever call me that again." Her eyes were level on his, the look direct, so filled with remorse and pain that he brought her hard against him.

"It is not your fault." His words were fierce, his tone muted, as if the room had somehow become a hallowed place where he must whisper. "For all the sins of the English, you are blameless."

Would that I were blameless, Judith thought, but the words were not spoken aloud. She was too much the coward for that. Instead, she allowed him to envelop her in his embrace, as if his warm flesh could block out the world. She snuggled closer to him, wishing that she was as pure as Anne, as gentle, as unused by life as Alisdair's first wife.

Life had used her too well.

Almost of their own will, her hands curled against his skin, seeking the tactile reassurance of him. He kissed her on the nose, a nonthreatening gesture of affection. Judith lifted her lips for a fuller kiss, leaned into him.

If Alisdair had not studied her so avidly for the past months, if he had not come to know just when those loch-shadowed eyes of hers hid what she felt and when they revealed her emotions, Alisdair would have said that Judith was feeling the same singular lust he was now experiencing, that what she wanted was mind-numbing pleasure, a respite from the world around them. But there was something more urgent in Judith's eyes than simple passion, something desperate that demanded satiation, some wild emotion which caused his heart to skitter in his chest and made him hold her even closer, an embrace comprised of fear and loss and something even more precious.

At this moment, with the silence of night falling about them, with the activity of Tynan fading belowstairs to a simple muttered goodnight greeting, a scrape of boot against a stair, the screech of the bronze doors as they were closed, Alisdair MacLeod recognized that there was a new emotion in the lexicon of his feelings. He knew its name and all its myriad facets. He appreciated its strength and its demands, but knew its rewards were worth any sacrifice. He loved Judith Cuthbertson Willoughby Henderson MacLeod, and the barbarism of it, the sheer melodramatic protectiveness of it rolled his stomach and curled his toes.

They were held together by the savagery of a kiss too quickly ended, by the tenuous bond of her hands clasping his shoulders.

And by words spoken by a man who had always been gentle, but whose tenderness brought the spiking of tears to her eyes.

"You have the softest lips, Judith," he said, and his tone made her shiver. It made her want to move her lips against that finger, capture it in her mouth, taunt him as well with words spoken as if they were the greatest truths in a voice meant to seduce.

One long callused finger touched her cheek, following the path of her skin to the edge of her nose and then to the top of her upper lip. He watched his own finger as if it had a will of its own, not empowered by his mind's wishes.

"My beautiful Judith."

She said nothing, her eyes fixed upon his mouth, upon the way he framed his words. How could a man's mouth be so alluring? How could he speak and she want to touch her tongue to the full contours of it, to taste his speech?

He rolled off the bed and removed his clothes, oblivious to the cold, to his own nakedness illuminated by candlelight.

"With that wicked smile, MacLeod, you look more like Pan than a Scots laird." She lay on her side, watching him.

"The Greek god of woods, fields, and flocks? Except that Pan had a goat's legs, horns, and ears. I prefer my own, thank you." He lay down again and pulled her fully clothed astride him. She looked down at him, at ease beneath her, hands now propped beneath his head. Without thought, she brushed back a tousled curl of black hair which fell against his forehead. Her fleeting smile made his breath catch.

She leaned down against his chest, her chin in her folded hands. Both his large hands were involved in slipping free her garments, one lace at a time, one stocking at a time, her nakedness sweetly and unabashedly accomplished inch by inch.

"I know better than to claim duties or chores," she said, to hide the fact that his fingers were tracing a pattern upon her skin that made her shiver. He could rouse a dead woman with his touch, she thought.

"Then you have learned something during your tenure in the Highlands, my love. There is nothing more important than this."

She didn't know if it was him calling her "my love" or the feel of exploring fingers which caused her flush. It prompted his gentle laughter, a teasing sound from such a large man. She squirmed and moved from him, but he only followed, his ease at changing her mind not at all surprising. She had long suspected her husband had once been a rake.

When he rooted between their bodies to grasp her hand, she did not flinch. He touched her fingers with gentle reverence, a large man who knew his own strength and yet never abused his power.

He levered her hand up to his mouth, blew gently on her palm as a stallion might nuzzle a trainer's hand. He had it backwards, did the MacLeod. It was submission from her he wanted. Trust. He wanted her to believe in him, and that she did already. What he did not understand was that she could not believe in herself.

"I can lift timbers to a rooftop, Judith," he said, refusing to look anywhere but at the palm of her hand. A hand which carried it own scars, softened over as they were by the lanolin from the sheep's fleece. "I can lift a broadsword over my head, walk for miles without tiring." He looked up, finally, at her face, and his eyes seemed licked by flames like a snifter of brandy backlit by a glowing fire. "Yet, here, in this room, in this bed, I am equal in strength to you."

"Me?"

"Did you not know that there was one place where men and women are equals?"

Nights of brutality flashed into her mind. If the words had been said by anyone but the MacLeod, she would have struck out at him, either verbally, or with her fists, so angered was she by the trite falsity of his words.

"What happened to Meggie was not lust, Judith. It had no place in passion's games." He smiled, a gentle, teasing smile, as if to tame her from her anger. His voice was so low that she leaned towards him to hear it. His breath brushed against her cheek, the warmth of it infused the air between them.

"In love, Judith, men and women are equals."

The silence was measured by the beat of her heart, a living metronome. How many seconds, minutes, eons, stretched between them before she could bear to look into those flame-tinted eyes again? How many seconds did it take to lift her gaze past that aquiline nose to those impossibly long-lashed eyes? Her heart beat steadily, faithful heart, but rapidly, as if straining to make up for the space in eternity in which all time stood still, rocked on its axis by Alisdair MacLeod and tenderness.

"This is to be shared, Judith," he said, his teasing gone, his look so direct and without artifice that it was difficult to stare full face into it, like gazing at the sun.

The air was cold against Judith's back, but she was warm everywhere else, a curiosity no doubt brought on due to Alisdair's encompassing look. He seemed fascinated with her nakedness, although there had been many times in which he'd seen her without her clothes. And his hands. Curiously tender for such large hands, his fingers explored and dipped and warmed themselves in places she'd not thought heated.

The flush which suffused her face seemed to start at her toes, he thought.

"I but await your summons, Alisdair." Judith buried her cheek on the pillow beside his face. What was he about, that he should say such things to her?

"I do not wish a dutiful wife in my bed, Judith," he whispered, leaning over to plant a gentle kiss on the shell of her ear. "I want a woman who wishes to be here, not one who ascribes it as only her wifely occupation."

"I do not see it as a duty." Her words were muffled by the pillow. His smile was pure devilment.

"Do you not?"

She raised up and frowned at him. When she didn't speak, he wondered at her stubbornness and her fear. One day, the fear would be banished. He traced a line from her chin, down her throat to her shoulder and around to the sweet curve of armpit. She shivered and he chuckled.

His fingers stroked her breast, following the edge of the curve to where it began and then finally to the straining nipple. Judith felt a tug in her middle when he licked his lips. She could feel his tongue on her flesh even before she bent forward. An arc of pure fire raced from her breast to her womb, spreading molten tongues of flame in its path.

He relinquished her breast only to cover the other one with raining kisses, unconsciously lifting himself up to meet her softness.

"I do not know what you want, Alisdair."

"I want what you want, Judith. Do what you feel like doing."

She felt like kissing him, and she did. Not the childish peck he half-expected, but a full-throated heady kiss as pungent as burgundy wine, as addictive as lust itself. Her tongue sought his, darted across the seam of his lips, demanded surrender a millisecond before he would have willingly laid down his arms. When she raised up and looked at him, her own lips were swollen and pinkish red as if she'd savored the same rich Bordeaux.

"Enjoy me, Judith. Enjoy your own power."

The idea was so ludicrous that she nearly laughed. When had she any power? Her knees brushed the edge of the mattress, and she shifted on her strange perch. At the feel of him, she frowned. He was aroused, erect, but he was doing nothing about it. Once again she met his eyes, and once again, she was the one to look away. An experimental motion on her part brought a groan to his lips.

"Do not unman me, love," he said, with a half-laugh. "Use me, but do not, I pray you, abuse me. At least not for too long a period of time."

Again that lopsided grin which made her heart beat faster.

It was an odd feeling, this. And in that moment, she realized what a gift he gave to her. Secure in his masculinity, he was ensuring she felt safe in his arms. He did not loom over her, but allowed her to set the pace. She did not take from him, he gave of his own free will. She was overcome not by his strength, but in his relinquishing of it.

His hands, however, refused to stay limply upon the curve of her waist. His fingers were particularly intrusive, dedicated and talented. They teased her at the juncture of her thighs, timid little darts of touch, fleeting and so quick she might have imagined them. They seemed to come in waves, those touches, each one successively longer, so that she grew to anticipate them and half-rose from her perch upon him that they might have greater access to her heat. He smiled at the pooling wetness, the unconscious seduction of her movements, the undulation of her body upon his, an arching rhythm to which she responded without conscious will, as if it were induced by a siren's call.

He raised his knees, creating a natural cradle for her, a saddle of flesh for her to ride. He half-rose, encouraging her movement, a rhythm she grasped, established, made her own.

She was swollen and wet, an inner rain urging passion, daring release. He held her by a grip on her thighs, watched her, head back, eyes closed, swaying to some internal beat he couldn't hear, realizing that the sound of it was female and mysterious and as inviting as sin itself. His fingers gripped her thighs, his thumbs parted her, stroked her, worked in rhythm to that music she obeyed, hoping in some purely masculine and needful way that she would not crest without him, but carry him along with her.

The passion beat was transferred effortlessly, the urge of it echoed by blood alone. He hurt with the need to be buried in her swollen depths, the head of him, arrow-shaped, flanged, scraping her internal walls. He wanted to plunge and rear like a maddened stallion. Gone was the thought of beguilement, of gentle seduction, of play. She had unleashed the monster of his lust, shocking him, and yet pleasing him in a visceral, pagan way. His mouth was wet and an answering wetness was echoed on her nipples, their petulant crowns deeply red. Again, she felt that sharp tug in her belly. His voice was unsteady, his plea reinforced in the uncontrollable thrusts of his hips against her.

Judith did not remember parting herself for him. Did not recall his entry, slick and sleek, made welcome by desire. Nor did she know that her downward plunge onto him almost made him cry aloud, so ravenous was her demand from him. She was not aware that her voice was shunted into a high-pitched punctuation of their move-ments, that each downward thrust elicited a moan, that each upward pull a cry of need. All she was aware of was the feel of him, and a yearning, almost pain, to end the friction between them. She wanted it, and she did not want it to end.

She slid her hands up his muscled torso, thumbs pressed upon male nipples, fingers curved into the hollows beneath his arms, gripping, branding with their nails. Her head arched back as Alisdair let her ride him. He was trapped in a web of longing. Not to simply end this maddening need, but to watch her as she peaked, to let her soar, to ride with her to whichever place she sought as destination.

He was too big, too intrusive, he filled her, invaded. A grimace pulled her lips back from her teeth even as she pressed down on him to take more. She moaned, a sound of feral need, demanding, thrusting, complete in its abandon.

Judith's hands clung to his shoulders, nails raking against his flesh as if to scar him. She fought the duality of her own emotions as she struggled against the fierceness of this new and staggering need. Men had brought her pain. Men with their strength and their threats. But not this man. Never this man. Alisdair had taught her that her body could scream with release, not just terror, that her eyes could glisten with tears of joy and not just pain.

She leaned down, nipped his shoulder with her teeth, an act of possession and one of anger at the same time.

He was still a man, and she couldn't forgive him for it.

If he hadn't felt her anger, Alisdair would have soothed her with a touch. But her rage surprised him at the same time it freed him. He let her lead the pace, not demurring when she demanded, nor flinching when her nails cut into his skin or her teeth bit too sharply.

She disappeared into some nameless void, concentrating only on sensation, enamored of it, welcoming it. Secure in it, because she knew, as she knew that each moment led her deeper and deeper inside herself, that somehow he was with her. When the darkness eased, and her panting led to shouts and her frustration culminated in blinding sensation, Alisdair was there, holding on and protecting her from herself, him, and always the world.

Her face was damp with tears, her cheek sticky as she lay it upon the pillow near his face. His hand stroked her from her buttocks to her shoulders. Tears wet the side of his face and he clenched his teeth against improvident, silly words.

Long moments later, Judith surfaced long enough to become conscious of his breathing. It was deep and regular. Not that of a man relaxed, but that of a man struggling to appear so.

Judith levered herself up, and it was only then that she became conscious that he was still solid and aroused within her. His lips smiled, but the look in his eyes was not contented, nor was it amiable. It was predatory, needing, as she sat upright and welcomed his gaze upon her flushed chest, upon her nipples, rock-hard points, upon the spot where they joined.

She moved down on him suddenly, a gesture as subtle as a brick falling upon his head, and as daring as the most sophisticated courtesan. Their coupling was fierce, brilliant, and thoroughly exhausting, bathed with tears of release. Alisdair thought that his quick-witted wife showed a penchant for delightfully wicked ways.

And Judith came to the conclusion that saints were overrated.

Chapter 29

Judith knocked softly on the door, and when the voice bade her enter, she walked in unsurprised. She'd already spoken to Lauren, one of the women from the village sent to take Meggie her meals when Judith was occupied in the weaving shed. It was Lauren who told her that Meggie had begun to speak, to turn away from the broth, and had, instead, begun to tease her about being intentionally starved.

"It's as if she's decided to join the living, sweet lass," Lauren said.

Now, Judith walked into the room at Meggie's summons and closed the door behind her, waiting for the other woman to speak. She was framed against the window, her back to Judith, her gaze focused on the undulating expanse of the sea, much the same way Judith had often stared. As if the ocean held the answer to so many questions in her life. Why me? What now?

So simple, so easy to voice, questions still unanswered.

Meggie was dressed in the simple dress she'd been wearing when attacked, although much mended and laundered—clothing was not such a simple thing to replace in the Highlands.

Meggie turned, glancing at the jar of heather ale in Judith's arms. A grin replaced the solemnity of her expression.

"Aye, an' it's a pure Scots lass ye're now, Judith?"

Judith smiled tremulously in response. "Sophie sent it up, but I urge you to use it judiciously. I find it has quite a kick."

Meggie's smile lit up her face. "Aye, I remember."

Judith was grateful for the memory which sparked such a smile, even if the amusement was at her expense. She wondered if the entire clan had heard about her debacle with heather ale, and supposed they had. There were few secrets in the glen, which would make the coming months so much more difficult for Meggie.

"Come then, an' we'll savor the brew."

"One tumbler only, Meggie," Judith cautioned. "I've no wish to lose my head again. Or find it twice as big tomorrow."

"Aye," she said, smiling softly, "my Robbie would say the same."

"Your husband," Judith said.

Meggie nodded, and turned back to the window, as if the view were somehow compelling. In a way, it was. Heaven and earth. Land and sea. Judith wondered if Meggie felt the way she'd often felt standing there. As if her own problems were infinitesimal compared to the sheer size of the world. That she was only a puny human being compared to the majesty of the rolling sea.

"It's a strange thing, life, isn't it?"

Judith didn't answer, any words she might speak being less important at this moment than silence.

"I ne'er would have thought my life to be so verra different from my mother's or her mother. I'd not thought to be so verra different from the rest of the women I know. I loved Robbie with a' my heart. I hated the English for killin' him, an' my da and my bruthers, too. An' then ye came, Judith, an' I thought maybe the English aren't so bad, after all. Tha' it was just war.

"Ye tried to save me, an' I realized it wasna because ye were English, it was because ye were Judith."

She turned and looked at Judith and held out one hand. Judith took it, set the heather ale down upon the floor, and went to stand in front of the window beside Meggie. A small, sad smile appeared on Meggie's face.

"Ye musna blame yersel'," Meggie said, when she saw Judith's tears.

"I'm sorry, Meggie." Sorry. What a futile word. What a useless word.

"Aye, me, too," Meggie said, and it wasn't her rape she meant. Judith looked down at the sill, at the sight of her hands clenched there.

So, she *had* heard.

It was one thing to speak to a lump in the bed, quite another to face that expression on Meggie's face. Horror, mixed with compassion. She might have looked the same had Meggie told that tale.

"I was layin' in that bed wonderin' how to go on, feelin' as I did the shame of it. As if something evil had been borne inside o' me, crept inside my womb. Yer words crept inside my heart, instead, Judith. I'll no tell anyone, ye can rest easy."

"I never thought you would, Meggie," she said, her gaze still intent upon her clenched hands. How did she tell the other woman that words were easy, it was the living that was difficult? That some days, she felt as ancient as the ocean itself, as though one more step was too much, one more breath beyond her capabilities.

"Next, we'll be cryin' like bairns, Judith," Meggie said, her smile a little shaky, but no less bright. "Wi' all this fine heather ale, seems such a pity." She reached out to the other woman and enveloped her in a swift, hard hug.

"What are you going to do, Meggie?"

"Do? What should I do? I'm the same person I was before, Judith."

''Will you stay here, then?''

Meggie smiled. ''Runnin' won't make things easier. I've my memories here—Robbie, an' Janet. Why should I let the English chase me from my home? Besides, I can't run from myself. I found tha' out layin' in this bed. I had to wake up sooner or later.''

''You are so much wiser than I, Meggie,'' Judith said, humbled by the profound wisdom of the other woman's words.

''No, I'm not,'' Meggie said, gripping Judith's right hand tightly with her left. Her smile was determined, strong. ''I've lost too much to lose myself, Judith. I'm all I've got left.''

For Meggie, recovery would come, because she was surrounded by people who loved her, with whom she belonged.

She would not have to hide, to pretend. Above all, she would never need to act in desperation and fear.

And bear the burden of that secret for as long as she lived.

Chapter 30

It was a perfect autumn day. Even though the ever present dark clouds marred the horizon, above Tynan the sky was clear and blue. The air was cold, the breeze from the ocean chilled the bones, but Judith would never remember the climate or the dark clouds. She would look back on that day as a time of magic, hours in which she had no worries, no thoughts of the past.

If anyone had asked what was the single greatest pleasure of that day, she would have unhesitatingly stated being with Alisdair. An Alisdair who could laugh like a young boy, for all that she never forgot he was a man. Alisdair, who admired her toes and kissed her elbows and told her she was lovely. Alisdair, who pushed her down among the late blooming wildflowers and the heather which had turned to seed and tickled her until her laughter echoed through the glen.

He'd awakened her with a kiss. "What would you say, wife, if we were to absent ourselves from chores for a little while?"

"What would we do?"

"There is that, of course," he said, laughing at her slitted look, "but there is also the promise of sunshine for an hour or two. Shall we loll about like earls and pretend to have pots of gold?"

She had thought Alisdair capable of charm before, but she had never been the recipient of it for a whole day. It was pure enchantment, this time out of adulthood, a day imbued with the sheer joy of being a child, not a lonely one, but one granted a companion of the heart. It was a time taken selfishly, a moment she stole from reality to enjoy, to savor in the future, much like Granmere took out her jewels and relived a memory.

Judith saw the man behind the responsibilities, the man whose laughter sparked an answering smile on her face, who told stories of kelpies and brownies, and who attempted, to her utter befuddlement, to teach her Gaelic.

He began with a toast, which sounded as unintelligible as an ancient foreign tongue.

"No, no," he said, laughing and reaching out one hand to form her mouth into the right shape, "it's *na h-uile la gu math duit, a charaid!*"

"It's no use, Alisdair, my mouth won't go that way!"

They were seated at the end of the promontory, the trees at their back, their legs stretched out before them casually, as if a sheer drop did not exist only inches from their feet. She wiggled her cold toes, luxuriating in the unexpected freedom of being without shoes despite the chill. If Alisdair watched from time to time to ensure their paradise was not intruded upon by English soldiers, it was a vigilance of which she was ignorant.

"I don't even understand what it means," she said.

"May all," he said, interspersing the translation with swift kisses to her pursed lips, "your days . . . be good . . . my friend!"

"All right," he said, finally resigned to the fact that at Gaelic, she was a failure. "Then we'll teach you how to talk like a Scot."

"You don't talk like a Scot, MacLeod." She frowned at him, but her fierce look was softened by her smile.

"A gangin' fit will ay get somethin', gin it's naethin' but a thorn or a broken tae," he said, in a perfect imitation of Malcolm.

"A fit will get you something, even if it's nothing but a thorn or a broken toe, but what's gangin'?"

"Loosely translated, to go, as in gang yer ain gait—go your own way. So, a selfish fit will get you something."

"Oh," she said, still smiling. "I'll try to remember that when next you throw a tantrum."

"I'd prefer you'd remember this one," he said. "It's ill wark takin' the breeks frae aff a Heilandman."

"True words, MacLeod," she said, and tilted her nose into the air.

"What about—a blate cat maks a prood moose? Him that hes a muckle nose thinks ilka yin speaks o't, or wha' wad sup kail wi' the deil wants a lang-shaftit spune?"

"Enough," she cried, holding her hands up to stop him. "I'm impressed, you sound as proficient as Malcolm. No, no," she said, reconsidering as he lunged at her, intending to tickle her again as he had awakened her this morning. "You're much, much better than Malcolm! You're the greatest-sounding Scot in the entire world. Please, Alisdair, stop!"

He let her go when her laughter echoed down the long drop to the sea. He pulled her into his arms and they sat watching the blue gray ocean waves in perfect peace.

"Alisdair," she said softly, "tell me about your family." It was a brave thing she asked of him. He'd never spoken of his lost kin. All of her information about them had either come from Granmere, or from Malcolm.

He did not answer, and it was only when she turned and glanced over her shoulder at him that he spoke.

"There was only Ian and myself," he said finally. His eyes were fixed on the expanse of ocean, as if it mirrored his past. "I think my father would have wanted more children, but Louise was not about to do anything that would mar her looks," he said sardonically.

"What was your father like?" She squirmed back against

his chest and he held her there, his chin resting on the top of her head.

"Father?" He thought for a moment. "He was forever laughing, although looking back, I realize he had little to scorn about his life. He had everything he could have wanted, a beautiful French wife, two sons, a heritage of land as far as you could see, and adequate funds to procure anything he might wish for."

Not like his son, she thought, who had inherited a ruined castle, a decimated clan, and empty coffers, but who still found the ability to smile and to laugh.

What was Alisdair's early life like, when Tynan gleamed with the richness of wealth? Guests would arrive for week-long parties, torches lighting their way, the iron-rimmed wheels of their lacquered carriages announcing their presence before Tynan's bronzed doors. The women would wear taffeta and silk, stiff panniers and kid leather slippers, while their male companions would be attired in kilt and jacket, jabot and lace. Had young Alisdair peered from the battlements with his brother to spy the arrival of those carriages? Did he have a favorite pet who stood by his side, mouth open in tongue drooling ecstasy, his young master's hand softly rubbing the special spot between his ears? Did he and Ian play as boys upon this very place where they sat? Did he read a favored book here, or dream of being a physician?

There was so much Judith did not know about this husband of hers. She found she wanted to know everything.

"Ian was my father's favorite, I think," Alisdair continued, with no rancor in his voice, "and when I see my father, I see Ian, too, in my mind."

"And your brother? Were you close?"

He thought of Ian, how looking at him would serve as a mirror, alike in features, although Ian's hair was as blond as his own was black. How, despite the fact that they were separated by two years, they had been close until adulthood, until only debate and divisiveness marked their meetings.

"He was my best friend, I think, until I went away to study." He did not mention how his brother drank to excess, that he loved every woman who crossed his path, that he espoused rebellion with a single-minded fervor he'd otherwise spent chasing those women. "Granmere used to say that he would never make old bones. Maybe he knew it, so he lived each hour with a full measure of minutes." His smile was tipped in sadness.

"You miss him, don't you?"

"Aye," he said, softly. "I regret the fact that we had not settled our quarrel. It is difficult remembering that our last words were those of anger. He was zealous about the rebellion; I was against it. He loved and admired the Prince; I had little liking for him. It seemed as though we were forever at each other's throats. Even that last morning."

"And what of your mother, Alisdair? Why do you never speak of her?"

She was excessively curious, he thought, with a smile. "The lovely Louise? Ah, now there's a different story." The overindulged and cosseted daughter of a duke believed she had married beneath her. Silk was fine enough to touch her white skin, but soft kisses from her child were too rough. His mother had demanded music from violins, but had banished the pagan, whorled sound of the pipes. She had looked around at the majesty of the land that belonged to her and denied it, the same way she repudiated the love of a second son who so resembled her husband and not her own blond looks and blue eyes. With her son's and her husband's fall at Culloden, Louise had assumed the mantle of grieving wife and mother only until she could flee Scotland for a safer place. A week following Culloden, she had been far from Tynan, sparing no thought to the clan who had protected her with their own lives.

"You do not wish to speak of her, do you?"

He sighed. She always cut to the quick, he thought, with a touch of humor.

"It is not that I do not wish to, Judith, it's that I do not know how to. How do I explain my mother? She insisted upon speaking French, although my father did not wish it spoken. She spent wild sums of money, and gave elaborate parties both here and in Edinburgh.''

"Did it displease your father?"

He thought back to his earliest memories. "No, as I said, he was a happy man."

"Then perhaps it was she who made him happy."

He considered her statement.

"It does not matter, she soon got over his death. She never spoke of him after that day, and God knows did not allow much time to elapse between his burial and her departure for France." His words were tinged with bitterness.

"Perhaps," Judith said, wishing that his mood had not changed, "it was because she could not bear it. Maybe her grief was such that it would have torn her apart to remain here, and live with memories."

"Perhaps." He nuzzled her hair with his chin. "You are too compassionate sometimes, Judith. I don't think Louise a worthy object of it."

"She is your mother, Alisdair," she said softly. "And therefore extremely worthy." He smiled, and kissed her quickly.

"What were you like as a little boy?"

"Oh, so now it is my turn?"

"Of course, did you think yourself spared? I can picture you as a scamp," she said, turning and smiling at him. At this moment, Alisdair thought, she looked as young as a child herself, her eyes aglow with happiness. He wished he could freeze this moment, so that she would always look this way, her lips curved, her glorious eyes sparkling, her face softened into joy.

"Did you get into trouble and refuse to obey? Did you kiss all of the little girls and make them dream of you?"

"Every single one. I was the only boy to go off to school and have my own entourage of playmates following me, weeping into their bonnets and crying at their nurses' knees."

"I can believe it."

"Of course," he said, looking offended. "And I was the best of children. I obeyed everyone, listened to my elders, ate my porridge, and everything else put before me, I must admit."

"You have grown into a lovely man."

"Lovely? Woman, you make me sound like a flower. I would have you call me handsome, brave, stalwart, dashing, debonair, but not lovely, I beg of you."

"No, lovely," she said in the tones of one who has decreed it and it will be so, "I've decided. From now on, it's Alisdair the lovely!"

This time, he tickled her until she admitted that she might have been wrong about calling him lovely, and yes, yes, yes, he was all of those things he'd said.

He showed her his favorite hiding place when he was a little boy, the cave which was overgrown by brush and only reached through low tide. She shook her head emphatically when he asked her, with a wiggle of his eyebrows, if she wanted to explore it.

They walked on a beach strewn with boulders the size of the massive blocks of Tynan. They played like children in the surf, only to stop and race to the top of the hill, breathless.

He showed her the tree he had marked as a little boy and the spot where he had killed his first deer, although, even now, he looked a bit shamefaced about the action.

"I did not like it much," he admitted, "especially the blooding, when they touched me on both cheeks with the deer's blood. I tried to be manly, although I never acquired a taste for hunting. I have, however, acquired a taste for something else," he leered, abruptly changing the tenor of the conversation.

He reached for her, and she giggled and then flushed as his hands stroked across her bodice and he whispered provocative suggestions into her ear.

"Shall we return to our room?" he asked softly.

"Is that all you can think about?" she protested, backing away from him.

"No, but it occupies a fair share of my mind," he admitted with a smile. "But it is your fault, after all."

"How do you see that?"

"If you weren't so responsive, Judith, and so hot in my arms, I could wait a few hours." There it was, that flush he'd teased into life.

He scooped her up in his arms as if she weighed no more than a lamb and followed the track away from the village.

He had suspected he would like this woman when she emerged from her self-imposed restraint, but he had not expected to be captivated by her. He'd felt compassion and pity for her, a curious understanding, and an aching desire. How odd that he reveled in simply being with her. He knew when she entered a room, because the very air seemed to shimmer with her presence. He felt her pain when others spoke of children, and he remembered the look in her eyes when Douglas was passed around to be cuddled. He knew by her scowl when she was in a fierce temper, or when she was hurt and hiding it. He'd seen the laughter in her eyes and wanted to replicate it every day of his life. And the blush which started at her toes and tipped her nose pink, he wanted to summon it forth, also.

He set her down inside an abandoned crofter's hut, one of those built into the side of the craggy hill, half its structure shale and stone. It was pitch-dark and smelled of animals; the only light was from the chimney hole and from the open sky peering in between the gaps in the thatch. The only furniture was one sagging cot, wedged into a corner.

Alisdair closed the warped door as much as it could be shut, but anyone walking by could easily see the interior. As a trysting place, it was barely adequate. Still, when he spun her around and pulled her into his arms, suddenly neither the damp, dark smell, the sounds of mice, nor the lack of privacy disturbed either of them.

He gently placed both large hands on either side of her head, raised her face with his thumbs beneath her chin. Even in this dim light, her face looked luminous. Her eyes sparkled with remembered laughter, her lips curved sweetly.

He bent his head and with his tongue traced the outline of her smile. She leaned closer to him, her hands on his arms. He deepened the kiss suddenly, mated his tongue with hers, coaxing a bemused response, a slight, hesitant moan emerging from her lips.

She extended her arms around his neck, as if suddenly needing a support. His hands slid up from her waist, pressed tightly, possessively against the sides of her breasts until they were pushed up against the wool of her bodice.

Judith heard the rumble of thunder and discounted it. There was always rain in the Highlands. Alisdair kissed her closed eyelids, swept down the fine line of her nose. His fingers slid through her hair, his fingertips pressed into her scalp, and although the touch was domineering, fierce, it was yet curiously gentle. She leaned into him, her hands braced against his chest, feeling the hardness of his muscles, the radiant warmth of his skin. It was quiet joy she felt now, not fear.

The first drops of rain didn't disturb her. Nothing mattered at this moment but the taste of Alisdair's lips and the sweet, heady wonder of the hard strength of his body pressed against her. How odd that the fear she had felt for so long at the thought of a man's touch had mellowed to a sweet, piercing anticipation.

The rain continued, not in a soft, gentle patter like English rain, but sheets of gray, transforming the path outside the hut into a muddy trench. It saturated the thatch roof, cascaded down one side of rock, a waterfall created from man's interference and nature's complicity. The hut, abandoned for its habit of flooding, became a wet cave redolent with the odor of dung and fur.

Alisdair pressed his thigh against the softness between

Judith's thighs, rotating, sliding, until she moved against him, willing to go where he led.

The chimney hole served as a funnel for the sheets of water that instantly flooded the hard-packed earthen floor of the cottage.

Alisdair was aware of the penetrating rain, but was too bemused by eager lips, by the warm, wet cavern of Judith's mouth and the budding passion of her response to him. Although cloth denied him passage, his memory recalled the feel of her, hot, wet, willing. Still, the insistence of the irritation managed to penetrate the fog of desire. Judith stirred, the annoying sensation of being drenched by the downpour slowly penetrating the ardor of his embrace.

They separated, finally, and looked at each other.

She took a step backwards, and nearly fell in the ankle-high water. He reached out an arm to steady her, pulling her back into his arms. She leaned her forehead against his sodden shirt and began to laugh weakly. His rumbling laughter echoed hers.

"Perhaps I have not chosen a suitable spot for trysting," he admitted wryly, the uncomfortable fit of wet trousers gloving his arousal reminding him of his loss of control.

She only giggled.

"Although, it could be worse, I suppose."

That set her off again.

"How?" she asked finally, leaning against him, not bothering to brush the tears of mirth from her eyes. She was so wet, it did not matter.

"Well," he said, considering, "it could be winter."

She howled.

"Or," he whispered, "we could be naked."

She looked at him suspiciously, the laughter in her eyes softening her glance. She took one step back, stumbling on the wet length of her skirts. She fell backwards, barely missing the wooden frame of the sagging cot.

She did not, however, avoid the mud.

His laughter shook the walls of the cottage with as much ferocity as the storm itself. He knelt beside her, oblivious to his own state, and raised her up. She was coated with mud, a slippery, oozing mass of clinging odor. He sniffed her and began laughing again.

The coarse wool of her dress itched and the weight of her skirts, along with the sucking mud beneath her feet, conspired to make every movement difficult. She brushed his hands away and attempted to stand, but he only pulled her down beside him.

On her next attempt to rise, he merely held onto the collar of her dress, and the old wool separated easily. So did the chemise. The sight of her, coated with mud and spitting mad did not encourage his laughter, it diffused it.

He rose and clasped her wetly against him. His mouth searched hers, felt its mutinous contours, softened them, gentled them, until she forget her anger and allowed them to fall open under his onslaught.

He stepped away long enough to pull off his sodden shirt and fling it to the floor. Bits of leaves and grass fell through the gaps in the roof and stuck to his skin. His trousers left nothing to the imagination, especially since the bulge there seemed to enlarge as she stared.

Her rain-slicked breasts slid against his chest and the mat of his hair heightened the sensation. Judith moaned against his mouth; he encompassed the sound with his lips.

Rain splattered on her shoulders and dripped relentlessly down her skin. Alisdair bent and licked each droplet that fell from her puckered nipples and felt her response in the sudden arching of her back. He stood apart, disregarding her muffled protest, and stripped off his remaining clothes. He flung them into the corner, not noticing when they floated among the debris of the flooded hut.

He returned to her, pulled her close, then lifted her until her waist was level with his.

"Put your legs around me, sweet," he husked, and she did, feeling herself open for him. He lowered her until she was impaled, and then he turned. The force of the rising water made it impossible to walk, but not impossible to move. She hung onto him as he continued to turn in slow circles. His motion made him move gently within her, hard and large and hot. The rain pouring down her back was only an incidental sensation, inconsequential next to the feelings he was drawing from her.

He was the only warmth in the suddenly chilled, wet cottage. She leaned against his shoulder and did not notice when her teeth grazed his skin. He did and her abandon almost made him lose what control he had left. But he vowed that he would not find his release first.

He held her by the waist while she clung to him. His hands slipped upwards, the rain only aiding his passage. They were both sheeted with water. No matter how he turned, he could not avoid the torrent. His thumbs brushed her nipples, pushed in, and rotated against them. He shifted slowly around, the action thrusting her down upon him even further. Each successive step intensified her pleasure, until she was whimpering against him.

He pushed her up against the earthen wall, transformed by the rain into a slick sheet of mud. Judith didn't protest as he ground against her. It was as though she were a part of the earth and part of him. He thrust again and she could only cling wetly to him as the shudders began. When they peaked, the feeling was almost painful in its intensity. His climax came only seconds later.

Alisdair finally stirred, but only enough to cup her buttocks in his hand and move them carefully, inch by inch, onto the sodden cot. The wooden frame sagged, as he deposited Judith into the middle of one large, cold puddle. He shifted beside her, placed his broad arm around her, and pulled her closer to him. They sat, watching the flotsam of the cottage floor float around their feet and through the partially open door of the hut.

Alisdair MacLeod, chief of the clan MacLeod and the last remaining heir of a long and distinguished warrior dynasty, sat on a sodden cot with his English wife and laughed aloud. It had just occurred to him that his trousers had long ago joined the ranks of the leaves, twigs, and other debris that now floated through the ditch in the middle of the village.

Judith looked at him sideways. She could not help the answering smile on her face, his humor was so contagious. Besides, she felt too contented to be anything but amiable at this moment.

He smoothed the mud from her cheek. She smelled. Horribly. Alisdair thought it was a strange thing indeed, for him to have wanted her so, even covered with grayish mud and smelling of the barnyard. No, perhaps it was not so strange after all.

He leaned down and kissed her gently before he broke the news. "Do you remember when we walked back to Tynan naked?"

She shuddered. "In full view of the clan? Perfectly, Mac-Leod, in glorious detail. Such a thing is not that easy to forget."

"I'm afraid, Judith, that we must repeat the act," he said softly, a devilish smile wreathing his lips.

She looked wide-eyed at him, and then to the corner where her clothing had been tossed. Granted, he had easily ripped the old wool gown, but she would have been partially covered had she worn it. It, however, had floated away, along with the MacLeod's trousers.

"I don't believe it," she moaned.

"Believe it, Judith," he said, chuckling. "And believe this, also. The storm has stopped. Prepare yourself for another audience."

She hit him on the arm with her balled fist.

"It is very well for you to say, MacLeod, you have less to expose," she said, exasperation clouding her eyes.

His booming laugh could shake the roof down upon their heads, she thought.

"Ah, Judith," he said, still laughing, "what you have to learn about men." He stood, and she saw what he meant.

The MacLeod was in a glorious state. She glanced up at him with a frown on her face.

"Cannot you comport yourself decently?"

"It does not have a string, little general," he said, smiling.

"Well, do something about it."

"There is, fortunately, only one thing to be done."

In the spirit of human kindness, she allowed as how she could assist him. Judith discovered that the MacLeod had marvelous powers of recuperation which were supplanted only by her own. She also discovered, and it was knowledge that she tucked away for later, that he could make her forget the most outrageous circumstances, such as a puddle of muddy water at the small of her back, and a steady drip of water upon her face.

The MacLeod strolled naked through his village, with his exhausted English wife in his arms. He could not help the smile that broadened his face, or his cheerful nod at the memory-tinged looks of the old men. He only chuckled at the women, most of whom tossed their aprons over their faces and scurried back into their own cottages.

There was something to be said for having an English wife.

Chapter 31

Judith knelt beside Granmere's bed, took her frail hand in hers, and sobbed with an acute sense of loss. She bowed her head, tears slipping unchecked down her face. It had been a gentle passing, in her sleep, as quiet and devoid of fuss as if Sophie had planned it.

Alisdair's touch upon her shoulder, as he moved to kneel beside her, roused her finally. Words were without comfort, but she could be here. She placed her hand over his, the other stretched upon the bed to touch Granmere's arm, feeling the fragility of her bones, as if she weighed no more than a feather.

Sophie had been the first person to welcome her to this land, her staunchest ally. Judith had felt such love for this tiny woman with her indomitable will and a spirit far more robust than her physical strength. If she were grieving so, what was Alisdair feeling?

"I wish I could have saved her," he said, his voice low and tinged with loss, "but I've no treatment for age."

"She was ready, Alisdair. She had prepared herself."

"How do you know?" He turned to look at her and Judith almost wept at the sadness in his eyes.

"By this," she said, rising. Judith retrieved the casket of jewels she had been instructed to give to Alisdair. "She wanted you to have these," she said, handing the small box to him. It was ornately decorated with pearls and its rounded top was encrusted with tiny, sparkling bits of glass.

He held it in his large hands, a small smile touching his lips. "I was ever intrigued by this when I was a boy," he said softly, and then searched for one spot on the side of the casket. He pressed one rounded jewel and a secret drawer slid free.

He stared at the contents for a long moment. There were two objects lovingly placed there. On one side rested a drawstring bag containing Granmere's small collection of unmounted jewels. Nestled on the other side was her wedding ring. She had not removed it since she had come to Scotland as a bride. Indeed, he had not noticed its absence from her finger until now. Alisdair pushed the drawer back into place, understanding full well his grandmother's last request.

He wished he did not.

Her duty not yet complete, Judith went to the small vanity his grandmother had used all of her life. From the top drawer, she extracted another article and returned to Alisdair's side.

She could not prevent the tears, nor the sudden lump in her throat.

"I charge you, Alisdair MacLeod," she said, in the somber tones the oath she'd memorized decreed, "Chief of the clan MacLeod, laird of your people, with the honor, duty, and obligation of your station. Do you, Alisdair Mac-Leod, promise to protect and shelter your people, provide for them with your might, and by the right of your birth?"

"What is this?" He extended his hand to hers, to what lay shining in her palm, but she withdrew it.

"Please, Alisdair, just answer."

He had known the laird's pledge for as long as his memory served him. It was strictly a ceremonial oath, given during solemn occasions, when the mantle of responsibility fell to the living, on the night following the death of the current laird. He had not had the time, nor had it been thought of, following the battle of Culloden.

He nodded.

"You must speak it, Alisdair," Judith said softly, tears roughening her voice.

"I do so say, and I will do so," he said, repeating the ancient response.

"Then wear this badge proudly," Judith said, repeating the words Granmere made her learn. "The blood of your fathers protect you, the love of your mothers surround you, the pride of your clan sustain you." She reached over, brushed his hands away, and pinned the crested badge upon his shirt.

He looked at its shining surface mutely and then at Judith in confusion. He had not seen this since his father had worn it during that final battle. He had supposed it had been lost. He did not know how his grandmother had come to have it, but he knew well the gesture she had forced Judith to make. At her death, she was telling him that she found him worthy.

It made her last request more vital.

He would do it, but his spirit and his heart rebelled.

Judith wanted to be alone, a difficult feat at Tynan this evening. She finally slipped away from Alisdair's watchful eyes and Meggie's vigilance. There was no danger of her being so stupid as to wander alone on the lonely paths surrounding Tynan. She had lost her innocence in England. She would not lose her life in Scotland. It had already claimed her heart.

Although she had thought the request ghoulish, Judith had met with Malcolm and conveyed to him Sophie's last wish.

"She had no right askin' this o' me. It's a sacrilege."

"She wants the weapons buried with her. That means

all the ones you've already taken from their hiding place, the ones hidden in the crofters' huts.''

Malcolm's look of surprise was almost worth Granmere's request.

"She knew?"

"That you wanted to arm the glen? Yes, she knew."

"An' I'm thinkin' she shouldn't have been tellin' an Englishwoman the secret o' the MacLeods.''

"Would you rather that Douglas died, then, Malcolm? Or Fiona?" The words were cutting, but not as sharp as the look Malcolm shot at her. "What price is a child's life, Malcolm," she continued, "or the women of your clan, or the boys not yet grown to men? Tell me, then, Malcolm, who you will sacrifice for a lost cause. Then go and slit their throats, for it is a kinder thing you do than what the English will do to all of the MacLeods if they find such contraband.''

Not one word passed between them, then. He did not mention that he remembered her tale, that he'd been unable to forget what English soldiers had done to a young woman with eyes the color of Scotland. She did not tell him that she'd given her word to Sophie and despite the fact that her past held secrets and her soul was tarnished, it was a bond of inestimable value to her. Malcolm finally nodded curtly.

Now, Judith wanted a quiet space of time without the chatter of other women. This morning had been difficult; the preparations accompanying death often are, but during the ritual, Judith discovered that the Scots were a superstitious sort. They grieved for Sophie's passing, of course, with a deep and genuine sense of loss, but their sorrow was curiously mixed with what appeared, at least to her, bizarre customs.

Each one of the women summoned to prepare Sophie had tried to explain, their contempt for her replaced by necessity, death taking precedence over rancor, it seemed.

"One's for the body. 'Tis the other for the spirit," Lauren said, after placing a wooden platter upon Sophie's breast. Upon this platter were two separate mounds, one consisting of the soil of Tynan, the other of salt.

"Aye," Meggie added, she being the one who had assisted Judith in the laying out of Sophie's fragile body in the rusty black dress. "We dinna believe it's a bad place ta go, heaven. " 'Tis a better place an' all." She smiled down at Sophie and then, with a tender parting gesture, bent to kiss the withered cheek.

All of the women had made a point of kissing Sophie, an action they said would prevent dreams of her and also to prove to the world that they had no cause in her death. In fact, if Judith could believe their stories, each had seen evidence of Sophie's imminent passing.

" 'Twas the cock crowing," Sara stated emphatically. Had she not heard it in the wee hours of the morning?

"An' old Willie's hound, too," Meggie contributed. "He howled last night."

One of the other women had heard the sound of a bird tapping at the window, followed by a strange and unaccountable rapping on her roof.

Judith thought she would scream if she heard one more premonition. If the Scots had been truly gifted with such abilities, it's a wonder that the horror and the suffering of the past four years had not been prevented. Still, she'd managed to smile politely at their stories and listen to their instructions with temperate grace, all the while praying that her resolve would last long enough to escape to blessed silence.

She walked on, careful of the distance between the great brooding shape of Tynan to her rear and the nearest path. Only when she saw the twins, did her guard relax a little. David—or was it Daniel?—waved to her from the fence line, and she waved back. Even in the midst of sorrow, there were duties to be performed.

She leaned against the fence and watched the great milling flock of sheep, for once their sound not grating to her ear, but lulling to her mood. Because of these sheep and her father's accidental largesse, the MacLeod clan would be able to carve a future for themselves. She smiled, thinking of it.

She would miss Sophie so much. In just a matter of months, she had taken the place of Judith's mother, of the confidante she'd never had. She'd been uncritical, without judgment, as if nothing Judith could say or do would be untoward or unacceptable. It was the first time in her life she'd ever felt that kind of unquestioning love from anyone. At home, she'd been singled out as strange. Even her gentle mother had despaired of her oldest daughter, a fact which Judith had realized from an early age. Peter's affection for her had lasted until his mother's first tirade, and Judith doubted that Anthony had felt love for anyone, except perhaps his brother.

Judith recalled the first time she had seen Granmere, shuffling from the shadows of the courtyard, her imperious cane marking her passage. She smiled at memories of Sophie's resolve in the face of her and Alisdair's stubbornness, the three-month bargain which had been coined at her insistence. She thought back upon their conversations, when Sophie's gentle compassion had purged her of unwelcome and bitter memories, and when old, wise eyes had sparkled with laughter. She remembered sitting quietly by the fire as Sophie sewed yet another garment, a gift of generosity and caring.

"Ye'd best return to the castle, missus," one of the twins said, and held up his arm for his brother. It was uncanny the way his twin seemed to turn at the exact moment his arm went up in the air, as if having sensed that he was needed.

She was not so idiotic as to argue with him. Meggie's rape and her own near assault still burned too fiercely in her mind. The problem of Bennett, however, was postponed this one night. Granmere came first.

Judith entered the great hall and slid beside Alisdair without saying a word. He looked down at her, determined all was well, pulled her close and continued his conversation, all with no noticeable gap in his speech.

Meggie nodded at her from across the room, as if comforted by her appearance.

The clan was assembled for the first part of the ceremony marking Sophie's death. Judith looked around the room, recalling the last time everyone had been assembled. Then, suspicion had colored the looks from every pair of eyes. Suspicion and not a little hate since she'd just been exposed as a widow of one of Cumberland's veterans. If there was hatred now, it was masked civilly, or she had become too inured to feel it. Plus, the act of being pressed against their laird's side might have mitigated what anger remained. Old Geddes was there, and Malcolm, Alex leaning against the wall with his crutch and leg propped against one step, Hamish being led into the room. Sara was holding court in the corner, no doubt regaling some poor innocent with another hideous recipe or chastising someone for daring to speak before she'd finished. Fiona held Douglas, the little boy squirming to be let down so that he could explore and practice his new trick of walking.

She and Alisdair were the first to perform the lykewake. The fire was extinguished in Sophie's room, and only when the ashes were cold and swept clean, did the women move to leave. They removed every polished surface, including the small bronzed mirror that Granmere had used each day. Judith was left with a candle, enough food to last the night, and a small bottle of whiskey that one of the crofters had received in trade for a length of unused linen.

She and Alisdair were to wait for the dawn to be relieved of their duty, for there was to be no coming or going in the dark. "For fear of what ye might see," Meggie said, slowing shutting the door behind her.

Soon, Alisdair would join her, and together they would mark the passage of time in a silent homage to the spirit of the woman who had loved them both. It was not strange to Judith that she felt as though Sophie's spirit knelt beside her in that cold room.

She felt Alisdair's touch on her neck and looked up at

him with a small, sad smile. He bent to kiss her before kneeling beside her, gripping Judith's hand tightly.

When they were relieved of their duty at dawn, Alisdair and Judith mounted the wheel staircase in the corner of the laird's room, brushing past the cobwebs from a hundred industrious and rarely disturbed spiders.

"Careful, here," Alisdair said, leading her around a hole in the floor. They ascended yet another level, until the pink and yellow dawn shone brightly through the roof. Up one more until they emerged on the battlements, where they could see for miles.

Fires still burned brightly along the track to the village, a ceremony, Judith was told, that dated back to Viking times.

"Our land used to stretch as far as you could see," Alisdair said, extending one hand as if to encompass the horizon itself. "Now, it ends at the other side of the promontory and at the far end of the fishing village."

She didn't ask who owned it now. Either the English, or absentee landlords who cared as little for the land as the people who subsisted on it.

Alisdair turned, extending one arm around her, pulling her into the warmth of his embrace, cradling her against his chest. It was less a sign of passion, than it was a need for comfort.

"She loved you, you know," he said in a low voice. "Else she would never have told you about the treasure."

"You knew?" She looked up at him.

"I am laird, Judith, it is my business to know. I had not realized, however, how much had been moved from the secret place." The night had been filled with stealthy activity, he was certain of it, as Malcolm and his ill-assorted band of would-be patriots gathered up their cache of hidden weapons, placing them in Granmere's coffin. It was a strange request his grandmother had made of Judith, yet she'd accomplished it, a feat which did not surprise Alisdair at all.

Sophie was buried amidst the cairn stones which marked

the graves of Alisdair's ancestors, in the spot set aside for her beside her beloved Gerald. Half a score of men helped Alisdair carry the coffin bearing Sophie's fragile remains. If the wooden casket weighed more than it should, or if each man labored under the effort, none spoke of it.

There was no minister present, no one to say the words appropriate for such a ceremony. As they shoveled the earth over Sophie Agincourt MacLeod, Alisdair pronounced the benediction. "She was loved," he said simply, his voice deep and resonant, his eyes hooded against sudden emotion.

Judith thought it was an epitaph Granmere would have wanted.

Alisdair clasped his arms tightly around her, almost painfully so. He would do his duty after the burial. He disliked it, yet he could do nothing less. Granmere had demanded it of him without a word spoken.

Chapter 32

Judith entered the lord's room with no premonitions.

Meggie had passed Alisdair's message to her. Discounting the strangeness of it, she had mounted the stairs, grateful for the respite. Tynan was overflowing with people. Instead of leaving after the funeral supper, the women had stayed to clean, while the men continued to drink brandy toasts to Sophie's memory, to the calling of the clans, to the honor of the MacLeods, to the past, the present, and the uncertain future.

The walls had rung with cheers, even though there was an occasional surreptitious wiping of an eye, or a smile that momentarily lost its gaiety and slipped into bittersweet memories.

Life goes on.

If there was one thing that Scotland had taught her, it was the resilience of the human spirit. Husbands perished, lovers disappeared, children grew ill and died, but life, itself, never relinquished its cycle. It continued and would always continue, as the sea itself would never cease its relentless pounding upon the cliff rocks, and its ageless tides would never suspend their rolling gait to the shore.

Alisdair had slipped from the great hall sometime earlier during a raucous, and dangerous, toast to the Bonnie Prince. He stood at the window, his back to her. How tired he looked, she thought, as she noticed his slumped shoulders.

Although he heard her entrance into the laird's room, he did not turn. He had been given a respite from this chore by the ceremony of the wake and funeral. Yet, such rituals had merely delayed his duty, not prevented it.

It had occurred to him, in the hours following Sophie's death, that his grandmother had been right. Judith had never been given a choice. She had been married twice because of the whims of her father, found herself banished to Scotland for the same reason. Nor had their marriage been a voluntary union. If she stayed at Tynan, it would be because she wished it, not because circumstance, the English, or Squire Cuthbertson decreed it so.

It was only fair to give her that choice, now.

But what if she chose to leave?

"Alisdair?" she said quizzically, when he did not speak, remaining motionless by the window. She went to him, then, and placed her arms around his waist, leaning her cheek against his back, feeling the solid warmth of him. She sighed, closed her eyes, and wondered if she would forever be able to summon him to her mind by the scent of newly washed linen.

Alisdair moved from her embrace, stepping closer to the windows. She only stared at him, confused. When he still did not turn, she began to realize that something was terribly wrong.

"What is it, Alisdair?"

"Granmere is dead, Judith," he said without inflection. "That leaves only one witness to our declaration." Still, he did not face her, which was better, perhaps, then seeing his expression. She did not want to see the counterpart to this cool voice in the amber gleam of his eyes.

"What are you saying?"

He turned then, just when she wished he wouldn't.

She stared at him without speaking as he went to the armoire and retrieved Sophie's jeweled box. He sprung the secret drawer and removed both the small pouch of jewelry and the wedding ring.

She had neither moved, nor spoken since his words. She was too pale, her eyes wide and dark.

"It was not your wish to find yourself here, or married to a Scot," he said, not meeting those eyes. They betrayed too much confusion, too much emotion. It was not his choice that mattered right now, but hers.

"But I would have you make the decision now as to which future shall be yours." He spread open the bag and dumped the contents into her reluctant hand.

Judith stared down at the sparkling gems on her palm. Small diamonds winked alongside green emerald chips and perfectly formed rubies as bright as droplets of her blood. She blinked several times, but did not speak.

"If you choose to leave, the sale of these will bring you more than enough to keep you for several years. Perhaps you might purchase a shop, or emigrate."

Time was suspended, strangely slow. A movement of a hand took achingly long seconds to accomplish. A breath was weeks long. She licked her lips, felt their arid surface too hot and sensitive. All time and sensation was out of place, skewed.

"What about the English Colonel? Will he think my defection as innocent?" Even her words seemed from far away, the effort of speaking them almost beyond her.

Alisdair's smile was small, infinitely sad, she thought. "I'm sure the good Colonel will understand your desire to visit your family. He needn't know the visit is permanent."

"And if I do not wish to leave?"

"Then," he said, careful not to alter her decision by his own emotions or desires, "if you do not, we will contrive a marriage between us."

She stepped back when he would have placed something in her other hand. She clasped the stones with a hand that did not heed their sharp edges, craving the pain of it, because it proved she was still breathing, that this was not a dream, that this was real.

His black hair fell down upon his brow again, the chiseled chin was now lowered as he stared at her hand. He would not meet her eyes, but she could see the sweeping length of his lashes, the noble, etched line of jaw.

Alisdair reached out, forced open her other hand, and gently placed Granmere's gold ring on Judith's palm. He closed her fist around it tenderly, turning away before she could read the expression in his eyes.

"Take your time, Judith," he said, his tone, despite his intent, betraying his inner emotions. "Decide well. If you choose me, you choose Tynan, an uncertain future, a land of harsh beauty but infinite promise. If you choose freedom, you choose comfort, your own country, and a future of your own making."

He did not wish her gone. The joy she felt was instantaneous and rapturous, as nerve-biting as a shard of ice, as spirit-plummeting as the truth. She could not escape it, after all. He wanted her here. She could not stay.

"You told me once that no one was free." Why did her voice sound so odd?

"You would be less so, I'm afraid. You would be the laird's wife, a Scot instead of an Englishwoman waylaid because of a few ill-chosen words."

"And how would you have me choose?" The words were important, the sentiment behind them doubly so. She did not tell him it would be all she had of him, words to last a lifetime.

"With your heart," he said softly, to cover the sudden rasp in his throat. "You once said 'I wonder how many women would trade their husbands for their freedom and being taken care of for the ability to care for themselves.' I give you that freedom, Judith. You must choose if you wish it."

She stared at him, unable to speak.

Judith looked down at the wedding ring she held in her hand. Choices. He offered her a choice. A lonely future, or being his wife. On the surface of it, it seemed no choice at all. Unless, of course, she gently pushed back one layer of self-knowledge, a thin veneer of composure, and peered into the person beneath.

Alisdair offered her his home, his life, and although he did not make the gesture, it was as if he opened his arms and stretched out his hands, palms flat and open, easily granting her his kingdom and his future.

Such generosity deserved a reward, did it not? And what recompense had she given him? She had opened the door and invited the Devil in for tea. She had summoned Bennett Henderson to Tynan by her very presence.

One word would keep her here, but that same word would seal Alisdair's fate. She was under no illusions as to Bennett's nature. He thrived on misery, flourished on despair. He would not rest until he had destroyed anyone or anything which represented happiness or peace to her. And this time, he had English law on his side. A man who would terrorize those weaker and less apt to strike back would not hesitate to twist and mold the law to suit his own purposes.

Bennett would not hesitate to avenge his brother.

Dear God, do not let this be happening. How many times had she prayed that? How many times had she made bargains with God if only He would let the hell she was experiencing be a product of an overactive imagination, too many half-penny novels, too many comfits. But it had happened and wishing it away would never make it disappear. The memories could not be burned from her mind. Her own actions could never be disavowed.

What would Alisdair say? He had embraced and protected her, had defended her against his clan and the English, cherished her enough to offer a choice—what would he do if he knew what she truly was?

He had brought such hope into her life. He had made her feel clean and whole once more, when once she had despaired of ever feeling whole and clean again.

Judith had not thought it possible for a man to be gentle,

and yet, Alisdair had shown his tenderness in a hundred ways. She had not thought it possible for a man to be selfless, to think of others before he thought of himself, but Alisdair worked without complaint so that others could carve a future in this ruggedly beautiful land. She had not believed that a man could be intelligent and yet not boast of his wits; handsome and not preen. Most of all, she had not realized that a man could possess a sense of family as strong and as abiding as the tides that rolled in each day.

She had realized many weeks ago that he was a special man, someone to cherish and value.

Judith didn't want to be noble or gracious or self-sacrificing; she only wanted Alisdair. Right at this moment, she wanted to smooth back his hair, or touch his shoulders, or be surrounded by his muscular arms and pretend that he had not offered her this onerous choice. Because, after all, there was only one thing she could do.

The burden of being self-sacrificing was doubly hard now. To leave after she had learned what love truly meant was almost too much to ask of her. Or was it the very meaning of love itself? To turn her back on Alisdair after she'd sampled life on his terms was asking her to walk into hell naked.

Unconditional love. Love that sacrificed, that gave with no expectation of receiving. The kind of love Sophie had given her. If she truly loved Alisdair, she would bring him peace and joy and simple pleasures, not mark his life with danger, uncertainty, threat.

But how did she say goodbye to him? How did she part her heart from her chest? How did she walk away from the only happiness she'd ever known?

In the end, it was a simple decision. She loved him more than she loved herself, and that is why she did what she did. Her steps were almost soundless as she approached him. Pulling his hand to her, she pressed his fist against her chest and forced it open as he had done with hers. She looked deep into his eyes and then smiled, a tremulous smile so filled with love that he closed his own eyes for a moment.

"I love you, Alisdair. I will always love you," she said tenderly, gently, lovingly, and then dropped Granmere's ring onto his palm.

She stumbled from the room, tears blocking her passage. She stopped outside the door, and leaned weakly against the wall, incapable of descending the sloping stairs.

She did not hear the sound from the laird's room, the muffled noise of a clenched fist striking the stone walls of Tynan.

Chapter 33

Judith left Tynan as pale and wan as she had looked on her arrival; only this time, she left accompanied only by Malcolm, not following a great herd of sheep.

Malcolm disliked his errand and the fact that both the MacLeod and Judith had insisted upon it this night, as if another few hours at Tynan was a horror neither could bear.

If not for the fact that they possessed only two scrawny, tired horses, Malcolm did not doubt the MacLeod would have sent the whole clan to escort his wife to Inverness. As it was, only he was charged with that duty, in the dark of night with the English patrols still abroad. Still, it had not seemed a wise thing to argue with the lad, recalling how the MacLeod's face was set and expressionless. It wasn't all for grief of Sophie, Malcolm was thinking.

She was too quiet, he thought, glancing over at Judith. Her self-control, once laudable, now masked too many secrets. This he remembered only too well.

No, there was more to this story than either of them was telling.

Judith rode beside Malcolm, her mind numb, her vision

turned inward, oblivious to her surroundings. Once, the idea of being independent would have been heady; this occasion joyful, not steeped in pain. Now, however, freedom stretched out before her like a long and winding road down which she would travel alone.

She would be free, but at what cost? And what had she given up to attain it?

In this stark and harsh land of savage beauty, she'd known unquestioning joy. Its people had gifted her with memories to last a lifetime. Sophie had given her affection and love from the first moment she held out her hand. She'd kept her grip unfailingly tight and reassuring until the moment of her death. From Meggie, who seemed to embody the spirit of Scotland—strong, resilient, accepting what life gave her, never fighting it, but overcoming just the same—Judith had been granted an earthy wisdom. And from Alisdair, she'd learned acceptance, courage, hope.

Too much to give up, too much to lose. She did not think she could survive this.

Not even having nobility as a cloak to draw around her added to Judith's misery. She did not feel innocent enough to be noble, nor clean enough. Yet, somewhere, beneath the pain of this, it was enough to know she had made the right choice. The only choice. The knowledge did not make the journey easier, nor make her wish each clopping step Molly took to end it, to speed her swaybacked mount back to Tynan, rush up the steps, and beg for Alisdair's forgiveness.

Yet, she could not change the past. And it was the past which held danger for the future. She was no enchanted princess, no faerie queen, despite the sorcery of the past few months. A spell had been cast upon her, had it not, then just as quickly taken away.

Her blue eyes would now be only blue, not the color of midnight, as Alisdair had once whispered to her. They would no longer have the power to sparkle, or to rage, or to open wide with wonder. Her hair would revert to simple brown, devoid of the gold and red highlights he said he loved so much. Her legs would only be legs and not marble columns he had once claimed, laughing and nibbling at her knees. She raised her hands and looked at them objectively, seeing not aristocratic-looking fingers, as he had said, but only chapped and red hands. She remembered the actions of these hands, as she cupped them close to her face, breathing deeply, as if she could still smell the scent of him on her palms. Judith opened them wide, remembering how they had traced a path on his back, how they had gently cradled his manhood, how they had smoothed down his black hair, or playfully tweaked his nose. She remembered holding his hand, as they had laughed like children, running through the woods bordering Tynan. From this moment on, they would only be hands.

And life would only be existence, as it had been before.

Hours passed, their mounts were kept to the center of the road, the clopping cadence of the horses' hooves became both a lulling sound and a signal of safety. Darkness added danger even to a road well traveled.

Malcolm's self-deprecatory curse was enough to tell Judith that something was wrong. She glanced to her right, and that's when she saw them, their blood red uniforms turned black by the faint moonlight. She and Malcolm had both been so singularly involved in their own thoughts that neither had noticed the patrol until it was almost on top of them.

Bennett's smirk was glowingly evident even in the darkness, as was the dull gleam of the saber extracted from its sheath with a hiss of metal against metal. Five mounted men followed him, each of their faces bearing the same feral, expectant look. Their hunting party had found prey. Judith wondered if they were the same men who had raped Meggie, or did Bennett change companions as easily as he did coats? Were there that many amoral English soldiers billeted in Scotland?

The dread she'd lived with for years, which had been noticeably absent in Alisdair's care, was summoned from some dark part of her mind. It rose, like bile, to lodge in her throat as Bennett cantered forward, easily halting her swaybacked mare. Molly seemed to sag in relief at his gesture.

It was the strangest thing, Judith thought, that she should feel so calm right at this moment. It was not fear she felt, but certainty. A knowledge she held to the core of her like the conviction that the sun would rise in the morning. There was danger here, possibly death, certainly the promise of pain. Yet, the horror she'd lived with all those years was gone. No longer would she live her days waiting for Bennett to visit his atrocities upon her. No longer would she live in the sickly miasma of fear at the thought of him touching her. Whatever happened from this moment on in her life, whatever outcome this night brought, it would never be as bad as what she'd already experienced.

Leaving Alisdair had left her empty, a husk of flesh from which the spirit had departed. She had given up everything that was dear to her because of Bennett's abuse. Love, safety, sanctuary, a feeling of being able to come to grips with her past, a promise of being able to forge a better future—all these things she had sacrificed because of his perversion, his cruelty, and to keep safe the one person she loved. She would no longer cower. What was it Meggie had said? *I've lost too much to lose myself, I'm all I've got left.* Judith had lost Alisdair, a promise of tomorrow, a hint of joy, days of wonder. She had lost the possibility of forgiveness, the promise of love.

The fear Bennett induced no longer had its ominous power—she had nothing left to lose.

"Dear Judith," he said, his voice tinged with mockery, "we meet again."

She did not speak, simply looked into his shadow-cloaked face with all of the contempt and disgust she had always kept carefully masked. She despised him with a loathing that she had otherwise reserved for Anthony, for unlike the other drunken molesters, Bennett had enjoyed her struggles and her screams. He feasted on them the way a bird of prey would, the meal so much more delicious if the victim still lived.

With a contemptuous flick of his wrist, Bennett beckoned the rest of his entourage closer. As they reined in, Judith could see from their glassy eyes and slightly askew uniforms that this was no ordinary patrol. Not with the smell of spirits wafting from them and a leering look from even the youngest of the five, a boy barely past his first shave.

Malcolm slitted his eyes and looked at the leader. No, this wasn't good. An English patrol was one thing, damn their Sassenach hides. A drunken English patrol, with their leader making insulting noises towards the laird's lady, now that was something else.

Malcolm edged his horse closer to Judith, slid his dirk alongside the edge of her boot. Aye, it was all well and good for Sophie to wish peace in the Highlands, but there were just some things that a man had to keep for . . . well, sentimental reasons.

Judith felt Malcolm's hand and did not veer her gaze from Bennett.

"Is there a reason you've stopped us, Bennett, or have you lost your way?" Her scornful tone was due to two things—she desperately wanted to prevent Bennett from realizing exactly what Malcolm was doing, and secondly, she no longer cared if Bennett realized the depth of her antipathy. Alisdair was safe from him now.

"I am an instrument of English justice, dear Judith."

"The two words do not seem to belong together, Bennett. English and justice." Her smile was cold, a mere upward slash of lips. "You are more likely an instrument of English lust." Malcolm thought her words an act of courage. Bennett reasoned she was bluffing, her ridicule nothing more than bravado. Judith knew them to be only words, simple words, incapable of measuring the depth of her loathing.

"Let's see what you say after a visit to the magistrate, my dear," he softly intoned, his eyes gleaming with anticipation. Only at the beginning had she ever defied him; this rare show of courage added a growing thrill to this chase.

"What will your English magistrate say about the crime of rape, Bennett? Do you go without punishment?"

"If a few English soldiers were entertained by a lusty Scots wench, that is human nature, Judith. Surely not a punishable offense."

His indifference infuriated her; he had never had any thoughts for anyone other than himself.

"Is rape the only way a woman will willingly allow you to grow close?"

"You've grown brave, Judith. I admire your spirit; it will make the game so much more refreshing."

"And you've grown coward, Bennett, hiding behind your uniform."

With his entourage milling around him, perhaps she should have been more cautious about her words. Yes, they had strength in numbers. Yes, there was only her, and one aged Scot who would have roared in protest at that appellation. Yet, Judith knew something they did not. She had absolutely no intention of repeating the past.

She would gladly die first.

Bennett waved his companions away, and only his coarse words to the group convinced them that he was adequate to handle one old man and one slightly used whore.

He had plans for Judith. Plans that did not require witnesses. And if the old man had to die first—so be it. What was one more Scot? Bennett Henderson had no intention of letting his former sister-in-law leave Scotland alive.

He had relished his plans for so long now that he almost gloatingly took in every detail of her appearance, almost ghostly in the pale moonlight. She was prettier now than she had been in London, more fully fleshed. Would she feel the same? Would her satin skin still feel as good? Would her screams still excite him as they had before? He intended to find out and then, once he had pleasured himself in her body one more time, he would kill her slowly. As slowly as his brother must have died, in as much agony.

Malcolm sidled up to Judith, his horse shouldering her mare aside. He had enough of this foolishness. If they were to be arrested, let Henderson try. If it was other sport he was after—again, let him try.

He peered at Judith through the shadows, at her pale face, the only part of her visible above her black dress. She turned, watched him wiggle his eyebrows at her and then motion down to her boot with a point of his angular nose.

She understood. A weapon would at least even the odds.

Bennett's saber sliced through the air, as if cutting away a portion of the night, surprising Judith almost as much as the sudden, fierce pain shocked Malcolm. He pressed his hand over the wound in his shoulder, staring at the Sassenach who had drawn first blood without warning. He spurred his horse around the mare, leaving Judith free to escape. But she had no intention of leaving Malcolm.

An ungodly howl punctuated the silence as Malcolm launched himself at Bennett, screaming and shouting as his dirk slashed through the air with maniacal fervor. The battle cry of the MacLeods had last been heard at Culloden, multiplied five hundred times, but the sound uttered by one old and angry man was enough to raise the hair on the back of Judith's neck.

Judith eased her hand down to the side of her boot and gripped the dagger with a suddenly sweaty hand. Its sharp edge cut into her skin, the dots of blood shining wet and black. She rubbed the side of her hand against her skirt.

Malcolm was no match for Bennett's youth, or the reach of the saber. Bennett slashed again and a long line of red appeared on the side of Malcolm's face. He roared and leaned to the side, plunging his dirk wildly into the darkness. He was reaching to stab again when Bennett's saber flashed one more time, almost contemptuously cutting off the old man's ear, severing it from his head.

Judith did the only thing she could think of, reasoning in that split second of time left her that the stallion's pain was a small price to pay for Malcolm's survival and her freedom.

She grasped the dirk Malcolm had slipped her, closed her eyes tight, and with both hands plunged it hilt deep into the rump of Bennett's horse. The stallion screamed in agony, pawed the air, and not even Bennett's centaurlike grace could control him. Bennett slid from the saddle with an unearthly elegance, rolling when he hit the ground and easily eluding Malcolm's thrown dagger.

He was not fast enough, however, to escape the killing hooves of the pain-maddened stallion. The horse reared, an unearthly silhouette against a moonlit night, a demon of fury and agony. Judith would be able to remember the sounds of that night for years to come—Bennett's screams and an animal's shrieking terror.

Was it hours or only minutes until the frenzied horse finally raced, riderless, over the moor, spooked and wild-eyed by the scent of the blood spattered from his hooves to braided mane.

Malcolm dismounted heavily, looked down at the injured Englishman and then back up at Judith, still seated on her mare.

"Come here, Judith," he said, in a soft tone, unlike any she'd heard Malcolm use. He had to coax her twice more before she tremblingly obeyed, sliding from the sway-backed mare and resting against her side for a moment until her legs stopped shaking and she could support her own weight.

He pulled her down by one arm until she nearly toppled onto Bennett's inert body. His chest was crushed; the stallions' well-shod hooves had done their work well. Malcolm raised Bennett's head. A bloody froth oozed from the corners of his mouth and his eyes were glazed.

"This mon had done ye grief, lass," Malcolm said gently, beckoning her closer with one bloody hand. "Ye need to help him die."

He held out his dagger, the handle coated with blood—his or Bennett's? In the moonlight, the blood appeared shiny and black.

Judith took it, wiped the handle clean, held it tightly gripped in a trembling hand. How many times had she wanted to kill Bennett? How many times had she felt powerless, helpless, the victim? How many nights had she prayed for just such an opportunity, for just such a moment?

Malcolm shook the dying man until his eyes opened in protest or sudden awareness. Judith forced herself to look into Bennett's eyes.

There was death here; she could hasten its coming. With one short stroke she could kill, send this demon back to his hell. For all the nights of agony, she could repay him, for every bruise on her soul she could be avenged, for every moment she'd been degraded, she could force him to atone.

At what price to her already damaged soul?

Her hand would not move forward, her arm was frozen into place, her eyes remained as fixed and staring on Bennett as if she, herself, were close to a corpse.

Malcolm said nothing, watching her with hooded eyes. Still, she didn't move, not even when Malcolm shook the dying man again. A glimmer of recognition was all she saw before it faded and Bennett slumped against Malcolm's hold.

For a long moment, she did nothing. Then, slowly, she stood, holding out the dagger to Malcolm, who replaced his dirk in his boot. Judith stripped a length of material from her one remaining dress, helped bind Malcolm's wound, tenderly wiping the blood from his face. All of this was accomplished in the most perfect of silences, as if the sound of the blood leaving Bennett's body was not an accompaniment to the moonlit night.

When she finished binding Malcolm's wound, Judith began to cry. Tears flowed down her face unchecked, and it was only then that the old Scot opened his arms to her.

She grasped his coat, buried her face against his bloody shirt, and wept.

Malcolm wavered between unconsciousness and a pain-filled observation that his judgment wasn't wrong after all.

He had thought she had promise.

Chapter 34

It was a sad and dispirited pair they looked, Alisdair thought.

Malcolm rode into Tynan's courtyard, Molly plodding docilely beside him. Judith sat atop her swaybacked mare, exhausted and more than a little concerned about the crusty Scot at her side. The journey to Inverness would have been too much to expect of him, wounded as he was. Twice, he'd swayed on the saddle and would have fallen if she hadn't held on to his waist. They'd been on the watch for the rest of Bennett's patrol, but Malcolm reasoned they were no doubt passed out on the side of the road by now. The retracing of their journey seemed to take forever, too slow for the state of Malcolm's wounds.

Even so, the old Scot made use of the time.

"Lass, doubt me all you wish, but don't doubt the Mac-Leod. Who are you afraid of, lass? Him, or yersel'?" She'd looked at him in puzzlement. "It's no' an easy thing ta love a Scot," he said, by way of explanation.

"You've wished me gone for weeks, Malcolm. Why do you argue with me to stay, now?"

"I'm thinkin' he could do worse," he muttered, which

was the greatest compliment he'd ever given any woman, had the daft lass the sense to know it.

She'd refused to back down, although he'd given her nothing but sour looks for weeks. She'd refused to become conciliatory, had matched him look for look, the way a good Scot would do. He had heard her story at Meggie's bedside, seen her real grief at Sophie's passing. And when she had unerringly and without hesitation thrust the dagger into the horse's rump, he had almost kissed her feet. She was more Scot than English, and of course she was a worthy mate for his laird.

Now, if he could only convince the two of them.

"You do not know, Malcolm," she said somberly. "I am not what you think I am."

"Because ye were marrit ta a cruel mon, Judith? Who used ye in foul ways? I'm no' so hurt I canna remember." She bowed her head and stared at the neck of her long-suffering mare.

"Give the lad a chance, Judith." It was a statement he had made more than once on the dark road.

Outside Tynan's gates, he'd tried once more. "Ye don't need to go, lass," he said finally, "now that the bastard's dead." He gripped his lips tight against the pain of his wound. He did not want her to turn her back on Tynan. "You canna do this to him, lass. He needs a wife."

"Inverness is that way," Alisdair greeted them, pointing to the west.

"Aye, lad, and don't we know it."

The emotion Alisdair felt at Judith's return was immediately supplanted by concern, as he saw the makeshift bandage wreathed around Malcolm's head. He bounded down the steps and peered into his old friend's face. Blood matted the bandage and the front of his shirt.

"Judith?" His eyes scanned her figure, but there was no sign of injury.

"I'm fine, Alisdair. Malcolm is the one needing tending." For a flash of moments, Judith allowed herself a fantasy. She was returning from a necessary journey and

Alisdair awaited her. His frown was for the days apart, for their blessed end. His arms were reaching out to hug her, not to scoop Malcolm from the saddle. His radiant anger was for the presence of others. Blessed welcome, a promise of a warmer greeting later.

Alisdair had no time to frame the question before Malcolm turned on him.

"It's an English wound, MacLeod. I'm lucky the brainless bastard dinna cut off my nose. I'm sure he was aimin' for my heart."

"How did it happen?" Alisdair unwound the bandage, inspected the wound. The old man's slight moan was not the only sign of his pain. He began a series of voluble curses which grew in volume as they entered the bronze doors, Judith following behind.

"You left here intact and returned without an ear. I'd congratulate you on your sleight of hand, but I'd rather know what happened."

"I'll tell ye for a spot of brandy, lad," Malcolm said wearily, the pain-filled journey having taken its toll.

"The brandy would be better served to bathe your wound, Malcolm."

"Nae, it'll better serve my stomach."

He swore as Alisdair helped him onto the kitchen table, eyeing the beams above his head with distaste. He knew their shape well. Judith had shamed him into climbing a ladder and ridding them of their festoons of webs. Now, she simply stood beside the table, holding Malcolm's bonnet and the bloody strip of dress she'd used to bind his wound.

" 'Twas the English patrol, lad, come upon us near to Inverness."

Alisdair shot a look at Judith. She didn't look at him, merely kept her gaze riveted on Malcolm. There were words that needed saying, but not now, not when Malcolm so urgently needed medical attention.

"Ye'll do fine with only one ear, you stubborn old fool,"

Alisdair said as he wiped away the crusted blood from the side of Malcolm's head.

"Aye, the better ta ignore ye," Malcolm grumbled.

It was a good thing his old friend wasn't a lady's man, Alisdair thought, as he stitched what he could. The remainder of Squire Cuthbertson's brandy was used, not to bathe the wound, but to soothe the victim. Still, it was not a pleasant procedure, and Malcolm made sure his displeasure was well known. Alisdair had not realized how voluble his old friend could be, and in how many languages.

When he finished, Alisdair surveyed his handiwork. Like a war-weary mongrel, Malcolm would win no prizes for beauty. The other wound took less time to suture, the saber having gone clean through Malcolm's shoulder, missing any vital organs.

Only then was Malcolm established in Ian's bed—it crossed Alisdair's mind that it had almost as many visitors recently as when Ian was alive and had a penchant for sneaking his lady loves in and out beneath their parents' noses.

"Are you going to tell me what happened, or will I have to drag it from you word by word?" The question was asked with a nonchalance Alisdair was far from feeling.

"I'm thinkin' that's a question ye need to ask of yer wife, MacLeod." Malcolm's statement was softened by the liberal amount of brandy he'd imbibed. The alcohol, the feeling of warmth and the softness of the bed upon which he lay, induced in him a feeling of mellow comfort.

He did not see the stricken look Judith sent him, or the swift study his laird made of his wife.

The bench on which she sat was crafted from pine, the wood new, the splinters not yet smoothed by the plane. Still, it was one of the few pieces of furniture in the Great Hall; the others were charred or nearly ash from the fire which had seared the heart of Tynan.

She'd never spent time in this room, it did not urge the

inhabitant to linger. The walls were thick, the ceiling high, shadows occupied the corners. Its dimensions were too large to feel cozy or secure. Upon the blackened walls were round iron handles, once used to hold the shields and claymores of the MacLeods. The weapons were contraband now, the room itself denuded of its ornamentation. Only the black smoke and the stench of burnt wood remained, traces of the inferno which had raced through Tynan at the Duke of Cumberland's command.

It was the perfect place for this conversation.

Alisdair had not moved from his position near the mullioned windows. The glass had cracked from the heat of the fire, splintered apart, and then glazed back together. It was an odd, fragmented picture, backlit by the sun filtered through a thousand shards of crystal. He had not looked anywhere but at her since he'd led her to this room, a scrutiny she was unprepared to face.

"You must curse your luck, Judith, for bringing you back to Tynan." She had returned due to circumstance, not inclination, that was obvious.

"Malcolm needed you."

Malcolm needed you. The words swirled in the air. An indictment of such delicacy that he was surprised at the pain he felt, as if speared by it.

"And you, Judith, do you not need anyone?" Anger was an easier emotion to swallow than despair, and he'd had a bellyful of that.

Alisdair didn't know if this confrontation was wise, or foolhardy. All he knew was that he had to understand. Why had she turned her back on Tynan, on him? Once that was answered, once she told him, he would be able to leave her alone. Banish her from his mind the way all the other ghosts of his life had been expunged.

A wiser man would let her go. A saner man would not question why she'd left him. A prouder man would not, even now, hope to convince her to stay.

Life, however, was not lived on the brink. It was a pool into which you plunged, headfirst, immersing yourself to the neck. He could no more have loved Judith in half measure than he could have turned his back on his clan and Tynan.

She did not answer him. He was unsurprised by her eternal silence, prepared for it. What she did not realize was that he had time and endless patience and a budding rage that fueled them both.

Her knees were pressed together like a child learning decorum, her feet planted on the floor next to each other, toes aligned perfectly. Back straight, the angle of her chin a testament to military precision. She was a perfect example of ladylike manners, but he didn't care if she had a board strapped to her back. Her hands were clenched before her, not folded calmly. Nor was she otherwise composed. He saw how tightly she held herself, as if she would shatter into tiny pieces if she did not. She'd learned to school her features, to exhibit an incredible stillness which masked her emotions to everyone but him.

Her eyes, however, never failed to give her away. Pain dwelt there, surface deep. Pain and resolution.

He would have gone to her then, had not her hard-won dignity and composure been so apparent. He would have encased her in his arms and led her to a cozy corner, near a fire where she would feel safe and warm and protected.

But he did neither, only stood and watched and felt a premonition of doom steal over him, as strong and as eerie as the morning he'd stood beside Ian on Culloden field and waited for the battle to begin.

He saw the half smile she gave the room, and wanted to shake her. She was being so damnably English right now.

Did he know how fragile her composure was? She suspected he did, and she also suspected he goaded her to see an end to it.

"What do you want from me, Alisdair?" she asked, forcing the issue.

"The answer to a riddle, Judith."

She tilted her head, a questioning gesture, and he complied.

"Why did you leave me?" Not why did you choose to leave Tynan? Not why do you want your freedom? He had personalized the question, made it intimate, real, painful.

She closed her eyes against the sight of him standing there with his hands clenched at his sides, the pride etched on his face so strong a blind man could see, the softness of his eyes an odd counterpart to the resolve there. He towered in the room, even as large as it was. He overwhelmed her by his very presence, but in the end it wasn't his size, or his formidable strength, or even his beauty which compelled her to tell him the truth. It was the soft curve of his mouth, the compassion in his eyes. A compassion she did not deserve.

For a long moment, she stared at the ruined flagstones of the floor, her gaze fixed not upon them, but upon some distant vision imprinted upon her soul. She was summoning the courage from a thousand places, where it had splintered like the glass in the window.

There was always something restrained, he thought, almost hidden about Judith, as if she were careful to keep a part of herself shielded from him. There was a control about her that still appeared even in their most intimate moments, as if she were afraid of him gleaning her thoughts. He wanted to crush that control, break her silence in two, extract the real Judith from the hard shell she encased herself in, as if she were a nutmeat.

"And Henderson?" he asked, when she remained eternally silent. "Why did he hate you so much?" Why had he attempted to hurt her from the beginning? Too many times, he'd wondered about the antipathy that boiled between them. Too many nights, Alisdair had waited for her to tell him.

She glanced at him, knowing that the words must come now. Somehow, they must be spoken.

"Because he knew I had killed his brother," she said,

the words dropping like large, heavy raindrops into the parched silence. "I killed my husband."

He didn't move, didn't react in any way to her pronouncement.

"Or I would have, had Providence not decided to end his life that night."

She took a deep breath, swallowed, tasting the heaviness of tears. Did she cry for herself, or for Anthony? Dear God, even now she could not lie to herself. She had shed no tears for Anthony. Not even then.

She could recall that moment with pinpoint accuracy, as if the scene replayed itself, ghostlike, in her mind. The flailing arms, the look of terror as Anthony realized he was choking, clawing at his own throat until the skin grew bloody—all these silent, shrieking moments were part of her nightmares. In her dreams, she felt the horror. At the time, she'd felt nothing. She'd stood and clasped her hands over her apron and watched his struggle, thinking of all the times he'd given her to his friends, payment for a debt owing, or simply to see her raped. She thought of the nights Anthony beat her, with a belt or a chain, simply because she'd done something to anger him, or others had, and she was a satisfactory scapegoat. And, too, she thought of Anthony watching as Bennett thrust her across the threshold of hell and laughing as she screamed.

It was only later that she learned he had not died of the poison.

Judith had managed to restrain her hysterical laughter when the regimental surgeon had looked into the stiff and arched throat of her husband and pronounced Anthony's death due to an errant chicken bone lodged in his throat—misadventure—not murder. Still, the intent was the same.

Her eyes were almost black, Alisdair noted, blurred by unshed tears. Her tale, as she told it, was relayed dispassionately, as if the continual rapes happened to another, as if the sadism and bestiality visited upon her had been perpetrated upon someone else.

"I could not bear any more, you see," she said finally,

the tight rein on her composure slipping a little in the face of his continuing silence. He had not moved, nor had he spoken at all during her tale. How odd that it grew easier with the telling of it. For so many years, to have hidden the truth of her marriage, and within three weeks to have told it twice.

Bennett had suspected her all along.

"I confess to plotting Anthony's death, may God forgive my eternal soul. If the poison hadn't worked, I was going to cut his throat open in his sleep." Her eyes were haunted, exposing all the pain once hinted at, all the naked self-loathing.

Courage was not the act of bravery without fear, it was being confronted with the starkest, deepest terror and refusing to retreat. Alisdair had seen many examples of courage on the battlefield—men whose fear resulted in loosened bowels and sweat-drenched faces, who had taken up another bloodied sword and marched on despite their trembling panic. Even now, as Judith waited so bravely for him to reject her, to repudiate her, he found himself wondering how much courage it had taken to live in such fear from day to day.

She bowed her head, her hands gripping each other so tightly that her knuckles shone blue white, waiting for him to speak.

He moved closer, his steps cautious as if afraid of frightening her, and in a way, he was. He reached out one hand as if to bridge the distance between them. She took it, and he knelt beside the bench. He held her cold hands between both of his, as if the act of warming them would bridge the terrible chasm between them. He bent his head until his forehead rested against her knees, stretched out both arms along the outside length of her legs from knee to thigh. It was a curiously restrained embrace, yet intimate in its imprisonment.

She looked down at him, kneeling before her as if he were the lowliest supplicant and she the queen.

Banishment was more than a fitting atonement, an apt

punishment. To never see this man again, the only man she had ever loved, the only man who had ever loved her, surely had to be a penance equal to her great sin. To never look upon this man, his black hair as deep and dark as a raven's wing, his long, brown arms flexed with muscle and bristling with hair, his scent as clean as the windswept moors surrounding Tynan, this would be the truest torture of them all.

God might as well cauterize her brain with a sharp heated sword, blind her to the beauty of the world, and take from her the sense of touch and smell and hearing. And please God, take her memory, also, bleed her mind dry of any recollection of Alisdair MacLeod. It would be the only way not to suffer so.

"Alisdair," she said, her hand reaching towards him as if listening to a will of its own. Her fingers stopped just an inch from his bowed head, just a small distance, really. She clenched her fist and withdrew her hand, the very skin of it aching to touch him.

"Alisdair," she began again, her voice filmy with tears, "I am not worthy of this." She spoke of his kneeling before her, of his kindness to her, his humor. She meant the love she'd seen in his eyes, the compassion she'd always seen on his face since the day the English came to Tynan.

"Shall I banish Meggie, then?" He raised his head, his eyes blazing gold as he demanded an answer of her.

"What?" Once again, he'd managed to confound her.

"She has been soiled, Judith, touched by men not her husband. Should she be sent away now?"

"She was an innocent. She could not help their actions." As Judith spoke the words, she expected his response.

"So were you."

But Meggie was so much more innocent. She had not killed.

He enfolded her hands in his own, his grip almost painful; his words, when he spoke, were harsh with impatience, perhaps fear.

He could feel her slipping away from him, could almost

see it. It was as if she were wishing these past months away, forgetting them deliberately, ignoring their import. There were no nights entwined in each other's arms, no tender laughter, no friendly camaraderie. No teasing, no passion, no love.

"Do you want confession, Judith? Then I give it to you. Freely, willingly, totally. I'm a man who has pledged to heal, and yet I've killed. I can remember the face of each man who died at my hand. I can recall the look in each man's eyes as I took his life, his future, his hope. I wonder at the women I made widow, and the mothers who cry because of me, and the children left fatherless. Each time I killed, it was the most terrible act I've ever committed. Yet, I would do it again, in order to survive. I wanted to live and I was given no other option. Is that confession enough?" He held out his hands, palm up, studying them as if he saw them coated with blood. "I spent so many years learning to wield these hands as tools of mercy. In five short hours, they became brutal instruments of death." He bowed his head, studying the threadbare cloth of her skirt as if he found the words he needed there.

"As to absolution, I don't know about such things. Or eternity or damnation. I am only a man. Leave the idea of judgment to other minds more capable of deciding these truths, or to the angels, I don't care." When he raised his head, his eyes gleamed with their own tears.

He smoothed the hair back behind her ears, then cupped her face with his hands. He looked into her eyes so deeply she feared Alisdair could probe her soul. His voice was earnest, direct. Soft.

"We have all fought in war, Judith. There is not a man or a woman in Scotland who has not felt the bite of battle. Do you not see that you have been engaged in war, nothing less? Our weapons, our adversaries were different, but we each have struggled to survive. I told you once that I do not think the less of you because of your scars. Either on your flesh or in your soul."

Restraint was overwhelmed by the need to have her close.

He stood and pulled her into his arms, placing her cheek gently against his chest. She should always be here, right next to his heart.

"Perhaps bringing us together was a form of absolution, Judith. Two people who could not forgive themselves. Perhaps we can forgive each other. Who are we to question such things?"

For a long moment, he didn't speak. These words must be perfect. They must convince her to throw in her future with the ragtag bunch of MacLeods, to banish the thought of England and freedom.

"Scotland is a harsh land, Judith," he finally said, his breath warm against her ear. "Our people have a penchant for lost causes which defies logic. They work hard, with industry and purpose. They have survived against odds that would break the less hardy. Scotland requires sons and daughters who fight for life. I think you well equipped to take on that challenge."

Alisdair didn't know what else to say to ease her mind, wished he knew something wise and profound to say at this moment. He wanted to show her how it could be. He wanted to bathe in the cove with her and stand on the battlements and watch the sunset. He wanted to outlast the winter and relish the spring. He wanted to hold her in his arms until his joints ached with age and he creaked and groaned and grumbled. But these were all dreams unless Judith dreamed with him. Life was more than the simple absence of pain, or of terror. He wanted to share all its faces with her.

But, in the end, what he wanted was not as important as what she chose.

"I'll not force the pace, Judith," he said, his voice rumbling against her ear. "There is more than one way to coerce, and I'll not be guilty of it. You still must choose, I'll not do it for you."

Her vision was blurred. She could not speak.

He tilted up her chin with one gentle finger so he could see the watery brightness of her beautiful blue eyes. "You decide, Judith, but make your decision on what you want for your future, not what has already happened in the past."

She gazed at his face, seeing more than strength or kindness, seeing love in all its guises. Teasing laughter, gentleness, wine-deep passion, blazing possession.

She felt the faint beat of her heart escalate until the pounding of it would surely be audible to him. But it was not, because he slipped from her with a final, soft smile, and left the Great Hall.

She found him standing at the cairn stones, at the small enclosure which marked the graves of his father, Ian, Gerald and Sophie. His head was bowed, his stance that of a man carved from rock, a statue of pride and purpose and a resolution almost too strong too touch.

He turned and the look on his face was so fierce Judith recoiled from it. Only for a second, before she gained what courage she still possessed and glued it to her backbone.

"Alisdair . . ." It was a tentative peace. She held out her hand. In her face was resolve, in her eyes was the answer he'd dreaded. Her face was awash with tears, and the sight of them made this even more difficult.

He hated her in that moment with all the passion he'd held in careful restraint. Hated her for visiting so much more pain upon him, at a time when he could barely hold in check the grief he felt. Hated her for being unwilling to chance a life with him, for believing him incapable of giving her enough love and laughter and promise to offset any burdens they might share.

"Go wait in the courtyard. I'll summon the twins. They'll see you safe to Inverness." The ugly harshness of his voice reflected his rage. It surprised him that the words were not coated in flames, they burned him so.

Her face was stark white, yet she did not turn, nor heed his unspoken warning. Did she not realize how close he was to tearing out of his self-imposed cloak of patience and tenderness and understanding? The man who faced her now was not kind. This was the man who'd returned from Culloden battle-scarred, soul awash with what he'd done, who'd carried his dead father and brother in a rickety cart many long miles that he might bury them on Tynan's soil. The man she stared at now was devoid of hope and stripped of dreams. But she did not move, this stubborn Englishwoman, her eyes dark with tears, the fatigue evident in her face, her very stance.

"Yesterday, a woman laughed, and I thought it was you." Of all the words he could have spoken, she did not expect these. "I began to crave the sounds of an English accent, only one clue to my insanity." He turned back to the cairn stones.

"Is that why you're still here, Judith, to witness my submission?"

One day, and he'd longed for her like a callow boy, ached for her as if she carried a string to his heart in her possession, tugging on it each hour as if to remind him of her absence. One day, and he'd been reminded of all the days she'd been in his life, all the weeks and months he would be without her. One day, to realize how much she meant to him.

"I love you, Alisdair."

"Yes, I know," he said harshly. "The last time you left me, you said the same. A simple goodbye would suffice."

"Forgive me."

His answer was a soft sigh. Still, he did not turn.

"When I was a little girl, all I wanted was to belong somewhere." Her voice was a warm and gentle breeze blowing over his soul. He did not want to soften to it. He did not want his anger to melt, his hearing to be so acute he could sense the very hesitance of her speech. "All my life, I've been known as different, strange. Even my own father thought so." She took one hesitant step toward him. He flinched at the sound of it. If she touched him, it would be too much.

"After Anthony died, I lived within myself, knowing that

the world would never understand what happened, that God would never forgive me, that no one would ever look at me the way you did just now.''

The tears in her voice were too much to bear. He turned and wanted to shout at her to finish this death knell, but for the look on her face.

It was as if a sun dwelled in Judith, she was that luminous. The tears that fell down her cheeks flowed freely, but they were only a backdrop for her watery smile. Alisdair felt his heart clench at the sight, the rage and pain he'd felt transformed, as if by sorcery, into something cleaner, more pure, distilled of love and hope.

"I wish, with all my heart, that I could come to you without one stain on my soul. I wish I could offer myself to you without memories, without regrets." She extended her hands to him, palms up. He could not help himself, he reached out for her.

"Did you hear nothing I said, Judith? None of us are pure." He held her prisoner by the tips of her fingers; she held him captive by the look in her eyes.

"Please. Do not send me away, Alisdair." In her eyes was hope, a tiny flicker of it. It was, he thought, enough to fan a flame.

"I could not bear it, Judith," he said solemnly. It was as much a declaration as she needed.

He held out his arms and Judith walked into them, holding onto him as if he were the anchor she needed to keep from floating away.

Chapter 35

Malcolm MacLeod was not one to ask for the Almighty's intercession in his life. He much preferred to handle his affairs the way he wished to and call upon the stern God of his youth and endless days in Kirk only on special occasions. The death of his wife had been one of those rare times, as had been the morning of Culloden. The rest of the time, he and God had an arrangement. Malcolm would muddle through, and God would leave him alone. Therefore, it was with great irritation that he finally called upon his Maker to protect him from one very determined Englishwoman.

He sighed, tried to ignore the stench coming from his wool- and water-covered feet. He, Malcolm MacLeod, who'd been a reiver in his younger days, who'd stood on many a battlefield and not retched at the sight of blood, or gore, or streaming entrails, barely escaped gagging at the smell of washed virgin wool. Since daybreak, he'd been stomping around the large banded oak washbasin, while buckets of wool had been alternately thrown in and fished out of the yellowing water.

Called him up before the clan, Judith did. Asked him

the question in front of twenty women. Told everyone they needed a braw, strong man, and wouldn't he fit the bill? Fell for it, he did.

"Och, Malcolm, have yerself a bit of bannocks, or yer frown will curdle yon wool." He knew the grate of that voice before he turned.

"Sara, what ails me willna be cured by food," he said, lowering his chin nearly to his chest. It was his pride that needed tending.

Sara's beady, pigeonlike eyes scanned him, following his line of sight. Clumps of wet wool adhered to his feet and floated on top of the water. Occasionally, one of the village women would bring another bucket of warm, soapy water and carry away some of the wool. All in all, it was a sad chore for a warrior.

If Sara frowned, Malcolm could not tell. The woman's face was permanently lined with a dour expression, as though she had smelled something foul in infancy and had carried the memory of the stench with her into old age.

"I've brought ye my boiled chicken dish, Malcolm," she said, gesturing to where a covered plate was placed on the rise of ground not far away. It was close enough that he could smell the odor of it, and once again, he felt the bile rise in his gullet. "No' that I had time, mind ye, what wi' the work I've ta do," Sara continued, oblivious to the fact that Malcolm's complexion had whitened a little more.

"Thank ye, Sara," he said, smiling with effort. Sara's cooking was the worst in the glen, but none had the heart, or the courage, to mention it to her. Consequently, she spread her efforts towards all equally, and every one of the MacLeods had been faced with the dilemma of either eating it, or secretly burying her efforts. Malcolm was not so hungry that he thought it might be edible. Especially not after sniffing the air again.

"I made it wi' two potatoes, an' a bit o' greens. No time ta make a new batch of bread, but how a body's supposed ta do all Judith expects an' still have time ta be goodwife, I canna ken.''

"I'm sure it will be tasty, Sara, an' I thank ye for thinkin' of me."

"Hah! Was told ta feed ye," she said, scanning the hill where Judith's figure was visible. "Told me, she did, that the wool came first. Bossy bit of goods, she is. Still, she's turned into a good wife, I ken."

The easiest way to rid oneself of Sara's presence, Malcolm had discovered many years ago, was to simply agree to everything she said. Today, however, that gambit was not working. Sara remained firmly entrenched in front of him. Him, with his rolled-up pants an' his legs white an' naked-looking like they'd never appeared beneath a kilt. Him, with white clumps of wretched-smelling wool sticking to his feet an' the odor of Sara's cooking sticking in his craw. He nearly gagged again.

"She's the talk o' the glen," Sara said, stubbornly scowling up at the figure on the hill. "Stubborn, she is. Just like the laird. Never saw a body work like she does." There was approval in the grumbling, as Malcolm well knew. Sara, who had been the first to condemn the ways of the lass, was now among her staunchest supporters.

Malcolm had not known on that day so long ago that he would marry his laird to a demon in a dress. He wished the MacLeod would hurry back. She was becoming uncontrollable, she was. First, she had changed the run-rig system that the two men had labored over for many a night. Then she had set the sheep loose to cavort over the hills, explaining patiently that they would never fatten unless they were allowed to forage to their heart's content. Then she had worked with Alex, of all people, to train border puppies, and a sillier sight he'd never seen but those damn dogs and their protective stance around the sheep.

Nor had she stopped there. And the MacLeod only gone a month.

She had ordered the old loom in the weaving shed chopped down and made into firewood, and bartered for two more looms. She had traveled from glen to glen with Meggie, visiting with the old women, inspecting looms that had never been torn down, studying old patterns that sat rotting on the frames, learning about different dyes made from lichen, the bark from the alder trees, bracken root, and elderberry.

She was driving him daft, she was, what with all her questions, and those damn tears which seemed not to have stopped since the MacLeod had left, first for Inverness, and then England. Malcolm couldn't remember ever seeing a woman cry so much. Either she was crying, or she was angry, and the woman refused to cook when she was angry. Worse, she vented her rage on anyone nearby, which meant that he was the recipient of the brunt of it.

She'd nearly the temper of the MacLeod and the frowns to match.

The MacLeod wouldn't have gone, if the English patrols hadn't swept wide by Tynan. The session with Colonel Harrison had its tense moments, but the English were satisfied with the outcome of their investigation. No one could dispute the sharp hoof marks on Bennett Henderson's chest. Malcolm also suspected that Colonel Harrison would not miss his captain overmuch. There were rumors of unexplained deaths of young women where he had patrolled, enough to wonder if the MacLeods were left alone by way of apology for Bennett Henderson.

Although Malcolm knew he would have to come to grips with the English domination of Scotland one day, he opted for the MacLeod's revenge—winning small battles with English merchants, which was one of the reasons the Mac-Leod had ridden away, only a month ago, leaving Malcolm in charge.

In charge? Hah!

It had taken her only one day to assume the role of laird.

Malcolm merely grunted, wishing that Sara would take the hint an' leave. At the set, determined look on Sara's face, he knew he was doomed to partake of the noon meal with his clanswoman, an' be forced to listen to one complaint after another for hours.

He preferred wet wool.

Judith thought Malcolm's normally taciturn features looked even more woebegone than earlier, but then, he was being romanced by Sara. She wondered if she dared tell the old Scot that Sara had designs on him. She smiled and thought not. Although Judith had a soft spot in her heart for the stubborn Scot, she thought it might do him good to be the object of a woman's determined pursuit.

It might take his mind off the changes she was making in the glen.

It had been a steady alteration. At first, she had toiled along with the village women, harvesting their potatoes, using the fork to turn the mounds as another bent and extracted the root crop from the hard soil. Her hands had developed more blisters, but they were an honest sign of work and disturbed her not one bit.

She bent until she grew breathless, pulling the green leafy tops of the turnips, helping the women to store them in the special cellar Alisdair had devised.

Each morning, she donned her clean apron and met with the other women beside the village well. She neither complained nor explained her actions, until they began to accept her presence as they would one of their own. She worked until one day rolled into another. She did not see their sidelong glances, nor did she hear their muttered words, but when Meggie came and led her away to a soft spot on the moors, and brought her a tumbler of water, bathing her sweaty forehead with her own kerchief, she understood they had discovered her secret.

"Ye canna do this, Judith," Meggie said, with censure in her voice. "Ye'll hurt yersel'."

"No, Meggie," she stubbornly replied. "I am one of you and I'll work like the rest of you. Janet did."

"Janet lost her babe because o' it, Judith," Meggie retorted. "An' probably died because o' it, too. Do ye wish the same?"

"This child is undoubtedly as stubborn as his father."

"O' her mother," Meggie responded.

Her working was infinitely preferable to sitting at Tynan and wondering what mysterious errand had taken Alisdair from home, only a few weeks after the thaws had begun.

She consented to leave the hardest work to the others, not bothering to tell Malcolm—who had stood in front of the door and would not let her leave until she promised—that she had accomplished her goal and that spending the time in the weaving hut was what she wanted anyway. Yet her determination and constant presence among the women had broken down their reserve, brought them closer. At first, only Meggie joined her in the weaving. Then Grizzelle appeared one day, followed by Sara. By the end of two weeks, most of the women of the clan were occupied with wool, in one form or another, and by the talk and laughter in the weaving hut, no one would have guessed that there had been dissension between Judith and the other women.

She began to realize what Alisdair's sacrifice had meant to the lives of these people. If she was not loved by them yet, with the fierce love they reserved for their laird, at least she had finally been accepted, enough to be grumbled at by the older matrons and to be scolded by the younger ones. She listened to their advice and she heard their stories and she began to feel as if she were a new member of a large and loving family.

Judith had found acceptance in this strange land. First, from its laird, who had taken one look at her past and not fled in horror. Instead, he had surrounded her with his love, his humor, his strong arms. Then the clan MacLeod had reached out to her. She didn't feel alone when she walked through the glen anymore. Her smile was readily received and just as easily answered.

Although the clan structure of the Highlands was gradually and inexorably being swept aside due to the rule of the English and economic conditions, here it was still in force and Judith suspected it always would be, as long as there was a MacLeod at Tynan.

The crowded huts had been torn down and replaced with structures that boasted windows. Small, yes, but still, they let the light in, and were airy and comfortable due to the fact that the chimney smoke was now diverted into corner hearths.

Alisdair had arranged for a hospital of sorts to be devised. Their village now numbered over three hundred people, and never a day passed that some injury or another was not reported.

The children were being educated by a young teacher hired from Edinburgh. Before his first class, however, Judith removed the birch and paddle from his collection of teaching implements and threatened him with being dismissed summarily from Tynan if he ever thought to use them.

Tynan seemed to be the likeliest spot for the unlikeliest of men, traveling north in search of work. Alisdair hired these sheep men, young men who labored in the fields and did not seem overwhelmed by the pace he set for them. Meggie was planning on marrying a MacLared, and Sara had her own plans for Malcolm. Even Fiona had ceased to be a burden, choosing to reside with her aunt in Inverness while she shopped for a husband.

Judith did not miss her.

She did miss Sophie. A small brick enclosure had been erected around the cairn stones, and Judith went there often in the first days and talked to Granmere, not noticing the swift, compassionate looks directed her way. Somehow, it eased her mind to be there, as much as the tears she shed when no one saw.

This was a strange place, Scotland, full of rolling hills and tall peaks etched with snow, and the sea which never remained the same color. There were pines which seemed to scratch the sky itself so tall were they, green gorges of valleys, layered hills of slate and rain which fell continuously, making the Highlands a gray and black place, warmed only by courageous hearts.

Judith learned to love the chill days, and the stark beauty of the sea flowing into the cove. She stood on the top of the moor and welcomed the change of seasons with joy, anticipating Alisdair's warmth in the coldest winter nights, the spring beauty of an awakening landscape, the summer smells of rich, fertile earth, and the poignant farewell of autumn.

She began to love this land, and with each passing day she began to realize something else.

It was home.

When the wagon finally pulled into the courtyard a few days later, more than one prayer was answered. Judith was ecstatic; Malcolm was jubilant.

Alisdair threw down the first of the trunks lashed to the top of the wagon. There was barely enough room in the courtyard for the second wagon, he thought, but somehow he would manage it. Both conveyances were filled to overflowing, accompanied by a menagerie that looked to have come straight from Noah's ark.

Malcolm greeted him with an almost hysterical fervor. He flung his arms around his laird and squeezed Alisdair tightly, which was as effusive a greeting as he had received in his lifetime from his dour clansman. He insisted upon shaking his hand, too, and it was only Alisdair's insistence which finally ended their clasp.

"Is everything well, Malcolm?" Alisdair asked. That set Malcolm off again.

"Aye, now that the laird is home, it is," he chortled. "Aye, aye." He would wait until later to inform Alisdair of how unruly his wife had become, even rounded with child. Stubborn lass.

A new litter of border puppies barked at a cage filled with spitting cats, pets of his companion. Alisdair yelled at both sets of animals. Judith only laughed as she carefully descended the steps and threw herself into her husband's arms.

Granted, his eyes were shadowed, as if he had not slept much, and his face needed a shaving, but he looked tall and strong and fit, clad in his usual attire of white linen shirt and black trousers. She sniffed the air experimentally. Clean, soft linen.

"What are you doing, wife?" He picked her up and whirled her around in his arms.

She laughed, bending down to meet his kiss.

Malcolm leaned against the bronze doors, shook his head at the sight, prudently closing his eyes. He opened them long moments later, but they were still kissing and the young lass sitting primly on the wagon seat looked more than a little lost. He sighed, went to her, and held out his arms, and she allowed him to help her down.

"Elizabeth!" Judith screamed, as she disentangled herself from Alisdair's embrace. She hugged her sister, turned her round and round in inspection, and then hugged her again.

"Oh, Alisdair, how? Why?" Judith's overbright eyes were brimming with tears; Malcolm snorted in disgust. He'd seen enough of those these days.

"I share Malcolm's feeling about your father, love," Alisdair said, noting Malcolm's disgruntled look. He could just imagine what his old mentor was thinking. But Elizabeth wasn't just one more Englishwoman, she would always be a child, incapable of understanding more than a child would, but with an innocent's grace and charm. But Squire Cuthbertson was still a stupid man and had bargained once again with the Scots. David and Daniel would be arriving in a few days with more free sheep, and the MacLeods had been blessed with another of his daughters.

Malcolm turned away from all of them and shuffled up the stairs burdened by one of the heaviest trunks. The puppies swarmed around him, racing in search of the kittens. "I'll not handle this on my own, man," he roared at his laird. "Give me a hand! How am I ta wrestle with this bunch of surly creatures?"

Alisdair could not prevent the grin that touched his mouth. The normally quiet courtyard was marred by hissing, spitting, and barking.

"If you will look to that green trunk, Malcolm," he called out with a broad smile, "you will find a store of brandy and other spirits which once belonged to Judith's father." He didn't bother telling Malcolm he'd bought the lot; somehow purloined brandy tasted better.

Malcolm brightened, his ire transformed magically into rapture. Aye, things were looking up after all.

Alisdair had been home five hours before he was able to be alone with his wife. There was a welcome to be had and that small matter of a rounded belly to investigate. But Elizabeth needed to be settled, and while Judith took on that responsibility, Alisdair apportioned the supplies, then reported to the elders as to their profits. When, finally, every question had been answered, every duty either performed or delayed, Alisdair went in search of his wife.

He found her in the laird's room, bending to fluff the covers on the bed. When Judith saw him standing framed in the doorway, she straightened, the sheet still clutched in her hand. The dazzling sun entered the windows, shone brightly over the large bed, the chair in the corner. The air wafted in from the sea, forever chilled, laden with heavy moisture and a salt taste.

He did not coax her into his arms, but pulled her there impatiently. She laughed as he jerked her closer. She raised her face and drank in the sight of him with wide eyes. Her hand smoothed over his bristly cheek, her palm gently abraded by the touch of it. He closed his eyes at her touch, and that one small gesture deepened the blue of her eyes and caused her tremulous smile to shift a little.

Her tears made slow, delicate tracks down her cheeks. She touched the line of his neck, up to where it met his jaw. His skin was soft there, then turned rough with a day's growth of beard. The tip of a finger brushed against his feathery lashes, as long and as black as a crow's plumage. Two fingers brushed across his brow and down the arched expanse of his nose to that jutting chin with its cleft. She reached up and placed a tender kiss there, right at the spot where it stubbornly faced the world. She mapped his face with her fingers, and her wide, wide eyes.

She angled her head, clasped her hands around his neck, and brought his mouth closer to hers. He lapped at her tears, and the roughness of his tongue brought a smile to her lips, a smile that soon vanished under the tender onslaught of his mouth.

"Alisdair," she whispered, "oh, Alisdair." It was a litany of love.

Her other hand entwined in the hair at his nape, but he needed no urging.

He brushed his lips against hers, tasting the moisture still there, the salty remnants of tears and kisses. His tongue traced the outline and her lips opened spontaneously.

His hand brushed back her hair, that glorious mane of red and gold and brown which swirled around her face. He placed his lips on her forehead as if in benediction.

How they disrobed, she could not remember. It somehow did not seem important, the only reality in the world was the touch of his naked body against hers. She did not demur as he carried her to the great bed in the middle of the room.

They both knelt on the bed, equals in love. Her palms slid up his forearms and he cupped her elbows in his hands. They sat only inches apart, her breath exchanged with his, his smile a broad echo to her own tremulous one. He did not imagine the pulse racing beneath her skin.

It would be hours until it was dark in the room, but she said nothing as he studied her, made no protest as his brandy eyes burned a path from shoulders to hip. She was as avid in her own exploration, eyes and fingertips, as if searching for a sign that the weeks apart had changed him in some detectable way.

He placed his hand against her rounded belly, his eyes filled with wonder, joy, fear.

"You did not tell me." His fingers traced a path across her skin. His child.

"I did not know." She bent her head until her forehead nestled into the space between shoulder and neck. "I am supposed to be barren, Alisdair," she whispered. "I am not supposed to be full with your child." She leaned back and smiled at him. There was no more beauty in the world than Judith in love.

"It's all the practice, Judith," he said with a grin. "And being Scots."

He leaned down to touch her breasts with his fingertips, and then his lips, and she moaned softly as he caressed the delicate curve beneath one breast.

His hands reached around her waist and slid down her hips. One of hers strayed to his back, feeling the taut strength of those firm, long muscles. He lowered his lips to hers and she traced the outline of their warm wetness with her tongue.

He spread her hair across her breasts, to where it ended at her knees. She stroked that pelt of hair on his chest and smoothed both palms across it.

He slid his hands up from her knees to the tops of her thighs. Where they parted, she was wet, and it was that wetness his fingers sought even as his tongue delved deeper into the grotto of her mouth. She leaned weakly into him, and he became her support.

He placed both hands on her shoulders and pulled her closer until her head was leaning against his chest. His heart was beating in hammer strokes against her cheek. When he pulled back, she protested, a slight whimper of negation. He only smiled and kissed the tip of her nose.

He left her then and she watched him as he walked to the other side of the room, not as curious as to his errand as admiring of his form. Was there ever a man more gloriously made? The bright sunlight would have exposed any flaw, but as she studied him, she could see none.

When he returned to his position on the bed, his smile was rakish.

"Would you like me to turn around, so you can complete your inspection?"

"I've seen enough," she said, smiling softly, "and there is nothing I would change."

"Be certain of that, my love," he said, his easy teasing replaced by a more somber tone, "I'll not give you another chance." With one hand, he opened her palm, in the other he held Granmere's ring.

"Alisdair, what are you about?" she whispered.

"Something I should have done a long while ago. Judith," he said gently, "there are four ways to wed in Scotland. Since I do not see a Kirk nearby, and since we have already been wed by declaration, and lived together as man and wife, I feel that we must seal the deed again by marrying thrice over." He smiled. "Therefore, my sweet and lovely wife, we are performing the last way of marriage left us. Declaration of intent followed by coupling."

She smiled tenderly.

"Will you live with me and be my wife? Will you love me, my clan, and my home? With no regrets and of your own free will?" he asked softly, the rasp in his voice betraying his emotions.

She nodded her head, her heart too full of love, and her throat too choked with tears to speak. He slid Granmere's ring onto her finger.

He lowered her onto the bed, and stretched out beside her, one hand gently resting on her breast, the other supporting his head. He did nothing else for a long moment, as if creating a space for her to breathe.

She wanted no respite.

She pulled his head down, trying without words to thank him for his tender care of her. Small sounds, not quite words, punctuated their kisses, each soft stroke of finger, of mouth. In those moments, they created a cocoon of comfort, bathed in yellow sunlight, a perfect delicacy of feeling, carved from life itself.

When her liquid warmth flowed around his fingers, Alisdair slipped slowly into her, filling her so full that he checked his movement to give her time to adjust. Judith had other ideas. She clasped her arms around his hips and pulled him into her. With his invasion, she became neither the conqueror nor the conquered. She was simply loving.

Each separate step of this dance of love had been ordained from the beginning of time, yet it felt fresh and new between them now. He arched his hips back at the same time his tongue began to stroke hers. She lifted her hips up against his, a tender tyrant, imploring him to fill her again. A gasp slipped from her lips as he reached down with one hand and stroked her open wetness. Faint tremors of need shook her as she clutched his back.

Her fingers traced weak patterns on his flesh, her mouth opened against his skin, tasting, licking, gently scraping with teeth and tongue. He traced her full lips with one finger, then traced his handiwork with his tongue, savoring her winsome smile. Her hands roamed from his wrists to his shoulders, to the corded muscles and their strength.

Through it all, he moved slowly, gently, coaxing her to soar with him, invading, relinquishing, moving, creating a sweet and unbearable feeling of need within both of them.

Why was it possible to feel his exhilaration as she felt her own, a thrumming that began in her core and sparked outward into a dozen small fires? Judith gasped, crying out his name as she sank into oblivion for moments, unafraid, even now aware that he held her and protected her. Aware, too, that he followed her into bliss, his own cry muted by their kiss.

His smile melted into hers.

"Alisdair," she whispered.

"Yes, my love?"

"Although I admire most of Scotland's customs, and not that I doubt the finality of this sort of wedding, I'd just as soon settle for a parson."

He chuckled, thinking she would be surprised at the arrival of the visitor from Inverness. The minister would be here in a few days, to celebrate their fourth, and final, bonding. No couple would be more wed than he and Judith.

She sighed finally, holding him close when he would have pulled away.

"Do not leave me, Alisdair," she murmured when he moved. Since he was intimately joined to her, he only smiled, and held her close. She raised her face and drank in the sight of him with misty eyes.

"Never, my love," he said gently, and she smiled at the way he framed that word, a tender and gentle endearment.

Epilogue

"You look like a young girl readied for bed," Alisdair said, smoothing his hand over the silky length of her hair, newly brushed. She was dressed in a clean gown and the sheets had recently been changed. He smiled at the sight of her, propped up in the bed like a little girl, instead of a lovely but tired woman who had just given birth.

He had not wanted Judith to see the depth of his anxiety, but she'd discerned it anyway, which is probably why she'd not told him she was in labor until their son was nearly born. He'd no time, towards the end, to recall either Anne or Janet, or any other birthing tragedies. He'd been too busy asserting his rights as laird, physician, and husband—although not necessarily in that order—in order to remain in the room with his wife. He should not have worried—Judith excelled in childbirth.

"It's being a Scot," she said, smiling at him when he said as much.

Judith leaned back against the pillows and sighed. She was exhausted, and it would be only moments until she succumbed to the deep sleep which beckoned.

She knew that her presence as mother of the heir was

superfluous at this particular moment. Over the last two years, Judith had discovered that the industry of the Scots was expended in merrymaking as much as it was backbreaking labor. Right now, they were doubtless waiting for Alisdair's presence in the Great Hall for the celebration to begin. Elizabeth was there, excited beyond measure by the smiles and laughter. She was performing those chores given to her by the women of the clan, looked after and coddled, and forever loved.

Gerald Malcolm MacLeod had been born during the wee sma' oors, which meant, according to Grizzelle who seemed to be an authority on the subject, that the MacLeod's son was expected to be as intelligent and stubborn as his father.

His first journey must not be down towards the warmer rooms, Judith had been told, and since the lord's room was the top most habitable room, Alisdair proudly took his son on his first journey up the steps of the wheel staircase, to where boards prevented further passage. Only then was he taken to the warm kitchen, where he was washed and readied for his first suckle. His right hand was left untouched, so that he would never know poverty, and each visitor was required to place a coin in his hand for good luck. Her son gripped the coins tightly, and the women laughed, saying that he was to be a tightfisted, wild, intelligent man.

Judith only sighed and hoped she was up to the challenge.

Gerald was returned to the cradle beside her bed, where she turned and watched him with such love that it shined in her eyes. It was Janet's cradle he rested in, because on no account must his first sleep be in any but a borrowed bed. Alisdair had, during her labor, walked seven times around the perimeter of Tynan, or as much as was possible due to the presence of the cove, to safeguard the child and protect him from being stolen by fairies. A knife was placed at her son's feet, for the same purpose, and each of the women who attended her knew not to carry fire out of the house until her son was at least a week old. She, herself, must never leave the house after sunset for at least a month, lest she be stolen to nurse an ailing fairy child who could not return to health unless suckled on human milk.

Judith thought that the superstitions surrounding the birth of her child much more difficult than the actuality.

She had felt little pain at first, which had changed drastically towards the end of her labor. She had felt constrained by the interested faces of the women of her clan, who had watched to see if she was a soft Englishwoman at this critical juncture, or a stoic Scot. She had been a stoic Scot, and she wasn't going to let them forget it.

Their son was worth all of the discomfort and pain.

While Alisdair held her tenderly within his arms, they both kept vigil over the newest MacLeod.

"I did not realize I could bear a child, Alisdair," she admitted, "until I came to Scotland. I did not know a great many things about myself."

"Like what?" he smiled tenderly at her.

"For example, I seem to have a bit of a temper."

"Aye, Judith, that you do." He didn't care if she saw his smile. She had the devil's own temper when she was riled.

"Yet, you've always let me speak freely."

"We Scots are like that," he said, brushing back the tendrils of hair from her face. "We appreciate independent thinking." Aye, and courage, and pride. She had all these qualities and more, his wife.

"Shall I ever be a Scot, Alisdair?" she wondered, her cheek against his chest, feeling in that one perfect moment all the joy she'd never expected to feel.

Alisdair closed his eyes against the power of the emotion which swept through him then.

"I think you've always been one, love," he said softly, and held her gently within his arms.

A few minutes later, he sighed and kissed the top of her head. "I wish to build you a home, my Scots lass," he said tenderly. ''A small home with two floors and a neat, thatched roof.''

''We would leave Tynan?'' She raised herself up and looked at him in the light of the candle. He had scandalized the women by refusing to sleep apart from her, even in the last stages of her pregnancy, and was planning to sleep next to her tonight. It was spring in the Highlands, he had complained, and he needed her warmth. None of the women were taken in by such a flimsy story.

Judith would always remember the sight of him, then, his face softened into tender lines, the somber gleam of his amber eyes overlaid with one of mischief.

''I seek a home without the scent of burned wood, Judith. A place to begin again.'' He looked at her seriously. ''Will you miss being the mistress of a castle?''

''The incessant scrubbing and the sounds of mice? I think not.''

''We do not have mice at Tynan,'' he grumbled.

''Of course not, Alisdair,'' she said, smiling gently, and curled up in his arms, feeling as if she had always belonged here.

Judith would sometimes come to Tynan in search of her children, a wild Scots-English horde led into mischief by their eldest brother. Gerald loved playing Robert the Bruce, using the castle as a place of made up stories, while his sisters and younger brothers were relegated to minor English parts.

She would stop sometimes and glance into the empty cavern which used to be their kitchen. Stone dust lay inch thick upon the floor, undisturbed except for tiny mouse footprints. She would smile and wander into the room Sophie had called hers, now stripped of its heavy French furniture and delicate lace. No ghosts lingered here, even though the silence sometimes echoed with the click, click of an ivory-handled cane.

The steps were still uneven and steeply canted, but Judith took them slowly, passing Ian's room, and up one landing to the laird's chamber. It was empty now, and dusty, filled with long-

ago memories that seemed to whisper in the swirling light from the open windows.

In the silence and perfect peace, Judith would feel the greatest serenity and comfort, as if a golden blanket of warmth had been placed around her shoulders. The air itself was rife with solemnity and a curious benediction, almost tasting of forgiveness. In those moments, she felt touched by tenderness, humbled by the sensation of it. It was as if Heaven answered her many prayers, promising a future filled with joy, laughter, and love.

I hope you've enjoyed Judith and Alisdair's story. The time following Culloden was one of deprivation and hardship for the inhabitants of the Highlands. Yet, I like to imagine that a lonely and isolated place like Tynan could still provide a future bright with hope. Once, I stood upon the battlements of a deserted castle, watching the ocean change color in the face of an oncoming storm. Is it any wonder that my heart envisioned a happier fate for such a glorious place, and imagined the presence of two people who could coax joy from despair?

I would love to hear from each and every one of my readers. Please write me at:

Karen Ranney
P.O. Box 701622
San Antonio, TX 78270-1622